The SECRET HOURS

Also by Santa Montefiore

Meet Me Under the Ombu Tree
The Butterfly Box
The Forget-Me-Not Sonata
The Swallow and the Hummingbird
The Last Voyage of the Valentina
The Gypsy Madonna
Sea of Lost Love
The French Gardener
The Italian Matchmaker
The Affair
The House by the Sea
The Summer House
Secrets of the Lighthouse
A Mother's Love
The Beekeeper's Daughter
The Temptation of Gracie

The Deverill Chronicles

Songs of Love and War
Daughters of Castle Deverill
The Last Secret of the Deverills

Santa Montefiore

The SECRET HOURS

**SIMON &
SCHUSTER**

London · New York · Sydney · Toronto · New Delhi

A CBS COMPANY

First published in Great Britain by Simon & Schuster UK Ltd, 2019
A CBS COMPANY

1 3 5 7 9 10 8 6 4 2

Simon & Schuster UK Ltd
1st Floor
222 Gray's Inn Road
London WC1X 8HB

Simon & Schuster Australia, Sydney
Simon & Schuster India, New Delhi

www.simonandschuster.co.uk
www.simonandschuster.com.au
www.simonandschuster.co.in

A CIP catalogue record for this book
is available from the British Library

Hardback ISBN: 978-1-4711-6962-5
Trade Paperback ISBN: 978-1-4711-6963-2
eBook ISBN: 978-1-4711-6964-9

Typeset in Bembo by M Rules
Printed and bound by CPI Group (UK) Ltd, Croydon, CR0 4YY

For my dear friend Emer Melody,
who embodies everything I love about the Irish

Chapter 1

Nantucket, 1960

Last night I dreamed I was at the castle again. In real life I have never been to such a place, yet in my dream those grey-stone walls are as familiar to me as my own skin. They envelop me in a keen embrace as if they have arms to hold me, as if they want to draw me in, as if I have been away a long, long time and am returned home at last. And I yearn to be held. I ache to luxuriate in this sense of belonging, this sense of home, as if everything that has come before is but a dream and only *this* is real, where I want to be, where my heart is. And as I wander into the great hall there is a baronial fireplace where flames crackle and flicker and throw dancing shadows across the walls. Everything is majestic, as if I am in a royal palace. There are paintings in gilt frames, Persian rugs on the flagstone floor, a grand staircase that leads me up into dark corridors, enticing me deeper and deeper into the castle, and I run now, because I know that I am close.

Candlelight illuminates the darkness. I reach a gap in the wall and take the narrow staircase there. This is the core of the castle, the oldest wing, the only section to survive the fire. I know this as if it is part of my own history. I climb the uneven wooden steps, each worn into a gentle hollow from centuries of treading feet. Now I place mine into those hollows and slowly ascend. My heart accelerates and I am suddenly afraid. At the top there is a sturdy old door. It is blackened with time and smoke and the iron hinges and studs are from another age, when men wore plumed hats and boots and carried swords at their hips. I put my fingers on the latch and gently lift it. The door opens without protest; it is used to my coming.

Inside, with her back to me, stands a woman. She is slim with thick red hair falling in waves down to her waist. She is staring into the fire, one pale hand on the mantelpiece, the other hanging by the side of her long green dress. She has been expecting me. She turns and looks at me. I gasp, horrified. Those grey eyes, that sweet smile, the freckles that play about her white skin, the rosy apples of her cheeks, the lustrous red hair, are mine, all mine.

She is me and I am staring at myself.

From the swing chair on the veranda I gaze out over the sea at the translucent dawn sky, the last fading star and the vaporous wisps of pink cloud and know that the castle in my dream is far from this shore. This big house on Nantucket, with its dove-grey clapboard walls, tall windows and white widow's walk where lonely wives once kept vigil for their mariner husbands, has been in my father's family since the first Claytons arrived in America from Ireland in the early nineteenth century, and yet it feels less familiar to me than the castle I have only ever visited in my sleep. It is a strange feeling and one I am unable to shake off. I don't even know where this castle is. I assume it must be in Ireland, although I have never been there. I would ask my mother, for she was born in Co. Cork, but since her stroke some five months ago she is unable to speak and I don't want to burden her with what is, after all, only a dream. I tell Temperance instead, as I have told her my thoughts and feelings since I was a child. She is originally from South Carolina and has worked for my mother for fifty-six years, from the age of fourteen. She is seventy now, twelve years my senior, but she doesn't look old to me. She looks as she always has done: black skin plump and smooth, voluptuous body all curves and softness, brown eyes round and shiny like chestnuts. She's a big woman. I've always thought that she needs to be big to accommodate such an enormous heart; Temperance is all unconditional love and compassion and the most noble person I've ever met. She's like an angel put on earth to heal it. I wonder, with such a nurturing, maternal nature, whether she would have liked to marry and have children of her own, but I don't suppose my mother would have been happy with that. Arethusa Clayton is a very needy woman and has always wanted Temperance to herself. Not that she's unkind. In fact, I'd say she's kindest when Temperance is in the room – there's something about her that brings out the best in my mother. However, her affection for Temperance makes her selfish, and Temperance has spoiled her rotten.

Temperance brings me a mug of milky coffee, sprinkled with chocolate and other secret spices she won't reveal in spite of my asking. She only smiles, waves her long fingers and says, 'That's a secret, Miss Faye, and a secret's not a secret if you share it.' I notice her hands as I take the mug; they are the only parts of her body that betray her age. The skin is rough and dry from household chores, the shell-pink palms etched with deep lines, which, according to her, denote an old soul. 'Sit with me a while,' I say.

She sinks with a loud sigh into the chair opposite. Her soft body melts into the wicker frame and I find comfort in this quiet routine, for every morning we meet like this, just the two of us, waiting with patience and trepidation for the old woman in the downstairs bedroom to die.

I push myself off with my toes and gently swing. Temperance looks tired. Her eyes are rheumy and the sorrow in them makes me feel guilty. I think Temperance loves my mother more than I do. Or perhaps she needs her more. After all, I have a husband and children who, in spite of being all grown-up now, demand my attention; Temperance has only Mother. She has given her life to her, every drop of it, and, knowing my mother as I do, she will have taken it greedily. I wonder whether Mom has ever thanked her. I doubt it. I doubt Mom has ever considered Temperance and the loyal service she has given her. Temperance would not expect thanks; she loves her all the same, unconditionally. Love is a mystery, I muse, Temperance's love for my mother more of a mystery than most. I know one thing, Temperance's love is closer to God than mine. I shouldn't feel sorry for her, I should feel awed.

'I had that dream again last night,' I tell her. 'I must have had it a dozen times since Mom had her stroke. Why do you think that is?'

Temperance always has an answer for everything. She nods and smiles and folds her rough hands in her lap. 'They say, Miss Faye, that recurring dreams are past-life memories unleashed from your subconscious. You are simply remembering your past.'

I laugh affectionately at her. Temperance is all spirits, magic charms and enchantment. I love her for that, but I was brought up in the Catholic faith and feel more secure remaining close to the teachings of the Bible, which say nothing of reincarnation, or any of her other pagan beliefs. 'I think it's just anxiety, Tempie,' I reply, taking a sip of coffee. No one makes coffee like Temperance and I sigh with pleasure, suddenly caught off guard by the chocolatey taste of my youth and the nostalgia that comes with it in a sudden onslaught of images, sounds and smells. I am a little girl again, in the kitchen, sharing my thoughts with Temperance, and she is listening to me with patience, her round face full of wisdom, her big eyes brimming with love. I hold on to the feeling and in it I can smell the sweetness of her baking and hear the resonance of our laughter. I can even see the dress I am wearing and feel the seersucker fabric against my skin. I am filled with wistfulness, which is nostalgia's companion, as I reflect on the passing of time, the transience of life and the tender moments lost for ever in the wake of constant change.

Mom's passing will be the natural order of things for my brother Logan and me, but for Temperance, it will be the end. We will look after her, of course; she is like family. But this house, where we have spent every summer of our lives and to where my mother retired after my father died, will pass on to the next generation, and it will never be the same again. Ted Clayton, my father, was the eldest of seven brothers and sisters and the Governor of Massachusetts in his younger days. A big, burly man with a short temper, a quick mind and a formidable character, he was a person who did not suffer fools and liked to have total autonomy over his world – even after his death eleven years ago his cigar smoke is still embedded in the fabrics and furnishings so that I continue to smell him as if he is still sitting in his chair, barking commands. He was king and everyone else his loyal and obedient subject, except Mom, his queen. His worshipping of her was his only weakness, and the source of her power. While Mom continues to live here, Ted's rules still apply. When she goes, their reign will end and new rules will grow up over the old ones. It will no longer be my home. It will no longer be Temperance's, either. It will be Logan's and he's not sentimental like I am. His wife will gut it, transform it and it will cease to smell of cigars.

I hug my mug of coffee and look at Temperance, anxious to show her the compassion she has always shown me. 'You've been a saint, Tempie, looking after Mom all these years. She's never been easy, has she?'

'She is a good woman,' Temperance replies reverentially, eyes shining and face aglow with admiration, as if she's speaking of an angel and not my self-centred mother.

'Since her stroke she has been strangely peaceful,' I say, reflecting on the remarkable change in my mother's nature. She went from cantankerous to meek overnight, as if she realized she was nearing the end and had accepted her fate without question or complaint.

'She will die with a clear conscience,' says Temperance. 'She has banished her ghosts and will rise into God's light with joy.' I'm not sure what ghosts Temperance is referring to. I know little of Mother's past. She came from Ireland, from a poor farming family, to escape poverty and start a new life in America as so many did in those times of hardship and famine. That much she told us. She never elaborated and we weren't curious to know. Only now, as she is on the point of dying, do I wonder about her beginnings. I know she had two brothers. Whatever became of them? Did they leave Ireland too? With all my uncles and aunts on my father's side and more cousins than I can count, it now seems odd to know not one of my mother's relations. She came to America alone and will leave alone, and we will be none the wiser.

Mother has two nurses looking after her around the clock,

but she insists on having Temperance by her side too. It is plain that she needs her even more than she needs me, her daughter. I'm a little jealous, but that is only natural. Temperance has been with her constantly, but I married and moved away when I was twenty-two. I bear no grudges, have no regrets. Mom and I have had an easy relationship only because I have always bowed to her will. I have been dominated all my life, by my father and then by my husband, so I am used to accommodating stronger characters. I'm as flexible as a reed in a pond. I don't resist. I do as I'm told and I don't complain. I know what is expected of me. My father was a direct man who left no room for doubt. To be a good wife and mother were, to him, the highest aspirations of any well-brought-up girl and I desired nothing more than to please him and make him proud. But something in me is shifting now as if, like the earth, I have tectonic plates of my own; I feel movement deep within me.

I am a woman of fifty-eight and I realize, as I sit on this veranda in the morning and gaze out over the sea, that I have pleased everyone all these years, except myself. I reflect on life and the lack of impression I have made with mine. My footsteps in the sand are shallow and will fast disappear when the waves finally wash over them, for I have done little besides raise my three children, look after my husband and be a gracious and charming hostess. My mother is dying and that makes me think of life and death and our purpose here. I realize in a blaze of clarity that I have been living for everyone else and not for me. I consider my dream once again. It makes me uneasy because I sense it is trying to tell me something. My subconscious prompting me to take a closer look at myself, perhaps. Unlike other dreams, it does not fade, but remains with the obstinacy of a dog determined to stay at his dead master's side.

I am at my mother's bedside when she passes. My brother Logan has made it from Boston in time and the two of us hold her hands while Temperance looks on, her face wet with tears, her bottom lip glistening and trembling as she mumbles inaudible prayers. Arethusa Clayton was a strikingly handsome woman once – she was never considered a beauty, her features were too strong for that, but her looks were arresting and men found her irresistible, even when she was no longer a young woman. Now, in death, she is serene, benign, passive, which is strange for me and my brother because she was never any of those things in life. She looks sweet, gentle even, as if she has given up a fight. As I gaze at her the word 'fight' rises in my thoughts like a cork in water. It is insistent. I wonder what she had to fight for, why she had to fight at all. The fight is over now, for sure, she is at peace. But I can't help wondering why it was there in the first place.

Her death hits me in unexpected ways. It is complicated, like a tangled ball of wool I had expected to be tidy. I feel sadness, a hollow, aching sadness, but I am also relieved for she has been released from her suffering and I have been released from her dominance. It is a thorny thing to feel both sorrow and relief at the same time. I feel guilty for feeling relieved and then I feel regret for all the things I never said. All the love I didn't realize I felt. And I feel terribly alone and a little lost, as if she has been the puppet master and I the ignorant puppet, oblivious of the strings that have, until now, held me up. Temperance is just sad and I know her sorrow cuts a cleaner wound than mine. For her there is no relief or regret or guilt. For her there is only mourning.

Now it is up to Logan, as executor of her will, to see that

our mother's wishes are carried out. It is up to Temperance and me to begin the laborious task of sorting out all her belongings. Her wardrobes of clothes and shoes and handbags, her jewellery boxes, make-up, toiletries and her desk of papers and library of books. Really, it is a daunting task and one I would rather hand over to somebody else, but there *is* no one else. Only the two of us, and, as the days go by, I feel we are getting nowhere. Mother clearly did not like to throw things away. What are we going to do with all this stuff?

There is one item which I find out of place among her things. It is an instrument that looks like a small violin, but the belly is round and the fretboard very long. Temperance gasps when she sees it and smiles with childish delight, as if she has just found a beloved old friend. 'That, Miss Faye, is a banjo,' she says, and her voice is full of wonder. Sensing she wants to hold it, I give it to her. She takes it with great care. Then she begins to play. Her fingers move deftly over the strings. I'm astonished. I didn't know she could play the banjo. I listen as she sings. Her voice is low and soft like whiskey and cream, and all the while she sings she looks at me, the emotion in her eyes raw and tender. I'm enchanted. But I'm doubtful my mother ever knew how to play such a thing. It must have been an unwanted gift she never got round to throwing away.

'Tempie,' I gasp when she is done. 'You play beautifully.'

Temperance's heart is bleeding on account of her loss and she cries easily and often. She cries now as she strokes the banjo nostalgically. 'My father taught me how to play when I was a little girl,' she tells me. 'He worked these strings like he was born for it. And he could dance, Miss Faye, tapping his feet, so light and graceful he was, like a fire spirit, and he could sing too. He used to play and sing to send me to sleep, but I would lie with my eyes wide open like a frog, not wanting to miss a single minute of it.' She gives it back to me. 'After he died I never played again. I regret that now.'

'It's never too late to start,' I say. 'Why don't *you* have it. It will remind you of your father.' I see Temperance then as a little girl, with her father, who I imagine to be handsome like she is, with her smile and the same tenderness in his eyes, and I wonder at the differences in our childhoods. Me with my white, privileged upbringing and she with prejudice and intolerance on account of her colour. The injustice of it makes my heart swell with compassion. America has come a long way since she was a girl, but still, old mindsets die hard. 'I want you to have it, Tempie,' I insist.

'You mean that, Miss Faye?'

'Of course, I mean that, Tempie. Mom would *want* you to have it.'

'I will treasure it, Miss Faye. And I'll play it too. I'll play it and remember the past.' Her eyes are moist. I'd like to ask her about her past. I'd like to hear more about her father, who she clearly adored. I'm aware suddenly of how very little I know about her apart from stories of her grandmother's cooking, and I'm ashamed by my lack of curiosity. My lack of interest. However, now isn't the time to ask. I don't want to upset her. Her grief is very close to the surface at the moment and the slightest thing will set her off. I can't cope with her tears right now. I'm barely coping with my own.

My children are wonderfully supportive. Rose, who is thirty-two and works in fashion in New York, offers to come and help, but I put her off. She has her own young family to think about. She insists she can get away and I know she really means it. She would cancel anything to come to my aid, but I assure her that Temperance and I are just fine on our own. Instead, she calls me every day. Sweet, considerate and patient, she listens as I tell her about the odd things I have found in my mother's closets. I know it's boring for her, but she's in no haste to hang up. She knows I need to work through my grief and gives me all the time I need. As for Edwina, she is two years younger and has just started a new job in California, making movies, so cannot get away, but I appreciate the telephone call and her sympathy. It's very typical of Edwina to offer to help, hoping that she won't have to. I love her ambition and her drive, but she is the selfish one of my chidren and won't put herself out for anyone. Walter, our son, is twenty-two and studying for his final exams at college. He wants to come up, but this is no job for a young man. He doesn't call very often. He's working hard, he has a girlfriend. I know his heart is in the right place but only Rose is truly empathetic.

They will all come for the funeral, however, along with their father, my husband, who telephoned last night to ask when I am coming home. I would usually put everything down and hurry to his side, as he expects me to do, even in this case. He cannot understand why I can't just leave it all to Temperance. But I want to be here. At last I am thinking of myself. I want to be here, so I shall stay.

Just when I think we are making progress, we are dealt a terrible blow. Logan and I meet with Mother's attorney, Frank Wilks, who comes to the house to read her will. He is a small, wiry man with a white moustache, bald head and high colour, which reminds me of the lobsters we used to catch and boil when we were kids. We take our seats in the dining room, at one end of the polished cherry-wood table, and make small talk while Mr Wilks opens his briefcase and lifts out a file, placing it in front of him with an air of solemnity and self-importance. He has looked after my parents' affairs for thirty-five years and is genuinely saddened by our mother's passing. Temperance brings in a tray of coffee, then leaves the room and closes the door behind her. Mr Wilks smiles as I pour him a cup, but it is not an easy smile. I guess that Mom has made some awkward requests. After all, she was difficult in life, why would she not be difficult in death?

Mr Wilks opens the document, inhales through his nostrils and informs us that Mother has stipulated in her will that she wants to be cremated. This is a shock, to say the least. Our father is buried in the Catholic church of the Holy Cross and it has always been assumed that Mother, who was also Catholic, would be laid to rest beside him. Ted Clayton did not believe in cremation. He made that clear, as he made everything clear (his dinner-table lectures were infamous and patiently endured in the same way that one endures sermons from the pulpit). When Judgement Day arrives, Ted Clayton will be complete in body and ready to rise again. No one doubts he will. If anyone can defy death and burst out of the earth it's Ted Clayton. But he did not think it possible to forge a body out of ash, however potent the power of resurrection. It is therefore unthinkable that Mother has chosen cremation over burial. We can't even argue that she was mad because she was of very sound mind when she rewrote her will, a few months before her stroke. Indeed, she hosted a fundraiser the day before she was struck down and everyone commented on her vitality and her charm. Therefore, as hard as it is to accept, cremation was her sane choice, but still we cannot fathom why.

'This is outrageous!' Logan exclaims. His face, still boyishly handsome, reddens with indignation. 'I won't accept it. Dad would turn in his grave if he knew.' He looks at me sternly. 'Did *you* know about this?'

'Of course not,' I reply.

He folds his arms and sits back in his chair. 'Ridiculous,'

he scoffs, hoping that by dismissing her request in this way her wish will not be taken seriously. 'No wonder she didn't tell us when she was alive. She knew very well how we'd feel.' He shakes his head, still luxuriously covered with wavy chocolate-brown hair, greying only slightly at the temples. 'Why would she want to be cremated? She was a devout woman. It goes against her faith. It simply doesn't make sense.'

'It's about to,' says Mr Wilks, pushing his glasses up his nose. We turn our attention back to the diminutive man who clears his throat and taps the page with his middle finger like a bird tapping wood with its beak. 'That is not *all* she has requested,' he adds.

'Go on,' Logan urges, dropping his gaze to the document in front of Mr Wilks. 'What else does it say?'

'She has requested that her ashes be scattered in Ireland.' Mr Wilks ignores another collective gasp and continues. 'To be precise, and her will is indeed *very* precise, she wants them scattered . . .' He leans over the page and reads what is written there. '*On the hills above Castle Deverill, with both a view of the castle and the ocean. Let the wind take me and the soft rain settle me into the Irish soil from where I came. And may my sins be forgiven.*'

At this point I feel as if I have just had the wind knocked out of me. The mention of the castle is an extraordinary coincidence. I put my hand to my chest and take a breath. I cannot share my dream with my brother, he is a sensible, pragmatic man and would think I had lost my mind. Goodness, I'm not even sure I can tell Temperance, only because she will read too much into it and I'm afraid of what she might say. I'm afraid of my dream. I'm now scared to sleep in case it comes again. I'm scared of facing myself there by the fireplace and of waking up in a cold sweat with my heart pounding against my ribcage and not knowing why I am so frightened.

Logan asks Mr Wilks to pass him the will and the attorney slides it across the table. My brother reads it carefully, lips pursed, cheeks the colour of bull's blood. 'This is crazy!' he exclaims. 'Why on earth would she want her ashes scattered in Ireland? I mean, we know her maiden name was Deverill, but she never spoke of a *Castle* Deverill. Did she ever mention a castle to you?' Again Logan looks at me and again I shake my head. 'Well, we know she grew up on a farm in Co. Cork and crossed the Atlantic to seek a better life in America, but we have never heard of a castle. It is one thing to cremate her, but quite another to scatter her in a distant country which she left over sixty years ago and barely ever mentioned.' He slides the will back to Mr Wilks with disdain. I know that Logan will want to ignore her wishes and lay her to rest here, alongside our father. Usually I would comply with his wishes. I always have, after all he is seven years older than me and I've never really voiced a strong opinion about anything. But for some unknown reason I feel very strongly about *this*.

'If she wants her ashes to be scattered in Ireland, it is our duty to see that it happens,' I say and Logan frowns irritably, surprised that I am not in accordance with him. I think of the castle in my dream and feel more certain than ever that the two are connected, perhaps even the same, and that *I* should be the person to take her. I don't tell Logan what I am thinking. It is much too out of character and he's had enough surprises for one day.

I haven't considered my husband. He is an obstacle too solid to contemplate right now.

There is one final demand. Mr Wilks clears his throat and seems to brace himself. His shoulders lift, almost to his ears, as if he wants to pull in his head like a tortoise. 'Mrs Clayton has requested that the servants' house be lent to Temperance for her lifetime along with a gift of two hundred thousand dollars.' Logan looks horrified. That is an enormous amount of money for a maid. Mr Wilks goes on regardless: 'A third of her wealth she has left to you, Mrs Langton, and a third to you, Mr Clayton.'

'And the other third?' Logan is quick to ask, ignoring the house and money for Temperance. I am curious to know as well. I lean forward, elbows on the table. 'Who else *is* there?' Logan adds with an impatient shake of his head.

Mr Wilks looks uncomfortable. Our mother has no doubt made another surprising request. 'Mrs Clayton was very clear about this,' he replies. 'She has stipulated that the identity of the third party must remain anonymous until you have been to Ireland.'

Logan looks as if he is going to burst. Even his ears go red and throb angrily. 'Anonymous?' He stares at me, brown eyes large and feverish, but before he can ask whether I knew of this, I reassure him that I didn't.

'I can't imagine who it could be,' I say quietly and I feel my own face redden with the shock of it. I am ashamed to admit that I, too, am a little put out.

'A third? Who, besides her children, is entitled to a third? Was she out of her mind? What on earth was she thinking?' Logan jumps to his feet and paces the room.

Mr Wilks clears his throat again. 'These are your mother's wishes and it is your duty, Mr Clayton, to carry them out.'

'What if I want to contest it?' Logan challenges, sitting down and leaning towards Mr Wilks, dwarfing him with his wide shoulders and attempting to coerce him with his sharp, predatory eyes.

'Which part of it?' Mr Wilks replies coolly, returning his gaze without blinking.

'All of it,' says Logan.

'Logan,' I protest. 'You can't do that. It's the law. These are Mother's wishes. You can't ignore them.'

Logan stares at me in surprise. I have voiced an opinion and it is not what he wants to hear. 'I will do all I can to ignore them, Faye.'

'On what grounds will you contest the will?' Mr Wilks asks sensibly. I don't imagine Logan would be able to build a very convincing case. I think he knows that too. He steeples his fingers as he ponders what to do. Mr Wilks catches my eye but neither of us smiles. We are both anxious to do the right thing. Logan is only thinking of himself. He only ever thinks of himself.

'Very well,' he says at length. 'I will not fight her wish to be cremated, although it goes against our father's wishes and the wishes of her family. As for her ashes being scattered in Ireland, I find the whole idea ridiculous. She remains here, where she belongs. As for the final part, hell will freeze over before I allow one third of Mother's wealth to go to—'

'A ghost, Logan,' I interrupt. 'Because until we know who it is, it might as well be a ghost.'

Mr Wilks coughs into his hand. 'Before we bring the meeting to an end, there is one more thing.'

Logan and I stare at him. What else can there be? Mr Wilks leans over and lifts his briefcase off the floor and places it on the table. I hold my breath as he opens the clasps and raises the lid. Inside is a brown envelope. It doesn't look like much but I dread to know what is inside. He places it on the table with great importance, as if it contains something very valuable. Logan and I look at it, hoping that it is innocuous, that it won't give us cause to argue.

'Mrs Clayton has left specific instructions that this be left to you, Mrs Langton.' He slides the envelope across the polished wood. Logan leans over. He wants to take it from me and open it himself, and he probably would if Mr Wilks wasn't watching and making sure that everything is done by the book. I would like to carry it off to a private place and open it on my own, but both Logan and Mr Wilks are observing me closely, so I am left with no option but to unseal it in front of them.

Inside is a black, leather-bound book. Without asking, Logan takes it from me and flicks through the pages. 'It's in some kind of code,' he says at once, dismissing it. 'What good is that?' He hands it back. I open it and look closely at the writing. I can't even tell if it is Mother's. It does not appear to be her hand, nor is it legible.

'I can't read it,' I comment with a sigh. But part of me is relieved. If it is anything like her list of wishes, I'm happy not knowing.

'Well, at least it doesn't have teeth,' Logan quips mirthlessly. 'Thank you, Mr Wilks, for coming. I will be in touch. In the meantime, Faye, Mother's gift to this anonymous person is to remain between us. Do you understand?' I nod. 'Good.'

I don't think this is the right moment to tell him that I intend to go to Ireland.

Chapter 2

The cremation service takes place in a small, impersonal crematorium that lacks both charm and intimacy. I find the industrial nature of the building distasteful. It is too clinical, too cold. I begin to wish that I had given in to Logan's demand and buried Mom beside Dad, after all. However, I put on a brave face for the sake of my children and for Temperance, who quietly sobs, dabbing her streaming eyes with a white handkerchief and gently blowing her nose. My husband Wyatt is not comfortable with emotion so I clench my jaw and try to hold back my own tears. It is Temperance who takes my hand and squeezes it. I try not to look at her. I know I will cry if I do. It is a relief when the ordeal is over and I can remember Mom in a more charming service, which takes place later the same day in the local church.

I have not had time to grieve and here in this church, in front of my parents' remaining friends and Dad's family, is not the place to start. The Claytons are a tough lot and I am one of them and must be tough too. However, clearing out Mom's things, sorting out her affairs, arranging this service and being strong for Temperance have taken their toll and I feel drained. It is no surprise that there is not a single member of Mom's family present, but it does feel strange. Perhaps they all died in the famine. Or they moved away in search of a better life like she did, or remained to rot in their cold cottages on farms where nothing grew. It is quite possible, now I think of it, that Mom suffered a past so traumatic that it hurt too much to talk about it. Why has that never occurred to me? She was, by her own admission, a woman who wanted to live in the present. But now that she has requested her ashes be scattered in Ireland, I can't help but turn my thoughts to the past she wanted to forget. If her heart was here, with all of us, why wouldn't she want to remain? Why return to Ireland in death if it had meant nothing to her in life?

My curiosity is aroused. I realize, to my shame, that I know nothing about my mother, nothing at all. It's not that I suspect she kept secrets; it's not that. It's simply regret, and sadness at my lack of understanding. I feel a swell of grief building in my chest. It's sudden and takes me by surprise. I stifle a sob and drop my gaze to the floor where I focus hard on the flaws in the stone. Yet, still the questions arise. I know nothing of Mom's childhood, nothing of her growing up, nothing of the struggles and hardships she endured. I know nothing of her parents, her siblings and nothing of her home. Arethusa is gone. There is no one left to tell her story. I feel as if her whole family has died with her, swallowed into oblivion. There is a void now, a black hole, a nothingness in the place where my mother once was. And I regret very much that I never had the curiosity, or the courage, to ask her.

After the service we head back to the house for the reception. The congregants stroll the short walk from the church. Dressed in black they look like a flock of crows making their way slowly over the fallen leaves. They enter the house where

I have hired waiters to offer them glasses of wine and girls in dark dresses to relieve them of their coats. Temperance watches from the shadows with her bottom lip out and her hands on her wide hips, guarding her mistress's home possessively.

I position myself by the door to greet them. I long for it to be over, for everyone to leave. I'm tired of talking, shaking hands and thanking people for their sympathy. The drawing room is stuffy, I can barely see the other end of it for the cigarette smoke, and the noise of chatter is loud and invasive. I yearn for quiet. I suddenly want very much to be left alone, to process my loss, to remember Mom in my own private way. I want to flee from the compassionate, probing looks and questions, which, although kindly intended, are an intrusion.

I find a quiet moment by the window in the drawing room and look out over the garden where the trees are scattering scarlet and golden leaves into the wind. I love the fall. It's my favourite season. I love the rich, contrasting colours, the soft light, the wistfulness of it as summer slowly dies and winter creeps in with its long nights and hard cold. Today its beauty soothes me.

'I'm glad that's over.' It's Logan, standing beside me now, swigging his glass of wine.

'Me too,' I agree with a sigh. I know he's referring to the cremation, but I want *this* to be over too.

'Well done with the service. It was sufficiently glamorous without being ostentatious. She would have enjoyed it.' He smiles and I'm glad to see he's not cross with me anymore, but slightly teasing, as he always is. I study him closely. At sixty-five his good looks have only been enhanced by the deepening of the lines around his mouth and at his temples. However, the years have not endowed his face with wisdom or character, if anything they have exposed his superficial nature and his vanity. There is something of the fading film star trying too hard to hold on to his beauty, which is oddly pitiful. In spite of his temper and his bullying I realize now that he is really rather benign. I turn my eyes back to the darkening skies and wonder why I am suddenly seeing the world and those in it in a different light.

'In spite of being cremated, I believe her soul's up there with Dad's,' I say. 'With her family, too, I guess.' I gaze up at my brother, who is very tall, and search for emotion. I wonder if her death has moved him. It doesn't appear to have done. Besides anger, indignation and pleasure, Logan seems to be a man who does not feel things very deeply. He never shows a vulnerable side, at least not as far as I know. Perhaps he lets his guard down with Lucy, his wife. But somehow I doubt it. She's a cold fish as well. They are both as unsentimental as each other. 'Do you ever think of her family?' I ask.

He shakes his head. 'No. Why, do you?'

'I haven't until now. Have you noticed there's no one here from her side of the family? No one at all.'

'That's no surprise.'

'But don't you find that a little sad? Not one family member to say goodbye.'

'Well, they weren't here during her life so it would be pretty odd if anyone turned up for her funeral.'

'Are any of them left?' I ask, throwing my gaze back onto the falling leaves and waning light and feeling an unbearable sense of emptiness. 'They can't *all* have died. There must be someone out there who knows her story.'

'She didn't want to remember it, otherwise she would have told us.'

'Yet she wanted her ashes scattered in Ireland.'

'A whim,' he retorts dismissively. 'Absurd.'

'A very emphatic whim, Logan. She's incredibly specific about where she wants us to scatter them. If she didn't care about her past she would have been content to be buried beside Dad.'

Logan does not want to think about this. His jaw hardens and his lips thin. 'She can't really have expected us to go all the way to Ireland,' he says and for a moment I believe him. It is, indeed, a substantial request. I am so used to looking up to the men in my life – my overpowering father, my older, more beautiful brother and my clever, assertive husband – that for a moment I do not think to question him. Yet, something pulls at me, a nagging feeling, like an invisible hand tugging at the hem of my dress, demanding to be noticed.

'She wants us to go, Logan,' I say, and in that second everything becomes clear, like water after the mud settles. 'Of course!' I mumble, my voice rising with excitement. 'She *wants* us to go. She *wants* us to know her story. That's why she is sending us there.' A look of irritation darkens his face. 'I know, it sounds crazy. But I have a strange feeling—'

'She got nostalgic, that's all,' Logan interrupts, gazing at me down his long nose. 'Old people always get nostalgic.'

'No, it's more than that,' I insist, tearful because he does not understand and I *want* to go to Ireland, very much. 'I feel it in my gut,' I add quietly, putting a hand on my stomach.

He pats my shoulder. 'Your gut needs a little wine, I think. Come on, we can't stand at the window all afternoon ignoring our guests. Have you talked to Aunt Bernard? She had me in a corner for ten long minutes and I know she wants to talk to you too.'

I sigh at the prospect of Aunt Bernard, Dad's sister. All the

Clayton girls have boys' names because their father, Clinton Clayton, had only wanted boys. I do not wish to see Aunt Bernard. I haven't got the strength for her strident personality. In fact, I do not wish to see anyone. I feel low because I anticipate not being allowed to go to Ireland. I have the money, my father left me a great deal, but I don't have my independence and I am afraid to assert myself, because I have never done so before. I anticipate my husband telling me I can't go. Logan telling me I can't go. I see myself, in my mind's eye, bending to their will, as I always do. It is a pattern that is both familiar and depressing. I'm appalled at my own weakness. *That* makes me feel lower than anything, my inability to stand up for myself.

I want to sit on the swing chair outside and hold on to that tugging feeling, because there is something strangely comforting about it. I don't know why. The room is too noisy and full of people for me to be able to think. I need peace and quiet. I turn to face the throng, hoping to weave through the people and escape onto the veranda. To my dismay, Aunt Bernard is pushing her way past the guests, elbows out, jaw jutting with determination. Nothing is going to stop her. And because of her size, no one can.

Before I am able to escape, Aunt Bernard is staring up at me with her round, moon face and round, china-blue eyes. Everything about Aunt Bernard is round. 'Good! I've been looking for you, Faye. Now, what's all this about Tussy wanting her ashes scattered in Ireland? I mean, what in God's name was she thinking? And cremation! Ted must be turning in his grave. It's outrageous.'

I feel my fury mount. 'It's what she wanted and we are compelled to carry out her wishes,' I say, trying to be patient and not let my irritation show. I am used to the Claytons. They are as thick-skinned and insensitive as buffaloes, and the women are as tough as the men.

'She said nothing of it when she was alive. Did she say anything to you?'

'No.'

Aunt Bernard chuckles and her big bosom heaves. 'Of course she didn't, because she knew what kind of reception she'd get. No one can reach her where she is now, you see.' Aunt Bernard's eyes widen further, giving her the intense look of a madwoman. 'You're not going to Ireland, are you? You're not considering it?'

'Well . . .' I hesitate.

'Of course you're not. You know it's a silly idea. Bury her ashes next to Ted. They're meant to be together.'

'But she's been very specific—'

Aunt Bernard waves a chubby hand. Her nails are bitten to the quick and her fingers are short and square, like her body. 'She's just playing you for fools. She doesn't want to go to Ireland any more than you and Logan want to take her. She turned her back on that country decades ago and that was that. It seems mighty strange to me that she wants to return now, when she's nothing but ashes.' At the mention of my mother reduced to ash my eyes fill with tears. The thought of it is horrendous. Can that be all that is left? Aunt Bernard continues regardless, either ignoring – or oblivious to – my pain. 'I went there once, Co. Wexford. Pretty but wet. Rained all the time. I've never been so soaked in all my life. There's nothing to see in Ireland but hills and sea and rain.' She waves her fingers again. 'Bury her next to Ted. You will, won't you, Faye? It's the right thing to do. The family has to stay together and generations of Claytons are buried in that cemetery. It would be wrong to take her halfway across the world. You know that as well as I do. And trust me' – she chuckles and clamps those saucer eyes onto mine – 'you really don't want to go to Ireland.'

I lift my chin and hear myself declare, 'Actually, I do.'

Aunt Bernard blinks in astonishment. 'Sorry, what did you say?'

'I said that I *do* want to go.'

Two red spots of indignation flourish on Aunt Bernard's cheeks. 'You do?'

'Yes, I want to see where my mother came from.'

'Muddy fields and cold parlours, I suspect,' Aunt Bernard replies dismissively.

'Then I shall see those,' I say. 'And I shall find out who my mother was.' As I say it I realize, with a frisson of pleasure which takes me totally by surprise, that I have decided. It is done. I will stand up for myself and do exactly as I want. I don't have to take the ashes, I can go alone, that way Logan can't stop me, and if Wyatt objects, I'll simply say that I want to find out whether any of Mother's family are still alive. How can he deny me that? I only hope he doesn't decide to come with me.

I manage to extricate myself from Aunt Bernard and leave the drawing room. I flee to my father's old study, which was transformed by the children into a games room after he died, with a pool table, dart board and a card table in the bay window where his desk used to be. In there I find the cousins hiding out like naughty schoolchildren. Rose and Edwina are lounging on the sofa with their older cousin Maggie, Logan's daughter. They have kicked off their shoes and are smoking cigarettes, complaining about the inordinately large number of ghastly relations present. Logan's boys, Henry, Christopher and Alexander, are playing pool with my son Walter, who is

younger than them and easily led. When they see me standing in the doorway they stop what they are doing and look
at me guiltily.

I don't blame them, however. I wish I could take refuge in
there as well. But I can't. I am the hostess and I have to do my
duty. 'Have you seen your father?' I ask the girls. They shake
their heads. 'If you see him, tell him I'm looking for him.'

'Are you okay, Mom?' Rose asks. How like Rose to be
concerned.

'Oh, I'm fine,' I reply, forcing a smile. 'It'll be over soon.'

'Thank the Lord for that!' says Edwina, blowing out a puff
of smoke. 'If one more person tells me how wonderful my
grandmother was I'm going to slap them.' She flashes a mischievous smile, designed to win the support of her cousins.
'She was a prima donna of the first degree!'

They giggle, then glance anxiously at me to see if I have
taken offence. I haven't.

As I leave the room, taking care to close the door behind
me so that the young people will not be found by determined relations, I see, out of the corner of my eye, someone
hurrying down the corridor to my right. I realize that it is
Temperance. In her black dress with the white collar, short
greying hair and fulsome body, she is unmistakable. She gets
to the end of the corridor and turns left, disappearing into
the pantry.

I follow. I know how hard my mother's death has been on
Temperance, but I also welcome an excuse not to have to go
back into the drawing room. I find her leaning back on the
butler's sink, handkerchief pressed against her lips, eyes red-
rimmed. She is a pitiful sight and my heart goes out to her.
'Temperance . . .' I say.

Temperance shakes her head. 'I'm sorry, Miss Faye,' she

snivels. 'But I can't stand around there watching all them people without making a fool of myself.'

I go to embrace her. 'It's okay, Tempie,' I say softly. 'I wish they'd all go away too.' I put my arms around her and squeeze her hard. She smells of cake, having baked for the occasion. It clings to her hair and to the oil in her skin. I inhale the familiar scent of home and feel the same reassurance I felt when, as a little girl, I used to sit in her lap and allow myself to be gathered into her big arms and spongy bosom. But now it is *I* who am comforting *her*. She lets out a sob, then a shudder.

'I don't know how I'm gon' do without her,' she sniffs. 'I known her since I was fourteen. She's been good to me.'   ·

I reflect on my mother's short fuse, her endless demands, her impatience, her addiction to drama and her obstinacy. 'But you were good to her, too, Tempie,' I say truthfully. 'You put up with a great deal.'

Temperance lifts her face off my shoulder, leaving a wet patch where her tears have soaked into the fabric. 'She never meant to lose her temper, Miss Faye. She was just colourful. One minute up, the next minute down. Sometimes she was all over the place. But she had a heart of gold. There was not a more generous soul on the earth than Miss Tussy. She was never anything but kind to me.' I reflect on the servants' house and the small fortune my mother has left her and agree that she was certainly generous, at least in death. I don't remember her being especially generous when she was alive. Then, as if reading my thoughts, she adds, 'I don't deserve such earthly riches, but she's given them to me anyway.' She begins to cry again.

'Did she ever talk to you about her past?' I ask, changing the subject.

'In Ireland, you mean? She scarcely mentioned it.'

'She wants her ashes scattered there.'

This does not surprise Temperance. 'Of course she does,' she says, as if it is the most natural thing in the world. 'It's home, isn't it? Everybody wants to go home in the end.'

My eyes well and my throat grows tight. 'That's beautiful, Tempie,' I whisper. 'I hadn't thought of that.

'Are you gon' take her, Miss Faye?'

'Logan wants to lay her to rest beside Daddy.'

'That's no good,' says Temperance, her eyebrows coming together in a scowl. 'She don't wanna be buried there. You must take her to Ireland or she'll be stompin' and stampin' up there in the clouds like it's nobody's business and givin' us mortals no peace.'

'I think she wants me to go to Ireland,' I say, a warm, excited feeling firing up in the pit of my belly, dispelling my sorrow. 'I think she wants me to go and discover her roots.'

Temperance looks suspicious. 'You gon' find out about her past?'

'I want to.'

She taps a finger on my nose like she used to do when I was a little girl and looks at me steadily with her dark amber eyes. 'You be careful now, Miss Faye. You don't know what you gon' find.'

'A few old relatives, I hope.'

'And more, I suspect,' says Temperance darkly. 'Everyone has a past, Miss Faye, and I guess Miss Tussy had more of a past than most.'

But I am adamant now that I am going. I am sure that if I go to the place where my mother grew up I'll be able to come back with a strong argument in favour of fulfilling her wish and scattering her ashes there. I know it is the right thing to do, for Mom as well as for myself.

The tugging feeling is persistent. It is now in my heart, as if it has strings and someone is pulling them. I put a hand on my chest as I walk up the corridor towards the noise coming from the drawing room, and smile. It doesn't matter who is doing the tugging, or if it is grief causing my imagination to feel things that aren't really there, because I *want* to go. I want to go very much because I sense it will somehow connect me with my mother. Without her I don't know who I am anymore. She was the wind in my sail and I am now lost at sea. Perhaps if I go to Ireland and spend time alone, far from home, I will find my own wind, and learn how to use my own rudder.

Wyatt is talking to a group of men by the fireplace in the drawing room. They are smoking and drinking and laughing as if it is a party, not a wake. My enthusiasm deflates and I resolve to wait until the guests have gone and we're alone to tell him of my plan. I plunge back into the crowd and accept the condolences with grace.

At last everyone has left. Temperance has served us a light supper, for none of us are hungry. We are all staying at the house; Logan and Lucy and their four children, Wyatt and me and our three. Walter, who is the youngest and the clown of the family, imitates the more eccentric relations and we all laugh. It feels good to laugh, albeit a little inappropriate. When at last we are alone, upstairs in the bedroom which was mine as a girl and later as a married woman, with blue floral wallpaper and matching curtains, I tell Wyatt about Ireland.

He looks at me with a mixture of irritation and sympathy. I can tell he thinks grief has made me irrational. 'Logan says the ashes will remain here,' he tells me, untying his tie. I feel a pressure build beneath my ribcage as the two men rise up in my imagination as obstacles to my independence.

'I'm not going to take Mom with me,' I explain. 'I just want to go and see where she grew up. I feel like I didn't really know her at all.'

Wyatt sighs and puts his hands on his hips. I have been in Nantucket for almost two months, waiting for Mom to die, and after clearing the house with Temperance, so it is natural he should want me back in Boston. He is a partner in a big advertising firm and likes me to accompany him to work dinners and the endless social functions he insists we go to. Wyatt comes alive when he's surrounded by people he can show off to. 'I need you at home, Faye,' he says. 'Everything goes awry when you're not there. I'm bored of going out on my own and coming back to an empty house and it's been months since we entertained. Besides, it doesn't look good. People will start to talk.'

'I'm sure they'll understand.'

'What? You heading off to Ireland on your own? I mean, you don't expect me to come with you, do you?'

'Of course not. I know how busy you are at work.' Wyatt would never put himself out for me, or for anyone else for that matter. He missed Rose's graduation because he wouldn't postpone a game of golf. (Rose was sweet and said she didn't mind. Had it been Edwina all hell would have broken loose!)

'It's out of the question that you go to Ireland on your own,' he continues. 'What will people think?'

I can't help but chuckle at his archaic attitude. 'I hardly think a grown woman travelling on her own is going to raise any eyebrows,' I argue. 'They'll think what we tell them to think,' I add.

He shakes his head and steps out of his trousers. 'It's not safe,' he adds, picking them up and folding them carefully. Wyatt is very particular about tidiness.

'I'll manage,' I reply.

'It's not appropriate.'

'I'm hardly a scarlet woman.'

He brightens. 'I tell you what. I'll take you to Ireland. Next year, perhaps. We can go together.'

This does not suit me. I don't want Wyatt to come with me. If he comes, it will be all about Wyatt. 'That's a nice thought. It really is,' I say. 'I appreciate it, I do. But I don't want to wait. I want to go now. I *need* to go now. I have never gone anywhere on my own.' I look at him beseechingly. 'I've never asked you for anything, Wyatt. Not in all the years we've been married. So, I'm asking now. I want to go. I want to go alone, and I want to go now.'

Wyatt doesn't know what to say. He blinks at me in bewilderment. I hold my ground. I am quite determined. I'm not sure where this determination is coming from. My heart is pounding against my ribs, my hands are sweating and I can feel myself trembling in my skin and yet, I don't back down. 'I'll think about it,' he says at last.

'Wyatt, I'm not asking you to think about it. I'm *telling* you that I'm going.'

Wyatt has never been spoken to like this in all his life. His obedient little wife has always done what she is told. He has always been the alpha male in the family, the one who calls the shots, the man who makes the rules and all the decisions. He scratches his head and his face twists with irritation, all sympathy now gone. He is dealing with a rebellion and he wants to quell it before it gets out of control. He looks at me quizzically, as if wondering who I have been talking to.

Who has sown these seeds of subversion? 'Faye, I accept that this is a difficult time for you, your mother dying and all, but don't forget your place. You are my wife and I need you at home.'

'And I have lost my mother and I need to go to Ireland,' I reply, standing firm and quite astonished by my own tenacity.

'Fine!' He raises his voice now and I flinch. I don't like it when he's angry. But all the same, I don't back down. 'If you still feel the need to go to Ireland, go in the spring. But I suspect, by then, you'll have come to your senses.' He strides into the bathroom and closes the door behind him with a bang.

I nearly jump out of my skin at the sound, but I am triumphant. It is not what I wanted, but it is good enough. I will wait for the spring and I will not change my mind.

Chapter 3

Spring, 1961

Spring comes and I surprise Wyatt by announcing that I am booking my flight to Shannon Airport. I have arranged to stay in a small hotel in Ballinakelly, the town near the castle, called Vickery's Inn, and they have organized a car to pick me up at the airport. The duration of my stay will be two weeks. Wyatt is aghast. He can't understand why I want to be away so long. I'm not entirely sure myself why I booked two weeks and not one. I'm aware that there are darker reasons besides loss that propel me to go. They lurk like shadows around my heart, growing denser the more I wilfully ignore them. But I'm scared to look too closely. Scared of what I will find at their source. I tell myself that I need time away, to rest, recharge and reassess my life, and that in so doing those shadows will go away.

Logan is disapproving and I know he has discussed my trip with Wyatt, undoubtedly on the golf course. Wyatt doesn't know, because I have kept my word and not told a soul, that Mom has left a third of her wealth to a mysterious third party. Logan is trying to change the will, but he really hasn't got a leg to stand on. There *is* no argument. Until we find out the identity of this anonymous person, how can we complain? What if it is one of our children, for example? Unlikely, of course, but not impossible. We wouldn't want to object in that case. Mom has designed this elaborate will for a reason, and I'm pretty sure that going to Ireland will reveal what that reason is. But Logan is trying to alter it all the same. He is damned if he is going to share what he believes to be *our* inheritance with anyone else.

I'm pleased I'm going away. I don't like Logan's attitude and I'm ashamed, because, as much as I hate to admit it, *I* feel something of his outrage.

Unlike Wyatt, the children are not surprised that I am going to search for my mother's roots. They support my decision and are curious to know where their grandmother came from. Rose was the first to tell me that two weeks is the right amount of time, considering the distance I'm travelling. She laughed and said it was hardly worth going if I was only intending to stay a week. It is only Wyatt who thinks it's too long, and inappropriate for a wife to travel alone, without her husband. He is old-fashioned and loathes not being in control. But I am tired of toeing his line; it's time I toed a line of my own.

At one point I worried that Wyatt might decide to come with me, but I should not have wasted my energy. Wyatt is much too preoccupied with work, and with himself. He works hard, I'm sure, but he seems to spend most of his time playing golf. I joke with my girlfriends that he is married to Noble Price Golf Club, but really it is not very funny, because it's true. He's on the course at every opportunity and, knowing little about the game, I find his conversation, and the conversation of his fellow golfing buddies, very dull. I have played the gracious wife and hostess for over thirty years so why am I only tiring of it *now*?

A part of me would like to go back to the way I was before Mom died. At least I knew who I was then. I'm not sure who I am now, only that I don't like myself very much. I want to be someone else, but I don't even know who *that* is either. If Wyatt had the slightest idea of what is going through my head he would send me to see a therapist. But I know I don't need therapy, I just need to go away and find some peace, by myself. I need to work out what it is exactly that my mother's death has unleashed.

I say goodbye to Wyatt, who is sulking now. He's like a child who has not got his way. He accompanies me out into the street where a cab is waiting to take me to the airport and helps me with my suitcase, but he is quiet. Usually he talks about himself, confident that I'm going to listen and agree with everything he says; now he's not even talking. He's answering my questions in monosyllables and doesn't return my smile as I kiss his cheek. He flinches and I feel awkward. It doesn't feel natural to touch him. We are like strangers. I can't even remember the last time we were intimate. I suppose that part of a marriage dies eventually, corroded by familiarity and domesticity. We are like siblings – yes, Wyatt is very like Logan. They could be siblings too.

I feel sad when I climb into the cab. Wyatt doesn't wait or wave, as most husbands would. He goes back inside and I sigh and turn my attention to the wet tarmac, because it rained in the night. The glistening new leaves are just beginning to unfurl on the trees that line the street. They are delicate and the prettiest shade of lime green, almost phosphorescent. Purple and yellow tulips open their petals in the sunshine and the blossom looks like snow. Spring is exploding with colour and scent and yet I yearn to leave, as soon as possible. I am confused to find that I am crying. I wipe my tears and hide behind the back of the driver's seat so that he can't see me in the rear-view mirror. I'm heading to Ireland and I'm afraid. I'm wondering now whether I'm doing the right thing. Perhaps I do need to see a therapist, after all.

I am nervous travelling on my own. I've never thought about it before because I've always travelled with Wyatt. Wyatt arranges everything, the flights, the hotels, the car, the restaurants, the tours, he even looks after my ticket. We've been all over the world, to Italy and Spain, France, England and Africa, but here I am, at Boston Airport, nervously standing in line with my ticket and passport, anxious that I won't find my way to the departure lounge. I tell myself to calm down, that any idiot can find his way around an airport, but still my anxiety builds.

Once I am on the plane, in the window seat, I begin to relax. I have a glass of wine and feel better, even a little excited. I read, I sleep and I think, and I feel I have left all my worries on that landscape which is now far behind me. Below is only sea, the vast blue Atlantic Ocean, and on the other side is Ireland. In a way, I'm coming home. I've always considered myself American, but I'm Irish in my blood. Mom was Irish and grew up there and Dad's family originated there even though they have been in America for generations. I like to think of myself as Irish, even though I don't know what that means. It feels good, like I'm taking on a different personality or finding a new part of myself that I never appreciated was there.

We land in the early morning at Shannon Airport and I easily spot the taxi driver in arrivals, holding up a large piece of card with my name on it. He is a big man with broad shoulders and a slight stoop. He is wearing a grey cap, which matches the greying hair curling beneath it and the thick stubble on his unshaven face. His blue eyes shine brightly as he acknowledges me with a look of surprise. He stares at me as if he has seen me before. I notice the colour of his eyes at once. They are not ice blue like Wyatt's, but indigo. A rich, deep blue like lapis lazuli, and they dominate his face and twinkle beneath thick black eyebrows set low on a wide forehead. I smile and as I approach he smiles back and there is charm and a hint of mischief in the way one side of his mouth curls more than the other. Then, as if remembering his manners, he takes off his cap and nods. '*Céad míle fáilte.* Cormac O'Farrell at your service. Welcome to the Emerald Isle.' His Irish brogue is like whiskey. It is full-bodied and warm and instantly revives me after my long flight.

'It's lovely to be here,' I reply, and it really is lovely. Lovely to be away from home, away from the grim residue of Mother's death and away from Wyatt.

'Is it your first time in Ireland?' he asks.

'It is,' I answer.

There is knowing in his smile, as if he is withholding a secret, and mirth in those twinkly eyes. He appraises me. He's about to say something else. I frown. There's an awkward pause. Then he replaces his cap and takes my suitcase, thinking better of it. I presume it is my red hair that has aroused his curiosity. A woman of my age shouldn't really have long hair like I do. But Mother used to call it my crowning glory and said that, like Samson, my power lay in it and without it I would lose my allure. I'm not sure I have allure, but my hair is indeed lustrous and thick and even though I usually wear it up, I am used to people commenting on it.

Now I am wearing it down. Is that a metaphor for my sudden sense of freedom?

'The car's just outside,' he says. 'It's a good three hours to Ballinakelly, but you'll see a fair bit of the countryside on the way, so the time should pass quickly.'

The car is not a taxi. It is a green Jeep and not a comfortable one either. It smells of damp dog and there are black dog hairs on the seats and in the well beneath the dashboard. I wipe them off, sit in the front and we set off. After a little small talk we settle into an easy silence. I'm immediately engrossed in the intensely green countryside as it opens into smooth hills, damp villages and patchwork fields of sheep and cows grazing on the wild grasses that grow among the bright yellow gorse. Heavy grey clouds scud across a watery blue sky, but it does not rain. Every now and then the sun comes out and chases the shadows across the hills. It is a constant game that mesmerizes me, a battle between light and dark played out on an intensely green canvas. Ireland feels small, intimate, isolated. Why I should think this, I don't know. Perhaps because the lanes are narrow and the fields small, encompassed by grey-stone walls and woolly hedges speckled with budding fuchsias, which give it a quaint and old-fashioned feel. There is something about it that instantly appeals to me. I like to think it's because I have Irish blood running through my veins, but I suspect I am just happy to be here at last.

I see farmhouses and other small dwellings and wonder if my mother lived in a place like them. I consider how very different her life must have been, growing up here, compared to the life she made in America. I wonder how she must have felt leaving it, and whether she ever regretted not coming back. I'll never know the answers, but it doesn't matter. Perhaps I can ask around and see if anyone remembers her or knows where she lived. It would be interesting to find the house where she was raised. I might even find the odd relative, who knows? But I don't want to ask my driver. I want to spend some time on my own first before I talk to people. I'm going to be in Ballinakelly for two weeks; I'm wary of opening up to people too quickly and then being unable to shake them off. I've come here for some peace, so I'll keep myself to myself for the first half of my stay, at least.

We stop for gas. Cormac buys some Club Milks and offers me one. I don't really like biscuits but I take one because I'm hungry. When we get back into the Jeep he has decided it is time for a chat. He proceeds to give me a history lesson as we drive into what he calls 'Michael Collins country'. As the Jeep makes its way slowly along the narrow lanes that meander through the gentle folds in the land he tells me about the War of Independence and the Civil War that followed, when rebels fighting for an Ireland free from British rule plotted their strikes and staged their ambushes in these very hills. He tells me about the Easter Rising, the Kilmichael Ambush and Michael Collins' assassination by his fellow Irishmen at Béal na Bláth, which he translates as the mouth of flowers. At first I am irritated. I'm tired and I don't want to be talked to, but then I find my interest growing, and the way he's telling it, in his sonorous voice with its soft Irish lilt, is alluring. I gaze out over the wild and rugged slopes and imagine the rebels hiding out among the rocks. I ask questions and Cormac knows the answers, and he clearly enjoys showing off his knowledge. 'Where were you when all this was taking place?' I ask.

He grins. 'Up there,' he replies, giving a nod to the hills.

'Honestly?' I say, my curiosity suddenly spiked.

'As true as I'm sitting here,' he answers.

'How old were you, if that's not a rude question?'

'I was a lad of twenty-five in 1921.'

'Are you seriously telling me that you were a rebel?' He holds up his left hand then and I notice he is missing his little finger. 'My God!' I exclaim in horror. 'How did that happen?'

'The Tans took it when they tried to extract information.'

I am astonished that he is talking about something so terrible to someone he has never met, and so casually. 'How horrific,' I say, embarrassed because I don't have the right words. I have never met anyone who has lost a finger before.

'Oh, it's nothing. Many fared worse than I did. At least I'm alive.'

'Well, yes, that's definitely a bonus,' I reply drily.

We continue in silence for a while as I'm trying to digest what he has just told me. When I look out of the window I don't imagine faceless rebels among the rocks, but Cormac O'Farrell. I can't help but imagine him as a dashing young man; he is handsome even now and he is sixty-five, if my math is correct. I have never been very good with numbers. He's the same age as Logan and two years younger than Wyatt yet he looks considerably older than both. He's clearly not a man who preens himself like my husband and brother do.

At last the sea comes into view, sparkling beneath a big blue sky, and he breaks the silence by announcing that we are coming into Ballinakelly.

This is where my mother grew up. This town of shabby-looking houses, mostly painted white or not painted at all and left an austere grey, with sloping slate roofs and rows of chimney stacks, from where rooks gather and keep watch with suspicious black eyes. I wonder how much it has changed since she was here. Besides the telephone wires that criss-cross the street I don't imagine a great deal. Everything looks old-fashioned, from another age, and poor. The houses are small,

many of them could do with a fresh coat of paint. I peer
into the store windows and wonder at how little everything
is in comparison to America. We pass a pub with the name
O'Donovan's written in big gold letters above the door. A
group of rough-looking men loiter outside smoking, in caps
and jackets and heavy boots, and I imagine they must be
farmers. They break off their conversation to stare warily
at the Jeep as we motor on. Cormac raises a hand and they
acknowledge him with a nod and peer into where I am sitting.
They are very curious. Clearly no one has told them it is rude
to stare. We pass the Catholic church and I know, without a
shadow of doubt, that Mom would have spent much of her
time in there. She was a devout Catholic. I envisage her as a
girl, walking up the path and through the big doors. I decide
to attend Mass as soon as I can. I know I will get a sense of
her in there. I will also get a sense of peace.

We are obstructed by a dozen brown-and-white cows being
herded up the street by a woolly-haired farmer with a stick.
Cormac thinks nothing of it. He rolls down the window,
rests his elbow on the frame and shares a joke, as if he has
all the time in the world. They both laugh, something about
the night before at Ma Murphy's, but I'm not really listening.
I'm watching the cows as they wander nonchalantly up the
high street. There are a few cars parked on the kerb, locals
browsing the shops, life going on in its usual way and no one
seems in the least surprised to see cows there, in the middle
of the road. Even dogs don't bother to chase them but trot
alongside their owners, snouts to the ground in pursuit of
more important business.

At last Cormac draws up outside the hotel. It is a white
building with large sash windows and a wide porch, which
gives it a stately air. I imagine it must have been a private

house once, perhaps the mayor's or some other local grandee's. Cormac lifts my bag out of the trunk and escorts me inside. The lady at the reception desk takes her eyes off her finger-nails. As she registers the new guest she looks surprised. Her mouth opens. But she then checks herself and smiles in the way women like that are trained to do, with false charm. I'm puzzled, Cormac gave me the same look at the airport. Surely they've seen women with red hair before?

'Good morning,' she says, blinking at me through her spectacles with magnified eyes. She is middle-aged with curly brown hair, a freckly face and crooked teeth. A badge bearing the name Nora Maloney is pinned to her chest.

Cormac puts the suitcase on the shiny wooden floor-boards and answers for me. 'This here is Mrs Langton, from America,' he says.

'Of course. Welcome to Vickery's Inn,' says Nora Maloney.

'It was grand meeting you,' Cormac says to me, touching his cap. 'I'll leave you in Nora's capable hands. I hope you have a good stay.'

'Thank you for picking me up and for giving me a brief his-tory on the way.' I unclasp my handbag, expecting to pay him.

'That's all right, Mrs Langton,' he says. 'You can pay me when you leave. I assume you'll be needing to be driven back at some point?'

'Yes, I will,' I reply, not wanting to think of leaving, having only just arrived. 'Are you the only cab driver in Ballinakelly?'

He laughs and his skin creases at his temples and around his mouth. 'I'm not a cab driver, Mrs Langton,' he says.

'Oh, I'm sorry, I assumed ...'

His indigo eyes twinkle at me. 'Enjoy Ballinakelly, it's a grand town,' he says and he saunters out, hands in his jacket pockets, a whistle upon his lips.

I turn to Nora Maloney. 'Oh dear, I hope I haven't offended him.'

'Now why would you be thinking that? I don't imagine it's easy to offend Cormac O'Farrell.'

'If he's not a cab driver, what is he?'

She smiles and I notice the affection in it at once. I realize that Cormac must be one of those local characters who is beloved by everyone. 'He's a bit of an everything man,' she says, wrinkling her small nose. 'Now, let me show you to your room. Leave the suitcase here, Séamus will bring it. Séamus!' she shouts.

I follow her to the stairs and we climb to the second floor. My room is at the end of the corridor. She puts the key in the lock and I notice her bright red nails. She turns it and the door opens into a modest-sized room with pale floral wallpaper, a double bed draped in a light green quilt, a sash window looking out onto the street and an adjoining bathroom, which is just big enough for a small bath and a sink. 'Ah, Séamus, there you are.' I step aside as Séamus, a burly young man with tousled black hair to his shoulders and moody green eyes, puts the suitcase on the bed. 'You must be tired after your journey,' says Nora Maloney. 'If you'd like something to eat, we'll be serving lunch downstairs until three and then high tea from five to seven. If you need anything, just shout.' Séamus gives me a strange look, his watery eyes lingering on me longer than is polite.

'Thank you, but I think I have everything I need.'

Nora Maloney nods. She too hovers in the doorway as if she wants to say something else and regards me quizzically. But I thank them again and close the door, shutting them out. I wonder at their ill-concealed curiosity, as if they have never had a guest before or, at least, one who looks like me.

In America my hair is my greatest asset, envied by women and admired by men, but here it seems to be considered exotic.

I unpack what little I have brought, pleased that I have included sweaters and a coat, for although it is spring, it is cold and there is a dampness in the air that makes it feel colder. I guess it rains a lot here, that's why it's so green.

In the dining room I eat at a small table on my own. There are other guests, tourists like me, I imagine, but I take no notice of them. I'm content, sitting there by myself. I'm surprised how content I am with no one to talk to. I'm happy to be here, happy that I have two weeks ahead of me – two weeks with nothing to do but be.

After lunch I make a trunk call to America, because that is what is expected of me. Wyatt is in a meeting. I leave a message with his secretary to let him know I have arrived at the hotel. I do not leave my number; I do not want him to call me back.

I wander into the street. The sun is warm but it is cold in the shadows. I take the side of the street that is not in shade and stroll up the sidewalk. I stop in front of store windows and browse. There is a shoe store called Downey's, a woman's clothing store called Garbo's, a drugstore, a bakery, a bank, a post office and a newsagent. I enter Garbo's, out of curiosity, not with a view to buying anything, and the young salesgirl does a double take, much like Cormac, Nora Maloney and Séamus did on first seeing me. I smile at her and frown, hoping for an explanation, but she smiles back without giving me one. I decide to get to the bottom of it.

'Is it my red hair?' I ask, touching it. She looks puzzled. I continue, determined to find out what it is that's making everyone look at me strangely. 'You gave me an odd look when I came in, I thought it must be on account of my hair.'

'Oh no, I'm sorry for that,' she says, blushing. 'I thought you were someone else.'

'Ah, so that's what it is. Everyone's been giving me odd looks today.'

'That's because you look very like Mrs Trench. I suppose it's the hair, she has red hair as well, thick and wavy just like yours, and she wears it down her back. You have her face as well, or something of it.'

'How funny, I'll look out for her,' I say, relieved that *that* is all it is.

'Oh, you can't miss her. Indeed, it'll be like looking in the mirror,' she says with a laugh.

I browse. There are some very nice wool sweaters and skirts, but I'm not in the mood to try anything on. I just want to see the town. I thank her and walk back out into the street. I decide to make my way to the church. I feel it pulling at me for that is the one place I can be sure has not changed since my mother's childhood. Now that I know why people are staring at me, I am no longer uncomfortable. I'm happy to be in Ireland, in this quaint little town where my mother grew up. I don't think of Wyatt, save to appreciate the vast distance between us. This is the first time in my life that I am on my own in a foreign country and the feeling is intoxicating. I walk with a bounce in my step. I want to laugh, but I'm being looked at with that curious, surprised expression which accompanies every stare, so I hold in my laughter and acknowledge them with a smile instead.

I reach the church of All Saints. It's a grey-stone building built in the shape of a cross, probably hundreds of years old, with a tower that prods the sky. The big door is open and I walk inside. There are rows of wooden pews, an altar draped in a green silk cloth, a large statue of Christ hanging behind it and tall, stained-glass windows. It smells as all Catholic churches do, of incense and melted wax and years of worship. A table of votive candles is set up to the right of the altar, their little flames dancing jauntily in the gloomy atmosphere of this ancient house, and I think of the prayers that go with them and wonder if anyone hears. There are a few elderly women in black mantillas bent in prayer, but apart from them the church is empty. I sit at the back and think of my mother. As I picture her face I feel an ache in the core of my heart. It is a lonely, cold ache that is full of emptiness. I wonder where she is now and what she is seeing. I hope she knows I'm here in her home town, because I believe she wanted me to come.

I decide to light a candle and say a prayer for her soul. I'm not particularly religious. I haven't been to Mass in a long time, but I believe in God and am ashamed to admit that I only call on Him in times of need. I light the little candle and close my eyes. I need Him now. I need Him to hold Mom in His light, and to hold me in His light as well.

When I leave, I find a gathering of people at the gate. I wonder what they are waiting for. Was one of those old ladies someone important? But as I walk down the path I realize that they are staring at *me*. Most of them are elderly. The men stand with their caps in hand and look away when I catch their eyes, but the women are less abashed and simply stare. I wonder who this Mrs Trench is and why they are so intrigued by my resemblance to her. I say hello and walk, embarrassed, through the throng. I hear a woman say to another, 'Sacred Heart of Jesus, Mary, you're right. She has a double. They say if you meet your double, you'll be dead by midnight, God save us. I'm not in the better for the shock.'

I'm not sure I can take two weeks of this. I resolve to ask Nora Maloney about Mrs Trench when I get back to the hotel.

I'm not feeling so confident now and the bounce in my step has been deflated. I hurry back down the street, eyes to the ground. The sun has gone behind a cloud and I feel chilly. The town no longer looks so charming.

I dash into the foyer and look for Nora Maloney. She is behind her desk talking to a woman with long red hair. I catch my breath. Nora Maloney looks past the woman and nods at me. 'Here she is, Mrs Trench,' she says. The woman turns round, just as she does in my dream, and for a moment I believe I really am staring at myself. At a more beautiful me, I must add, for this woman has finer features and fuller lips and an air of confidence that I do not possess. She settles her grey eyes onto my face and is as surprised as I am. Her lips part and her hand goes to her heart. 'They said my double was in town, but I didn't believe them,' she says in an English accent. She approaches me, elegant in a pair of jodhpurs, fitted tweed jacket and boots. She looks as if she has just got off a horse.

She puts out a gloved hand. 'My name is Kitty Trench. And you are?' She is amused by our similarity and her penetrating gaze probes my more reticent one.

'Faye Langton,' I reply and shake her hand.

'You're American?'

'Yes, but my mother was Irish. She was born here, in Ballinakelly.'

'Then we will know her, for sure. What is her name?'

'Arethusa Deverill,' I say. No sooner have those words escaped my lips than Kitty Trench blanches. Now she doesn't look amused at all, more like astonished. She puts her fingers to her lips and exclaims, 'Good Lord!' before taking me by the arm and leading me away from Nora Maloney, who is listening to every word and gripped. 'You are Arethusa Deverill's daughter?' she asks in a whisper.

'Yes, I am,' I reply, wondering why the sudden secrecy.

'Then we are cousins,' she tells me. 'Arethusa is my father's sister. I think you'd better come with me,' she says in an urgent tone of voice. Then she turns to Nora Maloney. 'Would you arrange for someone to drive Mrs Langton to the White House.' She looks at me and grins. 'I don't suppose you brought a horse?'

Chapter 4

My cousin Kitty Trench, Kitty *Deverill*, trots off down the street on her horse, past O'Donovan's pub where the men doff their caps, and heads off into the hills. I see her, beyond the rooftops, galloping up the hillside. She is an accomplished rider. She looks as if she has spent her entire life on a horse. Her flame-coloured hair flies out behind her and she is seated confidently in the saddle. My admiration for her grows, along with my excitement. I have found a relation, a first cousin, and I have only just arrived. She is beautiful, self-assured and glamorous. She has an energy about her that makes me long for her company. I want to be in this gracious woman's light. I want to be like her. I *look* like her, although a less striking version, but I am not *like* her. I find it curious that she doesn't have an Irish accent and she does not look poor. She is obviously a Deverill who made good, like my mother.

While Nora Maloney tracks down someone to take me to Kitty's house, I go upstairs to retrieve my mother's diary. I don't imagine Kitty will know how to break the code, but I feel the need to bring it with me all the same. When I return to the foyer Cormac O'Farrell is talking to Nora Maloney and I know they are discussing me and Kitty, because they stop talking the moment they see me and look guilty.

'I understand you need to be taken to Mrs Trench's house,' says Cormac.

'Yes, please,' I reply. 'Thank you for coming so quickly.'

He smiles. 'I see you've met your double.' I now realize why he gave me such a strange look at the airport. It would have saved me a lot of confusion if he had just told me there and then that I had a twin in his town.

Nora Maloney is waiting eagerly for my response. I imagine whatever I say will be spread around town before I've even arrived at Mrs Trench's house. 'We are very much alike, aren't we,' I reply.

'The dead stamp of each other,' Nora Maloney agrees and I'm a little embarrassed because I'm sure they are both thinking what I'm thinking, that Kitty Deverill is a far superior version.

I climb into the front seat of the Jeep. I want to talk about Kitty Deverill and her family – *my* family. Cormac is only too happy to enlighten me. 'Kitty Deverill lives in the White House, which is on the Castle Deverill estate.'

At the mention of Castle Deverill I interrupt him. Mom wanted her ashes scattered in view of it. 'Castle Deverill?' I ask. 'Who lives there?'

'Why, it's their family seat. The Deverill family seat,' he says as if I'm very ignorant not knowing. As if everyone knows about Castle Deverill except me. I'm confused. I thought Mom was poor and now I learn that her family owns a castle. My dream flashes before me. I see the grand hall, the staircase and dark corridor and finally the little room at the top of the tower where I find myself. I shudder. Did my mother grow up in a castle? Am I somehow tapping into her memories? Is that possible? Temperance would certainly think so. 'Castle Deverill has been in the Deverill family since Charles II's day, when Barton Deverill, the first Lord Deverill of Ballinakelly, was given a title and lands as a reward for his loyalty to the King,' Cormac continues.

'Are they English then?' I ask.

'They are Anglo-Irish. Kitty would put more emphasis on the Irish than the Anglo, mind you, but historically the Deverills have considered themselves English.'

I'm amazed that my mother never told us about the castle. 'I'd love to see it,' I say, hoping that Cormac will drive me past it.

'You don't see it from the road. It's hidden behind a wall and trees. The best view is from the hills as it nestles nicely in the valley, overlooking the sea. I'm sure Mrs Trench will take you if you ask her.'

'I'm her first cousin,' I tell him proudly, because I'm so thrilled to be related to her that I have to tell someone. 'My mother, who recently died, was her aunt.'

Cormac keeps his eyes on the road. 'Your mother was Arethusa Deverill?' he asks, and there is wonder in his voice, as if I have just told him that I am related to Santa Claus.

'Yes, she left Ireland for America and never came back.'

'As so many did,' he replies. Then he shakes his head. 'Indeed, it was all very mysterious.'

'What was?'

'Arethusa Deverill. The forgotten Deverill.' He glances at me and frowns. 'Do you know why she left for America?'

I shrug, as if it's obvious why she left. But I stop myself replying. She wasn't poor, clearly, and she wasn't in search of a better life, if she lived in a castle. So why did she leave? 'I don't know,' I admit. 'Do you?'

'There were rumours. People like to talk and when they don't know something, they like to make it up.'

'What were the rumours?' I ask.

He shakes his head. 'I'm sure Mrs Trench will know all about it. Or at least, Lord Deverill will, her father.'

Not only do I have a first cousin, but I have an uncle too, and he's a lord! I'm finding it hard to take in, these sudden revelations. I can't imagine why Mom never told us. 'Are there many Deverills?'

He chuckles. 'Lots of them and lots to tell about them.'

'Do tell me,' I say, but Cormac steers the car through an open gate and up a drive towards a pretty white house that sits serenely at the top of the slope.

'Another time,' he says, pulling up outside the front door.

Kitty appears as soon as I get out. I thank Cormac and he turns the Jeep around and sets off back down the drive. Kitty has changed clothes – she must have ridden like the wind – and is now in a tweed skirt and soft green twinset, her thick hair is pinned at the back of her head yet loose about her face and neck. She looks effortlessly stylish. I envy her panache. Her smile is wide and welcoming. I feel as if we already know each other, but then I suppose I have seen something close to her face a thousand times in the mirror. 'Come in, Faye. I will call you Faye because you are my cousin. I hope you don't mind.'

'Of course you must,' I reply, following her into the hall. The house is beautifully uncontrived. Nothing matches. It is as if Kitty has thrown things together because they give comfort and colour, not because they match, and everything is flamboyant, like she is. The walls could do with a fresh coat of paint and the fabrics on the chairs and the rug on the floor are faded and worn. The furniture is antique and polished, but I can see the odd chip and scratch here and there. I don't think Kitty cares much for material things. She likes flowers, though. There is a large glass vase of white lilies on a round table and their sweet perfume saturates the air. And she likes light. Beams of sunshine stream through big sash windows and flood the house with a soft golden radiance. Kitty leads me into a square-shaped drawing room where tall windows look out onto a garden flourishing with daffodils, tulips and blossom, and to the sparkling ocean beyond. Big squidgy sofas and armchairs are arranged around a fireplace where a fire must have been burning for most of the day for the logs are covered in grey ash and gently smouldering, and the room smells of wood smoke and peat.

Kitty sinks into the sofa and I take the place beside her. She is still looking at me in disbelief, as if she can't quite believe her eyes. Yet there is a familiarity between us. We are already kin, we share the same blood, the same history, the same ancestors, now all we have to do is fill in the gaps.

We chat about America, my flight and my first impressions of Ballinakelly, but I know we are just biding time while the maid puts down the tray of tea and cake and fills two china tea-cups. 'You must try the porter cake,' says Kitty. 'It's very Irish and quite delicious.' I watch the maid cut a slice and hand it to me on a plate. It looks like fruit cake, but I can smell the alcohol in it. I fork a piece into my mouth. It is indeed delicious.

At last we are left alone. Kitty leans forward and fixes me with her intense gaze. It is the sort of gaze that has the ability to extract secrets. I expect she is going to extract all of mine. Even the ones I should not tell. 'I am dying to know,' she says. 'What has become of your mother?'

'She died last fall,' I reply, and I feel sad saying that word 'die', which is so final, so irrevocable.

Her face crumples with compassion. 'I'm so sorry,' she

says and I know she feels it. I know she has also suffered loss, because her empathy is deeply sincere. She touches my arm. Her fingers are long and pale, her nails cut short and a little ragged. They are the hands of a woman who spends much of her time outside, in the garden and the stables, I imagine. It is then that I notice she is wearing no make-up and that her hair, although pinned up, is unbrushed and tangled, greying slightly around the hairline. She gives the impression of being groomed and yet she isn't. I admire her more for her lack of vanity. American women are so polished, it is refreshing to find a woman whose beauty does not depend on that.

'My mother never spoke of her homeland,' I tell her. 'Or she said very little about it. When she died she requested in her will that her ashes be scattered in view of Castle Deverill.'

Kitty puts a finger to her lips and shakes her head. 'That's so touching,' she murmurs and her grey eyes begin to shine. I'm surprised at the depth of her emotion, for surely she was too young to know her aunt, who would have left Ireland before she was born.

'We had never heard of Castle Deverill before the attorney came to read the will. Mom told us she left Ireland because her family was poor.' Kitty nods but says nothing, so I continue, telling this woman I have only just met things I have not shared with anyone. 'The fact that she wanted to be cremated was bad enough. My father was a devout Catholic and it was always assumed that Mom would be buried beside him, along with all his other ancestors. But when she stipulated that she wanted to return home, we were astonished. We didn't think she liked her home very much. Why else did she never go back? Not in all her married years did she ever *want* to go back. And after my father died, she never even mentioned Ireland at all.'

'So you've come to scatter her ashes?' Kitty asks.

'No. I haven't brought them. I've come on my own. You see, my brother Logan does not want to bring her here. He wants to bury her beside our father. In fact, he disagrees with most of the will and is trying to alter it.'

'I see,' says Kitty thoughtfully. 'A bit of a conundrum.'

'Yes, it's complicated,' I agree. I sigh, because I really don't know how it will end. 'But I decided to come and find out where my mother was born and what sort of life she had here in Ireland. I didn't expect her to have grown up in a castle.'

Kitty's face flowers into an enchanting smile. 'And Castle Deverill is not just any castle,' she says, clearly enormously proud of it. 'It's one of the most magnificent castles in Ireland. I will take you to see it tomorrow. Sadly, it's already getting dark now. Much better to see it in the light, in all its glory.'

'Who lives there?'

'My brother JP Deverill and his wife Alana.'

'I gather the Deverills are a big family,' I say, but Kitty is grinning at me and I realize that they are not only a big family but an important family too. I feel foolish knowing so little about my mother and where she once belonged.

'We are many,' Kitty says. 'And now, with you, we are more. Do you have children, Faye?'

'I have three. All grown-up now, of course. Rose, Edwina and Walter. They'll be astonished when I tell them what I've discovered here. That their grandmother was an aristocrat living in a castle. They simply won't believe it.' I laugh and imagine their reactions in turn. Rose who'll be curious. Edwina nonchalant but secretly riveted and Walter, the actor, who will put on an English accent and go into character, entertaining us with his comedy.

'Why don't you come and dine with us tonight?' Kitty asks.

'I will ask my parents to join us. I know my father will want to meet his niece. He's not going to believe it when I tell him you're here.'

I'm excited at the thought of meeting my uncle. My mother's brother. 'I'd love to,' I reply eagerly. 'I know my mother had two brothers. Does the other one live here too?'

Kitty shakes her head. 'Sadly, Uncle Rupert died in the Great War.'

'Oh, I see. I'm sorry.'

'He was a real character. My brother Harry died in the last war, so we are not complete, but those of us who remain are very close. I have two sisters, one who lives here and one who lives in England and they have children and grandchildren. As I said, we are many. I know my father will welcome you into the family.' She laughs and then adds with a shake of the head, 'He is, after all, quite used to the odd long-lost relation appearing out of the blue.'

I frown, but she does not elaborate. I sense this family has more secrets than most.

'It will be nice to learn about her childhood,' I say. 'Your father must have lots of stories about her. I never expected to meet any of her relations. I thought they were all dead.'

'I think that's what she wanted you to think,' says Kitty. She is right, of course, but I can't imagine why. All those years we thought of her as an orphan of the Irish famine she had an aristocratic family who lived in a castle. It seems absurd now, sitting opposite her niece.

'I went to the church here in Ballinakelly and lit a candle for her. I wish she were alive so I could ask her why she left and never came back.'

'Which church did you go to?' Kitty asks, sipping her tea.

'The Catholic church.'

'I thought so. I don't suppose Arethusa told you that she wasn't Catholic, Faye.' Her voice is gentle. 'She was Protestant, like all Deverills.'

'Protestant!' I am shocked that my mother chose to lie about her religion. I am so appalled by this news that I begin to make excuses for her. 'Well, my father was Catholic, so I guess she converted. She was very devout, you know. A very devout and dedicated Catholic.'

Kitty looks doubtful and I hear how thin my justifications must sound to her. She doesn't say that her grandparents would turn in their graves if they knew that their daughter had con-verted to Catholicism, which is the sort of thing Logan would say; she doesn't have to. I know it. I know enough about Irish history to appreciate what converting to Catholicism would mean to a Deverill. It would be considered traitorous at the very least.

I am so consumed by my mother's secrets, emerging now into the light, that I have forgotten about the diary in my handbag. Remembering it suddenly, I reach down and lift it out. I look at it and run my hand over the worn leather cover. 'This was her diary,' I tell Kitty. 'She left it to me in her will. The trouble is, it's written in code so I can't read it. I don't even know why I brought it to show you. Probably because I hoped you'd be able to decipher it for me. Silly, really. Maybe your father knows the code she wrote in.'

'Let me have a look,' says Kitty, putting out her hand. She smiles at me sympathetically, aware perhaps that I have received a few too many shocks for one day. 'I don't believe things happen for no reason, Faye. You brought it to me because you were prompted to bring it.'

I look at her, unsure whether or not she's joking. She sounds like Temperance and has the same airy-fairy look on her face, which is always a signal for me to change the subject. Kitty opens the book and looks at the first page. 'You were right to bring it to me,' she says, a touch of triumph in her voice. 'It's mirror writing.'

'Mirror writing?'

'Of course. Did you know that Leonardo da Vinci wrote in mirror writing? It's written backwards, so you have to hold it up to a mirror.'

'Really? And you can tell just by looking at it?' I'm amazed and slightly uneasy now, because I'll be able to read it – and perhaps answer my questions for myself. I'm not sure that I *want* to know the answers.

'Absolutely sure. Look.' She stands up and holds the book open in front of the mirror which hangs above the fireplace. I follow her and gaze into the mirror with a mixture of fear and fascination. It is as if Mother is speaking from beyond the grave.

'You're right. It's so clear.' I read a short paragraph:

Poor Grandpa is sick today. Really, he's a terrible patient. Mama and I take it in turns to read to him, but he grumbles and complains and nothing is quite right. His tea is too hot, then it's too cold and he's furious he's going to miss the meet tomorrow. He likes nothing more than riding out with the hounds and is more courageous, and according to Mama, more reckless, than all the men in the county. The way he's carrying on one would have thought he was never going to ride again. But he'll be well in a day or two, Dr Johnson says so. It is nothing more than a common cold, but Grandpa might as well be dying for the fuss he's making . . .

'How extraordinary,' I whisper.

'Well, she didn't want anyone else to read it,' says Kitty. 'But now *you* can.'

'How do *you* know about mirror writing?'

'Because *I* used to write my diaries that way too.'

'It must be a Deverill thing,' I say in wonder.

She laughs. 'I'm not sure it is. I don't think anyone else wrote like this.' She hands back the diary. 'Now you can read her story for yourself.'

I sense *she* would like to read it too. But I don't offer to share it, at least, I won't until I have read it.

'I will,' I reply. 'I will read it slowly. After all, I have two weeks in which to do it.'

'How lovely. Two weeks to get to know us and for us to get to know you. Let me drive you back to the hotel so you can have a rest and change before dinner.'

'That's very kind of you.'

'Not at all. You're family. It's the least I can do. I will send someone to pick you up at seven.'

Kitty drives me back to Vickery's Inn. The sun has now set and it is dusk. The sky is a pale luminous blue, the hills silhouetted against it dark and mysterious. It is cold now and the air is damp. It smells of new grass and rich earth and smoke from the chimneys as families light their fires and settle down for the night. Kitty and I have much to talk about and yet we fall into an easy silence. I look out of the window while she drives and neither of us speaks. It isn't awkward. It isn't awkward at all.

Suddenly, I feel weary. I can't believe I have only just arrived. That last night I was on a plane and this morning I drove from the airport with Cormac O'Farrell, who isn't a taxi driver, apparently. I smile at that. I love Ireland already. At least, I love Ballinakelly. In spite of the fact that I understand my mother even less than I did when she was alive, I love it. It is in my blood, as it was in hers.

When I get to my room I lie on the bed and close my eyes. I don't have the courage to read Mom's diary. She told so many untruths: she wasn't Catholic, yet all the years I was alive she was more Catholic even than Daddy. She didn't come from a poor, starving peasant family either, she came from an old, aristocratic family, and she wasn't Irish. She was *Anglo*-Irish, and I know how different that is. If she lied about those three things, what else did she lie about? What would Logan think if I told him? *Am* I going to tell him? I don't know. The one person I really want to tell is Rose. I can just see her lying on my bed, her grey eyes wide with astonishment, her lips curling with amusement, and asking me how I feel about it, if I'm okay. Always unselfish, empathetic, so typical of Rose. I smile and think of her now and feel suddenly quite alone.

I barely have the energy to go out for dinner. Part of me wants to curl up in bed and go to sleep, but my curiosity gets the better of me and I heave myself up and bathe in the cramped bathroom. I copy Kitty and pin up my hair, leaving stray bits about my hairline. I stare at myself in the mirror, seeing something of Kitty in my reflection, but not enough to make me feel beautiful like her. I wonder what Wyatt would think of her? I think she'd frighten him. He likes a woman he can dominate. I doubt anyone could dominate Kitty Deverill.

At seven I am picked up by one of the Deverill retainers. He is a middle-aged man with jet-black hair and dark brown eyes. He looks surprised when he sees me, but I smile and climb into the back of the car. I wonder if my uncle is going to look at me like that as well. I relax against the seat and reassure myself that it won't be long before everyone in town knows who I am and then they'll stop staring at me like I'm Kitty Deverill's long-lost twin sister.

When I arrive at the White House Lord and Lady Deverill are arriving too. Their car has pulled up and Lord Deverill is climbing out. It is dark but I can see in the light shining from the windows of the house that he is still handsome, with a wide face and grey hair swept off a broad forehead. He walks stiffly round to the door on the other side of the car, which the chauffeur is holding open. Lord Deverill bends down and puts out his hand. A gloved hand reaches out and takes it. Then one satin shoe steps onto the gravel, then another, followed by an elderly lady in a pale blue dress and glittering diamonds who I assume to be Lady Deverill. I watch in fascination as the two of them make their way to the front door, arms linked, his hand on hers. They are talking. They don't see me in my car, waiting until they have disappeared before I get out.

I am nervous now. My uncle is a lord and I have never met a lord before. They are both elegant. He in a jacket and bow tie, she in a long dress. I feel very shabby in mine. I wish I had brought my diamonds and my best dresses, but I never expected to be dining with aristocracy. I wonder if there is anywhere in Ballinakelly where I might purchase a gown. I doubt it.

I am greeted at the door by a butler. He takes my coat and escorts me into the drawing room where I sat earlier with Kitty. The fire is ablaze and there are more people in the room than I expected. They turn their eyes on me as I step across the threshold, but Kitty welcomes me enthusiastically. 'You must meet my husband, Robert,' she says, introducing me to a stiff-looking man with thick greying hair that must have once been dark brown and a sombre face. He is handsome, but there is something bland about his features. He pales in comparison to Kitty's effervescence. He is not what I would imagine her husband to be. Before I can dwell on him I am introduced to Kitty's parents. 'This is my father, Bertie, *Uncle* Bertie to you, Faye, and my mother, Maud.'

Uncle Bertie's gaze falls onto my face and seems to devour it. I know he is searching for his sister, but I look nothing like her. I look like his daughter. 'By God, you're the image of my mother,' he says, and his aristocratic English accent is very pronounced.

'Yes, you're Adeline, unmistakably so,' Aunt Maud agrees, shaking my hand with her thin, cold one. Her eyes are icy blue; beautiful, pale, wintry eyes, surrounded by heavily made-up black lashes. She has high cheekbones, a sharp determined jawline, silver hair cut into a severe bob and thin lips, and yet she is striking. I imagine she must have been a ravishing beauty in her day.

I turn to Kitty for an explanation. Everyone is staring at me. This is what it must feel like to be an exotic animal in a zoo. Kitty laughs. 'We didn't get around to talking about our grandmother, Adeline. I look like her too, but you, Faye, even more so. Oh, how I would adore you two to meet.' Kitty sighs dramatically. An exuberant man steps forward and grins. He must be Kitty's brother, for he, too, has red hair, freckles, full lips and a cheeky and charming smile, although he looks young enough to be her son. His eyes twinkle and they are grey like mine and Kitty's.

'I'm JP Deverill,' he says and shakes my hand. He is strong and athletic and my bones are crushed in his grip. He has the same energy as his sister, only an intensely male version of it. 'And this is my wife, Alana,' he says, stepping aside to give her space. His wife is sweet-looking with fair hair and eyes the colour of an Irish sky. She has an easy smile, which she now settles onto me, and it is full of warmth. I feel accepted. I have only just met these people and yet I feel as if I am one of them. As if they have been waiting all my life to meet me, and to include me.

We are given glasses of wine and invited to sit down. I sit beside Alana on the sofa. There is a brief silence. No one knows where to start. They all have questions, Uncle Bertie more than anyone else, I imagine. This is a significant moment for *me*, but I haven't until this moment considered *their* feelings. My mother was Uncle Bertie's sister. She left home and never returned. Now she is dead. I look at his jovial, ruddy face and wonder how he feels about the unexpected arrival of his niece and the news that his sister is no longer alive.

'I have explained why you have come to Ballinakelly,' Kitty says at last. She looks at her father and smiles at him fondly. 'It is of great comfort to Papa to know that Arethusa wanted to come home, in the end.'

I feel moved. Kitty has no memory of her aunt because Arethusa left before she was born yet she appreciates what this means to her father. I imagine the family must have spoken of my mother a great deal over the years. They must have wondered about her. Where she was, what she was doing. And here I am, ready to tell them what they want to know. Only I'm not sure what I *do* know. Shortly, it becomes clear that they know the beginning of the story and I know the end, and yet there's a very big middle which none of us knows. I sense it will come to light when I read her diary. I sense, too, that that is why she gave it to me, to read here, in Ireland, with her family.

'Tussy was defiantly individual,' says Uncle Bertie.

'She was outspoken and ahead of her time,' says Aunt Maud.

Uncle Bertie agrees with a nod. 'She was obsessed with the

poor and used to take them baskets of food. She fought for the underdog and she rebelled against our parents' way of life,' he adds. 'They sent her to London, to live with Cousins Stoke and Augusta in Mayfair. They thought it would be good for her to get away from Ireland, to do a London Season, meet new people and find other interests besides visiting the poor and sick. From what I recall, she made quite a name for herself in the few months she was there. I believe she had numerous proposals while poor Ronald Rowan-Hampton, her intended, languished over here, forgotten. Anyhow, there was a drama, raised voices and tears. The next thing we heard was that she wasn't going to marry Ronald, after all, and that she'd run off to America in a huff. My parents never spoke of her after that. Her name was barely ever mentioned.' He frowns. 'I suspect my brother Rupert knew what had happened. He was very close to Tussy and went to London with her. But he never divulged anything and then he died in the Great War, taking her secrets with him.'

'Tell us about her life in America,' says Aunt Maud, placing a hand on her husband's. He is visibly upset as the memory of his sister's departure emerges out of the mists of the past like a ghost rising from the dead.

I tell them about my father, that he had been Governor of Massachusetts. I tell them that Arethusa converted to Catholicism and that we all believed she was from a poor Irish family and had come to America to start a new life. They listen intently. The room is so quiet, only the crackling of the fire can be heard burning in the grate. I have their full attention, but as I tell them about the Arethusa I knew, I begin to realize that I am perpetuating what is undoubtedly a myth. I'm only adding more layers to her lies. So, I stop. 'I don't know who my mother was,' I admit, and I feel my face burning with embarrassment. 'She didn't tell the truth about many things, I'm now suspicious about the things she *did* tell me – and the person she claimed to be. She was a socialite. She gave extravagant dinner parties. She was the best hostess in Boston. She was beautiful and glamorous, but she was also selfish and self-obsessed. We children were not her main focus, *she* was. Everyone adored her, but no one knew how difficult she was to live with. She was up and down, moody, temperamental and demanding. She fell out with friends and made new ones. She could turn on a dime. But she was flamboyant and thrived on drama. My brother and I were at her bedside when she died. We thought we knew her, but after the will was read, we realized that we didn't know her at all. I came here to discover who she really was. But meeting you has just raised more questions than it has answered. She left me her diary, which I will read over the coming few weeks.'

'She gave you her diary, Faye, because she wanted you to know who she really was,' says Kitty. 'And she wants her ashes scattered at Castle Deverill because she wants to be laid to rest at home.'

Uncle Bertie's pale eyes shine. He has gone quite pink in the face. 'You will lay her to rest here, won't you, Faye?'

I sigh. I think of Logan and his determination to bury her with Daddy. 'I will do my very best,' I reply.

'A Deverill's castle is his kingdom,' he says and his voice cracks. Aunt Maud puts her hand on his again and squeezes it. I see a deep affection pass between them and a surprising warmth glow in Aunt Maud's frosty blue eyes. Wyatt slips into my mind uninvited. Wyatt, who hasn't put his hand on mine like that in thirty years. I push him out.

'Let's eat,' says Kitty, standing up. 'I wonder, Faye, whether you have a Deverill's appetite!'

Chapter 5

Castle Deverill, Ballinakelly, Co. Cork
The Past

Arethusa Deverill awoke to a great commotion. She climbed off the big four-poster bed and hurried to the window. Sweeping aside the long velvet curtains she pressed her nose to the glass. There, on the gravel at the front of the castle, was a mob of unruly men in shabby black jackets and trousers, caps pulled low over furrowed foreheads, muddy boots on agitated feet. They jostled and elbowed each other, arguing among themselves. She recognized some of them from her trips into town. Husbands of the women she visited in a bid to ease their suffering with baskets of food and words of encouragement. Others were her father's tenants, their faces gaunt and ruddy from toiling on the land in bitter winds and reaping little reward. A few she did not recognize at all, yet they all shared the same hungry, desperate look and the same seething anger. It was early morning and already a few of them were drunk.

Curious to see what it was all about she rang the bell for her maid and hastily began dressing. By the time the girl arrived Arethusa had pulled on her stockings and undergarments and was ready for her corset. 'What's going on out there, Eily?' she demanded.

Eily, barely fourteen with black hair brushed half-heartedly into an untidy bun, blue eyes that were both watchful and sour and a sulky, petulant mouth that let out tuts and sighs in spite of her mother telling her over and over how lucky she was to be employed at the castle, pulled tight the laces of Arethusa's corset. 'They've come to sweep the chimneys, miss,' she replied.

'What? All of them?'

Eily let the laces slacken. 'No, miss. That's why they're fighting. Lord Deverill said he'll pay five shillings a chimney as old McNally has died, God rest his soul, 'n' there's no one to do his work. Now half the town's come offering his services.'

'Do hurry up, Eily!' Arethusa exclaimed impatiently. 'Can't your hands and mouth work at the same time?'

'Sorry, miss,' Eily replied, then kept her mouth shut as she concentrated on finishing the job. At last the corset was in place. Eily helped Arethusa into her skirt, which, as she intended to go out walking, was shorter than her other skirts, reaching her ankle. Arethusa fastened the small pearl buttons on her blouse herself as Eily clasped the skirt from behind with clumsy fingers.

'Your hair, miss?' Eily asked, stretching for the ivory brush and tortoiseshell comb which lay on the dressing table among pretty glass pots with silver lids and trinket boxes full of jewellery. Arethusa's thick brown hair was long and tangled but she didn't have the patience for brushing and she was too old now, at seventeen, to be told to do so by her governess.

'Later,' she said, hurrying out into the corridor and running down the stairs to the hall.

When Arethusa entered the dining room her grandfather

Greville, Lord Deverill, was at the head of the long oak table, speaking to O'Flynn, the butler. Greville's sweeping white moustache twitched as he listened to O'Flynn explaining the situation outside. 'You see, m'lord, we don't know who arrived first and they're all claiming entitlement to the job.'

Elizabeth, Lady Deverill, listened from her chair at the opposite end of the table. At seventy-four she was not only hard of hearing but a little on the heavy side too, which put pressure on her joints and gave her the need of a walking stick. Wrapped in shiny black silk with ruffles and frills rising up her neck like feathers, she resembled one of the exotic black hens she kept in the castle grounds (and allowed to wander freely in the hall in the summertime, much to O'Flynn's disapproval). Her pudgy, bejewelled fingers reached for her teacup, into which she had dropped three spoonfuls of sugar and poured a generous amount of cream. 'My dear, there are forty chimneys to be swept, why doesn't each man do one?'

Greville glanced at his wife and his moustache twitched now with irritation. 'No one will want to do a single chimney for five shillings, Elizabeth,' he said, raising his voice so that she could hear.

Rupert, the youngest of Arethusa's two brothers, who was seated beside Charlotte, Arethusa's dowdy governess, grinned at his sister. Typically, he was finding the conundrum highly entertaining. Aged twenty-three Rupert was handsome with chiselled, aristocratic features, glossy cocoa-coloured hair, deep-set brown eyes and full, sensual lips, which were always curling with amusement, usually at the most inopportune moments. Now was one of those moments because his grandfather was not finding the situation remotely funny. He did not want to be bothered with tiresome domestic matters. His interest lay in hunting, shooting, fishing and socializing with his neighbours, as it always had. This was really a matter for Lady Deverill, but as she had just demonstrated with her ridiculous suggestion, she was not, in his opinion, capable.

'You could always put names in a hat, Grandpa,' said Rupert with an apologetic shrug because he knew his grandfather would not appreciate his contribution to what was already becoming a 'bothersome situation'. It was well known that Lord Deverill had little patience for those. Greville grunted and ignored his grandson's unhelpful suggestion.

Arethusa sat down opposite Rupert, on her grandfather's left, and unfolded a napkin onto her lap. 'They're all frightfully cross,' she said, catching Rupert's eye and glowering at him. This just made him smile all the more. He pretended to rub his chin thoughtfully to hide it. 'They're hungry, their families are hungry and they need work. *You* may find this hilarious, Rupert, but for those men a week being employed to sweep chimneys might save the family from starvation.'

Elizabeth appeared to let Arethusa's impassioned words pass over her head, like she did with things that were uncomfortable or unsavoury, or perhaps she just didn't hear, and sipped her tea. 'We must pay them all, Greville. Problem solved.' She waved a hand to dismiss the subject like she would a butler or a maid.

'Five shillings is hardly going to sustain them for very long, Grandma,' Arethusa protested.

'What?' Elizabeth shouted, but Arethusa couldn't be bothered to repeat herself, or to argue with a woman who simply didn't understand. She caught Charlotte's eye, but the governess, who was as quiet and timid as a dormouse, said nothing. Charlotte might as well not have been there, for no one noticed her and she made no attempt to draw their attention, silently eating her breakfast with slow, careful movements as if afraid that any sharp action might remind them of her presence.

'We've bought a set of sweep's brooms, apparently, which join together like fishing rods,' said Rupert. 'Surely one of the footmen can do it.'

'And send those poor men away?' Arethusa exclaimed. 'How could you even suggest such a thing, Rupert?'

'Send who away?' asked Elizabeth, confused. 'Who are you going to send away? Not the chimney sweeps, I hope. We do need those chimneys swept or they'll catch fire. We don't want Castle Deverill to catch fire! That would be a great pity.'

Greville was now tired of the subject and his wife's inane comments. He put his spectacles on the bridge of his nose, opened the *Irish Times* and resumed his reading. 'O'Flynn, choose a couple of men and show them the chimneys.' He raised his eyes at his granddaughter, adding, 'We can't very well pay them all.' Then he was gone behind the paper.

Rupert and Arethusa dutifully changed the subject and began to argue playfully about which one of their grand-mother's hens laid the tastiest eggs. Charlotte listened but said nothing. She had been Arethusa's governess for ten years and knew her charge as well as a mother knows her child, but in the last few years Arethusa had grown distant and everything Charlotte did appeared to irritate her. As a consequence, she tried to do very little. She had never been good at asserting her authority.

The door opened and a fragrant spring breeze swept into the dining room, bringing with it Arethusa and Rupert's mother, Adeline, pink-faced and bright-eyed from her morning ride over the hills. Her Titian-red hair fell in thick unruly tendrils down her back, accentuating her small waist below it. In her black riding habit with its white collar and sharply tailored shoulders she cut a dashing figure. If anyone could draw Greville out of his newspaper it was his daughter-in-law, whom he both admired and feared, on account of her beauty and the improper feelings it aroused in him.

'What a beautiful morning,' she gushed, beaming a smile. 'I was accompanied on my ride by mavis and ouzel-cock, blackbird and mistle thrush. How I love spring and all the little birds who frolic in the gorse and bracken. It's such a joy to be outside. It's left me ravenously hungry, though. O'Flynn, I'd love eggs, scrambled, please, and bacon, crispy, almost burnt. You know how I like it.'

O'Flynn gave a bow and left the dining room.

Greville folded the newspaper and put it on the table beside him. He looked at Adeline and his tough old face softened and his eyes grew wistful. 'Did you hear the cuckoo this morning, my dear?' he asked softly.

Adeline took the chair between her father-in-law and Rupert and sat down. 'I did, Greville,' she replied. 'I heard it at dawn. It was still dark and yet, as I went to my window, the sun was just beginning to burn a hole through the eastern sky.'

'Beautifully put, my dear,' Greville muttered, shaking his head at the sheer wonder of this woman who appreciated nature like he did. All Elizabeth loved were her silly hens and cake. No one loved cake more, or ate it with more relish, than Lady Deverill. He raised his fluffy white eyebrows and glanced shiftily down the table, but his wife was much too busy buttering a third slice of toast to notice him flirting with his daughter-in-law.

'Did you see any fairies on your ride, Mama?' Rupert asked, affectionately teasing his mother who believed in leprechauns, angels and fairies and claimed to see the spirits of the departed with the same frequency with which she saw real people.

Adeline laughed. 'Darling Rupert, if I said I heard nothing but birdsong you'd be bitterly disappointed.'

'Or the banshee!' He pulled his face into a silent scream. 'Ahhhhhh!'

'Good Lord, you pair of sillies!' exclaimed Arethusa, rolling her eyes. 'With respect, Mama, you're very easy to tease. You know there were no ghosts or haunted houses until after the Reformation. They were invented by the new Protestants to make up for the lost saints. It's only primitive people who need to believe in all that rubbish.'

'I disagree, Tussy dear,' interrupted Elizabeth through a mouthful of toast. 'I've often seen spirits wandering the castle corridors. This place is full of them.'

Rupert chuckled. 'That's just Grandpa sleepwalking, Grandma,' he said.

Elizabeth, who could not hear above her chewing, missed his comment, but Greville heard it and he chuckled too. 'Well said, Rupert.' Greville only tolerated Adeline's love of the paranormal because she was easy on the eye. 'Fancy taking the dogs out with me this morning?' he asked his grandson. 'We could shoot a few snipes or the odd rabbit and hare – or take a shot at a poacher,' he chuckled again. 'What d'you say, Rupert?'

'I'd love to, Grandpa,' Rupert replied half-heartedly, putting his napkin on the table with a sigh. He wasn't keen on the great outdoors and was notoriously incompetent with a gun. Killing living things was not his idea of entertainment and, as for poachers, he didn't think it fair to deny hungry people a free meal every now and then. 'After I've done a bit of writing,' he added.

'Poetry?' Greville retorted with a grimace, as if writing poetry was an absurd thing for a man to do.

'Yes, I'm putting together a book of poems.'

'Very well, if you must.' Greville turned to Adeline. 'When's Bertie back?' Bertie was Rupert's older brother of twenty-five, who was made in the image of his father Hubert, and grandfather. While Rupert enjoyed sitting in the warm library (one of the only warm rooms in the castle) playing cards, composing poetry and reading, Bertie preferred to be outside, preferably on a horse, in pursuit of a fox or a hare. Bertie was the sort of man Greville understood, the sort of man he could share things with. Rupert on the other hand, albeit undeniably charming and witty, was a puzzle to him.

'Bertie and Hubert will be back from London the day after tomorrow,' said Adeline.

'Good. In time for the next meet.'

'They wouldn't want to miss that,' said Adeline with a smile.

'And neither would you, my dear,' said Greville, his voice heavy with admiration for there was not a single woman in the county to rival Adeline on a horse. She rode side-saddle with both elegance and courage, jumping hedges many men would not even dare attempt.

'I'm surprised they lasted this long,' said Arethusa of her father and brother who had now spent nearly a month with their cousins, Stoke and Augusta, known as the London Deverills. 'I couldn't spend more than a day with Cousin Augusta. She has the social endurance of an armchair.'

Rupert laughed. 'And the hide of one too!' he added mischievously.

At that Arethusa roared with laughter a little on the coarse side for a young lady of her breeding. 'The hide of a *leather* armchair,' she exclaimed.

'Now *you* two are being a pair of sillies!' said Adeline, trying to restrain her smile.

'Cousin Stoke is a very patient man,' rejoined Greville, then, glancing at his wife, who was enviously eyeing the plate of scrambled eggs and bacon O'Flynn was bringing in for Adeline, he added beneath his breath, 'As indeed am I.'

After breakfast Elizabeth went out to feed her hens, Greville to take the dogs for a walk over the glen, Rupert retreated to the library to write by the cold hearth (until the amateur chimney sweeps had finished cleaning and the fire was lit once more) and Adeline went upstairs to change out of her riding habit. Since her mother-in-law had grown old, and dotty, the responsibilities of chatelaine had fallen on *her* shoulders. This involved answering letters, keeping accounts, attending the Ballinakelly branch of the Needlework Guild and other charitable organizations, and receiving the poor who came to the castle door daily with their woes and their requests, to whom she would give a kind word and a sovereign.

Charlotte suggested she and Arethusa go for a walk, but Arethusa shrugged her off impatiently with a 'Not now, Charlotte, I'm going to visit my aunts' and put on her coat and hat and hurried off to the stables to ask Mr McCarthy, the groom, to prepare the pony and trap. She planned to go into Ballinakelly with food for the Coakley family, whose three children were so painfully malnourished it kept her awake at night worrying. Charlotte, who knew she should chaperone Arethusa every time she left the castle grounds, had no reason to disbelieve her and watched her go, knowing that she was powerless to stop her even if she wished to. Arethusa was strong, wilful and had become, of late, quite intimidating. The governess settled herself into her small sitting room, which was next to her bedroom on the top floor of the castle, and took up her needlepoint. She hoped Mrs Deverill, Arethusa's mother, would not think her remiss, but Adeline's sisters lived

very close, in Ballinakelly, and Charlotte did not think it necessary to accompany her there. Arethusa, in turn, felt bad; it
was so easy to get round Charlotte that it just wasn't sporting.

As Arethusa approached with a basket of food and milk, Mr
Duggan, the head gardener, put down his pitchfork and wandered across the stable yard to talk to her. He had a worried
expression on his weathered brown face.

'Miss Arethusa, might I have a word?' he asked, taking off
his cap and releasing a bounty of black curls.

'What is it, Duggan?'

''Tis the young Mrs Foley, miss. Her baby—'

'Is it sick?'

'No, 'tis not sick, miss, but there's trouble and 'twill be
worse tomorrow than it is today,' he added darkly. 'If 'twill
be living at all.'

Arethusa was alarmed. 'Then I must go to her at once.'

'Thank you, Miss Arethusa.'

'Perhaps I should call the doctor?'

Mr Duggan shook his head. 'I don't think it's a doctor she'll
be needing, Miss Arethusa. Indeed, I think you'll be better
than any medical man.'

Puzzled, Arethusa watched him replace his cap. She went
in search of Mr McCarthy. She found him in the stable block,
sitting on a stool polishing a saddle. 'Good morning, Miss
Arethusa,' he said, standing up. 'Will you be wanting the
brougham?'

'Pony and trap will do. At once. I need to go to the young
Foleys.'

Mr McCarthy nodded and slowly put the saddle on the
saddle rack. Arethusa paced the cobbles impatiently while Mr
McCarthy wandered off at a leisurely pace to attach the pony
to the trap. Arethusa, whose every movement was dynamic,

could not understand a man who went through life as if wading through treacle. She bit her nails apprehensively and wondered what the problem could be. Perhaps it was distant in mind, she mused, as one poor child had been whom Adeline had had to take to the Children's Hospital in Dublin. Arethusa often thought of asking her mother to accompany her on her missions, but Adeline, although sympathetic to the poor, did not like to get too close, fearful as she was of disease. If she knew how often Arethusa visited them and how close she got to the diseased, she would be horrified.

At last the pony and trap was walked round to the stable yard and Arethusa climbed up onto the seat and took the reins. With a brisk shake, the pony set off up the track.

How magnificent it is, Arethusa thought as she made her way round to the front of the castle. With its grey-stone walls and imposing towers and turrets, it had the appearance of a magical castle in a fairy tale. Barton Deverill, the first Lord Deverill of Ballinakelly, must have not only been fanciful but ambitious too, she mused, as her eyes rested for a moment on the family motto carved into the stone above the big front door: *Castellum Deverilli est suum regnum.* A Deverill's castle is his kingdom. The trap rattled past the castle and on towards the end of the long, curved drive where the big iron gates were open in anticipation of her departure.

Arethusa went down the lane towards Ballinakelly and looked into the dark, mossy wood that lined her way. She thought of the superstitions that made people fearful of going there. They said it was full of ghosts and wandering dead. Some claimed to have seen a woman in white floating through it, others the spirits of men killed by Cromwell's soldiers. Mr McCarthy swore he'd seen the ghost of a captain trying in vain to find the ocean. All Arethusa could see were ancient boughs bursting with new green leaves, rhododendron bushes about to flower into explosions of pink and red and purple, and birds and butterflies basking in the sunshine. She saw nothing that would incite fear, only beauty in the thicket of lichened, weather-beaten trees that dispelled all trace of it.

Ballinakelly was an ancient seaside town of no more than a thousand people. It boasted three churches: the Catholic church of All Saints, St Patrick's Church of Ireland and the Methodist church. At its heart was a high street of shops and public houses (which were always full) and a small harbour where fishermen kept their boats and mended their nets. On the road just outside Ballinakelly was a statue of the Virgin Mary, which was set up in 1828 to commemorate a young girl's vision. The locals claimed to have seen the statue sway, all on its own, but Arethusa did not believe it. Pilgrims came from distant places to see it, and many declared that they had been healed simply by looking at it, but, as far as Arethusa knew, none of the locals had been so blessed, and many of them could have done with a miraculous cure.

Once in Ballinakelly she stopped the horse at the bottom of a side street and hurried towards a small white cottage that shivered at the top of a steep incline. She knocked on the wooden door. As she did so, the door gave way and opened on its own with a creak. 'Mrs Foley?' she called through the crack. 'It's Miss Arethusa Deverill. May I come in?' Arethusa stepped into the dark room. A turf fire smouldered weakly in the hearth and an old kettle swung miserably above it. On the table was a mug and a cracked teapot. She called again. 'Mrs Foley, it's me, Miss Arethusa Deverill. I've come to help you.' She rubbed her hands together to warm them for the cottage was cold and damp.

Arethusa jumped. There in the doorway between the

kitchen and the rest of the cottage stood Mrs Foley. Thin and gaunt with purple shadows beneath hollow eyes she was a woman who was little more than rags and bone. In her arms she held a baby wrapped in dirty blankets. Arethusa wasn't sure whether the infant was alive or dead. It was not moving. 'Mrs Foley, is the baby sick?' She peered at the child's white face and felt an icy claw squeeze her heart.

''Tis not sick, miss. Just hungry,' she said, glancing down at it sorrowfully.

'Can you not feed it?'

Mrs Foley looked at Arethusa, her black eyes haunted and afraid. 'The night she was born there was a great storm. Paddy, the soft little man that he is, would not go out and untie the donkey. The baby was coming and I didn't untie my hair, God help me. I didn't untie my hair and Paddy didn't untie the donkey.' Her lips trembled as she spoke of the birth customs that she had not followed. Suddenly Arethusa understood. She had heard her mother speak of such superstitions. These people believed that if they did not untie the animals, open windows and doors and loosen plaits of hair the new spirit would not be able to enter the body, leaving it open for fairies to slip a changeling into its place. The only way to rid the baby of the changeling was for the baby to smile or sneeze or, as a last resort, to hold the infant by its feet over a fire until it screamed so hard the changeling jumped out.

The claw on Arethusa's heart tightened its grip.

Mrs Foley continued in a quivering voice, 'This here is not my baby. It cries all the time. My baby's soul was out there that night, tryin' to get in, and I didn't let it. 'Twas out there in the storm and I didn't let it in. Now I have this ... this ... *thing* in its place and it must be made to leave.'

'No, Biddy, no. You're wrong. This is your baby. The

changeling story is just made up. It's not real. God would never let another soul enter your child's body. It's simply not true.'

'The neighbours do be comin' askin' if it's smiled or sneezed and I tell them no, it just cries and screams and twists and turns and now nothing. Just quiet. They do be comin' tonight to hold it over the fire to make the changeling come out.'

'No, Biddy!' Arethusa exclaimed in horror. 'You must not let them do that. How can this poor baby smile if it is dying of hunger? You must feed it, Biddy. It is your baby and it's going to die if you don't feed it.' Mrs Foley, who couldn't have been more than sixteen years old, blinked at Arethusa and tears welled in her big, sunken eyes. 'When was the last time you fed it?'

'Yesterday,' she replied.

'Good Lord! Well, you must feed it at once or it will surely die.' Suddenly the infant squirmed and let out a weak wail. Mrs Foley looked at Arethusa and bit her bottom lip. 'If you let this child die you will be hanged for murder,' Arethusa added firmly. 'And you will have to answer to God.'

At that Mrs Foley sat down and undid her dress. She put the baby to her breast. The wailing stopped as soon as the little mouth began to suck.

Arethusa placed the basket on the table. 'I have brought you some food. Eggs, milk, cheese, bread, potatoes.' She began to lay them out. She'd have to return that afternoon with another basket for the Coakley family. 'You must eat and get strong or you won't have enough milk for your child.' After unpacking the food, she put another turf log on the fire and waited until the kettle had boiled to pour the water into the teapot to brew the tea.

Once the baby had finished feeding and fallen asleep on her mother's breast, Arethusa took it away to wash and put to bed. While she fussed about the house the mother went to tell the neighbours that there would be no ceremony tonight for she had recognized the baby as her own. When she returned, Arethusa watched her drink the tea and eat some of the bread and cheese. While she grew stronger she told Arethusa of her troubles and Arethusa listened and the weight of sorrow on her heart grew heavier. How could she help these people who had nothing? Why did they have nothing when she had everything?

She left the cottage feeling low. Sunshine expelled the shadows and warmed the shivering town. She ambled up the high street, lost in thought. There were too many cases like the Foleys and the Coakleys for her to make a satisfactory difference. The thought of all those sick and hungry children gave her an overwhelming sense of helplessness. Sure, the ladies of the county helped, like her mother – and her grandfather employed hundreds of locals at the castle, in the gardens and on the land – but more needed to be done.

Suddenly, she stopped short. She recognized those boots. She lifted her eyes and her mood lifted with them. 'Well, hello, Mr McLoughlin,' she said, giving him a coy smile.

'Hello, Miss Deverill,' he replied, looking down at her with brown eyes shining beneath a thick black fringe. 'What might you be doing in *my* neck of the woods?'

'*Your* neck of the woods?' she replied, lifting her chin and putting her hands on her hips. 'Ballinakelly is *my* neck of the woods, if you don't mind, or have you forgotten that I'm a Deverill?'

He inhaled through his nostrils as if savouring the smell of her. 'How could I forget that you're a Deverill with that arrogant expression on your face?' He grinned, revealing two pronounced eye teeth that gave him the look of a wolf. She laughed and her limbs grew warm beneath his lascivious gaze.

He lowered his voice. 'Might you have time in your busy day to meet me round the back?' he asked, arching an eyebrow suggestively.

'Maybe,' she replied, tossing her head and stalking off past the foundry where he apprenticed his father, the local blacksmith.

He didn't shout after her but waited for her to turn left into the alley and disappear. Arethusa trod slowly over the cobbles, hips swaying, knowing that he would be there, in the court-yard behind his father's foundry, as he always was. Her breath grew short with excitement and she forgot her fears for the poor and her sense of inadequacy.

A hand grabbed her around the waist and pulled her into a dark stable, sending her hat floating to the ground. 'Dermot!' she whispered as he pressed her against the brick wall.

'Tussy my darling,' he replied. Then his mouth was upon hers and it was wet and warm and eager. She closed her eyes and parted her lips so he could kiss her more deeply. She relished the vigorous, masculine feel of his body and ran her hands over his back and shoulders, feeling the muscles beneath his jacket and shirt, muscles developed and honed by long hours of hard labour. She pulled him closer, wanting to feel the weight of his body against hers, not caring that it was improper – she was way beyond caring about that now. His bristles scratched her neck as he kissed her there and traced her skin with his tongue. 'I want you,' he whispered as his hand found her breast. Tussy didn't reply. She wanted him, too. Her whole body ached for him. 'Marry me!' he said. He took his face out of her neck and looked at her steadily, his gaze heavy with lust. 'Marry me, Tussy.'

Arethusa opened her eyes and cupped his face with her hands. 'You know I can't marry you,' she laughed.

'But you love me?'

Arethusa sighed. Why did the men she kissed always ruin it by wanting to marry her? 'No, Dermot. I don't love you.'

He grinned, undeterred, baring his wolf's teeth. 'But you love what I *do* to you.'

She smiled back. 'Oh yes. I love that.'

'If you marry me I will do things to you that will make you cry out with pleasure.'

'Don't tempt me, Dermot.'

He took his hand off her breast and moved it down to her hip. 'Let me show you how a man *really* pleasures a woman . . .' Arethusa licked her bottom lip. She was curious to know what Dermot could do. He was, after all, a very good kisser. He began to lift her skirt. Arethusa didn't move. She knew she was now entering dangerous territory. She'd kissed lots of men, but she'd never allowed any of them to lift her skirt. She knew it was deeply wrong. She knew she should stop him, but the danger of it gave her a wicked thrill. It was forbidden, and yet delicious. Now his hand was beneath her skirt, on her thigh, just above her stocking. She felt his fingers on her naked skin and caught her breath. His mouth hovered above hers, their lips almost touching, and on his were words of encouragement, whispered softly, seductively, commanding her to remain still, to not move, to allow him to touch her there, in her most sensitive place; the place that would give her exquisite pleasure.

Arethusa's eyelashes fluttered. Her lips parted and on her cheeks flowered two crimson poppies. Dermot's soft caress was now edging slowly higher. Arethusa was sorely tempted to allow it, just to see what it would feel like.

'No, Dermot!' she said suddenly, pulling out his hand. 'Enough.'

'Don't tell me you don't like it.'

'I wouldn't lie to you, Dermot. But I'd better be going.'

'You're a tease!' he exclaimed.

'You like me just the way I am,' she replied crisply. 'You've told me so.' She touched his face. 'And I've never promised you anything more than a kiss. I'll be married off shortly and it won't be to a smithy's son. You know that, so don't look so pathetic.' She lifted her hat off the floor and slipped past him into the yard, smoothing down her skirt.

'You drive a man mad,' he called after her.

She put her hat on her head and laughed. 'I know,' she replied gaily. 'More's the pity.'

Chapter 6

It was customary at Castle Deverill for evenings to be filled with entertainment in the form of lavish dinners, numerous guests and after-dinner games. Greville and Elizabeth Deverill were hungry for the company of friends and relations because they were exceedingly bored by each other. For that reason, their son Hubert had not moved out after marrying Adeline, but occupied an entire wing of the castle with their children Bertie, Rupert and Arethusa, and their large retinue of servants. The Deverills were never happier than when the castle was full of candlelight and laughter. Greville had an enviable wine cellar stocked with the best vintages and was never slow to share them. Elizabeth, in her younger days, had been a demon at the card table, but since her mind had begun to wander she was more suited to taking up residence in a big armchair by the fire with her knitting. Her clumsily knitted socks and Guernseys were endured by the poor who were not in a position to complain.

On this particular evening Arethusa was happy to see her three aunts, Poppy, Hazel and Laurel Swanton, who were Adeline's younger sisters, known affectionately, and collectively, as the Shrubs. Regulars at Castle Deverill for bridge, whist and backgammon, they enlivened any gathering with their enthusiasm and charm. The two youngest, Hazel and Laurel, might have been twins for they shared the same round, rosy faces, as flat as plates, sweet smiles and big china-blue eyes that blinked in constant wonder at the world like a pair of kittens. Their hair was mouse brown and pulled off low foreheads, revealing tidy widow's peaks. Their skin was pale and freckled, their movements nervous like a pair of thrushes. Frightened of men and alarmed by what women were expected to do in the marital bed, neither had married, preferring to live together in a cosy cottage in Ballinakelly, a short carriage ride from the castle. Such was their closeness that they finished each other's sentences and anticipated each other's needs. As long as they were together and had Poppy and Adeline nearby, they wanted for nothing.

Poppy, on the other hand, had married young and been widowed a few years later, without having children to comfort her in her grief. Pretty, with thick, dark brown hair, intelligent eyes the colour of moss and a soft, curvaceous body, she, like Adeline, was the complete antithesis of Laurel and Hazel. Wise beyond her years, Poppy was confident, sensual and strong, and, having been born only a few years after Adeline (and a decade before the other two), she was her natural ally. They shared secrets, a love of nature and a sense of fun, but most importantly their belief in God and the paranormal. However hard life might be, and for Poppy it had already been exceedingly hard, they would endure it because of their unwavering faith in their divine purpose.

Besides the Shrubs, Greville and Elizabeth had invited Reverend Mungo Millet and his insipid wife Cynthia, who were an odd-looking couple, he being well over six feet and she barely five feet. They were middle-aged, affable and experts at working a room, for there was barely an evening in the month when they weren't guests at the grandest houses in the county. However, as often happens with couples, one was liked, the other merely tolerated. Reverend Millet had a wry sense of humour and a twinkle in his eye, which warmed people to him, as well as a belief in God which was reassuring. His wife, on the other hand, was lacking in appeal. If ever a person's appearance and personality were perfectly in tune they were in Cynthia Millet, who looked like a dried-flower arrangement left to gather dust in the corner of a cold room and had the character to match. People suffered *her* because they loved *him*, and she was totally oblivious to that fact and believed herself a very popular and beloved person indeed.

Greville and Elizabeth, at the request of their daughter-in-law Adeline, had also invited an exuberant young man who was no stranger to Castle Deverill or the hunting grounds surrounding it. Ronald Rowan-Hampton was a contemporary of Arethusa's brother Bertie, and a favourite of her parents on account of his pedigree and because he was a fine horseman and a paragon of Anglo-Irish ideals. He was a stocky young man of twenty-five with red cheeks, flaxen hair and sharp hazel eyes which missed nothing that might be of use to him. One of those things that might be of use to him was Arethusa Deverill. Arethusa, being equally sharp, was in no way blind to his ambition, or the ambitions of her parents who considered Ronald, the son of a baronet, a fine match for her. Arethusa was well aware that there would come a time, probably sooner rather than later, when she would have to accept a marriage proposal and settle down to a conventional life. She accepted that this was her lot and had no intention of rebelling against it. However, she was in no hurry to give up her secret trysts with the likes of Dermot McLoughlin in favour of the duties of the marital bed. She'd succumb when she was good and ready and not a moment before. Judging by her afternoon's encounter in the blacksmith's yard she wouldn't be ready for some time.

There was a commotion at the door as Rupert appeared in the drawing room half an hour after the guests had arrived. He apologized profusely, with his usual self-deprecating charm, and went around the room bowing to the ladies and kissing their hands with such cordiality that it was impossible to be cross with him. 'Aunt Hazel, you look resplendent tonight,' he said, his brown eyes looking at her so intensely that she believed she was the only person in the room he wanted to talk to. 'Is that a new hairstyle?'

Hazel's cheeks flushed at the compliment. 'My dear Rupert, you are too kind.' She patted her coiffure. 'But I've worn my hair like this for years.'

'For years,' Laurel added, wanting some of Rupert's light for herself. 'We've *both* worn our hair like this since we were twenty.'

Rupert settled his beguiling gaze onto Laurel and she seemed to swell beneath it. 'Then it can't be the hair, can it,' he said, watching her blush too. 'You *both* look radiant. If it's not the hair then it must be something else.' He grinned suggestively and the two women giggled. 'Is there something you're not telling me, ladies?'

'Oh Rupert, you are saucy!' gushed Hazel, smacking him playfully with her fan.

'Saucy!' repeated Laurel, putting her fingers to her lips.

'You're deliciously mysterious, the both of you!' He turned to allow Arethusa to enter the conversation.

'Are you flirting with our aunts, Rupert?' she asked, giving him a reproachful look.

'I only told them how radiant they are tonight,' he explained with a shrug. 'What can I do? I'm only a man.'

Arethusa pulled a face. Unlike her silly aunts *she* wasn't fooled by her brother's flattery. She wondered why women were so easily taken in. 'And they are, indeed, radiant,' she agreed, just to be polite, although 'red-faced and sweaty' would have been more accurate.

'As are you, my dear Tussy,' said Rupert, his expression now slightly mocking. 'But then you are being wooed, are you not?' he added, lowering his voice and shifting his eyes across the room.

The Shrubs looked at Ronald Rowan-Hampton who was standing in front of the fireplace, a glass of sherry in one hand, the other moving expressively through the air as he entertained his host and the Reverend with one of his anecdotes. Ronald always had an endless supply of anecdotes and was especially fond of telling them.

Arethusa sighed. 'I could do a lot worse, I suppose,' she said.

'Oh, he's very handsome,' gushed Hazel.

'Very handsome indeed,' echoed Laurel.

'A little on the ruddy side,' said Rupert. 'But he'll improve with age. Most men do.'

'What do *you* know of improving with age?' Arethusa asked.

Rupert gave a sniff. 'I have an aesthetic eye,' he replied. 'I appreciate the way things look.'

'Do you appreciate the way Ronald looks?' Arethusa asked, a mischievous gleam in her eye.

'Not really,' he replied in a lofty voice. 'He's too pink, too porky and too pinguid.'

Arethusa threw her head back and roared with laughter. It was so loud and ungainly that everyone in the room turned to look at her, including Ronald, who was more than a little irritated to have his story interrupted. Arethusa put her hand over her mouth and tried to stifle it, but her shoulders continued to shudder rebelliously. The Shrubs looked like they'd just been bitten, but Rupert grinned down at his sister, pleased to have induced so gratifying a reaction.

'My dear, it's not very ladylike to laugh like that,' said Poppy, relieving her sisters who fled to the sofa, where they were shortly joined by Cynthia Millet, the Rector's wife, who laughed discreetly, as ladies should.

'It's Rupert's fault, Aunt Poppy,' said Arethusa, catching her brother's eye and giggling again.

'Perhaps you should go and talk to Ronald, Tussy. Rupert, my dear, I want to talk to you. Have you finished that book of poetry you've been writing?'

Arethusa left them to discuss poetry and wandered over to Ronald, who was just finishing his anecdote.

'And that was the end of a very sorry affair,' he said.

The Rector shook his head. 'What an extraordinary tale,' he exclaimed. 'Quite extraordinary.'

'Served the lad right! The fool!' Greville exclaimed, knocking back his whiskey. 'He'll never do that again.'

'Never do what again?' interrupted Arethusa.

Ronald settled his glistening eyes onto her and all she could think of was 'pink, porky and pinguid' and had to bite her tongue in order not to laugh again. *Good Lord*, she thought, *if I have to wake up to that every morning I'll laugh myself into an early grave!* 'What was it that so amused you, Tussy?' he asked. 'I should like to hear it.'

'It was nothing. Just a silly joke between brother and sister,' she replied.

'Better than the two of you arguing, which is what we have to suffer most of the time,' said her grandfather. 'Reverend, let me show you that letter. It's in the library.' The two men left Ronald and Arethusa alone, quite deliberately, Arethusa knew.

Ronald leaned towards her and said in a low voice, 'You look very beautiful tonight, Tussy, if I may say so.'

'Thank you, Ronald,' she replied. 'I've been outside in the spring air,' she added, thinking of Dermot's hand on her thigh. 'It does wonders for the complexion.'

'Will you ride out with me tomorrow? I've bought a new mare and I'd like to show her to you.'

Arethusa couldn't think of a good enough reason to refuse, although she didn't much like riding (she'd rather walk), or the fact that her parents insisted she take Charlotte with her as chaperone. However, Ronald believed her to be an enthusiastic horsewoman, like her mother and all the other Deverills, both male and female, so she did not want to disappoint him. 'I'd like that, thank you,' she replied. 'I'd love to see your new mare.'

'She's a fine filly. She really is. Takes a hedge straight on and no hesitation.'

Arethusa chuckled. 'You sound like Papa.'

'I will take that as a compliment,' he said seriously. 'Your father is one of the finest horsemen in the county. To be compared to a Deverill is the height of my ambition.' *To marry one, the pinnacle,* Arethusa thought roguishly. He moved a little closer and lowered his voice, giving her an almost paternal look. 'It has come to my attention that you've been busy helping the poor,' he said, changing the subject. Arethusa read his face and understood very quickly that he wasn't admiring of her charity.

'And what of it, Ronald?' she asked, looking at him steadily.

Ronald straightened. He was not used to women being so bold, but then Arethusa was not demure like other women.

She had a fire in her, which was one of the reasons why he liked her so much, although he hoped that, once married, he'd manage to dampen it a bit, or at least direct it where it would be better served. A wife with too much fire in her was a dangerous thing. 'You must be careful,' he warned. 'They are riddled with disease.'

'You mean the poor?'

'Yes, Tussy. They are not clean. I'm thinking of your health.'

'Oh, I'm quite robust,' she replied frostily.

'But not immune.'

Arethusa put her head on one side and frowned. 'Have you ever been to visit the poor, Ronald?' she asked. 'Have you gone into their houses and seen how they live?' He shook his head dismissively, considering the very idea absurd. 'Have you seen how miserably they live? So many of them are literally dying of starvation. They have nothing. And we . . .' She took a breath and straightened her shoulders. She did not want to get emotional in front of Ronald. 'We have so much.'

'And we are grateful for our blessings,' he replied in a tone that revealed he had never considered them. 'No one is more grateful than I. There is much that one can do to help, through charitable organizations. One does not have to get one's hands dirty.'

'One doesn't,' she retorted, losing patience. 'But sometimes one wants to, Ronald.'

He put a hand on her wrist. 'I'm just looking out for your welfare. One can't be too careful and you're very precious.'

'Precious?' she repeated, fearing at once that he wanted to put her in a box with other precious things and lock her up.

His eyes shone with tenderness. 'Precious to *me*.'

He was gazing at her, his face shiny like a red berry, and all she could think of was 'pink, porky and pinguid' and she began to laugh again. Ronald was put out. 'I'm sorry,' she blurted, covering her mouth with her hand again. 'It's just . . . will you excuse me?' She fled the room in a fit of hysteria.

Arethusa could not stop laughing. She was furious with Ronald for confronting her about helping the poor yet at the same time tickled by Rupert's hilarious description of him. She sat on the sofa in the hall, opposite the baronial fireplace and the portrait painted in oils of Barton Deverill, the first Lord Deverill of Ballinakelly, and tried to compose herself. He was raffishly handsome was Barton, she thought, admiring his long curly black hair, green velvet breeches and ruffled shirt. She wished Ronald was more like him.

'Men were very dandy in those days, weren't they?' It was Poppy, now taking the seat beside her.

'Peacocks indeed,' Arethusa agreed. 'I think they took more trouble over their outfits than the women.'

She looked at her aunt squarely. 'Have you come to tell me off about laughing at Ronald?'

Poppy placed a hand on Arethusa's. 'My dear, no man likes to be laughed at, however good his sense of humour. Ronald is proud and he wants you to admire him, not make a fool of him.'

Arethusa began to laugh again. 'But Rupert said he was pink, porky and pinguid and . . .' She snorted. 'I can't stop thinking about it and laughing.'

'That's not very kind of Rupert, but typical.' Poppy narrowed her eyes. 'It's not typical of *you* to be unkind.'

Arethusa stopped laughing. She did not want to be considered unkind. 'Somehow Ronald knows I visit the poor. He said I shouldn't visit them because they are unclean and I'll catch a disease.'

'Oh, don't listen to him. He knows nothing about it. But

perhaps you shouldn't visit them on your own. You know your mother doesn't like it when you sneak into town unaccompanied.' Arethusa made to speak in her defence, but Poppy silenced her with a raised hand. 'Don't think she doesn't know about it, my dear. She knows every time that pony and trap leaves the castle gates and it isn't fair on poor Charlotte. It's her job to chaperone you, after all.'

'Charlotte's a bore. She's more terrified of disease than Ronald, so she's no help at all. I bet if I marry Ronald he'll stop me visiting or make me join committees, like Mama, and help from a distance. That's no good. If I hadn't gone to visit Mrs Foley, she would have killed her baby by frying it over the fire to chase out the changeling.'

'Good Lord!' Poppy was horrified.

'You see, we need to visit these people, if only to talk some sense into them.'

'Where was Father O'Callaghan?'

'Spread very thinly, I suspect. It's a large community and there are many people in need. He's run ragged, I should imagine.'

'Poor Mrs Foley.' Poppy sighed. 'I tell you what, why don't we visit together, you and I? I'm sure Ronald would be less concerned if you were accompanied. And I don't like to think of you having to deal with situations like the Foley one, alone.'

'That's a good idea. Mama can't complain either if I go with you.'

'Adeline is thinking only of your health, Tussy. She's on our side, I assure you.'

'Oh, she is. But she worries. I have to sneak off without telling her, otherwise she'll forbid me to go altogether. If she knew what I got up to while her eye is turned the other way, she'd be appalled.'

'Let *me* speak to her.'

Arethusa took her aunt's hands in hers. 'Would you? It matters so much to me.'

'And to me, my dear. You and I are cut from the same cloth. I know you don't believe it, but your mama is too. Don't forget that Adeline has a husband to think of and I dare say Hubert is cut from the same cloth as Ronald. Those sort of men do not like to think of the poor in case it ruins their fun. And Adeline has to obey, for that's what she vowed to do before God. But I can assure you, Adeline's heart is in exactly the same place as ours.'

O'Flynn announced dinner. Arethusa, contrite after having been ticked off by Poppy and not wanting to appear unkind, allowed Ronald to escort her into the dining room. Hazel and Laurel walked in on either side of Rupert, the Rector walked in with Lady Deverill, and Lord Deverill accompanied the Rector's wife, Cynthia. Poppy and Adeline walked in together, due to the shortage of men, their heads almost touching because, although they saw each other almost every day, they always had a great deal to talk about. Arethusa tried to make it up to Ronald during dinner by giving him her unwavering attention and asking him about himself. It seemed to do the trick, for he puffed himself up again like a cockerel and crowed with anecdotes, laughing heartily at his own punchlines. She did not let her eyes stray to Rupert, who sat opposite, because she knew she'd collapse laughing again if he so much as blinked at her.

After dessert the ladies left the dining room to convene in the drawing room while the men sat on, smoking cigars, passing the port and discussing politics – mainly Gladstone's land reforms, which they considered a direct assault on their ancient way of life, and the recession that saw grain and meat imported more cheaply from America, New Zealand and Argentina. As a consequence, tenants were increasingly unable to afford to pay their rent. Greville did not like to think of the tenants. He feared change more than he feared anything. He threw himself into his hunting, fishing and socializing with determination to maintain the status quo. He did not like to think of the poor either – and fortunately for him Elizabeth was not one of those women, like Adeline, who had a soft heart and a social conscience; Elizabeth only ever thought of herself and her own comfort, and disliked change as much as he did. As for the Fenians plotting revolution in pursuit of Irish independence from Britain, well, he didn't like to think of them either. If he rode hard, played hard and continued living as his family had done for generations, he believed the world outside the gates of Castle Deverill might be easily ignored and, if ignored, might just submit to his will, see the error of its ways, and surrender. He saw no reason why the order of things should be altered and only took his seat in the House of Lords at Westminster to ensure that it wasn't. He puffed on his cigar, drank one of the finest bottles of port he could find in his cellar and changed the subject to one of his favourites: the wily fox, which only the week before had nearly outwitted him, the little devil.

In the drawing room Laurel, Hazel and Poppy took their places at the card table and waited patiently for Rupert, who always made up the four. Adeline, dutiful and good-natured, sat beside Cynthia Millet and listened to her dull, long-winded account of her lost cat which was predictably found hiding beneath the altar cloth. Arethusa sat on the club fender beside her grandmother who had resumed her knitting, and held the ball of wool while her mind wandered to the blacksmith's yard and Dermot's audacious hand on her thigh. Just the thought of him sent her blood racing. Nothing raced when she thought of Ronald. Did that matter? Was it important to be attracted to one's spouse? Wasn't shared culture, interests and pedigree more important? Arethusa didn't want to marry Dermot, or any of the other local men she had kissed, but she couldn't help wishing that Ronald was a little more like him. The two could not be more different. Ronald was smooth, Dermot rough. Ronald was articulate, Dermot was not. Ronald was well-educated, rich and entitled. Dermot was a blacksmith and would always be a blacksmith, and barely had two farthings to rub together. Yet, she liked being kissed by Dermot. She imagined Ronald's kisses would be slippery and cold, like a snake.

'What are you thinking about?' Elizabeth asked, looking up from her knitting.

'Marriage,' Arethusa replied dully. 'I don't find the prospect of it very appealing, Grandma.'

'It isn't meant to be appealing. It's duty and duty is often a trial.' She chuckled like a fat hen. 'Ronald might not be a knight in shining armour, but the Good Ones never are.'

'Good Ones?'

'The Good Ones are the men who will make good husbands. They'll be loyal and respectful and look after you and that, in the long run, is more important than physical attraction. The Handsome Knights will only make you miserable because they're all passion and no substance.'

'I suppose Grandpa is a Good One?'

Elizabeth chuckled again. 'Oh yes, he's a Good One. More's the pity!' She lowered her voice and looked at her granddaughter slyly. 'The secret is to enjoy a few Handsome Knights before you give in to duty, Tussy.'

Arethusa laughed in surprise. She couldn't imagine her

grandmother being anything other than decorous. 'Ooooh, Grandma! You dark horse. Mama would strongly disapprove of that.'

'In a life of duty, my dear, it is only fair to have a few windows of pleasure.' Her grandmother's cheeks burned and Arethusa was not sure whether it was from the fire in the grate or the fire in the body, which Arethusa knew very well. Dermot made her cheeks burn like that too. 'The secret is to keep up appearances, Tussy. What the eyes don't see the heart won't grieve for. One just has to be clever. A woman's lot is a hard lot, make no mistake, so we must grab joy when we can, with both hands.'

'I like the sound of that.'

'If you don't marry Ronald, you'll marry someone else very like him. You'll marry a Greville or a Hubert, a Bertie or a Rupert – no, not a Rupert, you won't marry a Rupert.'

Arethusa was baffled. 'Why not a Rupert?' she asked.

'He won't marry anybody.'

'Of course he will.'

'No, he won't. Men like Rupert shouldn't. Many do, but they shouldn't. Ah, speak of the devil.'

Arethusa raised her eyes to see her brother slip into the room and take his seat at his aunts' table. 'What shall it be tonight, ladies?' he asked. 'Poppy, deal the cards, Hazel and Laurel, brace yourselves. Tonight I'm feeling lucky!' He laughed in his habitual way, hunching his shoulders and grinning playfully, like a boy.

'You see? He's not like the other men. They'll be passing the port for another half an hour at least, but Rupert prefers to play cards with his aunts.'

'Which means?' Arethusa didn't understand.

'He'll be playing cards with his aunts, just like this, in

twenty years' time. Mark my words. Although, of course, I won't be around to witness it.'

'I'm not sure I agree, Grandma. Rupert is so handsome; all the girls adore him. He'll make a wonderful husband, or are you suggesting he's not a Good One?'

Elizabeth's needles began to click louder. Arethusa turned the ball of wool to accommodate the increase of speed. 'He is very handsome, that's true,' Elizabeth continued. 'He's good-looking, charming, creative and sensitive, but if he marries he'll be miserable.' She glanced at the card table, wincing a moment at the noise coming from it. 'If he marries, his aunts will be miserable. If he doesn't, his mother will be.' She sighed. 'As for you, there's no choice. That's a woman's lot.'

Arethusa considered her lot. What if she could have both a Handsome Knight *and* a Good One at the same time? After all, in a life of duty there had to be windows of pleasure!

Chapter 7

Ballinakelly, 1961

I awake to fog. It is thick like wool and damp. The high street glistens and the slate roofs glisten too, and everything is wet and cold and miserable. Today Kitty is taking me to Castle Deverill, but how am I going to see it in this weather? I am bitterly disappointed.

I returned from dinner last night in such high spirits. I have another family. A family who has always been here, only hidden from me and Logan. Mother was not alone, after all. She had never been alone. She just chose to be and I don't know why. Perhaps I will find out when I read her diary. I *will* read it, only I have not had the courage to do so yet. I awoke with the excitement of a child who wakes up on Christmas morning to the satisfying weight of a stocking on the end of the bed. But then I opened the curtains and saw *this*. Grey cloud covering everything. Now I feel like a child who discovers that Santa Claus has not come.

I breakfast in the dining room downstairs. Nora Maloney has heard the story and I imagine the whole of Ballinakelly knows too, for she pulls out a chair and joins me at my table without being invited. I am too polite to tell her I would

rather be left alone, and I don't have a newspaper to hide
behind. She wouldn't be so forward if Wyatt were here. But
I'd rather have Nora Maloney's company than Wyatt's. It is
strange, but when I think of my husband he is a small, indis-
tinct figure in a faraway land. He is not part of Ireland. He
does not belong here either physically or in my imagination.
I think of him only occasionally and even then, he is a blur.

As for Rose, a part of me wishes she were here to share this
with me. All my children have Deverill blood, but Rose is
the only one who would really be interested in her Deverill
roots and the only one who would understand why *I'm* so
interested. She would love discussing all the characters from
last night's dinner. I can see her face now, pink-cheeked and
full of light, relishing the unfolding mysteries just like I do.
But she's not here. It's probably for the best, after all she's busy
with her young family. Still, I like to think of her. Somehow,
I know she's thinking of me too.

'I could have guessed you were a Deverill,' says Nora, interrupting my thoughts. She puts her elbows on the table and
rests her chin in her hands. She smiles and I notice she has lip-
stick on her teeth. 'With that red hair and those grey eyes,' she
says. 'You caused quite a stir yesterday. The old people thought
you were Adeline, Lady Deverill that was, come to life.' She
laughs. 'Indeed, they thought you were a ghost. *I* thought you
were a ghost, when I first saw you. The young thought you
were Mrs Trench. Then the two of you together, like sisters.
It wasn't a surprise at all when I heard that your mother was
Arethusa Deverill.' When she says my mother's name her eyes
widen and her face glows, as if she is articulating something
deliciously forbidden. 'Arethusa Deverill,' she repeats. 'After
all these years. I don't imagine the Deverills thought they'd
hear from *her* again.' She barely draws breath and I listen to

her in the hope that she might shed light on why my mother went away. There must have been rumours and, as the saying goes: there's no smoke without fire.

'What do you know of Arethusa Deverill?' I smile with encouragement. I feel I have a certain power in this place, being a Deverill. The way Nora is looking at me, with a mixture of awe, fascination and deference, gives me confidence.

'I only know what my nan told me. Your mam was the talk of the town once upon a time. My nan said your mam was a saint. I kid you not. She said she was a saint. She cared about people.'

'Did your grandmother know my mother?'

'She worked at the castle when your mam was young. Your mam brought food and medicine to her family and other families besides. They were as poor as tinkers in those days and your mam took care of them. My nan thought she was an angel.'

'Might I meet your grandmother, Nora? Would that be possible?'

Nora's eyes widen further. She is literally trembling with excitement. 'She'd be honoured to meet Arethusa Deverill's daughter. Wait till I tell her who's coming to see her. She'll be beside herself with excitement. Can you come this afternoon? I knock off round five. If you come to the lobby, I'll take you to mam's house myself.'

'If it's no trouble, I'd love to.'

I'm excited too. I don't know why I think that Nora Maloney's grandmother should know more than Arethusa's own family, but I want to meet everyone who knew her. I want to retrace her steps. I want to tread where she trod. I want to talk to the people she talked to. It sounds absurd and I'm so glad Wyatt is not with me, or anyone else for that matter, because I don't think they'd understand. My mother is a distant figure, she always was – inscrutable, unreachable, like a cloud – but here, in the place where she grew up, I have purchase. I feel as if I am putting out my hand and finding something solid to hold on to. Or the promise of something solid.

I am still at the table when Cormac appears in the dining room. He is wearing a dark grey jacket with a woollen V-neck sweater underneath, in the same shade of grey. He smiles when he sees me and his lapis eyes shine with joy. I wonder whether he is ever sad. He appears to radiate happiness that is not dependent on the outside world but the way he is on the inside. 'Top of the morning to you,' he says and takes off his cap. His hair is grey like his beard and sticks up in thick tufts. He runs a rough hand through it to smooth it down. 'Did you sleep well?'

I smile back. His happiness is infectious. I bet he didn't look out of *his* window this morning and feel disappointed by the fog. 'I did, thank you. It's a very nice hotel.'

'Oh, it's grand. Vickery's Inn is the best in Ballinakelly.' He is proud of his town and of this modest inn. I am used to the finest hotels in the world, but I don't tell him that. I feel ashamed that I should even compare – that I am the sort of woman who *does* compare. Wyatt would turn his nose up at Vickery's Inn. I don't want to be like Wyatt. 'I've come to drive you to the castle,' he says.

'How nice.' I'm pleasantly surprised. I had expected Kitty to send her driver again, but I'd rather Cormac took me. I enjoyed talking to him in the car. There's something very appealing about his gentle charm and enthusiasm. A strength in his quiet calmness, which I'm drawn to. 'I'm not sure I'm going to see much of it in this weather,' I grumble.

'Oh, it'll be just grand, you'll see,' he says. Clearly, he is used to fog and thinks nothing of it. 'You'll see it all right.'

I return to my room to fetch my raincoat and hat. I'm wearing corduroy trousers and a sweater so I don't get cold. I change into lace-up shoes because my slip-ons are too delicate for this weather. I tie my hair back into a ponytail. I stand in front of the mirror and look at my reflection. I'm not a Clayton. My features are too feminine, all the Clayton women look like men. I now know that I am a Deverill through and through. The thought of belonging to this big Deverill clan makes me happy. I'm glad I came. I'm glad I stood my ground and didn't back down. I think of Logan then, who is a Clayton to his core, and wonder whether I should let him know what I have discovered. Would he be interested? I'm not sure he would. I don't think he is curious about our mother's past. I decide not to tell him anything until I get back to Boston. A part of me wants to keep Kitty and Bertie, and Arethusa Deverill, to myself.

I sit in the front seat. I notice a dog in the back. It is a border collie and it is staring at me with indignation, as if I am trespassing on its territory.

'That's Kite,' says Cormac. 'She's my constant companion. I would have brought her with me yesterday, but I wasn't sure you liked dogs.'

'How do you know now that I like dogs?' I ask with a smile.

'I just know,' he replies.

I can't help but laugh at his certainty. 'You're right, of course. I *do*. My husband won't have them in the house, though.'

'Now why would he do that?'

'The mess, I suppose.' Cormac shakes his head, as if banning a dog from the house for that reason is an abhorrence. 'And he's allergic,' I add quickly, which isn't true, but I don't want him thinking badly of Wyatt.

Cormac starts the Jeep, Kite settles down on the back seat and we drive slowly out of Ballinakelly. The fog is still thick and light drizzle lands softly on the windscreen. Cormac turns on the wipers and it is swept away. 'The Ireland of today must be very different from the Ireland you grew up in,' I say as we leave the town and drive into the sodden countryside.

'We fought hard for our independence,' he replies.

'It's difficult to imagine. I mean, it's so peaceful here.'

'I thank God every day for peace. That our children can grow up without the fear and the violence that we grew up with. The twenties were a brutal time. After independence was won there was civil war. Brother set against brother.' He shakes his head and for the first time I see real pain in his profile which takes me aback. I did not expect to see shadows in his radiance.

'What was it like for the Deverills during the War of Independence?' I ask. 'Did they consider themselves British or Irish? And what did the Irish, people like you, think of *them*?'

'Their allegiance was to Britain, and to us they were British. We wanted them out, all of them. It wasn't about personality, but about what they represented. We wanted Ireland back. But the Deverills . . .' He considers them a moment. 'They were different.'

'How so?'

'Kitty was one of us. She fought alongside us in that war.'

'Kitty?'

He nods and grins admiringly. 'She's always considered herself Irish.'

'What did she do?'

'She smuggled arms for us. No one was going to search a Deverill. She could walk straight past the Black and Tans with a bag full of ammo and no one would turn a hair. She was invaluable to the cause. A brave girl she was.'

Kitty Deverill rises in my thoughts like an avenging angel. She is not just beautiful, but courageous and fiercely patriotic too. No wonder people stared at me in Ballinakelly. Kitty is not just a local woman but a local heroine.

'Many Anglo-Irish left their estates and moved back to England. Many had their castles razed to the ground. Castle Deverill wasn't spared. It was burnt like so many others.'

I remember my dream in a sudden rush of recollection. I *know* the castle was burnt. I *know* it. How could I possibly know that, unless it is a just a coincidence, as Cormac says, so many Irish castles were set alight and destroyed.

'I'm not proud of that,' he continues. 'The Deverills did not deserve to lose their home,' he says quietly. I am surprised to see him looking regretful. His forehead is furrowed and his black eyebrows are set low over his eyes. I feel his regret.

'But they rebuilt it?' I say hopefully.

'Indeed they did, Mrs Langton, in old stone, at great expense, in the late twenties.' He glances at me. 'But it's no fairy tale. It's been dogged by tragedy. Your family has had its fair share of suffering.'

'Will you tell me about it?'

'Aye, I'll tell you. But it's a long story. I'll buy you a drink in Ma Murphy's and tell you your family history.'

'Do you have a wife, Mr O'Farrell?' I ask, because I am aware that a wife might not be happy with her husband buying a drink for a strange woman in a bar. I know how Wyatt would feel, but Wyatt is not here to mind.

'I had a wife,' he says. 'But she died.'

'I'm sorry.'

'It was a long time ago.'

'Do you have children?' I don't want to pry, but I'm curious. If his wife died, I would like to think of him having the comfort of children. But I sense there is something of the lone wolf in Cormac O'Farrell.

He shakes his head. 'No children, just Kite.'

We fall into silence. It feels awkward because I don't know what to say. He turns off the lane and drives up what looks like a farm track leading into the hills. The car jumps about as the wheels roll over puddles and stones. I imagined a grand driveway, not a rough track like this, with two muddy lanes for tyres and long grass growing up in between. The fog is still dense and I can't see where we are headed. On either side of the track are grey-stone walls. The stones are piled on top of each other and there appears to be nothing to bind them. I change the subject and ask Cormac about the stones and he tells me that these walls have been around for hundreds of years, built by mountain men who were clearing the fields and building boundaries at the same time. They knew instinctively which stones would fit where and although one can see through them, for there's no cement to fasten them, they won't fall down. They'll last for ever, Cormac says.

At length, he stops the Jeep. 'Have we arrived?' I ask, disappointed, because if this is the front drive, Castle Deverill is not the one in my dream nor in my expectation.

He grins, the mischievous grin of someone who is about to share an exciting secret. 'Come, I want to show you something,' he says.

I climb out and follow him up the track. Kite runs ahead as if she knows the secret and is excited too. Cormac walks at a brisk pace and I find myself out of breath and struggling to keep up. He's very fit. I imagine he ascends these hills a lot. As we near the top, I see, to my joy, beams of sunlight shining down in shafts of gold. 'Ah, the sun is coming out!' I exclaim happily.

'Just in time,' he says. We reach the top and, as I catch my breath, the mist begins to evaporate. I put my hands on my hips and survey the sea, emerging out of the whiteness in a glittering expanse of blue. I inhale the sweet, weedy tang of the ocean and my spirits soar with pleasure. And then, to my amazement, I see towers, crenellated towers, looming out of the fog. They come and go in a tantalizing game of 'now you see me, now you don't' as the cloud is carried inland on a salty wind. And then miraculously it clears, as if the sun has burnt a hole in it especially for me. I gaze in wonder as the towers grow into turrets and sturdy grey walls. It renders me speechless. Its beauty is in its magnificence and in its position, for it has a view of the ocean and at the same time is nestled in the folds of the hills, watched over by ancient trees, thick woodland and gardens. I take a deep breath. So this was Arethusa's home. Not some cold cottage shivering in a bog, but a spectacular castle, the ancestral seat of her illustrious family, and she chose to turn her back on it. How is that possible?

As for my dream. This is indeed the very castle, or one similar to it. My excitement mounts.

'I wanted you to see it from here before you see it up close,' says Cormac. 'Takes your breath away, doesn't it?'

'It certainly does,' I reply, smiling at him with gratitude.

'The night it burnt, the whole valley turned red. It was as if the hills were on fire too. As if the fire was consuming the entire estate.'

'It must have been devastating.'

'It went on burning for days and then it was left to decay into the ground. It was a great sadness to see that fine building brought to its knees. It might have represented the British Crown, but it represented the heart of this town and when it was lost, we felt lost without it.' He shakes his head. 'Now you'll be thinking I'm a poet as well as a taxi driver!' He laughs and puts his hands in his trouser pockets. I laugh too. It's impossible not to be affected by his *joie de vivre*.

I gaze at the castle, bathed in a pool of light, and long to go inside.

Kite nudges her master with her snout. Cormac bends down to pat her. She revels in his attention, wagging her tail and her bottom with it. We walk back down the hill to the Jeep. The fog has lifted and patches of blue sky are appearing through tears in the cloud. With the sun warm on my back, the wind in my hair and the smell of the sea in my nose, I feel carefree. I have only myself to think about. My time is my own. For two whole weeks I can do whatever I want. I don't have to consider anyone else. If I had been nervous at the prospect of being on my own for so long, I am no longer nervous. I am elated.

Kite jumps in the back and Cormac drives us to the castle. The Jeep stops in front of big black iron gates. On top of the two pillars of stone holding up the gates are a pair of fierce-looking lions, their mouths open in silent roars. The man in the gatehouse waves at Cormac and we drive on through. I suppose everyone knows each other in a town as small as Ballinakelly. The gravel drive curves in a gentle sweep, through an avenue of tall trees and rhododendron bushes, bursting with red and pink flowers. It is a beautiful sight. We emerge out of the trees and the castle rises up before us in regal splendour and once again it steals my breath.

I see Kitty's car parked outside the big door and my heart lifts with anticipation. I can't believe that I am here, at the very same castle I have dreamed about, with a family I did not know existed. It is like stepping into another life, one behind a veil, which has only now been revealed to me. It is *my* find, *my* secret and I am thrilled that Logan knows nothing about it.

Cormac leaves me at the door and I pull on the cord that hangs beside it. As I step back and wait, I notice an inscription carved above it in Latin: *Castellum Deverilli est suum regnum.* I tell myself not to forget to ask what it means, for I never learned Latin at school.

I don't have to wait long. The door is unbolted. It opens and I am greeted by a young butler in a black tailcoat. 'Good morning, Mrs Langton,' he says, stepping aside to let me pass. 'Mrs Deverill is expecting you in the drawing room with Mrs Trench. May I take your coat?'

I shrug off my raincoat and hand it to him. I attempt to smooth my hair with my hand, conscious that the wind on the hill has blown it into a mess. Then I cast my eyes around the sumptuous hall. I am stunned. I have been here before. It is exactly as I have seen it in my dreams. My eyes are drawn up the stairs and I wonder, if I were to walk down those corridors, whether I'd come across that narrow staircase leading up to the little room at the top. And if I were to come across it, what would I find inside?

I turn my attention back to the hall where there are faded Persian rugs on the chequerboard floor, a large marble fireplace with an empty hearth and Old Master paintings in gilt frames hanging from chains on the walls. The ceilings are high and a chandelier sparkles above me in the light that now streams in through the tall windows on either side of the door. It is opulent. I bear in mind that it was rebuilt after the fire in the twenties, so little is left of the original building. Still, it is splendid and I am impressed. It has not disappointed. Not in the least.

The butler leads me through the hall and down a corridor, into the drawing room. Kitty gets up from the sofa when she sees me and we embrace like long-lost friends. Alana takes my hand and kisses my cheek. 'I'm so glad you've come to see where your mother grew up,' she says.

My eyes stray to a portrait that hangs over the fireplace. Kitty and Alana look at it too. 'That's our grandmother, Adeline,' Kitty says. I am astonished. It is as if I am staring at myself. She has the same hair, the same grey eyes, the same pale skin. If I thought I looked like Kitty, I was mistaken. I look *similar* to Kitty, but I look *just* like Adeline. No wonder my uncle and aunt commented on it last night. The resemblance is extraordinary. I wonder why my mother never mentioned it. Surely, she must have noticed. She must have seen her mother every time she looked at me.

'My grandmother,' I say when I finally find my voice. 'How I wish I'd known her.'

'So do I,' Kitty agrees. 'You would have adored her. She was like a mother to me. In fact, I was much closer to her than I was to my own mother. Maud was a very difficult woman, but Grandma was soft and sweet and wise. I miss her every day. I truly do.'

We are served tea and cake, that delicious porter cake that Kitty gave me yesterday. 'What do the Latin words carved above the front door mean?' I ask.

'A Deverill's castle is his kingdom,' says Kitty proudly. Now I remember my uncle reciting it at dinner last night.

'You cannot imagine what this castle means to your family,' Alana tells me. 'It is more than bricks and mortar. It is their family's very soul and they have suffered terrible things in order to keep it.'

'But here we are,' says Kitty brightly, taking Alana's hand. 'And darling JP is where he should be. After everything that happened, it all turned out for the best in the end.'

'Cormac told me it was burnt down during the Troubles,' I say. I look at Kitty and wish I hadn't mentioned it. It is as if I have prodded an old wound.

'Our grandfather died in that fire, Faye,' she says quietly. 'And our grandmother, Adeline, never fully recovered.' She takes her hand off Alana's and puts it on her heart, and in that moment she looks old and defeated. A little of her sheen is dulled then, but it does not diminish her; it only makes her more fascinating. 'Everything changed after that.' She sighs and I long for her to continue. For her to tell me the whole story, but she smiles sadly and says, 'I don't know whether your mother ever knew of the fire or that her father died in it. After she left for America Adeline never heard from her again. I can't imagine what that must have been like, to lose a daughter in that way. Tussy didn't die, she just decided to cut all ties, and that is worse than dying. I wonder now whether my bond with Adeline was in some way forged out of her losing Tussy. I was the daughter she lost. I was her comfort.'

'There must have been a terrible falling-out,' I say. 'Things must have been said that could never be forgiven.'

Kitty shrugs. 'Yes, there must have been. But I don't know why.'

'Perhaps her diary will tell me.'

'You will find out,' she says with certainty, as if she knows something I don't. 'Tussy left you the diary so that you would know her story. Why else would she give it to you? And why to you and not your brother? I think you are about to find out.'

I think she is right, but I am scared.

Chapter 8

Kitty, Alana and I wander around the gardens with JP's three enormous wolfhounds, who mob on the lawn and disappear into the bushes – in search of rabbits, I'm told. The skies are a bright cornflower blue. Kitty points out a heron as it flies over the castle towards the sea. Its magnificent wings cast a shadow that seems to have a life of its own as it moves swiftly across the lawn and into the shrubbery. There are song thrushes, plovers and swifts, and the ordinary blackbird with its extraordinary song. Kitty is delighted by them, as am I, for like Cormac's her enthusiasm is infectious – or perhaps it is simply that my deprived spirit is crying out for joy.

We walk round to the stables, which are part of the original castle for they were spared the fire. The bricks are old and weathered to a pale grey colour, mottled with lichen and softened by moss. There is a clock tower, but I'm told that the clock hasn't worked for years, and cobbles on the ground, polished smooth in places from centuries of wear. Kitty tells me that the stable yard hasn't changed at all since her father was a child, so I can imagine my mother here among the racks of saddles and bridles and other paraphernalia that mean nothing to me because I am not a horsewoman. It smells of manure and leather, ancient stone and dust, and I don't imagine that those have changed much either.

There is a walled garden with an orchard of fruit trees in blossom. Every now and then gusts of wind blow the petals into the air like confetti. It is very pretty, as if I am in a very pleasant dream. There are immaculately weeded beds of vegetables and two vast greenhouses, as big as small palaces, with pale green roofs shaped like blancmanges. They are spectacular. But Alana tells me they just don't have the workforce the Deverills had in the old days to fill them with plants and flowers. Now only one is in use and the other is for storage and overgrown with weeds. Kitty recalls that there were at least twenty workers employed to tend the gardens when she was a child. Now they only have four and they are barely able to cope, so they hire men from town to help during the busiest times of the year. It must cost a fortune to keep this place, I muse. I can't imagine what the costs must be. I know it is vulgar to think of money, but it is hard not to when faced with such splendour.

As we make our way back to the castle, I gaze up at the windows in the towers and wonder whether one of them looks into the little room in my dream. The one where I find myself, or perhaps it is Adeline who is standing there with her hand on the mantelpiece, gazing into the fire, as if she has been waiting for me for a long, long time. I want to share my dream with Kitty, but I don't want her to think her newly found cousin is crazy. I long to find that room, but I can't go roaming about the corridors on my own or they'll think I'm sly or taking liberties. I must wait until an opportune moment arises.

'Faye, would you like to come and stay with us at the White House?' Kitty asks as we reach the French doors that lead into the castle from the terrace. 'I don't like to think of you staying in a hotel. You're family, after all, and it doesn't feel right. It's a big enough house so you will still feel independent, and we don't sit on ceremony, Robert and I. It's for you to decide, but I know it'll be infinitely more comfortable than Vickery's Inn.'

'JP and I would also like to invite you to stay with us,' Alana adds. 'But we discussed it last night after you'd left and decided that Kitty's will be more restful. We have small children, you see.'

'My daughter Florence married an Englishman and they live in London,' says Kitty. 'Robert is a writer and barely comes out of his study these days. I would welcome the company.' Her smile is so warm and open-hearted that I am unable to refuse. I am wary of losing my independence, the two weeks of solitude I craved, but I also want to belong in this family of mine that I have just discovered. I think I now crave that more than solitude.

'Thank you so much, Kitty. I would love to,' I reply and I feel an expansion in my chest as my heart fills with gratitude.

'Then I will send Shane to fetch you. When would be convenient?'

I remember tea with Nora Maloney's grandmother, which is at five. 'Perhaps tomorrow morning,' I tell her.

'Of course,' says Kitty. 'You must be tired after your journey and in need of an early night. I forget you only arrived yesterday and we dragged you out for supper. It's funny but I feel as if you have been here longer.'

Kitty drives me back into Ballinakelly. As the castle recedes in the wing mirror I can't help but wonder again how my mother could have left and not looked back.

Nora Maloney takes me to visit her mother. We walk through the town. The sun is setting. The whitewashed houses turn orange and the air grows thick with damp. I wrap my coat about me and put my hands in the pockets. Above the buildings the rugged hills sink into shadow. Only the tops catch the light and glow a dazzling gold, rising like flames into a translucent sky. Nora's parents' house, for her grandmother lives with them, is a ten-minute walk up a boreen. Nora herself lives a few streets away with her husband who is a mechanic. She chatters without drawing breath. By the time we reach the door I think she has told me the ins and outs of her marriage, as well as all the scandals in Ballinakelly, of which there are a great many.

They are expecting us. Nora's mother sandwiches my hand between her warm, doughy ones and tells me how delighted she is to meet me. 'May God forgive me for comparing the living with the dead, but you are the stamp of Adeline, Lady Deverill. Lord have mercy on her soul and all the holy souls.' Her round cheeks flush scarlet. 'Poor auld Mam is all worked up that Arethusa Deverill's daughter is coming to visit. She can't believe it. After all these years. Come into the parlour, girleen, and take the weight off your feet. I've wet the sup of tea and I've made a cake especially. You're a Yank, aren't you, so you must taste a biteen of Irish porter cake!' Nora's father, in a jacket and tie, stands up when I enter the small parlour and shakes my hand. He is sturdy and strong with a black beard and black eyes and he doesn't smile. I think he is shy. He steps aside and I see a little old lady in a black dress and shawl sitting by the hearth where a turf fire smoulders in the grate. She lifts her eyes and stares at me. 'God save us! Is it the Last Day or what?' she exclaims. 'Lady Deverill is out of her grave and back from the dead.' She has no teeth and her Irish brogue is so strong I find it hard to understand her.

'No, Mam, this is Lady Deverill's granddaughter. Miss Arethusa's daughter,' says Nora's mother, taking the seat beside her.

'Lovely to meet you,' I say. No one has told me their names and I know Maloney is Nora's married name, so I simply take her grandmother's hand, thin and cold like a chicken's claw, and smile down at her. She stares up at me wide-eyed as if she has seen a ghost and grips my hand.

'I've told no one!' she says in a whisper. 'Not a living Christian, God help me. If I don't go gaga I'll take it to my grave. Like I promised.' I am not sure what she's talking about. It's a bit unsettling and I wonder if she's not a little crazy.

We all sit down and Nora pours the tea and hands around the cake while her mother asks me about my visit and for how long I'll be staying. I reply, take the china cup I'm offered and taste the cake, which is like the cake I had at Kitty's and surprisingly good. I know I have to be polite and make small talk but I'm longing to ask about my mother. All the while we chat I'm aware of the little old lady's beady eyes upon me, devouring me with both fascination and fear. She stares at my face as if trying to make sense of this woman who has turned up out of nowhere, looking like Lady Deverill.

Then she suddenly wakes from her stupor.

'I worked at the castle as a maid, you know,' she says, interrupting her daughter who is mid-sentence.

'Mam worked for Lady Deverill, Adeline Deverill, Lord have mercy on her,' says Nora's mother. 'She was a maid when your mother was a young woman and, as you can see, she is very proud of it.'

'Did you know Lady Deverill?' asks Nora's grandmother. I think she is confused.

Nora's mother puts a hand on the old lady's. 'No, Mam. This is Miss Arethusa's daughter. She's come all the way from America. She never knew Lady Deverill.'

The old woman's eyes widen. 'You're the dead stamp

of her,' she says, shaking her head and fiddling with her rosary beads.

Nora decides to move the conversation along. She knows what I'm after. 'Nan, do you remember Miss Arethusa?' she asks, articulating her words clearly so that her grandmother will understand.

The old lady chews her gums. I can almost hear the cogs in her mind beginning to turn. She nods. 'I was fourteen when I went to work at the castle,' she says. I listen carefully. I don't want to miss a word, but she is very difficult to understand. 'I was a junior maid. I looked after Miss Arethusa. I used to dress her in the morning and take her clothes to the laundry. I never opened her notes. As God is my witness, I never did. She had no complaint about me. None at all.'

I am excited with this piece of information and smile at Nora with gratitude.

Nora is pleased. 'You see, you do remember the past, don't you, Nan,' she says.

'What was she like, Miss Arethusa?' I ask.

The grandmother smiles and her gums are pink and shiny. 'A saint,' she says, her voice laden with admiration. 'If she hadn't been a Protestant she would have been declared a saint or at the very least a Blessed.'

Nora laughs. 'I told you, didn't I?' she says, turning to me. 'She thinks the world of your mother.'

'Oh, she does,' Nora's mother agrees. 'Mam, tell Mrs Langton how Miss Arethusa used to help the poor.'

The old lady's small eyes brighten and I sense she is warming to her subject. 'She used to steal into the kitchen and fill a basket of food to take to the poor. There was such hunger in those days. People were sick and dying from starvation and disease. We had nothing. Indeed, I got my first pair of shoes when I went to work at the castle. I thought I was on the pig's back with those shiny shoes on my feet!' She leans forward and narrows her eyes. 'I heard the arguments. Mrs Deverill trying to stop her visiting. She didn't want Miss Arethusa to get sick too, wasn't the whole country dying of consumption and the pox, and Miss Arethusa accusing her of not understanding and besting her. Miss Arethusa thought they'd all die if she didn't take them food. The common people had a name for her, Naomheen. That's Little Saint in Irish. In spite of being Protestant and not afraid of the old priest, Miss Arethusa would pick up old blind Richie Ryan every Sunday in her pony and trap and take him to Mass and stay with him until Mass was over and take him home, God bless her.'

'Was she sent away because Mrs Deverill feared she'd get sick?' I ask.

The old lady shakes her head. 'God save us, no.' She is very certain about that.

'Why did she leave then?'

'Didn't she tell you?'

'Tell me what?'

The old lady lowers her voice, as if she is afraid the walls have ears. 'She was carrying, God between us and all harm!'

There is a collective gasp in the room. Nora's parents cross themselves. Nora can see that I don't understand. 'She was expecting,' she says, staring at me with big, anxious eyes, afraid that I am offended.

I'm not offended. I'm incredulous. I wonder now whether the old lady has lost her marbles. I realize suddenly that I'm a fool to have come. 'That's impossible,' I say. 'I'm sure you're mistaken.'

'Oh Mam. You *must* be mistaken,' says her daughter, laughing nervously and catching her husband's eye, who coughs into his beard.

'Nan, you must be thinking of someone else,' says Nora. She turns to me. 'I'm sorry. She gets confused these days. She means no disrespect.'

But the old lady is adamant. 'Oh, she was, as God is my judge,' she says. 'That's why they sent her to America.'

'If she was pregnant. Who was the father?' I ask.

'Dermot McLoughlin.'

Everyone in the room now relaxes. Her suggestion is clearly unbelievable. 'Mam, that's just daft. Miss Deverill would never mix with the likes of a McLoughlin.'

'Evil gossip,' says Nora's father suddenly. It is the first thing he has said and the women listen to him. I am grateful he has now entered the conversation. Nora's grandmother chews her gums again and stares into the fire. 'May God forgive you, Eily Barry,' he adds in a low voice.

Nora's mother puts her hand on the old lady's again. 'It's all right, Mam. You're just addled. How can you remember so long ago?'

There is a long, uncomfortable pause. Nora smiles at me apologetically, her mother looks embarrassed, her father stares at the floor as if he wishes it had a mouth to swallow him whole.

Then the awkward silence is broken. 'It was November and we had just had the first frost,' the old lady says in a slow and deliberate voice, without taking her eyes off the fire. 'I remember like it was yesterday. I'm not so old that my memory has gone. She was sent to America to have the child. Then she never came back.'

Of course, this is ridiculous. There was no baby. But she has sown a seed in my mind, a poisonous seed, and I know I will not be able to dig it up and throw it out. It is there, planted deep, and it will fester.

The old woman's eyes burn angrily, and a little crazily, the rosary beads passing through her finger and thumb at great speed. 'Poor auld Miss Arethusa was banished for carrying a child out of wedlock,' she says in an indignant tone of voice. 'Well, she wasn't the only one. Didn't old Lord Deverill cock his leg for Bridie Doyle and gave her not one child but a brace, God save us.'

'Whisht, Mam, hold your tongue,' says her daughter firmly, patting her arm.

The old grandmother sniffs and goes quiet. The conversation resumes, but it is flat and awkward and I soon make my excuses and leave. Nora is mortified, as are her parents. They apologize profusely. I tell them I really don't mind. That she is old and muddled, and that I am not at all offended. But I leave to walk back to the hotel, grateful to Kitty for inviting me to stay with her. I don't think I want to be near Nora Maloney anymore and I don't want to see her family again either. Her grandmother is a mad old crone. I realize in order to learn the truth I must face my mother's diary. No one knows what really happened but Arethusa herself.

I walk back to the hotel. Hands in pockets, head down, eyes to the pavement. I can't get the image of my pregnant mother out of my mind. Of course, the idea is absurd. But still I turn over the possibilities in my head. If she had a baby and gave it away for adoption, that would explain why she never spoke about it. It would explain why she went off to America. On the other hand, why could she not have married Dermot McLoughlin? When the old lady had mentioned his name there had not been a person in the room who believed it, so what was this Dermot McLoughlin like? Why was it unthinkable that Arethusa should be associated with him? I tell myself to stop guessing and to wait until I have read the diary, but I cannot control my thoughts. They are running in all directions, like hounds searching the ground for the scent of fox, exploring every possibility, wanting very much to find a truth that is tolerable.

I reach the hotel and hurry to my room. I don't want to speak to anyone. I want to be left alone. I am relieved that I am not moving to Kitty's tonight. That I have the whole evening on my own to hold that book in front of a mirror.

I shrug off my coat and kick off my shoes. There is a small mirror hanging on the wall. I take it down and carry it to the bed, where I lie against the pillows with my feet up and open the diary. I am nervous. What if I discover that she *was* pregnant? What then? Do I track down the child, my sibling? Or do I leave it alone? Will I be able to leave it alone? Can life continue as before when such a thing is known?

I put on my reading glasses and open the first page. The words, that look so strange on the paper, make perfect sense in the reflection of the mirror. It is like magic. Mother's handwriting is neat, although it doesn't look like hers, but that must be because she was writing backwards. It is an impressive skill.

Once again I am taken back into the past. It is summer at Castle Deverill and I almost feel I am there.

Chapter 9

It was a damp, misty morning in June. Castle Deverill shivered in the soft rain while the birds tweeted gleefully in gratitude for the abundance of insects and the lawns full of worms. The fireplace in the drawing room was empty. The log basket, piled high with sycamore, beech and oak to fuel the winter fires, remained untouched now that it was summer. Arethusa, wrapped in a thick shawl, knelt on the rug with her mother, aunts and Charlotte, sorting through boxes of socks, which the women of the Ballinakelly Needlework Guild had knitted for the poor. Adeline, who was president of the guild, had bought the wool and paid the women a shilling a pair, but there didn't appear to be a matching pair among them. 'Can none of the women knit two socks alike?' complained Hazel, holding up a couple of blue socks, one with a long foot and short leg, the other with a short foot and long leg. 'I'm sure the knitter meant for these two to go together,' she said.

'It's not worth doing if one can't do it properly,' complained Laurel, sighing reproachfully.

'I don't think the poor will mind,' said Poppy, glancing at

Adeline, whose eyes were on the sky. 'Do stop looking out of the window, Adeline. The rain will move on by lunchtime, I assure you. It always does.'

'And I who *love* rain,' said Adeline. 'It's so silly. But the thought of having seven hundred tenants and their families for tea on a sodden lawn in the pouring rain is dreadful. I just want everyone to have a lovely time.'

'They'll be so happy with the cakes they won't mind,' said Arethusa, finding the smallest sock, fit only for a tiny baby, and holding it up with a grin. 'This is for one of your fairies, Mama,' she said.

'Oh, that won't do for a fairy,' said Adeline, putting away her worries about the weather and laughing at her daughter's impish game. 'It's much too big. It will swamp the poor thing!'

'A sleeping-sock then,' Arethusa added. 'You can put a whole fairy family in here and they'll be snug all winter.'

'Aren't you a tease, Tussy!' said Hazel.

'A tease,' gushed Laurel. 'One day you might see a fairy and then you'll laugh on the other side of your face,' she added.

'If I see a fairy with my own eyes, Aunt Laurel, I'll be the first to admit I was wrong – and I'll knit sleeping-socks for the whole bally lot of them!' Arethusa looked at Charlotte, quietly going about her work. 'Have you any fairy socks, Charlotte?' she asked.

Her governess smiled a small, timid smile. 'One or two,' she replied in a soft voice. 'But mostly, I've found pairs.'

'Then chuck me a handful from your box and I'll go through them. This box here is full of socks made for midgets.'

There was a knock at the door and O'Flynn appeared with a grim face. 'Madam, Mrs O'Hara says she needs to speak with you urgently.' He inhaled through dilated nostrils because he considered the daily calls from the needy excessive and tedious. 'She appears to be in some distress.'

The Shrubs looked at one another in alarm. It did not take much to frighten Hazel and Laurel, but Poppy, who spent much of her time with the poor, was familiar with their hardships and only feared for *their* welfare. The word 'distress' made her very anxious indeed.

Arethusa put down the fairy sock and Adeline pushed herself off the floor. 'Send her in at once, O'Flynn,' she said, taking a more dignified seat on the sofa and waiting apprehensively for the distressed woman to appear.

A moment later Mary O'Hara bustled into the room in a soaking black dress, its hem caked with mud from her walk over the hills, wringing her coarse hands in agitation. Her black hair was matted and her stricken face grubby with tears. She was pale and thin and visibly trembling. 'Forgive me for disturbing you, madam,' she said, composing herself as best she could in front of the ladies.

The sight of her made Adeline stand up. 'What is the matter, Mary?' she asked.

''Tis me daughter, she's been taken,' said Mary O'Hara.

Adeline was shocked. 'Taken, by whom?' she demanded.

'Nuns from America. They said that Almighty God was calling her to be a nun. They said the hottest place in Purgatory is kept for them that do not heed God's call.'

The Shrubs stared at Mary O'Hara with their mouths agape. Charlotte did not look particularly shocked, just sad. Arethusa got to her feet and rushed to the woman's side. She put an arm around her. 'We'll get her back,' she promised, trying to give comfort with a squeeze.

'Tussy,' said Adeline. Arethusa ignored the warning tone in her mother's voice. She knew she shouldn't be making promises she couldn't keep or touching this poor creature who might not be well, but she couldn't stand by and do nothing.

'This is terrible,' said Poppy, her empathy such that she felt the woman's pain as if it were her own.

'Wolves have descended on the fold,' said Laurel darkly.

'Pirates on our shores,' added Hazel with equal foreboding.

'And not just me Maeve, but others too,' Mary O'Hara continued. 'They've taken eight. The flowers of Ballinakelly. Gone.' She began to whimper.

'Mama, we have to *do* something!' Arethusa demanded. 'They can't just come and steal children!'

Adeline asked O'Flynn, who was standing in the doorway and listening to the woman's story with interest, to bring a pot of tea, then told Mary O'Hara to sit down and tell them the whole story from the beginning. 'Does Father O'Callaghan know about this?' Adeline asked, sitting on the sofa again.

'The whole town knows of it, but no one can do anything about it but you, madam.'

'It's kidnap,' exclaimed Arethusa, outraged. 'Pure and simple. Someone should call the Constabulary at once!'

'Not if the girls went willingly,' said Poppy, catching Adeline's eye.

'*Did* they go willingly, Mary?' asked Adeline.

Laurel and Hazel pushed themselves off the rug and settled into the sofas like a pair of timid birds. This would give them nightmares for weeks! Poppy took the club fender. Charlotte remained on the floor with the socks pressed to her breast. Mary O'Hara perched on the edge of an armchair, afraid to soil the pale fabric with her dirty clothes. 'Maeve wanted to go,' she said, dropping her gaze into her rough hands. 'She said she wanted to be a Bride of Christ. Them nuns had promised them sainthoods and eternal life in Heaven, God save us. Now I've lost me only daughter. What am I going to do without her? Me heart is as heavy as lead and in smithereens that I'll never see me beloved Maeve again.' She began to sob. O'Flynn came in with the tray of tea and cake and lingered for as long as possible, curious to hear more riveting details. Mary O'Hara gulped the tea and ate the cake, and Hazel gave her her own handkerchief, embroidered with the letter H, with which to wipe her eyes.

'Think of the good Maeve will do in the convent, Mary,' said Poppy gently. 'Think of the people she will help. The children, whose lives will be all the better for her good works. She will make something special of her life, Mary. She will tend the sick and soothe the broken-hearted. She will give hope to the hopeless.' But these words of encouragement, although well-intended, did not have the effect Poppy had hoped for.

Mary O'Hara flung wide her arms. 'But what will become of *me*, I ask you? Me, alone in the world, without a man coming in to look after me and neither chick nor childeen to lift me poor broken heart? God help me to carry me cross in me own Calvary.' There was nothing any of them could say to that.

When she was gone, with a large slice of cake wrapped in paper, a beam of sunlight shone through the drawing-room windows, flooding the room with light and warmth.

'You were right, Poppy. The rain has passed,' said Hazel cheerfully, kneeling once more on the rug and delving into the box of socks to pick up from where she had left off.

'Now the grass will dry and everyone will have a lovely time at the tea party,' said Laurel.

'But what of Mary and her daughter, and the other daughters besides?' Arethusa exclaimed, astonished that her aunts could so quickly dismiss such an upsetting scene. 'What will become of them? Will they really not see their daughters again, ever?'

Adeline put a hand to her heart. 'I cannot imagine the sorrow those poor mothers are suffering. It's too dreadful to comprehend. I wish to God there was something I could do.'

'When I worked for a family in America I heard a story about nuns going to Ireland to inspire simple Irish girls to be Brides of Heaven. It's outrageous,' said Charlotte. Everyone stared at her because they had quite forgotten that she was there.

'It is outrageous,' Poppy agreed. 'That's a very good word.'

'Sadly, there is nothing any of us can do,' said Adeline.

'Papa will know what to do!' Arethusa exclaimed. 'I'll go and find him.'

'I'm afraid he's as helpless as we are,' said Adeline sadly. 'Those girls are already on a boat bound for America, I should imagine. And if they went willingly, then we are truly powerless to stop them.'

'Father O'Callaghan should warn the girls about these devious nuns. They should be on their mettle.' Arethusa lifted her chin. 'And if it were *my* daughter, I'd swim the Atlantic to find her and bring her back.'

Adeline smiled tenderly at Arethusa's naivety. 'My dear, sometimes you have to let them go. If you love them, you have to respect their free will. The hardest part of loving is letting go, because love is rarely unconditional.'

'And those poor women don't have the money to sail to America,' said Poppy.

'And neither would we,' rejoined Hazel.

'We certainly wouldn't. We're as poor as church mice,' said Laurel with a sigh, picking up a sock and examining it with contempt.

'Church mice who live rather well,' Arethusa added drily, realizing that her silly aunts Hazel and Laurel had little idea of what it meant to be poor.

That afternoon, as sunshine blazed upon the lawns of Castle Deverill and dried the last raindrops on the surrounding trees and flowers, seven hundred tenants and their families, dressed in their Sunday best, swarmed onto the terrace to shake hands with their landlord. Lord and Lady Deverill greeted them graciously like a king and queen greeting their subjects. Lady Deverill, supporting herself on a stick, wore an enormous hat with feathers collected from her own exotic hens. Every time she nodded, the feathers moved up and down, giving the impression that something living had taken up residence there. The children found it especially funny and lingered close by, squealing with laughter each time the old lady moved her head. Lady Deverill, oblivious of her young audience, smiled at each tenant and repeated the same sentence over and over. 'Lovely day, how good of you to come.' She wore a pair of white calfskin gloves to protect herself from contagion as well as soreness, for by the end of the line she must have shaken over a thousand hands and some of them quite vigorously. She decided she would leave Adeline to shake them at the end of the day on her behalf.

Lord Deverill watched the final tenant shuffle off towards the tables of sandwiches and cake and turned to his wife. 'You didn't ask Father O'Callaghan, I see,' he said.

'Adeline wouldn't let me,' Elizabeth replied. 'She said he would ruin the day. Everyone's afraid of him. He's got a face like a trout.'

'Very well.'

'And he's probably trying to find those poor missing girls.'

'More likely in O'Donovan's, knocking back stout,' said Greville. He looked into the crowd and saw Adeline moving through it like a swan among moorhens. *Now there's a woman with grace*, he thought admiringly, hooking his thumbs into his waistcoat pockets and rocking on his heels. Elizabeth wasn't really capable of working the crowd like Adeline, he thought. His wife always managed to offend by saying the wrong thing. Adeline, on the other hand, could be relied on to have the right word, the appropriate look and the well-timed departure, moving from person to person with tact and elegance. He spotted his son, Hubert, talking to the stable boys, and his grandsons Bertie and Rupert, who both found these sorts of occasions a trial, not that one would know given the show they managed to put on. Arethusa, pretty in a pale blue dress and matching hat, was chatting to a pack of young men who surrounded her like wolves around Red Riding Hood. She was throwing back her head and laughing in a very unladylike manner. This Red Riding Hood was not afraid of wolves, it seemed. In Greville's opinion, his granddaughter was much too familiar with these people. *One must maintain a certain distance*, he thought to himself. *One mustn't get too close or they'll expect too much of one.* He decided to speak to Adeline about Arethusa's behaviour. It would normally be Elizabeth's duty to speak to their daughter-in-law, but once again, Greville did not believe her capable. It really wasn't proper to flirt with such men, he concluded. The sooner she was wed, the better.

He swept his eyes over the guests, reluctant to plunge in any sooner than necessary. The Shrubs had come to help, as they did every year. Laurel and Hazel in their wide hats with pastel-pink ribbons flying in the breeze, their eager faces flushed beneath frilly parasols, sillier than ever. Poppy with her earnest concern, deep in conversation with a group of women, listening to their gripes and their woes. *Women*, he thought with a disapproving sniff, *are much too sentimental*. At least in

that regard his wife was something of a relief. Elizabeth had
no time for gripes and woes and kept the common people at
arm's length. As he finally stepped onto the lawn he thought
the women in his family would do well to take a leaf out of
her book. But only that one, mind you.

Arethusa managed to extricate herself from the garden
party without being noticed. It was nearly over anyhow and
she had played her part (and worked all the young men into
a lather of excitement). Eily helped her change out of her
party dress in favour of a walking dress and she hurried off
towards Ballinakelly, knowing that Charlotte would assume
she was still in the garden. This time she wasn't on her way
to help the poor but heading across the fields for an entirely
different purpose.

Wheat was turning golden in the sun and on the hillsides
cows and sheep were contentedly grazing on the long grasses
and heather. A stream meandered down a slope, trickling
quietly over rocks, and overhead a pair of seagulls cried into
the wind. The rain had been blown away and now the sky
was a royal blue with only a few feathery clouds wafting
across it. Arethusa walked with a spring in her step, her skirts
dancing about her ankles with each stride, a merry tune on
her lips. When she reached the edge of the wood she stopped.
She put her hands on her hips and looked through the trees.
Then she saw him, emerging out of the thicket in a jacket and
cap, a cigarette between his lips, a smile in his eyes. 'Dermot
McLoughlin,' she said, sashaying towards him coquettishly.
'Aren't you a sight for sore eyes.'

'You managed to leave the party then?' he replied, blowing
smoke into the air.

She stood before him, lifted her chin and looked him
straight in the eye. 'I thought there might be something more

interesting to do in this wood,' she said, grinning at him flirtatiously.

He put his hand in the small of her back and pulled her towards him. 'If the lady would allow me to show her, I think she'll find much amusement in it.'

'Please do, Mr McLoughlin.'

Dermot led her into the shadows. Shafts of light streamed through the thick canopy of leaves above them. Birds sang in the branches and butterflies searched for nectar among the foxgloves and elder. 'Isn't it beautiful,' she said, treading softly through the bed of ferns and bracken.

Dermot took her by the waist and pushed her gently against the trunk of an oak tree. 'It pales in beauty when compared to you,' he said, pressing her into the soft lichen.

'Now you're a poet like my brother,' she laughed, but her voice was already husky with desire at the prospect of what he was going to do to her.

He put his mouth on hers to silence her mockery. She parted her lips and closed her eyes and felt her whole body respond. His beard scratched her chin and then, as he kissed his way down her neck to her throat, it scratched her there too, giving her delicious feelings in her belly. She couldn't imagine responding to Ronald in this way. Then, at the thought of Ronald, marriage and the dreaded marital bed, her determination to explore her sexuality with a man who aroused her grew fierce. Dermot ran his tongue over her collarbone and into the well at her throat. Then he began to unbutton her blouse, and instead of making him stop she allowed him to undress her. As he fiddled with the little pearl buttons, his breath grew hot and hoarse, and Arethusa heard her own breathing as it grew shallow and more rapid with anticipation. When her blouse was undone she gently pushed him away so that she could reach the metal hooks on the front of her corset. She could not expect him to know how to release her from that piece of armour. His dark eyes watched as one by one she unhooked them. Gradually her flesh was revealed until she dropped the corset to the forest floor with a triumphant smile, releasing her breasts for him to admire, and admire them, he did. They were full and soft and a creamy, flawless white. For a moment Dermot stared at them as if he didn't know what to do. As if he was suddenly aware of who was standing half-naked in front of him and was duly abashed. Arethusa took his hand and placed it on her left breast with a small gasp. His hand was big and warm and rough with calluses. A labourer's hand. No one had ever touched her there before and the feeling was exquisite. He moved it, tracing his thumb around her nipple, causing her to let out a low moan. She lifted her chin and found his lips as his other hand moved onto her right breast. The sensation was so heavenly that Arethusa could think of nothing but the mounting tension in her belly. She closed her eyes, took his hand off her breast and put it between her legs, in the place where she ached the most. Dermot did not need any further encouragement. He lifted her skirt and burrowed beneath it. He slid his hand into her drawers and reached between her thighs, which were warm and damp and parting for him eagerly. Arethusa's moans grew louder as once again she felt his fingertips on the skin above her stocking. This time she didn't stop him. She closed her eyes and gasped as his fingers began to caress her most secret place, causing her to lose herself entirely in the moment. Then she was on the forest floor, her back against the soft grass, her knees falling towards the grass without so much as a blush upon her cheek. He knelt at her feet and unfastened his trousers and she watched him with a steady, shameless gaze until he revealed himself with a triumphant smile. Then he was slipping it into her and she was delighting in her wantonness, as if, by letting herself go in this way she was at last giving expression to her own true nature. With every thrust her pleasure mounted until, at its height, something gave, spreading warmth and pleasure into every corner of her body.

She cried out with joy then lay limp and breathless as he reached the pinnacle of his own pleasure with a groan. 'Oh Dermot,' she sighed, wrapping her arms around him. 'If I had known what delights were to be had in these woods, I would have come sooner.'

'You don't regret it?' he asked, pleasantly surprised.

'Regret it? Why should I regret it?' She laughed. 'If I'm going to marry boring old Ronald, it's only fair that I have a little fun of my own before.'

'You're going to marry Ronald?' He rolled off her and lay on his back, staring into the thicket above him with disappointment.

'Of course. You don't think I can marry *you*, do you?'

'I was hoping . . .' His voice trailed off.

'That's just silly. You know I can't. Now, forget about marriage, Dermot. Live in the moment.' She rolled onto her side and traced a finger down his face. 'When can we do that again?'

Chapter 10

Arethusa was excited about her new discovery. So excited, in fact, that her enthusiasm for trysts in the woods swiftly replaced her desire to help the poor and, as a consequence, her forays into this forbidden world grew more frequent. Now her visits to the poor with Aunt Poppy were mere decoys to hide what she was *really* up to. She shared the pony and trap and brought a basket of food as usual, but instead of spending time with the families she visited, she simply put the food on the table, said a few sympathetic words, then hastened across the fields to meet Dermot. It was illicit and wild, and the most thrilling thing she had ever done in her life.

Arethusa was not unaware of the risks she was taking. She knew all about procreation, Charlotte had been very enlightening on the subject, and she had heard the local gossip about the odd girl in town who had got into trouble and had to hastily marry or flee to Dublin and God knows what happened to them then. Eily, her maid, was a real scandalmonger and loved nothing more than bringing her mistress the latest news, bad news especially. But Arethusa was bold, reckless even; she never expected Fate to be inconsiderate. Therefore, when her monthly arrived, as it always did, she was not at all surprised, or even relieved. It was as it should be. She expected nothing less. Dermot was for pleasure, Ronald for duty, and she was sure Fate would know very well which man would father her children. Everything was as perfect as a dewy rose.

Then, in the middle of August, Poppy got typhus.

Due to the high risk of contagion no one but her sisters was allowed in the house. The three of them took turns to nurse her and Arethusa, although desperate to be by her side, was forbidden entry.

'It's just preposterous! How many times did I tell her to keep her distance?' thundered Greville during dinner in the dining room. Elizabeth ignored him and continued to tuck into her large plate of goose at the opposite end of the long table. The rest of the family respectfully suspended their conversations and gave him their full attention. 'I dare say she is regretting it now,' he added, wiping his mouth with a napkin.

'Poppy does not think about herself,' said Adeline in her sister's defence. 'She only wants to help the poor.'

Greville turned his glassy gaze onto his granddaughter, who looked down at her plate for fear that he might see in her eyes her secret and know what she got up to in the woods with Dermot McLoughlin. 'And no more going to visit the poor for *you*, my dear,' he said to Arethusa, pointing at her with his wine glass. 'This is a clear example of what happens when one gets too close. I forbid it.' He thumped his fist on the table, sending the silver salt cellar and pepper pot jumping into the air and causing the candles to flicker and spill wax. His wife continued to tuck into her goose oblivious.

Arethusa did not argue with her grandfather. He'd had too much wine and when he was drunk he became bombastic and intolerant. She would find a way to see Dermot. It would be harder, of course, but the rewards would be all the greater for the challenge.

'Isn't it time Ronald made an honest woman of Tussy?' said Rupert with a smile, ignoring his sister's warning look across the table.

'Is that Ronald *Rowan-Hampton*?' asked Augusta, who was married to Greville's diminutive cousin Stoke Deverill, and had come from London to spend the whole month at Castle Deverill. Sparkling in diamonds and pearls, her white hair teased and curled and rolled onto her head in an extravagant coiffure, Augusta Deverill, fifty-eight and formidable, was big enough to swallow her husband whole without anyone noticing. She sat with her fluffy Pekinese on her knee, stroking his fur with chubby, bejewelled fingers.

'Ronald is Sir Anthony and Lady Rowan-Hampton's eldest son,' said Hubert, glancing at his wife, for although it was common knowledge that Ronald and Arethusa would most likely marry, Ronald hadn't formally proposed and Arethusa was reluctant to commit.

'All in good time,' said Adeline gently, eyeing her daughter. 'One mustn't rush decisions which are then set in stone for the rest of one's life.'

Arethusa's heart sank at the thought of anything being set in stone for that long – or indeed, at all. She pulled a face at Rupert, who grinned back triumphantly.

'But she is young,' said Augusta, looking at Arethusa with admiration, for Augusta was a vacuous woman who prized beauty above all else and Arethusa was an uncommon beauty.

'I agree,' said Bertie's fiancée Maud, who shimmered in pale blue silk like a lovely icicle. Indeed, Augusta considered Maud's beauty admirable also, if a little severe. There was no warmth in her face, which could have been carved out of marble. Her cheekbones were too sharp, her jawline too square and her lips on the thin side. However, her eyes were quite remarkable being so chilly a shade of blue and framed by such unfeasably dark eyelashes. Bertie, handsome with flaxen hair and the wide, insouciant smile of a man for whom life has only ever been fun and games, was very pleased with himself for having wooed her. Augusta did not imagine it had been easy. 'I am twenty-one and will be just twenty-two when Bertie and I marry,' Maud continued. 'I think that is a very good age for a woman to wed.' Bertie, who had been placed beside her, squeezed her hand lovingly.

'In my day we married *before* we reached twenty,' said Augusta. 'A woman of twenty without a husband was already going off, like fruit left too long in the bowl.'

'Times have changed, my dear,' said Stoke, who was a man of few words, mainly because his voice was always lost in the hurricane that was his wife's and he'd long given up trying.

Greville grunted and his moustache twitched like a walrus's. 'Girls are married off in good time to keep them out of trouble.' Again, he settled his imperious gaze onto his granddaughter. 'I dare say Ronald will break you in swiftly, give you children to fuss over and keep you out of cottages riddled with typhus!' Arethusa delighted in the knowledge that she'd already been well broken in by Dermot.

'Oh, I do worry about Poppy,' said Adeline. 'She hasn't a mean bone in her body. She's good through and through. I pray to God she recovers.'

'We will *all* pray for her, my dear,' said Augusta. 'It could happen to any one of us. Life is precarious. One must count one's blessings. One has to be lucky and poor Poppy isn't.'

'I'm sure Dr Johnson will put her right,' said Hubert hopefully. 'He's a fine doctor, from London, you know.'

'An English doctor, well!' Augusta gushed. 'She'll be right in no time. I would not be happy for her to be at the mercy of an Irish doctor.'

Elizabeth put down her knife and fork with a clink. She was defeated by the second helping of goose. 'Poppy will most likely die,' she said, picking up her glass and taking a gulp of wine.

Adeline did not reply but let her mother-in-law's comment pass over her like an ugly cloud. She was too weary with worry to concern herself with her mother-in-law's tactlessness.

'Oh Grandma!' Rupert exclaimed with a smile. 'We can always count on *you* to be so wonderfully optimistic.'

'Prayer,' interrupted Augusta stridently. 'When the doctors have done all they can, we must rely on prayer.'

And on a God who allowed her to get sick in the first place, thought Arethusa bleakly.

Soon it became clear that Poppy was indeed dying. In spite of Adeline's herbal tinctures which she lovingly brewed every day from the medicinal garden she cultivated in one of the greenhouses, it appeared that Poppy was slipping away. Arethusa was devastated. She couldn't imagine life without her favourite aunt. In despair at the unfairness of the world she strode down to the beach to cry alone where no one would see her. Fat clouds with grey underbellies scudded across the sky on a wind that was blustery and cross. Seagulls squawked and a pair of corncrakes squabbled on the sand over a dead crab. Arethusa marched up the beach, her skirts billowing like sails as the gale propelled her over shallow pools and wet dunes. The sun battled bravely and won the occasional patch of blue sky, but those moments were fleeting. A storm was moving in from the east. As she tried to bargain with God the waves crashed noisily against the rocks at the foot of the cliffs where pirates had once hidden their loot in caves and above, puffins took refuge in nooks. Arethusa cried and her tears dried on her skin as soon as she had shed them.

It was there that her mother found her. Adeline strode over the sand, her red hair swirling around her head as the wind tossed it about. Arethusa was not grateful for the company, but Adeline pulled her into her arms and hugged her tightly all the same. 'My darling, we have to put our trust in God,' she said emphatically.

Arethusa let her mother embrace her, but she did not embrace her back. 'A God that can take a soul as good and sweet as Poppy's is not a God I want to believe in, Mama.'

'There is a reason for everything, Tussy.' Adeline linked arms with her daughter and began to walk slowly up the sand. 'My darling, we're spiritual beings having an earthly experience. We have all come here to learn and grow in light. That is our purpose.'

'What does that even mean?' Arethusa found her mother's discourses on spirituality baffling. It was like she was speaking another language.

Adeline leaned towards her so that her voice would not get snatched by the wind. 'Think of your soul as light, Tussy. The more you learn to love, forgive, empathize and open your heart in gratitude, the brighter your spirit will become. That is why we are here, because we are moving towards the greatest light of all and that is God.'

'What's that got to do with Poppy?'

'Because Poppy is a soul of light, too. She is here to grow brighter and lighter and when she has completed her life she will go home. She will return to the place from where we all come. To you and me it will seem that she has been robbed of her future, but she won't have been robbed. *We* will have been robbed, but *she* will have done all she needed to do in this life and will be free. We have to accept that if she dies it will be her time. And through our grief we will grow too. It is through suffering that we learn the greatest lessons and grow the most.'

'I don't want to grow, Mama.' Arethusa began to cry again. 'I want Poppy to stay here.'

Adeline stopped to hug her again. 'So do I, Tussy, but if she goes, I will accept it as God's will. Life is often painful, my darling. We cannot avoid losing people we love, it is inevitable and designed to wake us up to our true, spiritual natures. But resistance will only make it harder to bear. We have to learn to accept things we cannot change. Acceptance is one of the very things we are here to learn.'

'Well, I can't accept this. She will *not* die. I *won't* accept it. God will just have to change his plans and give her some more years.' Arethusa pulled away from her mother and shouted up at the darkening sky, 'If you take Poppy, God, you will only teach me that it is wrong to look after the poor. Wrong to take them food and clothing and medicine. Wrong to touch them and comfort them. And I will never ever help another poor person again as long as I live. How do you like that, Mr God?'

Adeline took her daughter's hand. 'Come, Tussy dear. Let's go home. There are better ways to talk to God.'

'He doesn't hear our prayers so what's the point?'

'Of course He does. We are holding a special service tomorrow to pray for her recovery.'

'It won't make any difference. He's not listening. And anyway, why bother praying if God has already decided?'

'Because I'm willing to try everything.'

Arethusa shook her head. 'You see, Mama, you're not even sure of your own argument.'

The following day the whole Protestant community gathered in the church of St Patrick in Ballinakelly to pray for Poppy. All the upper servants of the castle who were Protestant attended also, the men in black coats and top hats, the women in toques. The farmers and gamekeepers wore bowler hats and the coastguard looked distinguished in their uniforms. Adeline had done the flowers, even though it was not her turn on the rota. No one had Adeline's touch when it came to arranging flowers but even *she* had exceeded her own talent with the ravishing displays of *Alchemilla mollis*, rose and lily, picked from the gardens of Castle Deverill and lovingly assembled in big glass vases.

Arethusa sat in the front row with her family, as was tradition, and behind her Ronald sat with his parents, Sir Anthony and Lady Rowan-Hampton, and his two fat, pink-faced sisters, Julia and Melissa. Ethel Hardwood, an elderly widow with a glass eye following an unlikely accident with a garden fork, played the organ in a jerky, hesitant manner, while Hazel and Laurel snivelled into their handkerchiefs. Arethusa could feel Ronald's eyes on the back of her neck, for her hair was pinned in a thick chignon beneath the rim of her hat. She knew it wouldn't be long before he proposed and then what was she to do? It had been a while since she'd been able to see Dermot. Right now, with Poppy slowly dying, Arethusa didn't have the desire for Dermot's brand of entertainment. Perhaps it was time to embrace her duty and begin the rest of her life. After all, she was going to have to start sometime.

Reverend Millet gave an interminable sermon about acceptance, which Arethusa thought sounded a bit like her mother's, although it was much longer and full of clichés.

When it came to the prayers, she knelt on her prayer cushion and followed Reverend Millet's words just in case God happened to be listening this time. The only light moment came when Lady Deverill nodded off during the sermon and began to snore. Arethusa got the giggles and couldn't stop. Bertie elbowed her hard in the ribs, which only made her laugh even more. Maud was horrified but a cold stare from her had no effect on Arethusa, who was now unable to control herself. Her laughter was infectious and caught Rupert, whose shoulders shuddered so that behind him Julia and Melissa (who thought him the most attractive man in West Cork) grew even pinker in the face and began to snort like a pair of pigs. Lady Rowan-Hampton was a formidable woman and silenced her girls by rapping Melissa on the knuckles with her prayer book, but Rupert and Arethusa were lost. It was only when Lord Deverill nudged his wife and she came round with a gasp that the two miscreants were at last brought to heel. It had long been a family rule that Rupert and Arethusa were not to sit together in church, but distance seemed not to make the slightest difference. Simply knowing the other was in the same room was enough to set them off.

'I'm not sure your behaviour in church is going to win you any points with my mama,' said Ronald when they walked out into the yard.

'I know, but I couldn't help it. Grandma fell asleep and started snoring,' she explained, smiling again.

'I rather sympathize,' said Ronald. 'I'd like to have slept through Rev Millet's sermon as well.'

'Is there no one who can entertain in the pulpit?'

'I think being able to give a dull sermon is one of the most important qualifications required for an aspiring rector. The entertaining men find something more interesting to do.'

'I'm sure you're right,' said Arethusa.

Ronald seemed to enjoy her agreeing with him for he put a hand on her arm and gave her a sympathetic smile. 'I'm very sorry about your aunt. Jolly bad luck.'

Arethusa's eyes revealed her pain. 'Everyone says she's going to die.'

'Typhus is hard to cure.' He looked at her steadily. 'I hope *you're* not going visiting, Tussy.'

'Grandpa has forbidden it,' she replied gloomily.

'Good.'

'I don't have the heart to do anything at the moment, except wait for news. Of course, I'm not allowed to go to her bedside. I have to stay at home and pray. It's very frustrating.'

'I am praying for her too, but I do wonder whether God hears.'

Arethusa's interest was piqued. 'I'm not sure he does,' she agreed, eager to speak about her disappointment in God to someone who understood. 'Surely, if he cared, good people like Aunt Poppy wouldn't get sick in the first place.'

'There's too much misery in the world for God to exist.'

'You're right! If there really was a God of love as Mama insists there is, he would make Aunt Poppy better at once.'

'I don't imagine your mama's herbs are doing much good either.'

They shared a knowing smile. 'Of course they're ineffectual,' said Arethusa, rolling her eyes. 'But she brews them anyway. Her greenhouse is full of all sorts of plants with long Latin names. She believes there's something in there for every ailment. But I know better.'

'You're a sensible girl,' Ronald said admiringly. 'You're more practical, like your father.'

Arethusa lowered her voice. 'Mama is secretly pagan, but

don't tell Papa. In the olden days she'd have been burned at
the stake for a witch. If you could hear the rubbish she spouts,
ghosts in the castle and spirits contacting her from the dead,
you'd be sorely tried.' They laughed like a pair of conspirators.
'Mama really is away with the fairies!'

'*She* is not my concern.' Ronald gave Arethusa a meaning-
ful, affectionate look. 'You and I agree on many things, Tussy.
We're more alike than you realize. I like your pragmatism. A
man can talk to you. Most women's heads are full of nonsense.'

Arethusa was suitably flattered. She liked to think of herself
as pragmatic and more intelligent than other women. 'Thank
you, Ronald. I'm glad you appreciate my finer qualities.' She
was not going to enlighten him on the *less* fine ones. If her
visiting the poor was his only criticism she could perhaps find
another way to help the needy.

That afternoon Adeline received an unexpected visitor.
It was Old Mrs O'Leary whose son Niall was the local vet.
Adeline did not have the strength to listen to complaints
today, but O'Flynn told her that the woman had said it was of
an urgent and personal nature. Adeline sighed despairingly,
but, aware of her duty as chatelaine and too soft-hearted for
her own good, she felt she couldn't very well refuse her. She
agreed to receive her on the terrace where she was with Hazel,
Augusta, Maud and Arethusa, while the men were out hunting hares. At least, if Old Mrs O'Leary was tiresome, Adeline
would have her family around her for support.

The ladies waited, seated in a semicircle, looking out over
the lawn, while O'Flynn led the visitor through the garden
in a slow, stately fashion. They finally reached the terrace and
O'Flynn presented her in his usual formal manner, then stood
to one side. Old Mrs O'Leary stepped forward. She raised
her chin and smiled gently at the ladies. Arethusa noticed

the woman's eyes at once. They were the most extraordinary colour she had ever seen. A blend of green and turquoise, like agate. The ladies, who had been as unenthusiastic as Adeline, now sat up with interest.

Old Mrs O'Leary was an elderly woman in a black dress with a thick shawl draped over her shoulders, as was the custom for widows, and yet, what set *this* widow apart was her striking face. It was obvious that she had once been a beauty. Her grey hair was tied into a bun, emphasizing high cheekbones, wide-side eyes, a straight nose and a surprisingly full mouth. There was something foreign about her looks, as if she had come from far away, and a wisdom in her expression which made the five ladies curious to hear what she had to say. As she lifted a hand to arrange her shawl, Arethusa noticed her fingers, which were long, tapered and unexpectedly elegant.

'Madam, forgive me for coming at this difficult time,' she said in a soft, melodious voice, settling her strange gaze onto Adeline, who was visibly moved by her and baffled as to why they had not previously met. Adeline knew her son Niall, who came to look after her horses, but she had never met his mother.

'Please, Mrs O'Leary, what can I do to help you?' Adeline asked.

'It is *I* who have come to help *you*,' said Old Mrs O'Leary, and her smile was so full of knowing that it was hard not to believe she had the power to do so. She put a white hand into the pocket of her skirt and pulled out a glass bottle. 'This is water drawn from the Lady's Well,' she said. Arethusa caught Maud's eye and they shared a doubtful look. The Lady's Well was in the hills outside Ballinakelly where a statue of Mary stood in the centre of a well-trodden circular path where local Catholics and pilgrims walked 'rounds' with their rosary beads and prayed for miracles. Wishes were placed in notes beneath a hawthorn bush and, according to legend, if an eel popped his head above the water the wish would be granted. Arethusa, of course, thought the whole thing preposterous (in the same way she thought the swaying statue of Mary on the road out of Ballinakelly was preposterous) and was now in no doubt that the old woman was a witch. 'Give this to your sister, Miss Poppy, and she will be healed. The eel appeared and told me it will be so.'

Old Mrs O'Leary gave the bottle to Adeline, who smiled sadly but gratefully at the old woman's sweet thought. 'Thank you for your kindness,' she said. 'I will, and I will pray that it works.'

'Oh, on my life it will work,' said Old Mrs O'Leary, nodding with certainty. 'A lady such as yourself must know that the power of the water is not only in the water itself, but in the mind of the person who takes it. Tell your dear sister that this is miraculous water and she will be made well.'

Adeline frowned. 'I'm so grateful to you, Mrs O'Leary. Thank you. I'm surprised we have never met before. Your son, Niall, looks after our animals and often brings your grandson, Liam, with him. They are wonderful with the horses, both of them. They seem to have healing hands as well as an instinct to know immediately what is wrong. And now here *you* are, reaching out with your own healing hands and I'm terribly grateful for your kindness.'

'We might not have formally met, Mrs Deverill, but I know who *you* are. I am old now and prefer not to venture far. Like you, I am a herbalist. Everything we need for healing the body and soul is to be found in these forests and hills. We need look no further than here. I bless you and your family. May you live long and may your dear sister live out the rest of her days in peace.'

'I will hasten to Poppy's side immediately and give her this water,' said Adeline brightly, standing up. 'O'Flynn, please ask Mr McCarthy to drive Mrs O'Leary home in the pony and trap.'

'Thank you, madam. That will save my legs,' said Old Mrs O'Leary and before she departed she seemed to bless the ladies with a beatific smile.

'She's an angel,' said Adeline once she had gone.

'A witch, more like,' said Arethusa cynically.

'Did you notice her eyes?' Maud added. 'I didn't think a human being could have eyes of such an astonishing green.'

'I told you, she's a witch,' said Arethusa.

'She's most definitely a witch,' Maud agreed.

'If she's a witch then she's more likely to heal Poppy,' said Hazel. 'I'd sell my soul to the devil himself for a cure for Poppy.'

'Good Lord!' Augusta exclaimed fruitily, giving her Pekinese, who was positioned on her knee as usual, a biscuit from the plate on the table. 'One must not jest about such things, Hazel, or the devil may very well hear and seize the opportunity. I'm sure the devil is just waiting in the wings to steal desperate souls such as yours.'

Adeline turned to her sister. 'Hazel, I'm going right away. Are you coming?'

'I wouldn't miss it for the world!' Hazel gushed, pushing herself off the bench and hurrying after her sister.

If that water works, Arethusa thought, *I'm going straight to the woods to celebrate with Dermot.*

'If that water works,' she said out loud, 'I'm going straight to the Lady's Well to fill an entire can with it.'

Augusta laughed. 'My dear Tussy, if that water works I will eat my toque!'

Chapter 11

It was a great surprise to everyone except Old Mrs O'Leary when Poppy made a miraculous recovery. Dr Johnson was baffled. In his experience, a patient with such a severe form of typhus *never* recovered. Adeline put it down to Old Mrs O'Leary's holy water; Augusta insisted, stridently, that it was the power of prayer (and did not eat her toque); Maud and Bertie claimed it was God's will; Lord Deverill, Hubert and Stoke all agreed that it was simply the body's own natural way of fighting back; Rupert said, 'Good Lord!' and Lady Deverill said nothing. Arethusa wept with happiness and resolved to celebrate with Dermot – a part of her wondered at the little bottle of water Old Mrs O'Leary had given her mother, but her logical mind told her such a miracle was impossible. The cure must have simply been Poppy's own determination to get better.

The night after Poppy turned the corner, Hazel and Laurel sneaked off to the Lady's Well by moonlight. Two nervous creatures hurrying through the silver bracken and gorse with glass bottles in hand to fill with the miraculous water that had saved their sister Poppy from certain death. Frightened of the dark and panicked by the rustling noises of the night animals, but quite resolute, they held hands as they scampered along like a pair of mice, praying they wouldn't be seen. When at last they reached the well, they stood a moment transfixed by the white face of the Virgin Mary, eerily illuminated in the moonlight. However, when the statue didn't move or do anything spooky, they breathed again, filled their bottles with water and looked around for the hawthorn bush. Hazel and Laurel knew their hawthorn from their elder and spotted it at once. 'Have you got the wish?' Hazel hissed.

'I have,' Laurel hissed back.

'Where is it?'

'Here.' Laurel pulled a small piece of card out of her pocket. She handed it to Hazel who opened it. *God, send us a man, even if it's one between us.* She hastened to the bush and stuffed it into the branches where it lay hidden from all but the birds, along with the debris of hundreds of other notes gathered there over the years.

'No one must know,' said Hazel.

'No one,' agreed Laurel.

'God save me,' said Hazel.

'God save us both,' said Laurel.

Suddenly a loud plop resounded out of the stillness. They both turned to the well in alarm. There, peeping out of the water for a brief moment, was an eel.

'Did you see that, Laurel?' Hazel hissed.

'I did,' Laurel replied.

'An eel,' Hazel gasped. 'You know what that means, Laurel!'

'Oh, I do, Hazel!'

'I'm ready,' said Hazel.

'As am I,' said Laurel, and they set off down the path at a brisk pace, their glass bottles full of miraculous water.

When they returned to the warmth of their cottage, they poured themselves thimble-sized glasses of gin and made a vow, sealed with a solemn handshake, never to tell a soul what they had done.

Arethusa was so happy that Poppy hadn't died after all that she took the pony and trap into Ballinakelly to find Dermot. The sun shone, the sky dazzled a cornflower blue and the sea glittered beneath it like a quilt of sapphire. Overhead, birds of prey circled on the warm breeze and fat bees buzzed about the purple bell heather. It was a glorious day, made all the more beautiful by the thought of Poppy's recovery. Arethusa held the reins with one hand, occasionally holding down her hat with the other each time a gust of wind threatened to blow it off her head. She passed Mrs Hurley, the fish-woman, who was walking slowly up the hill behind a quartet of lobsters, which were scrambling along the ground in front of her. When one of them deviated from the path she eased it gently back with a bracken stalk. Arethusa waved and the woman waved back. In her basket Arethusa could see a slippery mass of silver fish. Mrs Hurley was obviously tired of carrying such a heavy load and had decided that the lobsters could walk some of the way by themselves.

Once in town Arethusa tied the horse to a post then set off up the high street towards the blacksmith's foundry. She found Dermot there, with his father, hard at work smelting iron over the furnace. She caught Dermot's eye as she sauntered past. His face flushed with delight at the sight of her. She winked, tossed him a coquettish smile and flounced off, swaying her hips as she went. A moment later they were reunited in the stable behind the foundry, hidden in the shadows. Dermot pressed her against the wall and kissed her roughly, his course beard scratching her chin and neck just the way she liked it. He lifted her skirt to discover, to his delight, that she was wearing no undergarments. His hand found only warm skin and soft thigh and she gave a throaty laugh, lifting her leg to give him easy access. 'Oh Dermot, I've missed you,' she moaned as he began to stroke her.

'No one else can do this to you, Tussy. Only me.'

Arethusa closed her eyes and relished the heat now spreading through her loins with the exquisite mounting of pleasure. 'I want you inside me, Dermot. I want to feel you inside me.' Dermot unbuttoned his trousers and released himself. Arethusa forgot about Poppy, Ronald and everything outside those stable doors as they moved as one towards their climax.

When they were satisfied they laughed at their wickedness. 'Aren't we beasts!' she exclaimed triumphantly.

'I didn't think you were coming back,' said Dermot.

'I couldn't while my aunt was unwell.'

'Are you back now? Or are you going to leave me again?'

'I'm here for the moment,' she said with a grin. 'Until I find something more entertaining to do with my time.'

'You're a tease, Arethusa Deverill!' He smacked her playfully.

She giggled and stroked his beard. 'But you love me, don't you, Dermot!'

'It is my misfortune that I do,' he replied, gazing at her with sentimental eyes.

'I'd better be going,' she said after a while. 'Mama will wonder where I've gone, and I'm not allowed to go visiting the poor anymore. We're going to have to meet in the woods as before.'

'That's grand as long as the weather holds,' he replied.

'Then we must make hay while the sun shines.'

As they walked out of the stable Dermot's father was stepping into the courtyard from the foundry. When he saw Arethusa, a look of surprise swept across his face. He slid his eyes from Arethusa to his son and back again. Then, remembering his manners, he doffed his cap. 'Good day, Miss Deverill,' he said, but the tone in which he said it had an edge of insolence to it.

'Good day, Mr McLoughlin,' she replied with a confidence she didn't feel. She raised her chin and pulled back her shoulders and turned to Dermot. 'Thank you for your advice, Mr McLoughlin. I will be sure to tell my father.' Then she strode around the corner into the alley that led out onto the high street. As she turned her back both Dermot and his father saw the powdery lichen from the wall clinging to her dress. Old Mr McLoughlin looked at his son and raised an eyebrow.

Arethusa was not happy to have been caught by Mr McLoughlin. She hoped he wouldn't tell. She did not need the people of Ballinakelly gossiping about her sinful ways. When she arrived back at the castle she gave the pony to Mr McCarthy and went inside. Adeline was arranging the flowers on the hall table.

'Where have you been, Tussy?' she asked without looking at her.

'Nowhere.'

Adeline frowned and continued to thread stalks into the vase. 'Do you need the pony and trap to go nowhere?'

Arethusa sighed. 'I just needed to get out.'

'And where was Charlotte while you just needed to get out?'

'I don't know. I wanted to be alone.'

'Darling, you shouldn't go into Ballinakelly on your own and it's not fair to disrespect Charlotte in this way. How can she do her job if you're running off all the time. You must be accompanied when you leave the castle. Your father is very adamant about that.'

'And do you just agree with him, unquestioningly, on everything?'

'Your father and I stand together on most things.'

'And on this? I bet *you* didn't take a chaperone every time you rode over the hills. You adore your freedom. Well, so do I.'

Adeline stopped arranging the flowers and looked at her directly. 'My dear, you're a young lady now. You have to behave like one. It's not seemly to race around the countryside on your own, nor is it safe. Poppy nearly died, don't forget. I doubt she's going to resume her work, helping the poor, in the same way. Neither should you.'

'I wasn't visiting, I promise.' She could speak the truth about that at least.

'Then what were you doing?'

Arethusa couldn't speak the truth about Dermot. 'I wanted to buy some ribbon for my hat.'

Adeline dropped her gaze to her daughter's empty hands. 'I see you didn't find any.'

'No, there was nothing I liked.'

'That's a shame, with so many different colours to choose from.'

'My thought exactly.'

As Arethusa made her way up the stairs, Adeline noticed the lichen on the back of her dress and her heart stopped. As far as she was aware, there was no lichen on the wall in Mrs Maguire's ribbon shop!

That evening before dinner, while Hubert, Bertie, Adeline and Maud were finishing their game of croquet in the half-light, and Greville, Elizabeth, Stoke and Augusta were talking on the terrace, Arethusa and Rupert went for a stroll along the beach, just the two of them. The setting sun bounced off the waves in silver spangles and Jupiter could just be made out as a faint star in the darkening sky. The wind was blustery, blowing in off the sea, bringing with it the smell of weed and brine, and birds settled down noisily to roost in the cliffs. Arethusa loved this time, just before twilight, when the colours changed so quickly, from indigo and turquoise to pink and gold. She loved the melancholy feeling it gave her as the day slowly died and night crept in with its dark and secret hours. Rupert, hands in pockets, strode up the sand beside her, feeling that same sense of melancholy and allowing it to permeate his being and give him a sense of wonder at the beauty of the world.

'There is so much misery on this earth and yet it is magnificent,' he said.

'Such a contradiction,' Arethusa agreed. 'It is hard to imagine unhappiness when the stars come out. But God should concern himself a little less with beauty and a little more with the poor, sick and needy. What good is a glorious sunset if people are starving.'

Rupert glanced at her sidelong. 'You're in trouble again, you know.'

'I know.' She sighed. 'And I wasn't visiting the poor today. Truly, I wasn't.'

'No, not the poor.'

Arethusa frowned. 'Rupert? What are you suggesting?'

He shrugged and chuckled. 'You need to be more discreet, my dear Tussy.'

She stopped walking. 'What have you heard?'

'Let's just say, Dermot McLoughlin has five brothers and three sisters. That's eight tongues capable of spreading gossip. Lots of tongues, Tussy. Lots of gossip. You need to be more careful.' Arethusa stared at him with her mouth agape. 'Have you ever heard any gossip about *me*?' he added.

'No.'

'Of course not. Do you think at twenty-three years of age I'm living my life like Father O'Callaghan?'

'I don't know what Father O'Callaghan's life is like, Rupert.'

'Celibate. That's what it is. It might not be sober, but it's certainly celibate.' He began to walk on. 'I'm not judging you, Tussy. I'm in no position to judge anyone. If I told you half of what I got up to in Ballinakelly, you'd consider your transgressions very minor indeed. The only difference is that I'm discreet and you are not.'

'Are you dallying with one of the McLoughlin sisters?' Arethusa asked, hurrying to keep up with his long strides.

He shook his head and laughed, as if the idea of dallying with the McLoughlin sisters was ridiculous. 'How little understanding you have of the world,' he said.

'Grandma says you'll never marry,' she exclaimed, hoping to exact some sort of revenge for his having suggested she was being improper with Dermot McLoughlin.

'Grandma is probably right,' said Rupert. 'I'm not the marrying kind.'

'She says marrying would make you very unhappy.'

'It would make my wife unhappier.' He looked at her again and smiled fondly. 'You'll be brought to heel by marrying Ronald Rowan-Hampton. I suggest you tie the knot sooner rather than later before you get into trouble.'

'How dare you, Rupert. I'm insulted!'

'This is me, Rupert, you're talking to. By all means play the insulted card when confronted by Mama and Papa, but don't waste your energy on me. You've been trumped. I know exactly what you've been up to.'

'I was only kissing him in the stable behind the foundry. His stupid father stepped out just as I was leaving. I suppose he's gone and told everyone. Lord, no one can keep their mouth shut in this town.'

'What were you doing in the stable in the first place, for goodness' sake? Are you out of your mind? In any case, it doesn't matter now, because Grandpa has told Papa to marry you off. Here beginneth the rest of your life, Tussy. As they say in Ballinakelly, God help you!'

'Oh, shut up! I won't marry Ronald. I'm not ready to marry anybody. Aunt Hazel and Aunt Laurel aren't married. Why should I get married at all?'

'Aunt Hazel and Aunt Laurel were not being indiscreet with the rough and ready of Ballinakelly, Tussy. Soon you won't have a reputation to patch together.'

'What do you suggest I do?' she asked.

'Do you really want to know?'

'I do,' she said, dropping her shoulders.

'It's an awful thing being a woman,' he said. 'But as you are a woman, you might as well make the best of it. If I were you, I'd appeal to Augusta and ask her to invite you to do a London season. That way you get out of Ireland before the rumours catch up with you, and you may meet someone more exciting across the water.' He pulled a face that made Arethusa smile. 'I don't imagine it'll be hard to find someone more exciting than Ronald.'

'I hadn't thought of that,' she said, brightening a little.

Rupert took her hand. 'I suppose we'd better get back. Grandma will no doubt have fallen asleep by now and Grandpa will be wanting his dinner. We're probably in terrible trouble.'

'You're *never* in trouble, Rupert,' said Tussy enviously.

He chuckled. 'And *I* have the potential to give them all more trouble than this entire family put together. But I won't, because I'm careful. After all, isn't the *Eleventh* Commandment "Thou shalt not get caught"?'

After dinner Arethusa pulled Augusta into her grandmother's study, which was a cold, barely used room decorated in shades of green and positioned on the far side of the library, with views of the lawn. Lady Deverill had once written her correspondence in there and liked it because she said the room was like an extension of the garden, being so green and full of light. Now she never entered it. She did not enjoy writing letters, nor did she enjoy being apart from the rest of the family. She preferred the library, which was warm and busy with the coming and going of people.

'I need your help,' said Arethusa, knowing that Augusta would relish the chance to be needed.

Augusta did not sit down. She did not intend to linger in such a cold, unfriendly room. 'What can I do for you, my dear Tussy?' she asked, holding her Pekinese close to her bosom as if it were a hot-water bottle.

'Please will you invite me to London?'

Augusta smiled broadly. 'But, my dear, you don't even have to ask. Of course I will invite you to London. The men in your family come all the time. Why shouldn't you?'

'Because Mama wants to marry me off to Ronald,' said Arethusa dispiritedly.

'And that's not an appealing option, I don't imagine.'

'Not yet. I'm sure it will be more appealing after a season in London!'

Augusta looked at her quizzically. 'More likely you'll find someone who does take your fancy. A lively girl like you would be a sensation.' She narrowed her eyes, contemplating the reflected glory of Arethusa's success.

'So can I come, please?'

'I will talk with your mother, but I don't see why not. You're young and pretty. It's only right that you should show yourself in London, be presented at Court, enjoy a little attention and learn a bit about the world. You're much too isolated here in Ballinakelly. You certainly can't marry without tasting a bit of the Big Smoke, surely! My first season I received six marriage proposals. Six! It wasn't uncommon and it shall be so for you. Trust me, under my supervision you will have the pick of the bunch.'

Arethusa clapped her hands excitedly. 'Oh! How thrilling! Will you tell her so!'

'Indeed I will. Now let's please hurry back to the drawing room because I can no longer feel my toes.'

Arethusa was not confident that her parents would allow her to go to London, therefore she was pleasantly surprised when they announced, a few days later at breakfast, that after much deliberation they had accepted Augusta's very generous invitation. Arethusa would set off for London the following April. They had asked Rupert to go with her and he had agreed. Arethusa was elated. With Rupert as her escort, she'd be free to get up to all sorts of mischief. Then, as if her mother could read her mind, she announced that Charlotte would accompany her also, as her chaperone. Well, she managed to run rings around Charlotte in Ballinakelly, so why not in London? With Rupert as her ally, poor, dull Charlotte didn't stand a chance!

There was much to learn before April and Arethusa threw herself into her training with spirit. She had to learn how to get in and out of a carriage with grace. How to curtsey and how to back out of a room while holding a long Court train, which would be no less than three yards, the length required for presentation at one of the Queen's four afternoon Drawing Rooms. Augusta sent long letters of instructions from London. Having no daughters of her own, only sons, she seemed to be taking Arethusa's coming out personally and was adamant that she did all that was required in order to 'profit from this exceptional opportunity'.

Adeline had not prepared Arethusa for this, and she read Augusta's letters with concern. Adeline had prepared her daughter for the life she expected her to lead, which was the same as her own. The wife of an Anglo-Irishman must know how to ride, hunt, dance and entertain, and manage a cold and draughty castle, of course. Playing the piano, painting, speaking French and being able to list the top two hundred families in England were not high on the Must Do list. She had brought up Arethusa with few boundaries and a sense of independence which most English girls did not enjoy. Arethusa was ill-disciplined, headstrong and wild. Adeline worried that she would disgrace herself when she failed to play by their stringent rules, and she knew from Maud, who relished recounting tales of her own coming out and the girls who either failed to find a husband or shamed themselves while trying and were shipped off to India, that English Society was most unforgiving. But Arethusa laughed at her mother's concerns and said she'd not regret sending her off when she returned to Ballinakelly engaged to a duke.

When the time came for Arethusa to leave Ballinakelly she said goodbye to Ronald. She pretended she was reluctant to leave Ireland and promised she would write regularly. 'Every young man in London will want to marry you,' he said bitterly. This thought delighted Arethusa, who was excited at the prospect of fishing in a fresh pond, but she feigned disinterest.

After all, she didn't want to burn her bridges; she might very well need Ronald if she didn't meet anyone more appealing in London. 'I might come to London myself,' he said, glancing at her hopefully. 'If you'd like that.'

Arethusa's heart sank. 'I'll write to you every day,' she reassured him, praying that the promise of regular correspondence might quell his desire to follow her.

'And I shall await each letter with eager anticipation,' he replied.

Saying goodbye to Dermot was infinitely more fun. They met in the wood the afternoon before her departure and revelled in each other until dusk. 'I suppose you'll marry an Englishman and never return to Ballinakelly,' said Dermot as they lay side by side on the grass, gazing up at the canopy of oscillating leaves above them.

'I might very well marry an Englishman,' Arethusa replied, 'but I'll always come home. Ballinakelly is where I belong. I don't wish to live anywhere else.'

'You're full of the old blarney, Tussy!'

'I mean it,' she insisted, rolling onto her side and looking at him fondly. 'We've had fun, you and I.' She took his hand and put a finger in her mouth. He grinned at her as she twirled her tongue around it suggestively.

'You're a naughty girl, Arethusa Deverill. One day you'll look back and accuse me of being the devil incarnate.'

'Why? For teaching me how to enjoy myself? For training me how to pleasure *you*? Certainly not.' She lifted her skirt and climbed astride him. 'Look how quickly you come to life again!' She laughed and reached down to guide him inside her.

'And some poor man will discover on his wedding

night that you've already been ruined,' he said, putting his hands on her hips and letting out a groan as she began to gently gyrate.

'I will pretend. I'm very good at pretending.' She bent down and kissed him on the mouth. 'But I've never pretended with you, my darling Dermot. Every moan of pleasure has been true.' She giggled as he deftly manoeuvred her onto her back.

'Then let me hear some more of it, to ensure that I never forget you.' And he thrust deep inside her, smiling wistfully as the woman he loved and was about to lose shut her eyes and moaned again.

Arethusa was not sad to be leaving home, she was only sad that she had to bring her boring governess with her. Clearly, her mother did not trust her to behave herself in London. If she had any idea of what she got up to in Ballinakelly, she would marry her off to Ronald as quickly as possible and make an honest woman of her while there was still time. But London beckoned, with all its glamour, excess and possibility, and Arethusa was only too ready to turn her back on this provincial town and look into a new and brighter future.

She hugged Bertie. 'Keep Ronald busy,' she whispered.

'I will make it a priority,' he replied and Arethusa smiled in gratitude, knowing that her brother had misinterpreted her intention.

She kissed her new sister-in-law's frosty cheek. 'I will shortly be following you to London,' Maud told Arethusa. 'You may find you need a friend who knows her way around. London can be quite bewildering to a newcomer.'

'I'm sure I will quickly learn the ropes,' Arethusa replied loftily. 'After all, how hard can it be?'

Maud smiled, her thin lips curled with knowing. 'For a girl like you, Tussy, it won't be hard at all. That's the problem.'

Arethusa embraced her parents and grandparents and the Shrubs who had come specially to wave her off. Then she climbed into the brougham to sit beside Charlotte, who looked pale and anxious. As well she might, thought Arethusa inconsiderately, for she was going to be positively ignored in London.

Greville took out his pocket watch and flicked open the gold lid. Rupert was late as usual. He grunted. Elizabeth sighed, she'd really rather be feeding her hens. Adeline glanced at Hubert. Hubert shrugged. At last Rupert bounded out of the castle full of apologies and self-deprecating remarks so that it was impossible to be cross with him. Everyone smiled, touched as usual by his irrepressible charm. He swept his mother into his arms so that her feet dangled above the gravel. He kissed his aunts' rosy cheeks and embraced his father and grandfather fiercely. Bertie received a hearty slap on the back and Maud's hand was kissed with a subtly mocking deference, for Rupert found his sister-in-law pretentious and unsympathetic. Then he climbed into the brougham where Arethusa grinned and Charlotte looked at him warily. 'Isn't this jolly!' he exclaimed, beaming a smile at Charlotte, who lowered her eyes shyly. 'Don't worry, Charlotte my dear. Keeping Tussy out of trouble is not a job for one. We will share the burden together.' He winked at his sister and Arethusa swallowed a laugh. 'And in that regard, I would say that *I* am quite the expert.'

Chapter 12

Ballinakelly, 1961

So, Mom was not sent to London because she was pregnant, after all.

I take off my glasses and rub the bridge of my nose. I'm suddenly overcome with exhaustion. I put the mirror on the bedside table and close the diary. I feel an enormous sense of relief. Nora Maloney's grandmother is wrong. I have no half-brother or sister to worry about. There is no long-lost sibling to find and make peace with. Mom had secrets, lots of secrets, but that isn't one of them.

I have a quick bath and curl up in bed. I am too tired to think about supper. I don't feel hungry. It is a relief to shut my eyes and allow my mind to wander. Ballinakelly is quiet. So quiet. I sink into the silence, relishing the feeling of approaching oblivion. It is like sinking into a pool of feathers, light and soft and comforting. I don't feel any animosity towards Nora's grandmother. I'm so relieved to have discovered the truth, from my mother herself, that I feel nothing but good-will towards an old woman who remembers only gossip and rumour. In a small provincial town like this I imagine the gossip mill was in overdrive and Eily was young and naive and believed it. But it doesn't matter. She is wrong and *that's* what matters. Mom was sent to London because her parents were worried she would get sick like her aunt Poppy had done, from close contact with the poor. I understand their concern. As a mother I would probably feel the same way. The fact that Arethusa was enjoying a romance with the son of the local smithy is irrelevant, but it makes me smile. I'm glad she enjoyed herself before she married my father, whom she must have subsequently met in London. I wish I had had her fearlessness before I settled down with Wyatt. I wish I had had her capacity for pleasure. But I've always been too concerned with making everyone else happy that I've missed out on my own fun. I've never put myself first. But it's not too late. Here I am, alone in Ireland, with only myself to think about. I'm going to be selfish for the first time in my life. I'm going to do as I please. I'm going to be more like Mom.

With that delightful thought, I sink further into the feathery silence and a dreamless sleep.

The following morning I am happy to see the sunshine. The sky is a forget-me-not blue with round, cotton-wool clouds bumbling across it on a blustery breeze. I breakfast in the dining room downstairs. Nora Maloney is quick to join me at my table and apologizes again for her grandmother's outburst. Normally I would reassure her that I am not offended. I would put her comfort above my own and go to great lengths to make her feel good. But now I look at her steadily and tell her that I have read my mother's diary, which has given me the true account of why she went to London. 'I don't blame your grandmother for listening to gossip,' I say. 'But you should tell her that the gossip was wrong, as gossip often is. Arethusa Deverill left Ballinakelly to enjoy a London season and that's the truth. Not that I ever doubted it.'

'Of course, it was gossip. Malicious gossip,' Nora agrees, emphatically shaking her curls, keen to show me that she never believed it either. 'Nan is old and muddled. It was a long time ago. She's probably remembering someone else's drama.' I nod and Nora leaves me in peace. I imagine she is relieved that I am checking out of the hotel too. The situation has become awkward. She probably wishes she hadn't invited me to meet her grandmother. It would have been better for us both if I had declined.

Kitty sends Shane to collect me at ten and I pay the bill and leave for the White House. It is my third day in Ballinakelly but I feel I have been here for much longer. So much has happened. To think I had anticipated spending time on my own, retracing my mother's footsteps. I never expected to be swept up into her family. If the next two weeks go as fast as the first few days I shall be back in Boston before I've had time to catch my breath. I do not want to think of Boston. I do not want to think of Wyatt. Right now he is a blur. I don't want him to become clear and solid again. I'm not yet ready for that.

When I arrive at the house Kitty is there to greet me, dressed in her riding clothes. Her cheeks are flushed and some of her hair has come away from the ponytail and is loose about her hairline. I can tell she has already been out with her horse. I can also tell that riding is the thing she loves doing best. Her eyes sparkle and she is exuberant. She is sixty years old and yet she radiates an energy that is much younger than her years. With her I feel younger than my years too, as if her *esprit* is infectious.

Robert wanders out of his office to welcome me into his home. He is a quiet, thoughtful man with a serious face. I noticed the other night when I first met him that he has a stiff leg. I assume he had polio, or something similar, and feel sorry for him. Growing up with any disability is difficult. Being married to a woman as feisty and able-bodied as Kitty must have made it even more so. It is hard not to compare them and to conclude that they are as different as two people could possibly be. He is her opposite. As if she deliberately went out of her way to choose a man whose even, muted nature neutralized her passion and fire. As if she wanted a steady hand at the helm of her marriage, leaving her to be the sail in the wind. Of course he is handsome, in a conventional, bland way, but Wyatt is handsome too and one gets used to that after a while and ceases to be impressed by it. It is a person's character that counts and what ultimately moulds the contours and planes of the face. I look into Robert's but I can't seem to find his character. I wonder how he managed to win Kitty's heart.

'Faye, I'm going to take you riding,' says Kitty with a grin. 'Would you like that?'

'I haven't ridden in years,' I respond, but the thought of setting off into the hills on a horse thrills me.

'Robert doesn't ride,' Kitty adds, and I imagine that's because of his stiff leg.

'I'm the only member of the family who doesn't,' Robert interjects and he gives a dry smile. 'But as my wife enjoys riding out on her own, it's probably just as well.'

'Today I'm going to ride out with *you*,' she says to me, setting off up the stairs. I follow. Robert calls for Shane and asks him to carry up my case.

My bedroom is pretty with two large sash windows that look out over the garden. The walls are papered in a faded green-and-white pattern, the curtains bleached down the edges by the sun. The double bed is sumptuous. It is luxurious compared with the little room I occupied at Vickery's Inn. 'And tonight I'm going to take you for a taste of Irish culture.'

Kitty opens the window, letting in a cacophony of birdsong and a gust of honeysuckle.

'Oh?' I'm intrigued.

'It's Friday night,' she exclaims, turning to face me. Her eyes gleam with excitement. 'Folk night at Ma Murphy's. As you're new to Ireland, it's essential I take you.' I recall Cormac telling me he'd buy me a drink at Ma Murphy's and find myself wondering if he'll be there.

'Are you a regular at folk night?' I ask.

She shakes her head and averts her gaze. 'No, Robert won't come, he likes to stay at home, but now you're here I'm going to make the most of it. I grew up here, you see. I know the locals. Robert is English. He keeps himself to himself. He doesn't mix.' She sighs with resignation and smiles. I notice a touch of sadness in it. 'But tonight I'm going and you're coming with me. It'll be fun. You'll experience the real Ireland. It's full-bodied and bold. You'll love it.' From the look on her face I can tell that *she* loves it more than anyone.

Kitty lends me a pair of jodhpurs, riding boots and a thick beige sweater. I tie my hair into a ponytail like hers and admire myself in the mirror. I enjoy the new me. I look like a Deverill. I *feel* like a Deverill; I hope I can learn to ride like one.

We step into the hall and Robert comes out of his study again, drawn by our laughter. We find our resemblance to each other hilarious and can't stop laughing. We are laughing like sisters, with abandon. I don't think I have laughed like this in forty years!

'I can't wait to see people's faces as they see us ride by,' says Kitty.

'Most of them are drunk and seeing double already,' says Robert, and I'm surprised by the wide smile that melts onto his face. Perhaps he's not so dour, after all.

I would love Rose to see me like this, light–hearted and merry. I wonder what she would make of Kitty and me setting off into the hills on horseback. Edwina would wave her cigarette in the air and say that she doesn't see the point in riding; Walter would definitely give it a go, being athletic like his father; Rose, my darling, gentle Rose, would just fear for my safety.

At the stables there are already two horses saddled up and waiting for us, along with a huddle of grooms in caps and jackets, watching us curiously. Kitty greets them and they doff their caps, their dark eyes sliding from her to me and back again in wonder. I can tell that Kitty is amused, as am I, but she goes straight to the animals and explains that the grey mare, which I am to ride, is called Shimmer. I run my gloved hand down her face and pat her neck and she snorts and sniffs me with her big nostrils. She's a fine horse. I tell her, in a whisper that only she can hear, to be kind and not to bolt.

Kitty's is a dashing chestnut called Jupiter. He's handsome and alert with shiny black eyes and a bright white blaze. As she deftly mounts him, one of the grooms comes to my aid and I step into his hands and swing my other leg over the saddle. Once I am seated, he gives me the reins. 'Shimmer's a grand mare,' he says, giving her a pat. 'She'll take care of you. Just relax and let her guide you. She knows these hills. She won't need any direction from you.' He looks up at me and his gaze lingers on my face. I know that he is baffled by my likeness to his boss, although he must have heard that Kitty's cousin has arrived from America; the whole town must know by now.

'Thank you,' I reply. 'That's encouraging.'

'You okay?' Kitty asks. I nod. 'Let's go then.'

We set off. I realize that riding a horse is much like riding a bicycle. One doesn't forget how to do it, even after not having ridden since childhood. I relax into the saddle and leave the reins loose so that Shimmer can follow Jupiter without my nervous twitching on her bit.

The hedgerows are thick with white-flowered elder and hawthorn. Small birds dive in and out in play and I relish the opportunity to watch them. Their dainty song really does have the power to lift the heart. We head down to the beach where long marram grass sways in the briny wind blowing in off the sea. The cliffs are high and rugged, covered with heather and thrift. Their nooks and crannies are home to seabirds who are busy building their nests. Kitty points out plover and shearwater, and the ubiquitous gannet who dive for fish in the choppy waves. Then she points across the ocean and laughs that the next parish is America. She tells me of a Spanish galleon sunk three hundred years ago, and of the odd silver ducat that still washes up from time to time on the sand. We leave the strand and take a snake path into the hills. Tiny cabins nestle among the gorse and bracken and narrow streams trickle through the grasses to the sea like silver ribbons discarded carelessly over the land. Cows and sheep graze on wild flowers and heather, lifting their heads every now and then to watch us as we ride by.

Ireland is so beautiful, it pulls on the heart. It is as if nature has delicate fairy fingers that reach in and touch me there, where I am most fragile, where my grief is still tender. I feel my eyes watering. My chest expands and the sorrow there is released. Kitty glances at me. I think she knows, and if she knows it's because she's experienced this sense of release too. This wondrous way nature has of connecting us to our deepest selves.

We reach the summit of the hill. From there we can see the wide expanse of ocean, as far as it goes, until it merges with the sky to become one hazy blue blur. We gaze about us in silence. The wind is blustery. The horses snort and toss their heads. 'I love it up here,' says Kitty, without taking her eyes off the horizon. 'Everything changes, but this always remains the same.'

'I don't think I've ever seen such beauty,' I tell her. 'It's overwhelming.'

'It's healing,' says Kitty firmly. 'I've ridden these hills since I was a child. This wind has taken every sorrow, every regret, and the splendour has mended every broken heart.' I notice her jaw stiffen. She bites her lip. 'Or at least it has helped,' she adds softly, almost to herself.

I wonder whether she'll mind me bringing up the War of Independence. I decide to take the plunge. She'll either answer or change the subject. Kitty is not a people-pleaser like me. 'Cormac O'Farrell told me that you fought with the rebels in the war,' I say.

She turns to me and smiles proudly. 'I did my bit,' she replies. 'Cormac did more than his.' Then she turns back to face the sea. 'It feels like another life now.' She sighs heavily. 'Another life. I feel like another person sometimes. It's hard to reconcile the woman I am now with the girl I was then. It seems so distant and unreal. But it happened. I have the scars to prove it.'

I don't know what to say. I want to know what kind of scars. Does she mean physical ones or emotional ones? I want to know more about what she did and how she did it. I'd love to hear of her adventures. But she just blinks into the wind and says nothing. I watch her profile, the strength in her jaw, the dignity in her cheekbones, the emotion in her eyes, and I sense there is too much experience for her to share in a few words. And perhaps words would fall short anyhow.

At length, she pulls the band out of her hair, so that it hangs loose in long tangled waves about her shoulders. 'Take your hair down,' she tells me. She grins and there is mischief in it. I do as she asks and shake out my hair. 'Now, let's gallop.' She turns her horse and sets off. I have no option but to follow for Shimmer has already decided that a speedy gallop is what she is going to do. I squeeze my knees against the saddle and grip the reins and we race behind Jupiter. I am at once injected with a feeling of elation. It breaks inside me, as if some internal restraint has snapped. I am flooded with joy. Not the constrained sort of joy I am used to but a wild, reckless joy that is new to me. The rhythmic drumming of hooves is in my ears, the movement of the gallop vibrates through my bones. The wind takes my hair and it blows cold upon my face and I hear myself laughing out loud. I feel outrageously happy. Gone is Faye Langton – the gale has taken her – and in her place is Faye Deverill. Well, haven't I Deverill blood in my veins the same as Kitty? I feel it now. It is hot and passionate and pumping into my heart, which has cracked open like a duck's egg and is sucking in this joy and this pleasure as if it has been starved of both.

When at last we stop, Kitty turns her glowing face to me and laughs. We laugh together. She pats Jupiter's flank and I do the same to Shimmer. 'How did that feel?' she asks, but she already knows.

'No wonder you love to ride so much,' I say, panting. 'I don't think I've ever had so much fun. Truly. I've never felt so uplifted.'

'That's because you were living in the moment,' she says. 'And when you're in the moment you have no cares. There's no room for them.'

'Well, that's true. I was much too busy holding on for dear life to think of anything else.'

'Happiness comes when you get out of your head, Faye. Living in your head is a very dangerous pastime. Galloping takes me out of mine. It's the one time I'm really in the moment and it's magical.'

'Then let's do it again!' I say and Kitty needs no encouragement.

Robert joins us for lunch. We eat at the dining-room table. We don't talk about Arethusa. I get the feeling that Kitty tries to shield her husband a little from her overwhelming family. She asks him about himself, how his book is going and they talk about Florence, their daughter. It is only when Robert leaves us to have our tea in the drawing room that we discuss my mother. I tell Kitty what Nora's grandmother told me and what I later discovered in the diary.

'Although she was having a secret fling with Dermot McLoughlin, the blacksmith's son, she wasn't pregnant. She left for London on very good terms with her family.'

'So, the falling-out was later,' says Kitty.

'I could flick through her diary to find out, but I don't want to miss anything. She wrote in great detail and very regularly and I'm enjoying reading it.'

'Yes, don't leap ahead. With every page you are learning something else about your mother. You will find out eventually why she left for America.'

'Perhaps her parents found out about her fling with Dermot McLoughlin. I suppose they would have been appalled that she was being romanced by a working-class Catholic, wouldn't they?'

'Our grandfather would have been appalled, but our grandmother less so. You know, when I was a child, I played with the local Catholic children and Adeline turned a blind eye. My mother would have been horrified. She's a terrific snob.

But Adeline always believed that humans are equal. That we are all spiritual beings living earthly lives, and class, race and religion are earthly qualities, present for our learning and growth, and when we die we leave those things behind with our bodies and are all one. She never considered anyone less valuable because of their class and didn't understand why we all couldn't get along and tolerate our differences. I'm sure she would have baulked at Arethusa's lack of modesty, being a woman of her time, but she wouldn't have minded her mixing with the blacksmith's son.'

'Is Dermot McLoughlin still alive?' I ask.

'Yes. He married and had children. He's in his eighties or early nineties now and still lives in Ballinakelly.'

'What happened to Ronald Rowan-Hampton?' I'm curious about the characters my mother wrote about. 'She obviously didn't marry him.'

Kitty sips her tea. 'Ronald married a woman called Grace who was very beautiful and charming – and ruthlessly selfish.'

'Oh, poor man.'

'Yes, she also joined the war and helped fight for independence, but her motives were very different to mine. She didn't care about Ireland. She thrived on the thrill of adventure and excitement. She lived the sort of life you only read about in novels. Ronald inherited his father's baronetcy and became Sir Ronald. Lady Rowan-Hampton had an affair with a local man and Ronald divorced her. He later sold their home and moved to London. Grace still lives in Ballinakelly with Michael Doyle, her lover. A pair of old soaks, they are now. Michael always struggled with the bottle and Grace was driven to it when she lost everything. They keep themselves to themselves. They've never married. Mama says they live in sin, but that's just nonsense. They live quietly, in the way they want to, and they don't give anyone any trouble, which is a change as both of them caused a lot of people a lot of trouble back in the day!'

I wonder what sort of trouble they caused. Kitty has a way of opening the door a crack, allowing one to glimpse the past, but leaving one wanting more. I wait for her to elaborate, but she doesn't. She changes the subject.

That evening we go to Ma Murphy's, which is a pub in the centre of town. Kitty is wearing a teal-coloured skirt with a cream silk blouse and a purple cardigan draped casually over her shoulders. She has put her hair up into a chignon, which looks elegant and sleek, and she is wearing small diamond drops on her earlobes. She is all grace and femininity. I wear the same green dress I wore to dinner the other night. I did not bring evening wear because I never imagined I'd need it.

Robert does not appear. Kitty drives and we chat all the way into town. She is excited to be going out. I don't imagine she goes out much, for Robert is clearly anti-social. I can tell that she is relishing the chance to see and be seen now that I am here to give her the perfect excuse. Her anticipation is infectious and I find myself feeling excited too, although I'm not sure what to expect of folk night at Ma Murphy's.

The pub is just what I imagine a typical Irish pub to be like. Low ceilings, dark wooden beams, red walls covered in framed pictures and black-and-white photographs, and a long sturdy bar behind which are shelves crammed with shiny bottles stacked in front of giant, finely distressed mirrors. It is full of people. When we enter, every eye turns to look at us and the conversations dwindle and then die. But I don't shrink with embarrassment. The fact that I'm with Kitty emboldens me and I put my shoulders back and follow her across the floor to the bar. She walks with her head high as if she is aware of her standing in this place, as if she knows she is admired and respected. She smiles at some of the locals, who smile back, and says the odd word here and there. She is gracious and dignified. Looking around at the clientele I wonder whether it is usual for a woman of her status to frequent this pub. They all look surprised to see her, and even more surprised to see *me*. I notice people whispering to each other. I know they are remarking on our likeness. I'm thrilled to look like Kitty, even a less beautiful version of her. Some of her magic dust has fallen on me and I feel beautiful in her reflection.

We take two stools at the bar and Kitty orders brandy and Babycham mixes from the barman, which sounds revolting, but she assures me is delicious. She begins to talk to the barman, but is interrupted by the starting up of music. She swivels round on her stool and nudges me. 'You're going to love this,' she says, beaming a smile. Then I see the group of musicians at the far end of the room. They are sitting in a semicircle, tapping their feet on the floorboards as they play. There is a guitarist, a violinist, a drummer and, to my astonishment, Cormac O'Farrell on the accordion. My interest is suddenly aroused. He's in a blue shirt with the sleeves rolled up, his greying beard is neatly trimmed, his hair swept off his face. He is handsome and I cannot take my eyes off him. Then he winks at me and I blush. My face is so hot and I imagine so red, that everyone must notice. I am a fifty-eight-year-old woman and I am blushing like a teenager. Yet, no one is looking at me, they are looking at him as he starts to sing. I am smiling with pleasure. His voice is rich and deep and thrilling. I am transfixed, and that wild and reckless feeling I had on the horse that morning returns and I have never felt so alive.

Her eyes they shone like the diamonds
You'd think she was queen of the land
And her hair, it hung over her shoulder
Tied up with a black velvet band.

Cormac is well into his third song, having enjoyed a rapturous applause from the audience after the first two, when the door opens and a couple walk in. I wouldn't have noticed them were it not for Kitty, who turns to look, and then does not turn back. I notice a change in her energy. She does nothing. She doesn't have to. I can feel her stiffen. I can feel a shift inside her, even though on the outside she remains unaltered.

I watch the man, who must be in his sixties. He is tall, bearded, with dark brown hair falling over his forehead and curling about his neck. His eyes are the colour of washed denim and he has a chiselled, attractive face. He sees Kitty and a flicker of surprise lights up his face. He nods at her, then averts his gaze and concentrates on finding a table. The woman he is with is, I imagine, his wife. She is fair-haired and sweet-looking. She, too, notices Kitty, but unlike her husband she smiles and waves. Kitty waves back. I can't see her face, but I think she must be smiling too. When she turns back to the musicians, I ask her who they are.

'Jack and Emer O'Leary,' she replies. 'Alana, their daughter, is married to JP.'

I turn my attention back to Cormac, who is now singing a song about the war.

At Boolavogue, as the sun was setting
O'er the bright May meadows of Shelmalier
A rebel hand set the heather blazin'
And brought the neighbours from far and near

I must have misread Kitty's body-language, for Alana's parents are family. However, I'm certain I saw something pass between her and Jack. Something awkward, but intimate. Perhaps it's the Babycham and brandy, an odd mix, but Kitty was right. It is delicious.

Chapter 13

The musicians take a break and Cormac puts down his accordion and comes to the bar. He stands beside me and grins boyishly. 'So what do you think?' he asks, but he knows I am impressed. He can see it on my face.

'I thought you were the local taxi man,' I reply provocatively.

'I know you did,' he says. He asks the barman for a Murphy's stout. 'Well, looks like I'm the local bard as well.'

I find myself grinning like an idiot. 'Is there anything else you do?' I ask.

'Jack of all trades, master of none.' He shrugs.

'I'd say you're master of both.'

He notices Kitty seated beside me. 'Hello, Kitty,' he says.

'You sang beautifully, Cormac,' she replies. 'I love those old folk songs.'

'They were written with broken hearts,' he says.

'They were indeed,' she agrees. 'And when something is written with that kind of emotional integrity, it goes on touching people through the generations.'

Just then, Jack and Emer O'Leary come to the bar and I find myself being drawn away from Cormac and introduced. They comment on my likeness to Kitty and we all laugh. Emer was born in America, which is where she and Jack met and married. She talks of it fondly, but her heart is here, she says. Ballinakelly is home. She has no desire to ever return to the country of her birth. Kitty jokes that *I* will stay in Ballinakelly too. 'There's a magic in the land that some people find irresistible,' she says. Then she looks at me steadily. 'I think you're one of those people, Faye.' I consider my mother; she obviously wasn't.

'Unfortunately, my husband has no desire to come to Ireland,' I tell them.

Emer frowns. 'You've come without your husband?' she says, not unkindly.

'Yes, my mother died and I needed time alone. I wanted to come and find her roots,' I tell her.

'She has a lot of roots,' says Jack with a grin.

'Did you expect to find so many?' Emer asks.

'I expected to find none,' I reply.

'But you found your twin,' says Emer with a chuckle, looking at Kitty.

'That's very kind of you,' I say, glancing at Kitty who is strangely quiet. 'I'm a less beautiful version of my cousin, but I will accept the compliment.'

Emer pulls a sympathetic face. 'Oh, come now. You're lovely,' she says and Kitty agrees.

'At least I now know where I get my red hair from. Mom had brown hair and Daddy was fair. None of our children have red hair. Only me.'

'Well, you've got the whole town talking,' says Emer. 'Not a lot happens in Ballinakelly these days, so when it does, everyone gets very excited.' The way she says 'these days' suggests that once a great deal happened. I think of the door that is only ever open a crack and wonder what did happen. I want to throw it open and know everything.

As we chat I notice that Kitty and Emer are at ease together, but there is definitely an awkwardness between Jack and Kitty. I wonder whether anyone else perceives it, or whether I'm reading too much into it. After starting my mother's diary I think I'm beginning to imagine secrets and intrigue where there is none.

When I turn back, Cormac has moved off. I search for him in the crowd. He's not far away, talking to a group of people at one of the round tables in the middle of the room, but I'm disappointed he's gone. I wonder whether I'll get another chance to talk to him. I find myself wanting to talk to him very much.

I rejoin Kitty's conversation with the O'Learys and observe. Jack lights a cigarette, while the women talk about JP and Alana and their small children. Emer dominates, although she is gentle and quietly spoken. There is something very soothing about her presence. While Kitty is all effervescence and movement, Emer's pace is slow and unhurried. Shortly, Emer is called over to a group of women at a table and the awkwardness between Kitty and Jack evaporates. I realize then that the self-consciousness is not between *them*, but assumed in front of Jack's wife. Now she is gone, they are very natural together.

I drink my brandy and Babycham and my head grows pleasantly light. I notice a tenderness between Jack and Kitty as they talk to each other, an intimacy that is not in their gestures – they don't touch each other – but in their eyes and their smiles and in the air between them. Whatever their history, there is no doubt that these two people are very fond of each other. I wonder whether Jack is the reason Kitty was so excited about coming here this evening. From their conversation, I have picked up that Kitty never comes to Ma Murphy's, or to any other pub for that matter. Jack teases her and I notice too that he refers to her as Kitty Deverill, not Kitty Trench, and at one point he says 'you Prods', so I assume that he and Emer are Catholic. I assume that most of Ma Murphy's is Catholic. His teasing is affectionate and familiar. How much more suited to Kitty would this man be than the one she married.

I would love Kitty to open that door a little so that I could see into their past.

Cormac and his band return to their posts and the music starts up again. Emer and Jack go back to their table. I don't know whether it is the brandy and Babycham but I gaze at Cormac and feel something stir inside me that I haven't felt since college. I know I must have felt it for Wyatt, but I can't recall. Or I don't *want* to recall. I certainly don't want to think about Wyatt. I stare at Cormac. I sway to the rhythm and am deeply moved by the passion in his voice, and I wish it would never end. That I could sit here for all eternity with him in my view and his singing in my ears.

It is not long before everyone is joining in, even those who have no ear for music. They sing loudly, joyfully and with so much enthusiasm that I join in too. It's easy to pick up the words of the choruses and the tunes are catchy. Kitty knows all the words by heart and she links her arm through mine and encourages me with her smile. We sing together and I don't think I have felt this happy in a very long time.

I don't get to talk to Cormac again. I watch him move around the room. He is popular. Everyone wants a piece of him and he indulges them with his crooked smile and his wit, and I wish that he would come over and indulge *me*. But he doesn't. I'd like to go and talk to *him*, but I know that's not appropriate. Even the Deverill in me, released in the saddle that morning, knows that it's not seemly for a woman to approach a man, especially a *married* woman. So I remain on my stool and I talk to the people Kitty introduces me to and I soon realize that they are not aristocratic people like the Deverills, but they are *her* people all the same. Even though she doesn't share their broad Irish brogue, she is one of them and I admire her so much more for that.

As the evening draws to an end the room goes quiet. Even the lights seem to dim. The atmosphere turns from buoyant to wistful. The bartender announces last orders. They collect their final glasses of stout and whiskey, light their last cigarette, and then they demand one more song.

The band put down their instruments. Only Cormac plays his accordion. I can tell from the first bar that it is a sad song. A deeply sad song. The room is so quiet that, if one closed one's eyes, one might be fooled into believing there is no one in it but Cormac. He sings 'Danny Boy'. It is one of the most famous Irish ballads. I have heard it before, but it is like I am hearing it for the first time because Cormac's voice is so tender. His eyes shine and his voice breaks with emotion. He is giving it a new expression and I am transfixed. I look around the room and see that many have tears in their eyes, and then I look at Kitty and she is crying too. She might not share their way of life, but she shares their history, that's certain. And she shares their love of Ireland. My thoughts turn once again to my mother and I wonder how she could have left this country and never returned.

> *Oh Danny boy the pipes the pipes are calling*
> *From glen to glen and down the mountain side*
> *The summer's gone and all the flowers dying*
> *'Tis you 'tis you must go and I must bide*

But come ye back when summer's in the meadow
Or when the valley's hushed and white with snow
'Tis I'll be here in sunshine or in shadow
Oh Danny boy oh Danny boy I love you so

But when ye come and all the roses falling
And I am dead as dead I well may be
Go out and find the place where I am lying
And kneel and say an ave there for me

And I will hear tho' soft you tread above me
And then my grave will warm and sweeter be
For you shall bend and tell me that you love me
And I will sleep in peace until you come to me

When the song is over the locals sing the National Anthem and then slowly get up and leave. Some go and shake Cormac's hand, others depart in silence. One or two need to be helped out because they are too drunk to walk. Kitty slips off her stool. 'Time to leave,' she says. I nod. I glance at Cormac, hoping I might catch his eye, but he is busy with his friends. Reluctantly, I follow Kitty outside.

The air is chilly and there is a dampness in it. I don't think we'll enjoy a sunny day tomorrow. I can feel the clouds above us. They are dense and low-hanging. There are no stars or moon to illuminate our way. As we drive out of town and into the lane it becomes very dark. The car headlights expose the odd cat or fox who stares out from the hedgerow with bright, glowing eyes.

'That was a beautiful evening, Kitty,' I say.

'I knew you'd enjoy it,' she replies.

'The people of Ballinakelly are so friendly and open to strangers.'

'You're not a stranger,' says Kitty. 'Not really. You're a Deverill.'

I laugh. 'After the initial curious looks, they seemed to accept me, didn't they?'

'Trust me, they're riveted. You're a celebrity. Didn't you notice how everyone wanted to shake your hand?'

'I thought you were introducing me to your friends.'

'Oh, I know them, of course, but they were bold in their determination to meet you. I don't imagine anyone has been talking of anything else. They were all taken by surprise when you showed up.'

'And when *you* showed up,' I add.

She sighs. 'Yes, I don't usually go to the pub. Robert dislikes them.'

I watch the road ahead and decide to test my luck. 'Jack and Emer O'Leary are lovely people. You are fortunate that your brother married into such a nice family.'

Kitty nods. 'You're right. I am lucky.'

'If they met in America, what brought them to Ballinakelly?' I ask, even though I have worked out the answer.

'Jack was born and brought up here,' she replies. 'His father was the vet and then he followed in his footsteps and became a vet too.'

'What was he doing in America?' I ask, hoping the door might open a little more.

'He left to make a new life. So many did. After the Civil War he wanted to start again, somewhere new.'

'Did he fight too?'

'Yes, he did.'

'Is that why you know the locals like him and Cormac? You all fought together?'

'That's right.'

'Did your family know you fought on the other side?'

'No.' She looks at me and lifts her eyebrows, and I'm glad I haven't offended her with my probing. 'I lived a double life, Faye,' she says.

'That's amazing, Kitty. You're like the heroine of a novel.'

She laughs. 'It would make a good story, I don't doubt it.'

'Does Robert know?'

'Yes. Robert is very understanding.'

I sense the door opening and persevere. 'When Emer said that nothing happens in this town any more, I got the feeling that once upon a time lots did. It's hard to imagine drama in a sleepy place like Ballinakelly.'

'I'll give you some good books on Irish history, then you'll understand what these people have gone through.'

But I don't want a book. I want her to tell me *her* story.

We arrive at the White House and the door to her past is now closed. There is to be no more looking back. We eat soup and bread in the kitchen and Robert comes to join us. We tell him about the evening and I notice that Kitty does not mention Jack and Emer O'Leary. I sense she doesn't want me to mention them either. So, I rave about Cormac and his beautiful voice. Robert listens as I go on and on about the music and the lyrics and how moved I was, and then he arches an eyebrow and says to Kitty, 'It looks like your cousin is being seduced by Irish charm.'

I blush. I feel it creep up my neck and flourish on my cheeks and there is nowhere to hide. I laugh dismissively. 'It's hard not to be,' I reply. 'For a foreigner, it's very seductive.'

Kitty comes to my rescue. 'Cormac has the charm of the devil,' she says with a smile. 'And when he sings, he's irresistible.'

'Isn't it lucky that Wyatt isn't with me. He wouldn't

appreciate my admiration for Cormac O'Farrell, not one bit.' I only mention my husband because I feel guilty. I have harboured feelings for another man tonight and believe, somehow, that by mentioning Wyatt those feelings won't count. I fall back into the safety net that is my marriage, and perhaps think that Wyatt's name will protect me from myself, from the devil, or the *Deverill*, that is the growing recklessness inside me – like a cross protects against vampires.

Yet, as I drift off to sleep, I think only of Cormac. I try not to. I try very hard, but he is persistent. In the end I give in. They are only thoughts, after all, and what is the harm in dreaming?

The following day Kitty and I go out riding again. It is an overcast, drizzly day. Indeed, soft rain falls upon our faces as we make our way into the hills where the beauty is not at all diminished by the weather. The sea is grey and rough, the wind playful and gusty. Seabirds squawk loudly as they wrangle over carcasses of crabs and other poor creatures on the sand. We gallop and the recklessness inside me grows. My thoughts turn back to Cormac at every pause in our conversation and I find myself thinking of ways to engineer a meeting. I can't go to the pub on my own and I can't wander about the town in search of him. I don't need a taxi to take me anywhere and I don't know where he lives, so I can't casually walk past his door. I know I'm being ridiculous. I'm a married woman. I'm in my late fifties! I'm too grown-up for this kind of crush. Yet, I can't stop myself. The harder I gallop, the louder I laugh and the more I bond with my cousin, the more the Deverill blood is pumped through my veins and the stronger I feel.

Then an idea pops into my head. Mass. I will surely see him at Mass.

That evening we go to Kitty's sister's castle for dinner. It is cold and austere, not at all like Castle Deverill, but Elspeth is sweet and keen to be friends, and I am warmed by her hospitality. JP and Alana are there too and my uncle Bertie and aunt Maud. They have invited their neighbours – other Anglo-Irish grandees who have titles and names I don't remember. I realize that Kitty is rare among her class. No one else seems to cross the class barriers, or religious barriers either, like she does. The Anglo-Irish stick together. They hunt together, dine together, go to the Protestant church on Sundays and intermarry. I wonder how JP managed to wed the Catholic daughter of the local vet. I wonder whether that was one of the dramas of the past that Emer alluded to. I can only deduce that, whatever happened then, the two of them are very happy now.

After dinner, while the men are passing the port, a ridiculous British tradition of men remaining in the dining room to drink, smoke cigars and talk politics (apparently, we women are not up to talking politics. Wyatt would fit right in!), I manage to get Alana on her own. We sit on the club fender in the chilly, smoky drawing room, with the feeble heat of the turf fire on our backs. I tell her that I would like to go to Mass the following morning but assume that Kitty and the rest of her family will go to the Protestant church. 'You must come with us,' she suggests. 'JP is Protestant by birth but he has chosen to bring the children up in my faith, so we go to Mass together.'

That is just what I wanted to hear. 'I'd like that, thank you.'

'JP's mother was Catholic, you know,' she adds.

At this I am confused. I look at Maud, beautiful, icy Maud, who is sitting on the sofa talking with one of the other women, and frown, for surely Uncle Bertie is Protestant. 'Aunt Maud is Catholic?' I say.

Alana puts her hand on her mouth and laughs. 'Goodness no! Maud is very Church of England.' Then she mimics an English accent. 'God forbid she ever hears you suggest she's a Left Footer!'

'But isn't she JP's mother?' I ask.

Alana leans closer and lowers her voice. 'No. JP's mother was a maid at the castle, called Bridie Doyle, who bore Bertie twins. One of those children was JP. Bridie was only young, and single, so JP was given to Kitty who brought him up as her own, while Bridie went to live in America. It's a very sad story and was scandalous at the time. I can't imagine her pain, having to give up her children and her life.'

'What happened to her?'

'Well, she came back a very wealthy woman and bought the castle. She never told JP that she was his mother, to protect him. He was very settled with Kitty and Robert by then, you see. Bridie was a selfless, godly person. How she must have suffered to have lived only a few miles from her son yet knowing she could never tell him the truth. Anyhow, she died eight years ago. But she left a letter for JP explaining the true circumstances of his birth.'

'Oh, that's so sad.'

'Yes, he never knew her. She left him Castle Deverill, though, and he built a memorial garden for her. Next time you come to the castle, I'll show it to you. It's a very peaceful little garden, with a bench, and it's always full of birds, even in winter.'

'What happened to JP's twin?'

'Well, they grew up not knowing the other existed. Martha, that's his twin, was adopted by an American family and raised in Connecticut. When she was about seventeen she

discovered, quite by chance, that she was adopted and set out
to find her birth mother. She was quite a detective, I can tell
you. It can't have been easy to track Bridie down. The convent
where Martha and JP were born had kept no records. But she
met JP in Dublin, by coincidence, which makes me believe
in Fate, and wound up here, in Ballinakelly.'

'Did she find her mother?'

'They met, but neither knew they were related. She found
her twin brother, and that was miraculous. But she only discovered who her mother was in a letter, after Bridie had died.'

I am so moved, I don't know what to say. I'm also astonished that Alana has no qualms about sharing this very
personal story. Then I remember Kitty saying that her father
is quite used to long-lost relations turning up out of the blue
and I imagine she must have been thinking of Martha. 'Does
she live in Ireland now?'

'No, she returned to America and married an American,
but she keeps in touch. She's family now. One thing you'll
learn about the Deverills is they're very tribal. They stick
together and look out for each other. Martha and JP are twins.
They'll always be close even if they're hundreds of miles apart.'

'So, Kitty is like a mother to JP?'

'Yes, but they are, in fact, half-siblings.'

'They look very similar.'

'They're similar in every way.' She smiles with tenderness
and I feel the love she has for her husband and envy it. I
wonder whether I ever smiled like that about Wyatt. If I ever
did, I don't anymore.

The men return to the drawing room and the women
move to accommodate them. As we get up off the fender,
I say to Alana, 'Are there any more family secrets I should
know about?'

She puts a hand on my arm and lowers her voice. '*Many* more secrets,' she says with emphasis. 'But most are irrelevant now and buried deep. The secrets we're all keen to know are contained in your mother's diary.'

'Ah, yes, the diary,' I say, promising myself that I will start reading it again when I get back to Kitty's house.

'We're all fascinated by Arethusa Deverill's story. I think we're going to find that *our* tales pale in the light of hers.'

'I'm not so sure. I fear you may be disappointed.'

With that she laughs. 'Oh no, trust me, the Deverills *never* disappoint,' she says. 'If there's one thing you'll learn about your mother's family, it's that.'

By the time I get back to Kitty's house it is too late to start reading Mother's diary. I get into bed and put my head on the pillow and the moment I do my thoughts are hijacked by Cormac O'Farrell. I'm excited that I'm going to see him at Mass in the morning. I don't imagine for one minute that he won't be there. Where I come from, everyone goes to church on Sunday. I don't believe it is any different here. I've heard the Irish are very religious.

The following morning JP and Alana pick me up and drive me into Ballinakelly. They have brought their three children with them: two boys and a girl, all under ten, who look at me with curiosity. Alana squeezes onto the back seat and lifts her daughter onto her knee, and I sit in the front. I have dressed up. I brought an elegant outfit for Mass, at least.

I am nervous. I know I am going to see Cormac. I'm anxious that I won't get to speak to him. That I'll see him from a distance only. That I'll leave disappointed. As we chat in the car, and the children ask me questions, being outspoken and

inquisitive as children are, I try to work out how to engineer a
meeting. If he doesn't come up to *me*, what excuse can I make
to go up to *him*? Is there something I can pretend to ask him?
Then I fear he might not be there. What if he doesn't go to
Mass? Or perhaps he goes to a later one? This is my fifth day
in Ballinakelly, I'm almost through the first week; what if I
don't manage to see him again? I don't think I can wait for
the following Friday folk night!

JP parks the car and we walk up the street to the church.
It seems like the whole town is going to Mass. They are all
dressed in their Sunday best, many of the women in small hats
or headscarves, the men in jackets and ties. Some of the locals
I met at Ma Murphy's smile at me and I smile back, grateful
for their kindness. I notice an old woman in a moth-eaten
fur coat, her grey hair is pulled off a coarse face which might
once have been beautiful but is now over-painted with badly
applied make-up. She is walking unsteadily beside a rough-
looking man with shaggy, greying black hair and a thick black
beard. He is tall and broad, she is slight and fragile and dwarfed
by his bulk. They look at no one and no one greets them or
gives them a wave. They are isolated and there is a dark energy
about them, as if they are enveloped by cloud. I keep an eye
out for Cormac O'Farrell, but I don't see him. Jack and Emer
O'Leary are there, and we choose a pew and sit with them.
The church is large and glowing in the light of many candles.

The priest starts the service and I feel deflated, because I
haven't seen Cormac. I'm not even sure he's here. Every time
I look around, I catch someone's eye and they smile, or nod,
thrilled to be acknowledged. I guess I *am* a bit of a celebrity,
after all. I try to concentrate on the Mass, but I'm not very
religious. Mother was, she went to Mass every morning. It
was the first thing she did, and sometimes on Sundays she

went twice. My mind drifts to her childhood, when she was Protestant, attending the church of St Patrick. I wonder what made her change her religion. Perhaps it was meeting my father, for he was a staunch Catholic. It wouldn't surprise me if she pretended she was Catholic, just for him. Certainly, there was never any mention of having ever been Protestant. I suppose she had the opportunity to reinvent herself when she arrived in America. It crosses my mind that she did it to spite her family. I don't imagine Greville, her grandfather, or Hubert, her father, would have approved of her changing her religion. If she fell out with them all, then she might well have done it to hurt them. I resolve to read the diary tonight. I tell myself that Cormac must not distract me from the purpose of this trip. But then, as I think of it, I know that learning about my mother's past isn't the only reason I came to Co. Cork. Perhaps it's not the reason at all, just covering for the real reason, which is to find myself. And if that is the truth, the bare and honest truth which I haven't, until now, been able to admit, then Cormac isn't a distraction at all.

I stand in line for holy communion. Jack and Emer are in front of me, JP, Alana and their children behind. I am conspicuous, there in the aisle, as those who have taken holy communion file past me on their way back to their seats. I feel many eyes upon me. Without Kitty beside me I am less confident. Then I see one pair of eyes I recognize. They are a deep, indigo blue and they are smiling at me. My stomach does a flip. He is here, after all.

Chapter 14

My thoughts are not with Christ as I partake of His body; they are in a far less spiritual realm. I return to my seat with my chin up and my shoulders back, aware that Cormac is in the congregation and might be watching me. I am injected with excitement while at the same time incredulous that, at my age, and married, I have a crush on this man. Crushes are for teenagers, not for women in their fifties. I know I should think of Wyatt, concentrate my mind on the straight and narrow path of marriage and duty and the proper behaviour expected of a person in my position, but I can't focus on anything but Cormac O'Farrell. Instead, I think of what I'm going to say when we talk outside the church. How can I extend it to more than a fleeting conversation? My heart beats wildly, the palms of my hands grow damp, anxiety takes hold. I am already anticipating disappointment. I have a crush on him; he has given no indication of having a crush on *me*.

Mass ends and we file out into the sunshine. Birds tweet in the plane trees but I don't hear them, I hear only the pounding of blood at my temples. I shake the priest's hand and he welcomes me to his parish. He comments on my likeness to my cousin and I go through the motions of being amused and complimented at the same time. He is much too polite to ask why it is that I am Catholic while my mother was raised a Protestant, but I know it is what he's thinking. As I look about me, at the many pairs of eyes that glance in my direction, I realize that they must all be thinking the same thing. But I don't know the answer yet either. It is another of my mother's secrets, and hopefully I will find an explanation in her diary.

Fortunately, JP and Alana are keen to mingle. This is a time for the community to get together and there is an air of exhilaration. Their religious duty is over for the week and now they can enjoy a day off work. The Deverill children scarper with the other children and I remain with Alana as she talks to the women. I try to concentrate on what they are saying, but I am hoping Cormac will come and find me, if only to say hello. At this moment, I do not expect any more than that.

At last I hear his familiar voice. 'Hello, Mrs Langton,' he says.

I turn and try to remain calm, but my stomach is full of butterflies. 'Oh, please call me Faye,' I reply, and as I take him in I am surprised at how much more handsome he has become since I've known him. His character is revealed in every line and contour of his face and it is very attractive. '"Mrs Langton" makes me feel old,' I add.

His lapis eyes twinkle with their usual warmth and his smile puts creases into his cheeks like his accordion. 'Faye it is.' He hesitates, then says what everyone is thinking. 'I did not think you'd be Catholic.'

'I did not think my mother would be Protestant,' I reply.

He chuckles. 'Deverills are all Protestant, with the exception of JP, who is an honorary Catholic on account of his wife.'

'My father was from a devout Catholic family so I can only assume that my mother converted when she married him.'

'And sent every Deverill turning in his grave.' He arches a black eyebrow and I laugh.

'I doubt they ever knew of it,' I tell him. 'Kitty told me that Arethusa left Ireland and never looked back. They have no idea what happened to her.'

'I'm sure you've filled them in.'

I sigh, revealing my frustration. 'I wish I could. *They* know the beginning and *I* know the end, but none of us know what happened in between.' Then I tell him about the diary. 'It's in mirror writing, so it's not easy to read, but I'm hoping it will answer our questions.'

'A right old mystery, then,' he says, putting his hands in his trouser pockets. 'You can be sure there was a lot of drama. The Deverills are a family who attract drama.'

'And make it, I should imagine,' I add.

'Indeed they do,' he replies with a chuckle.

I spot the woman in the moth-eaten fur coat walking out of the church. 'Who is that, Cormac?' I ask.

Cormac shifts his eyes to the church door. 'That's Lady Rowan-Hampton,' he says, lowering his voice. 'And behind her is Michael Doyle.'

'Oh, Kitty told me about them.'

'Now, they're a pair who make drama for themselves,' he says. 'But they've become harmless. They keep themselves to themselves at the Doyle farmhouse.'

'They seem sad,' I say, and I want to add 'friendless', but that's conjecture and I don't want to be unkind.

'Well, Grace is neither fish nor red herring and people are still afraid of Michael Doyle. A quare pair if ever there was one.' He looks at me and arches that eyebrow again. 'You're slowly learning what lies beneath the surface of this town,' he says. 'It's not all pretty.'

'With no help from you,' I tease. 'You promised you'd tell me about the Deverills, but so far I've only been given the odd, tantalizing scrap of information from my cousin. When are you going to give me the full story?'

'It's a *long* story,' he says.

'How much time do you need? I'm here for nine more days.'

He shrugs and pulls a face that makes me laugh. 'I can make a good start then.'

Alana is now standing beside me and I realize that it's time to go. She says hello to Cormac and asks after his dog. His affection for Kite warms his face as he talks about her, and to me he just grows more attractive. I agree that Kite is a special dog. 'Would you like to walk her with me this afternoon?' he asks me suddenly. 'I'll show you some of the sights around Ballinakelly.'

I am taken aback by his forwardness and wonder what Alana must think. But he's looking at me directly and I don't want to reveal my surprise, nor my elation.

'I'd love that,' I reply, my heart leaping like a grasshopper.

'Grand. I'll come and pick you up around four.'

I'm thrilled. 'Grand,' I repeat, imitating his Irish brogue, and I grin at him.

'We'll make an Irishwoman of you yet,' he laughs and watches us walk away.

There is a large luncheon party at the castle. JP and Alana have invited the entire family. I feel very privileged to be included. I enjoy being in the place where my mother grew up, even though little of it remains as it was in her day. I sit next to my uncle at lunch and ask him about my grandmother, Adeline. He tells me about her interest in the esoteric and how his father, Hubert, used to roll his eyes and call it 'ballcock'. He says that she and her sisters used to hold séances in the drawing room when his father was in Dublin and summon the dead. When I ask whether the dead ever came, he looks at me askance and replies, 'But do they ever come, Faye?'

'I imagine not,' I reply.

'If you were to ask Kitty, she would tell you that she sees the deceased all the time.'

'Really?' I look across the table at Kitty, who is deep in conversation with the rector.

'Oh, yes. She claims that she and Adeline shared a gift which enables them to see what they call the "finer vibrations of spirit".'

'We have a maid back at home who would agree with Kitty. She claims to see those vibrations too! Mother thought it all preposterous and would get quite cross with Temperance when she went off on one of her discourses about angels and spirits.'

'I dare say Tussy found Mama's obsession with all that nonsense somewhat trying. But it was part of her charm. She loved nature and adored putting food out for the birds and watching them feed. If she chose to see leprechauns and sprites in the woods, it was her business. It didn't bother me. In fact, I found it amusing. We teased her and she'd always laugh. She never took herself seriously. But it bothered Tussy. I think mother and daughter relationships are much more complicated than mother and son relationships. At least it's been that way in my experience.'

I look at Maud, who appears older in daylight, but striking nonetheless. I cannot imagine her being a mother at all. There is no maternal warmth there and I haven't seen her talk to the children. Some women are not designed for motherhood. I may be wrong, but I think Maud is more interested in herself than in her children and grandchildren.

'I wonder whether Mom ever knew that her home burnt down,' I muse.

'That I wouldn't know,' Uncle Bertie replies, wiping the corners of his mouth with a napkin. 'You see, after Tussy left for America under a heavy cloud my parents never really spoke of her again. Mama mentioned her only in passing, as if she was reluctant to erase her completely, but Papa was less forgiving. I don't think he spoke her name right up to his death—'

'In the fire,' I interrupt. 'I'm so sorry about that. It must have been devastating for you all. To lose your home and your father on the same night. I can't imagine . . .'

'The only part of the castle to remain standing was the western tower, to where Mama subsequently retreated and refused to leave.'

I put down my knife and fork. 'The western tower? Is it still the same?'

'It's the only part of the castle that is original,' he says.

I think of my dream and my excitement mounts. 'Might I see it?'

'Of course. If you're interested.'

'Oh, I am. I'm interested in my family's history. It's the only part of the castle that existed in Mom's day.'

'No one ever went in there, even then. It has always been cold and damp and pretty unfriendly.'

'Will you show me, all the same?'

'I'll show you after lunch,' he says and I hope he doesn't forget, because I want to go there very much. I want to see if it is the same tower as the one in my dream. I haven't had that dream since leaving Nantucket, but I remember it clearly. It is still fresh in my memory as if I dreamed it last night.

After lunch we drink tea and coffee in the drawing room. JP's big dogs charge in, having been released from their confinement in the kitchen, and their tails wag so vigorously that they knock the odd ornament off the sofa tables and thrill the children by pushing their noses into people's conversations in their desire to be petted.

At last Uncle Bertie takes me upstairs to see the tower. JP's eight-year-old daughter Aisling comes with us. She holds her grandfather's hand and skips along beside him, talking incessantly about nothing. She is as chirpy as a songbird. I recognise the corridor at once. It is long and there are doors along both sides. We go deeper and deeper into the castle and my anticipation grows.

I see the hole in the wall where the staircase is long before we reach it. I know it is there, and yet to the ignorant eye it is concealed. Aisling lets go of Uncle Bertie's hand and runs ahead. She disappears into the wall and I hear her footsteps clattering up a staircase. 'Here it is,' says my uncle and he stands aside to let me go first. I look down at the steps, they are just as I have seen them in my dream. Dark wood, worn to a light brown in places by centuries of treading feet, with a slight hollow in the middle of each one. I put my foot in the first hollow and up I go.

I catch my breath when I see the door. It is heavy and old and embellished with black studs and nails. Even the shape of it is the same as the door in my dream. It reaches into a gentle curve at the top, like the door to an old crypt. Aisling is already inside. She is by the empty fireplace, where the woman with red hair stands in my dream. Yet, the child has put her hands on the mantelpiece and is swinging with her feet off the ground. The room is the same size. The same window looks out onto the lawn. Only there is no one there. No one is waiting for me. Not Adeline nor a reflection of myself. Only Aisling giggling as she tries not to let go, her fingers slipping in the dust.

'Well, here it is,' says Uncle Bertie and I can tell that he finds it damp and cold and has no wish to linger. I absorb the energy in the room. It is very different from the energy downstairs. It's not a nasty energy at all, in fact it's pleasant in spite of the temperature. It's an ancient energy, as if one has stepped back in time to another age. I feel very strange. 'There are a couple of other rooms. Let me show them to you,' says my uncle. But I don't care about those. I only care about this one. Nonetheless, he opens another door to the right of the fireplace and leads me into what he tells me was once a bedroom. 'Mama insisted on living here after the fire. She refused to move out, even though it was uncomfortable and cold.' He puts his hands on his hips and shakes his head. 'It was a dreadful business. She lived out her last days here and eventually passed away.'

Aisling remains in the other room. I can hear her dancing now, her small feet lightly tapping on the floorboards. Uncle Bertie suggests we go back to the drawing room. 'This isn't a place one wants to loiter.' We go back into the little sitting room. 'Come on, my dear,' he says to his granddaughter, patting her head. 'Let's go downstairs, shall we?'

Uncle Bertie leaves the room. I start to follow. Then Aisling takes my hand. 'Aunt Faye,' she says.

I turn to her and smile. 'What is it, Aisling?'

'There's a woman in here who looks just like you,' she says. Her big eyes stare up at me innocently.

My heart stops. 'Sorry, Aisling. What did you say?'

'There's a woman in here with red hair who looks just like you.' I sweep my eyes about the room and see no one. 'She's often here,' she continues, as if she's talking about someone from the town and not a ghost. 'She's nice as well, just like you.' Then she smiles, lets go of my hand and skips on down the staircase, leaving me bewildered and a little afraid. I turn back to the chimney but see nothing except the cold black hearth and the dusty mantelpiece above it, marked with Aisling's fingerprints.

I am stunned by what Aisling has told me. I want to believe that she was making it up, but how could she know about the woman with red hair who I see in my dream? I am well and truly spooked. I return to the drawing room and am grateful that the talk is of earthly things like the weather, the hunt and the local gossip. I don't want to hear any more of ghosts.

I return to the White House with Kitty and Robert by foot. It is not far when one cuts through the estate and the weather is fine. I do not tell Kitty what Aisling said in the tower; not because Robert is with us, although I doubt he believes in spirits, but because I am afraid of what she might tell me. I don't want to believe the dead are around us. I like to think of them far away in Heaven. I have managed to avoid the topic for years, even though Temperance often slips it into the conversation or mutters under her breath. I don't want to be subjected to it here.

At four Cormac arrives in his Jeep. Kite is on the back seat. This time she does not regard me with suspicion but thumps her tail on the leather. I guess she has accepted me. Dogs sense when someone loves them. I lean over and scratch her beneath her chin. She lifts her nose with its pretty white blaze, shuts her eyes with pleasure and smiles. I swear she actually draws her mouth into a smile. I have never seen a dog do that before.

'I thought I'd show you the Fairy Ring,' he says.

'What's the Fairy Ring?' I ask.

'It's a circle of big stones on the top of the cliff. Legend has it that they were once people, turned to stone by an evil witch. At sunset they move. That's because the witch gave them a small window in which to become themselves again, and that's just as the sun touches the sea. Then they're stone again, poor devils.'

'Do you believe that?' I ask.

He glances at me sidelong and laughs. 'No.' I'm relieved. 'Pagans probably put them there for sun worship thousands of years ago. People love to invent elaborate stories, but the truth is no one really knows why they're there.'

We chatter on like old friends. I notice thick clouds blowing in off the ocean, slowly eating through the blue sky. Cormac parks in a field and we climb out. Kite races into the long grasses enthusiastically. There is a chilly wind and I'm glad I have my coat and scarf. I tie my hair into a ponytail to keep it from blowing about and rather wish I'd brought a hat. It's spring, but every time the sun goes behind a cloud the temperature drops.

Cormac is wearing a tweed cap. His grey hair curls beneath it. He looks like a farmer in his muted green coat and heavy lace-up boots. It wouldn't surprise me if he has cows and sheep as well as being the local taxi driver and bard. We head along a path that meanders through the purple heather and yellow gorse. Every time the sun comes out the flowers shine brightly. He bends down and picks a sprig of something and crushes it between his finger and thumb. 'What do you think this is?' he asks.

I take it and press it to my nose. 'Thyme?' I reply.

'Wild thyme,' he says. 'In the summer it blooms into purple and pink flowers. You'll find wild orchids here too, along with rosemary and other herbs. Once the sun's been on it for a while the smell is grand.' He inhales deeply. We walk on and every now and then he picks something else for me to look at, or smell. He points out birds, knowing them by name as Kitty does. There's a wagtail and a bunting, cormorants, chaffinches and curlews, and a flamboyant hoopoe which is apparently very rare. Kite is quick to spot rabbits but not quick enough to catch them.

'Tell me, who burned down the castle?' I ask.

'That's a very good question. It wasn't us,' he replies, shaking his head.

'So they never caught the culprits?'

He narrows his eyes. 'I suspect it was Michael Doyle, Faye. He had a hatred in him in those days, a hatred for the Deverills, and he was always on the bottle.'

'Who rebuilt it?'

'A cousin who lived in London. Celia Deverill. She poured money into it like there was no tomorrow, but her husband lost everything in the Depression of '29 and he hanged himself. Right there in the garden.'

'Goodness, that's terrible!'

'You see, the Deverills make a lot of drama.'

'Alana told me about Bridie.'

'Bridie was Michael's sister. Michael blamed Lord Deverill for getting his sister into trouble. It's a sad story. But Bridie came back from America a rich woman, married to a no-good Italian count, and bought the castle herself. Not long after that her husband was found buried up to his neck in the sand and drowned; murdered.'

'I don't suppose they ever found the culprits there either,' I say. I'm beginning to get a clear picture about this place. I imagine this town looks after its own.

'You're right. He was a gambler and a fraud, and a philanderer to boot. There were many who wanted him out of the way, I can assure you.'

We walk and talk and I am riveted by the history of this seemingly quiet little place. Cormac knows so much and I sense that, because I'm a Deverill, he feels it's my right to know my own family's history. I do not think he's a gossip. He takes no pleasure from the tragedies and scandals. When I ask him about Kitty's involvement during the War of Independence, he merely states that she was invaluable. I ask him about Grace and Kitty, whether they were friends, and he tells me that they were allies, fighting on the same side, but that is all. I would like to ask him about Kitty and Jack, but I don't dare. I imagine he does not feel it is his place to tell me about my cousin. I don't press him further. Kitty is a private person, a modest person too, so I will leave it at that.

We reach the Fairy Ring. It is high up on the cliffs and we can see for miles around. The sea is turning grey beneath the clouds, the waves growing big and angry. Seabirds soar on the mounting gale and Kite races after rabbits, which disappear swiftly into their holes, flashing their white tails at her triumphantly. I put my hand on one of the stones. It is massive, three times the size of me, at least. There is something rather special about touching this ancient stone. Perhaps because it has been here for five thousand years and who knows who has placed their hand here before me.

'If only these stones could talk,' I say.

Cormac puts his hands on his hips and nods. 'They'd have a few tales to tell, I should think.'

I sigh with pleasure and lean back against the stone. 'What's it like living in such a beautiful place, Cormac? Do you ever take it for granted?'

He shakes his head and our eyes scan the horizon together. 'I wake up with gratitude every morning of my life,' he says.

'How could my mother have left it and never come back?'

'You have to read that diary of hers.'

'I know. I'm afraid to.'

'Why?'

'Because of what I'll find out. Something terrible happened.'

'It's likely more terrible in your imagination than in her account of it,' he tells me wisely.

'She was very different in her youth to how she was as a wife and mother. I want to know her, because I realize now that I didn't know her at all.'

'Do children ever really know their parents?' Cormac asks.

'I don't know. Do they?' I think of Rose, Edwina and Walter and know that they would be totally unfamiliar with the Deverill side of me, which is only emerging now. I wonder what they'd think of it? I don't imagine children ever want their parents to change. They want us to remain as solid rocks to their anchors, while the rest of the world moves around them.

'I suppose it's only by stepping back and looking at them with detachment that one can hope to see who they really are. As long as you see Arethusa as Mother, and not as Arethusa, you'll judge her from the standpoint of a daughter, not a historian. You need to put your emotions to one side. It's not about you.'

Suddenly the sky darkens. The black clouds are upon us. The blue sky is all but gone and the temperature drops considerably. As it starts to rain, Cormac takes off his cap and puts it on my head. 'Come, I'll show you somewhere we can shelter until it's passed.' The rain hides my blushes. His cap is warm and there is something very intimate about having it on my head just after it's been on his. I feel like the college girl who is wearing her boyfriend's baseball shirt.

We walk briskly down the hill, keeping to the path. Kite does not mind the rain and leaps about, tearing into the long grasses only to emerge moments later with her tail wagging. I see an abandoned cabin nestled into the hillside. There are many of these uninhabited buildings, lying derelict in the grass like old bones. Cormac pushes the door and it opens easily. There's nothing inside, just a few empty sacks and a pile of dusty planks. But it is dry. Cormac puts a couple of sacks on the planks and we sit side by side. Kite lies in the open doorway and watches the rain, as do we. I am wet through. However, I don't mind. I give him back his cap and he replaces it on his head. We stare out in silence and I wonder whether he feels the romance of this moment as I do.

I know this is very out of character for me to be sitting here and feeling like this about a man who is not my husband. I barely recognize myself. But then I am discovering, as I trawl through my mother's past, that I am not only a Clayton and a Langton, but a Deverill too. And I'm beginning to realize that the Deverill part is stronger than any other.

Chapter 15

'You didn't come here just to find out about your mother, did you?' says Cormac. His candour takes me by surprise. Only a moment ago we were discussing the weather. But it is intimate in here, just the two of us, and I should be flattered that he has clearly given it some thought.

'What makes you leap to that conclusion?' I ask.

'Because you're here without your husband.'

'I didn't want him to come,' I reply quietly. 'He's busy working and he's not interested in Ireland or finding out about my mother. I had to come alone.'

Cormac nods. He is leaning forward with his elbows on his knees. He turns his head and looks at me. He smiles, not a jolly smile but a compassionate one, and I know he sees through me. I avert my gaze and stare out at the rain. 'After my mother died, I needed time on my own to grieve,' I tell him. 'She has requested in her will that her ashes be scattered here. Well, since she never talked about Ireland, I was curious. Mom was a very sociable, gregarious woman. She was difficult too. Not easy to get close to, on reflection. I realized that I never really knew her – the sociable, gregarious woman was hiding a lot of secrets. But coming here has dug up more questions than it has answers. Each secret that is reveals takes her further away from the mother I knew. I'm no closer to understanding her.'

'I think you came here to find yourself,' he says, still fixing me with those lapis eyes.

'How can you possibly think that when you don't know me?'

'You've changed.' He shrugs and knits his fingers. 'You're quite a different woman to the one I picked up at the airport and that was what, five days ago?'

I'm astonished and secretly flattered. 'Really?'

'Really.'

'I'm enjoying myself, that's all. Maybe I was sad when I arrived.'

'You're just different.' I can feel him looking at me more intensely and I keep my eyes on the sea. 'You're lighter. You know, it's okay to take time out to reassess your life. It's okay to be selfish. To think of yourself. You've likely spent the last thirty-odd years looking after everyone else, you're not even sure of your own needs. I'd say your mother's death has triggered something in you.' I drop my gaze into my hands, for he is right. Mom's death *has* triggered something in me. I know what it is. I'm just afraid to say it out loud, or even in my head, to myself. 'People don't always stay the same, Faye,' he continues. 'Life is a long road.'

'Wyatt hasn't changed.'

'That's not what I mean. *You* have.' I stare at him now, afraid that he is going to articulate how I truly feel. 'You came to Ireland to find your mother, but I'd wager you're going to find yourself.' He chuckles, releasing the tension that's been gradually building between us in this quiet cabin. 'I'd wager you're beginning to find the real Faye already.'

I smile, relieved that he is no longer talking about Wyatt.

'It is very healing to be here, in this beautiful place. I do feel lighter, much lighter. I like who I am here.'

'That's because you can finally be yourself.' I frown at him. 'Just a hunch.' He grins playfully. 'I don't *know* you, after all.' He is teasing me now. 'But perhaps I'm an amateur psychologist as well as a taxi driver and a bard!'

'And what of you, Cormac O'Farrell. How do you manage to be happy all the time?'

'Because I make a conscious effort every day to be grateful for my life.'

I'm surprised at the simplicity of his reply. 'Is that it? The key to happiness?'

He's not being funny. 'It's a choice we all have,' he says gravely and I can sense that after all he has been through he has worked very hard at this. 'I choose to live in the moment and not to be dragged back to unhappy times. Sure, I have a lot I could be sad about. I lost friends in the war. I suffered and was afraid. I loved a woman and I lost her. I'd like to have had children, but it never happened. I could go on. We all have reasons to regret and wallow in self-pity. But that's not who I am. I am who I choose to be today, right here, right now. So, I thank God for the rain, the beautiful rain. I thank God for the heather. For the gorse and the flowers. I thank God for my friends and my home. I thank God for Kite, who has healed the tears in my heart, indeed she has. I thank God for my life. It's beautiful.'

The tension has suddenly built again. The cabin is so intimate, it is almost unbearably so. His voice is a melody that is lovely to listen to. It is deep and gentle and wise. I am humbled. I only have to look at the stump where his little finger was to have an idea of how he suffered in the War of Independence and the Civil War that followed. What do *I* really have to be sad about? A marriage gone sour? A marriage that was never truly sweet?

'You make me feel like a fool,' I say quietly.

'You're not a fool, Faye.'

Suddenly, I want to tell him everything. This man I barely know but trust, somehow, to understand. I want to unburden my heart, because it is heavy and I can't carry it anymore.

'You're right. I didn't come here just to find my mother's roots. I came here to discover who I am without Wyatt. I came here because I don't want to be there anymore, with him.' Now I've said it, it really wasn't so hard. I take a deep breath to suppress the emotion that gathers in the centre of my chest like a ball of fire. 'I don't like who I am when I'm with him, Cormac. But I'm scared, because I don't know how to be anyone else.'

'You already *are* someone else,' he says softly and he looks at me with those clear indigo eyes and they are deep, like a well that is full of old pain and compassion.

The rain has lessened to a drizzle, the sky brightened a little. A bird warbles merrily in a nearby bush. I want to cry but not in front of Cormac. 'Come,' he says gently, getting up. 'It's almost stopped raining.' Kite anticipates her master setting off again and trots into the long grasses. We emerge into the light. I feel better for having unburdened myself. 'Don't think about the past, Faye,' he says. 'Don't think about Wyatt or anything else that exists outside of the now. Just be present. Yesterday is history, tomorrow is mystery.'

'I'll try,' I respond. He makes it sound so easy.

'Listen to the birdsong. Feel the wind on your face, the drizzle on your skin. Enjoy the view. It's magnificent. You're here, so don't be elsewhere in your mind.'

'I like being here,' I say. I like being with *him*. *That* I don't say.

We return to the Jeep and Cormac takes a towel out of the back and puts it down for Kite to lie on. He pats her affectionately and dries her a bit, before shutting the door and walking round to the front. I'm already inside. It's still drizzling. He climbs in, turns on the engine and the windscreen wipers sweep away the raindrops. 'I'm sorry you got wet,' he says as he drives into the lane.

'I'm not cold, though,' I reply. 'And there's something invigorating about walking in the rain. I'm soaked to the skin, but I don't mind. In fact, I quite like it.'

'That's the Deverill in you speaking. You'll be on a horse next, taking the hedges as if they're mere trotting poles.'

'I'm not so sure about that. I don't have Kitty's fearlessness.'

'Not many do. But you have ten more days to find it in you.'

'Nine,' I reply.

'Nine then. Nine more days to find it in you.'

'To find myself,' I reply.

'To find the Deverill.'

'Or the devil,' I add laughing.

He smiles back with knowing. 'It's one and the same,' he says.

Cormac drops me back at the White House and I wave goodbye. We have made no plans to see each other again and I wonder whether he'll make an approach. We grew close out there on the hill. It was a short moment, but an intimate one, and I shared things with him that I haven't shared with anyone. I told him about Wyatt. That I don't want to be with him anymore. I blush at the thought. I was uncharacteristically open. Did I reveal too much?

The house is quiet. It seems both Robert and Kitty are out. Perhaps they have gone for a walk. I go upstairs and run a bath. I'm suddenly cold. I take off my sodden clothes and wrap myself in a towel. It's raining again. The sky is grey and dark and the sea is grey and dark beneath it. I can't stop thinking about Cormac. I remember the way he gave me the thyme and the way he relished telling me about the birds. I look out of the window and see beauty everywhere. I resolve to focus on what I have, rather than on what I don't have, and I resolve to be grateful for my life. But I cannot remain present. I wonder when I'll see Cormac again. That's all I can think about. That's both the Deverill and the devil in me.

After my bath I sit at the dressing table and open Mom's diary to the place where I left off. I haven't read it since I was at Vickery's Inn. I take a deep breath, overcoming my dread. She was leaving for London and she wasn't leaving in disgrace. Far from it. She was leaving to do the season. I would like to leave it here, at this happy place, but I know I must read on. Not just for me and my brother, but for the Deverills too. Uncle Bertie deserves to know what happened to his sister. Kitty deserves to know what happened to her aunt. I realize that my mother wanted it so. Why else would she have left me her diary?

April
Oh! It is a delight to be in London. Rupert has entertained us all the way from Ballinakelly. I think he is more excited than I am. Charlotte was overcome with sickness on the crossing – it was frightfully rough – and had to be revived with brandy and water. Rupert said she turned as green as a frog and once the sickness had passed (we had to wait at the port for an hour for it to do so) he made silly jokes, asking whether she'd change into a princess if he kissed her. She was not amused. Rupert has the charm to make anyone laugh – but evidently not Charlotte. She is determined not to crack a smile and is doing a fine job of it.

We took the train to London. It was very civilized.

*I looked out of the window all the way while Charlotte
recovered in sleep and regained her colour. Rupert wrote
rhyming couplets about her because she slept with her mouth
open, like a corpse, which made me roar with laughter. Really,
he is mean, and I mean to laugh with him. He needs no
encouragement and should be ashamed of himself! Really, it's
very unfair of Mama to make me bring her. What am I going
to do with her in London?*

*Stoke and Augusta have a lovely townhouse. It is in
a leafy square in the heart of Mayfair, near Hyde Park.
Augusta is quick to point out that it is not only pretty but
fashionable too. Everyone wants to live in Mayfair, she says.
They also have a country retreat in Wiltshire called Deverill
Rising, which I shall visit in August. But I don't want to go
to the countryside, however lovely it is. Rupert says Augusta
is notorious for her grand house parties. She invites interesting
people like politicians and writers, and they entertain
themselves riding, picnicking, shooting (which is excellent,
according to Bertie) and dancing – well, it sounds just like
Castle Deverill! I've spent my entire life in the countryside,
doing all those things, and I'm now thoroughly bored of it.
I'm excited to be in the city. The greatest city in the world!
London. I have no desire to go anywhere else.*

*Fortunately, the house is big enough for me and Charlotte
not to have to share a room. Charlotte is on the floor above
(the house has six floors!). I hope she stays there! Rupert
is next door. I can hear him singing through the wall as I
write. There is a little desk in front of the window, which
looks out onto the garden at the back, and a dressing table
with a mirror. My trunk has arrived at last and a maid is
unpacking it. She hangs up my dresses on hooks – I have
brought day dresses, tea dresses, evening dresses, ballgowns,*

Augusta says in London a lady has to change four times a day
at the very least. The maid lays out my silver brushes and
tortoiseshell combs and I ask her to arrange water for a bath
for I'm dusty after the long journey. I feel quite at home here.
Unfortunately, I promised to write to Ronald. I'd rather not,
but considering his threat to come and join me here in town, it
is a small price to pay for freedom.

As for Dermot, I cast him a thought only because I miss
his caresses. I know I shall find amusement here which will
eclipse him. We have had fun, the two of us. It gives me a
frisson of pleasure to think how the knowledge of it would
shock Mama, and the Shrubs – even Aunt Poppy, who takes
my side on most things. Goodness, Papa would disown me!
I have a feeling Grandma would understand though, not that
she would approve of it becoming public knowledge, however.
But I sense she has experienced something of illicit pleasure
herself. Didn't she say as much that evening by the fire?

Tonight we remain at home to recover from our journey,
but tomorrow night Augusta is throwing a soirée for us. For
Rupert and me, so that we can meet people. Augusta says
London is such a small town everyone is bored of each other
and in search of new blood. Isn't that exciting? Tomorrow she
is going to take me shopping. She says the fashion in Dublin
is out of date and that I need to have frocks that show me to
my best advantage. I certainly don't want to look provincial!
Rupert says she is determined to find me a husband. I told
Rupert that if he's not careful, she'll find him a wife. He just
grinned at me and said that she's welcome to try.

Day two
London is a brilliant sight during the season. Augusta has
flowers sent up from Deverill Rising every week, along with

*hot house peaches and grapes. We are living like kings. This
morning we went to Rotten Row. It is where London's most
fashionable congregate, from eleven to one, to stroll, chat and
watch elegant ladies in braided habits riding side-saddle in
the park, escorted by dashing cavaliers in frock coats and tall
silk hats. Augusta tells me that every evening, by Grosvenor
Gate, people line up to see the Princess of Wales passing in
her carriage. I would very much like to see her and hope that
we shall go. But Augusta says we are going to be very busy.
Cards are already being dropped into the house. During the
season there are twelve postal deliveries a day. Fancy that!
The streets are heavy with traffic! Carriages and coaches and
omnibuses, horses and carts and people. The rustle and bustle
of a busy city, clattering over the cobbles. It is thrilling. I have
to comment, however, on the smell. It really is a very dirty
place. Mud piles up on the carriageways. Of course it's not
mud at all but manure from the horses, and little boys run in
between the carriages to shovel it away. I suppose the quantity
of horses makes it impossible to keep the streets clean! And
the sooty smog is thick too, and sticky. I cannot imagine what
it must be like in winter when everyone is lighting their coal
fires to keep warm. Augusta says one simply can't wear white
in the day, because it is grey by the time one returns home.
There is much construction work, the skyline is a forest of
scaffolding. It's very noisy too. Augusta took me down Oxford
Street in the carriage, just for the fun of it. I have never seen
so many shops and so much activity. We spent all morning
buying fabric and trimmings, then visited Augusta's tailor in
Piccadilly (the finest in London, according to Augusta) who is
now making me some dresses and is going to restyle a few of
my own to bring them up to date. If it's new blood they want,
it shall be rich and bright and dazzling.*

*In the afternoon we called on a friend of Augusta's, who is
so fat she makes Augusta look like a twig, and her surprisingly
pretty daughter, Mary, who is a few years older than me and
engaged to a very suitable man. Goodness, didn't I tire of
hearing about him. He's the son of a baronet (like Ronald)
and cousin (distant, I imagine, because there was a great deal of
hand-waving and vagueness) to the Duke of Northumberland.
Mary is very taken with him and clearly thrilled to have pleased
her mama (who goes pink in the face, like a beetroot, whenever
his name is mentioned). Mary has an older brother called
Henry who is not attached. Mrs Pilkington, for that is the
name of Augusta's fat friend, looked me over like I was a prize
cow at the country fair and Augusta, who has never mastered
the art of subtlety, listed my accomplishments (of which there
are few in comparison to those of these English girls who play
the piano, speak fluent French, paint and dance and sing like
wood nymphs) and those of my family – really, one would think
the Deverills were the ruling family of Ireland! If Henry has
inherited any of his mother's features he will be of no interest to
me. I already have an admirer who is pink, porky and pinguid!
What was far more entertaining, however, was listening to them
talk of 'poor, dear Jane Rutley'(whoever she is) who has lost
her heart to a man in trade. Oh the horror of a man 'in trade'.
What would they think of Dermot McLoughlin, I ask myself?
I think losing one's heart is a very dangerous thing. I will do
my utmost to avoid it.*

*Mrs Pilkington is overexcited about the 'Phaseolus
coccineus' as she calls girls from America who are invading
London in order to hunt for titled husbands. When she
explains that the 'Phaseolus coccineus' is an American variety
of climbing runner bean I am very amused. She is beside
herself with indignation. American women, she claims, are*

coarse, brash creatures who speak their minds, are much too independent and throw their money around. She laments that they will take the cream of our aristocracy. I dare say the impoverished aristocracy could do with their money. I wonder what Mama and Papa would think if Rupert came home with an American! Darling Rupert, I wouldn't put it past him to do something most outrageous. I secretly hope he will.

As for me, there seems little chance of me being given the opportunity to do anything outrageous. There are rules by which I must abide. I must not venture down St James's Street on account of the gentlemen's clubs there. If I do happen to pass in a carriage I must lower my eyes. I must not stray to the north side of Piccadilly for that is where bachelors have their chambers. Burlington Arcade, a delightful shopping street, is forbidden in the afternoons because it is frequented by street walkers. At balls, I must not sit out with a young man, or dance more than three times with the same one. Really, it's highly amusing. We girls are like fragile flowers and must be protected, watched over and guarded to ensure that we are pure on our wedding night. Well, this flower has a stain on her petals. Still, I am grateful to Mama for bringing me up in such freedom. Charlotte says English girls are not so fortunate.

I am very entertained by my mother's account of London. It is thrilling to read about the London season – and the invasion from across the Atlantic. I find myself laughing out loud at her irreverence and her hilarious descriptions of people. What I find the most fascinating is her lack of snobbery. The Arethusa Clayton I knew was a woman of high social ambition and acute observation. With one withering look she could strip a person of their pretences and reveal their shortcomings before they had even opened their mouth. I assumed that less attractive side of her was due to her upbringing in the bogs of Ireland, parvenues are always more critical than those born into wealth, but I realize now that it couldn't have been. I cannot imagine why she minded so much that I found a wealthy husband and Logan married a suitable girl. Those were my father's ideals, not hers. Maybe she took them on when she married him, as she took on his religion. He was, after all, a very strong, overpowering man. Yet, reading her words, I cannot reconcile the two personalities.

Kitty knocks on my door. She pokes her head round and smiles. 'Found anything?' she asks.

I sigh. 'Nothing to explain the falling-out. I haven't got that far yet. She's in London and it's all wonderful.'

'The calm before the storm,' says Kitty.

'I think so,' I reply. 'I'm being lulled into a false sense of security.'

'Come downstairs and have some tea. Papa has brought some old photo albums to show you. I think you'll be amused.'

'How exciting!' I close the diary and follow her onto the landing.

'Did you have a nice walk with Cormac?' she asks as we go downstairs.

'It poured with rain and we got soaked.'

'Oh dear. That's Ireland for you. It comes upon you without warning.'

'We had to take refuge in a derelict cabin.' She glances at me and arches an eyebrow, reminding me of Cormac.

I laugh. 'I'm a married woman,' I exclaim in mock horror.

'Isn't it lucky then that your husband isn't here.'

I am startled. I don't know which way to take her comment. But before I have time to reply we are in the hall and heading towards the drawing room. The butler has lit a fire

and there is a tray of tea and cake on the centre table. Uncle
Bertie rises to his feet to greet me. He is alone. I don't suppose
Aunt Maud is very interested in old photograph albums, or
perhaps she has seen them before. In any case, we sit down,
Uncle Bertie between myself and Kitty on the sofa, and open
the first album across our knees. I am riveted by the black-
and-white pictures of my mother. They are formal and posed.
She is a pretty young woman with a tiny waist, long dark hair
and, in spite of the stiff arrangements of the photographs, she
always has an amused look on her face. In fact, I comment
on it because she looks mischievous. Rupert is as I imagined.
Tall and broad with dark hair and eyes, and full, pouting lips.
Uncle Bertie was flaxen-haired and shorter than his brother,
but equally good-looking. No wonder Maud fell in love with
him. After a while I find my eyes searching for Adeline on all
the pages, because she looks so like me. Of course, the photographs are not in colour, but I spot her immediately in the
same way I would spot myself. I especially like the ones of her
sitting side-saddle on a horse, with her hair up and a veil over
her eyes, her long black dress falling down the horse's flanks.
She looks elegant and confident. Kitty tells me that *she* used
to ride side-saddle as a young woman and I imagine she must
have looked very much like her grandmother too. I catch her
eye and grin. I feel blessed to have found my family and blessed
to have been accepted by them. How very different my life
would have been had Mom not turned her back on her past.

Later, as I settle down to read more of her diary, I sense that
tonight I will find out why. I prepare myself for the advance of
the storm.

Chapter 16

London
The Past

Arethusa was swept up in a dizzying whirl of soirées, dinner parties and balls under Augusta's close supervision. With no daughters of her own Augusta relished having a young lady in the house to show off and spoil. Arethusa did not disappoint her new world. She was considered beautiful, entertaining and spirited, although a few of Society's matrons criticized her for being as outspoken and bold as the Americans. 'She has a brazen look in her eyes which is not ladylike,' said one disparaging observant. 'Well, my dear, you know what the Anglo-Irish are like,' said another. Indeed, the Anglo-Irish were famous for their wild hunts and reckless riding habits, but this reputation only served to enhance Arethusa's appeal among her suitors. When compared to the demure, subservient English girls, Arethusa was refreshing.

As for Rupert, he accompanied his sister everywhere, which made Charlotte, the miserable governess and chaperone, more miserable than ever for she felt redundant and unappreciated. She was left alone in the parlour to do her needlepoint, or to call upon friends whom she knew from her previous incarnations as governess to other well-to-do young ladies, all the while her charge blazed a trail around London on the arm of her brother.

Rupert and Arethusa threw themselves wholeheartedly into their new London life. In the mornings they rode in Hyde Park (for two people who didn't much like riding they put on a fine show of Anglo-Irish horsemanship for the admiring crowds who observed them). Arethusa, sitting side-saddle, cut a dash with her small waist, tight bodice and discreet veil, while Rupert, in pearl-grey trousers, frock coat and top hat, attracted gasps of appreciation from mothers and daughters alike. They went for daily carriage rides, greeting their growing circle of friends with smiles and waves, promenaded beneath the plane trees and watched the children playing rounders and bowling hoops in Kensington Gardens. In the afternoons they drove to Hurlingham, Roehampton or Ranelagh to watch the inter-guards polo matches, and stood in the Strangers' Gallery at the House of Commons to listen to debates. They were invited to the theatre and the ballet, to concerts, small five o'clock tea parties in private houses and elaborate garden parties thrown by ambassadors and visiting grandees from Europe, keen to rub shoulders with the English aristocracy. There was Royal Ascot and Goodwood, Henley Royal Regatta and Cowes Week. They barely had time to catch their breath.

Rupert was besieged by strident, ambitious mothers, determined to ensnare him for their daughters. Although he was a second son and not in possession of a great fortune, he was nonetheless of a good family (the brother of the future Lord Deverill of Ballinakelly) and devilishly handsome too. He charmed the mothers, flattered the daughters, but made not one proposal. By June Arethusa had received four. Had

Ronald known, he would have come to London immediately, bent the knee and proposed, but he did not. Arethusa
deliberately omitted that piece of information in her regular
correspondence.

At the beginning of June she was finally presented at Court.
A moment Augusta had been waiting for with much anxiety,
for once presented, Arethusa would have the Queen's seal of
approval and entry into the grandest houses in London.

Dressed in her finest low-cut, short-sleeved white gown
with its three yards of train, a trio of white ostrich feathers in
her hair, a diaphanous veil and long white gloves, Arethusa
set off in the family state coach, emblazoned with the Deverill
arms and driven by a bewigged coachman seated in front on
a splendid hammer-cloth, with Augusta by her side. Behind,
hanging on to embroidered straps at the back, were powdered
footmen in the Deverill family livery. Crowds of spectators
gathered along the Mall and at the Palace gates to watch the
debutantes arriving in their finest gowns and jewels. As they
queued to enter the Palace forecourt Arethusa noticed a portly
little man running from coach to coach in a state of great
excitement. 'He's a hairdresser,' Augusta informed her, with
a sniff of disapproval. 'Hurrying to make last-minute adjust-
ments to his clients' veils and feathers, I suspect.' She looked
at her charge with pride. 'With regard to you, my dear, one
cannot improve on perfection.'

Once inside, Arethusa was nervous. She knew what to do.
Goodness, she had practised her curtsey enough times and
how to walk backwards while holding her train, curtseying
again with every step. Arethusa knew that, as she belonged
to an aristocratic family, she was to receive the Queen's kiss.
Daughters of Commoners kissed the Queen's hand and had
to take off a glove beforehand prior to entering the Drawing

Room, which was most inconvenient. 'Don't be nervous, my dear,' said Augusta, as they waited in line. 'This is a proud, proud moment and one you shall remember for the rest of your life. When I was presented, the girl in front of me froze mid-curtsey and had to be rescued by a courtier.'

'I do hope that doesn't happen to me,' said Arethusa, wishing that Augusta had not mentioned it.

'Good Lord no! Strong, well-bred girls like you don't need any help sinking to their knees and up again. You're born to curtsey, Tussy dear.'

The waiting seemed to go on for hours. There were no refreshments or comforts of any kind in the stiff, formal atmosphere of the Palace. Arethusa waited, holding her bouquet of flowers and wishing the time would go faster so the whole dreary business would be over. When at last her name was announced, she walked confidently across the crimson carpet into the Queen's Drawing Room. There sat the Queen, looking weary, and, Arethusa thought, much like a trout. The room was full of courtiers, footmen, ladies-in-waiting and equerries, the air so stifling that Arethusa was very pleased when it was all over. She had curtseyed, been kissed by the Queen and had left the royal presence backwards without fault, as she had been taught to do. Augusta was very proud. 'However, I did notice that your walk has a little too much bounce in it,' she said, giving her charge a stern look. 'Had your governess taught you to walk with a book on your head, as English girls are taught deportment, the bounce would have been subdued.' But Arethusa had no intention of subduing her bounce and, that evening, she bounced merrily into the Duchess of Sutcliffe's ball with Rupert by her side and Augusta on Stoke's arm behind her, trying not to be alarmed by the confidence in her walk.

The house, one of the largest in London, was festooned with roses sent up from the Sutcliffe country estate. There were garlands winding up the banisters on the marble staircase and cascades trailing from the chandeliers in the hall. The Duchess herself stood at the top of the staircase with her flaxen-haired daughter, Lady Alexandra, to receive their guests, and as Rupert and Arethusa reached them, Lady Alexandra smiled at Rupert and blushed a deep scarlet. Rupert kissed her gloved hand and allowed his eyes to linger on her shiny brown ones for longer than was necessary. 'I think you have an admirer there,' said Arethusa as they walked on into the ballroom, which was gradually filling with guests.

'Pretty little thing, isn't she?' said Rupert casually, taking two crystal flutes of champagne and giving one to his sister. 'But easily outshone by her dashing brother Peregrine.'

'You mean your new best friend, Peregrine.'

'He's an interesting fellow.'

'Indeed, he is. Having a grand title and a big estate certainly helps,' Arethusa replied. 'Wouldn't Augusta be thrilled if I bagged a marquess and a future duke?'

'And I suppose you are going to pretend that you're impervious to such trivialities?'

'You know as well as I do that he wouldn't look at a lowly Miss Deverill, Rupert. He'll go for a woman with a fortune, and I, sadly, do not have one.' She grinned at him. 'I don't think you have one big enough for Lady Alexandra, either.'

'Well, isn't that a shame,' Rupert replied distractedly, running his eyes around the room. Being so tall he was able to see over all the heads. 'Ah, and there *is* the beautiful Marquess of Penrith. Come, let's go and say hello.'

They weaved through the throng, doing their best not to

get lured into conversation with anyone else before reaching him. When Peregrine saw Rupert he swiftly ended the conversation he was having with a dowager duchess and her simpering granddaughter and gave him a broad, grateful smile. 'Ah, Rupert old fellow, how good to see you.'

'Peregrine,' said Rupert. The two men shook hands with vigour.

Peregrine settled his gunmetal-grey eyes onto Arethusa and bowed. She gave him her hand and he kissed it. 'Miss Deverill, how nice to see you again.'

'And you, Lord Penrith. I do believe this is the most spectacular ball I have yet been to. The roses take my breath away.'

'Mama has spent months in the planning. She'll be thrilled that you appreciate her hard work.'

'Oh, I do, very much. It's quite the most enchanting ballroom in London.'

He turned his lovely eyes onto Rupert. 'Mama has hired a very special kind of entertainment for her guests tonight,' he said quietly.

'Ah, how like the Duchess to entertain with *entrain*,' said Rupert, knowing little of the Duchess and whether or not she liked to be original.

'Have you heard of the Madison Minstrels from New York? No? Well, allow me to let you in on a little secret, which won't be secret for much longer because they are due to start shortly after the Prince and Princess of Wales arrive.' Peregrine's eyes gleamed with excitement. He looked from Arethusa to Rupert, relishing keeping them in suspense. 'George and Jonas are brothers and they play the banjo.'

'The banjo?' said Arethusa. 'What's a banjo?'

'It's an instrument which resembles a small violin but is unique to America. It's going to be all the rage, you know.

After tonight everyone will want to play one. They are performing in London and then they are travelling the country.
Apparently, they're heading to Manchester after London and
on to Glasgow and Edinburgh. Mama heard them when they
gave a private recital for the Princess of Wales and managed
to get them to come tonight, before they begin their tour. It's
really quite a coup.' He looked from one to the other. 'Do you
know what makes them so very special?'

'I can't imagine,' said Rupert.

'They're black.' His eyes gleamed.

'Black?' Arethusa repeated.

'Well, that *is* exciting. I can't wait to hear them.'

'They are raising funds for a Christian school in New Jersey.'

'That's a noble cause,' said Arethusa approvingly.

'Indeed it is, which is why we must support them. I
think Alexandra is going to have banjo lessons while they're
in London.'

'Oh, I *am* jealous. I'd adore to learn how to play the banjo,'
said Arethusa. 'It would amuse me greatly to be able to list
banjo playing among my accomplishments!'

Peregrine laughed. 'I'm not sure whether or not you're
being serious, Miss Deverill.'

'Tussy is rarely serious about anything,' said Rupert.

'Oh, I'm perfectly serious about this,' retorted Arethusa.

Peregrine looked at Rupert and held his gaze. 'Perhaps it
can be arranged,' he said thoughtfully. 'We'd very much like
to see more of you, of *both* of you. You could *both* come. Mama
always has company for tea. You could help me entertain the
old ladies, Rupert. What do you say?'

'I'm very good at entertaining old ladies,' said Rupert.

'Good, I'll see what can be arranged. Now you must excuse
me,' Peregrine whispered. 'I must go and and stand with my

family. I will catch you later.' Arethusa noticed him lightly touch Rupert's arm before disappearing into the throng.

A moment later the ballroom went quiet. A frisson of anticipation rippled through the warm air. Everyone looked to the double doors in expectation. There was a murmur of voices and a rustle of silk as the Duke and Duchess, their daughter, Lady Alexandra, and Peregrine accompanied the royal party into the room, where they remained with every eye upon them. There came three bangs of a staff upon the floor and then the Prince and Princess of Wales were announced in a loud and pompous voice by a footman wearing Sutcliffe green-and-gold livery. The ladies dropped to the ground in deep curtseys and the gentlemen bowed.

The Princess of Wales walked in on the arm of her husband in a blue dress, as pale as a duck's egg, with an exquisite sapphire necklace sparkling at her throat. She had poise and dignity and a somewhat solemn air, but she was beautiful in a handsome way and Arethusa couldn't take her eyes off her. She radiated grandeur, serenity and majesty. The Prince swept the room with his big watery blue eyes and smiled at one or two of the prettier ladies, a smile that was barely perceptible behind his grey beard.

Presently the Duchess took to the stage, which had been set up at the far end of the room. Once again everyone went quiet. 'Your Royal Highnesses, my Lords, Ladies and Gentlemen,' she said. 'It gives me great pleasure tonight to welcome a very special pair of brothers, who have come all the way from America to bring their music to our country. I'm sure you will find them as entertaining as I do. Please will you give a very warm welcome to the Madison Minstrels.'

Arethusa would have clapped but she was holding a glass of champagne. She watched two men in crisp white shirts and black tailcoats step onto the stage with their little banjos and give a bow. Their skin was a rich, mahogany brown, such as Arethusa had never seen before, and lustrous, like satin. The two of them were so dark that the whites of their eyes shone brightly by contrast. They began to play. The twangy sound of the banjo made everyone smile. The smiles grew wider when, in clear tenor voices, they began to sing 'A Boy's Best Friend Is His Mother'. Arethusa couldn't take her gaze off them. The Duchess, who was standing between her son Peregrine and the Princess of Wales, laughed in delight. The Minstrels began to do a soft-toe dance, moving lightly across the stage. Soon toes were tapping in the audience and Arethusa was swaying to the rhythm along with everyone else. They sang 'Home, Sweet Home' and finally 'Star Of The Night Waltz'. When they stood to take their bow there was a thunder of applause.

'I must meet them,' said Arethusa to Rupert when the brothers were escorted off the stage.

'Then you need to find Lady Alexandra.'

'You have to come with me,' she insisted. 'She thinks you're marvellous.'

'Very well, come on then.' But they didn't get further than a few feet before they were accosted by Mary Pilkington and her friends Lady Clarissa Wellbroke and Lady Julia Almstead. Rupert, who had no intention of being waylaid by three such uninspiring young women, bowed and kissed hands before making a hasty retreat, leaving Arethusa in the awkward position of having to make polite conversation. 'Weren't the Madison Minstrels a delight,' she said.

'They were wonderful!' Mary Pilkington exclaimed. 'Did you notice the Princess of Wales's foot was tapping?'

'Yes, I did, and she was swaying to the music too,' added Lady Clarissa.

'I overheard Lady Alexandra saying that her mama has already booked her a lesson. Did you know that the Prince of Wales has requested one too?' gushed Lady Julia.

'How do you know that?' asked Lady Clarissa, put out.

'Because my mama had tea here yesterday and the Duchess told her.'

'Goodness, the whole of London will be wanting lessons,' said Lady Julia mournfully. 'I doubt they'll have time for me.'

'If the whole of London learns to play the banjo it won't be original anymore,' said Arethusa, whose enthusiasm for banjo lessons had suddenly deflated. 'It's only worth doing if no one else is doing it.'

At that moment her attention was diverted by the animated gestures of a vivacious girl she hadn't yet met. Her dress was exquisite and obviously expensive and her poise remarkable. There was something very *un*English about her that sparked Arethusa's interest. She was talking to an older, buxom lady Arethusa assumed to be the girl's mother. There was something brash about the pair of them. A brashness that appealed to Arethusa in the same way a glittery thing might appeal to a magpie.

'Who's that?' she asked, nodding in the girl's direction. The ladies turned to look, then stiffened and lifted their haughty noses.

'She's American,' said Lady Clarissa in a nasal voice. 'She's frightfully rich and after a duke, I suspect. I don't know what it is about these American girls, but Englishmen can't get enough of them.'

'They're bold,' said Lady Julia disapprovingly. 'Mama says it's the ones who can't make a success of themselves in New York who come over here to bag dukes. You know, some of them even pay vast sums for sponsors to introduce them to

Society. Then they return to New York and are welcomed with open arms by the grandest ladies in the city. Americans can't resist English titles, apparently.'

'Do you think her mama has paid a vast sum to get her presented?' asked Mary Pilkington, exposing her sense of superiority with a smug smile.

'Oh, I would say most likely,' said Lady Clarissa. 'And I dare say it will pay off. We're probably looking at the next Countess of Ronaldshay.'

'American women really know how to dress, don't they?' said Arethusa, ignoring their gossip and admiring the American girl's gown. It was embellished with small pink flowers that shimmered in the light of the chandeliers. 'I suspect it's from Worth.'

Lady Clarissa frowned. 'It's exceedingly *mal vu* to flash money in the way the Americans do,' she said crisply. 'I dare say she has fifty gowns by Worth. My mama says one can make the bottle as lavish as you please but if the wine's no good ...' She turned up her nose and inhaled through her nostrils, pursing her thin lips with displeasure.

At that moment Mary's fiancé appeared, as pink, porky and pinguid as Ronald, and Arethusa took the opportunity to move off. She decided to go and introduce herself to the American, even though, or possibly because, the three snooty girls she'd just been speaking to would think it very *mal vu*.

'I don't believe we've met,' she said. 'I'm Arethusa Deverill.'

The girl gave her a lofty took, but Arethusa could see the glimmer of gratitude behind it. 'My name is Margherita Stubbs,' replied the girl, 'and this is my mother, Mrs Stubbs.'

'How do you do,' said Arethusa.

'You're bold for an English girl,' remarked Mrs Stubbs,

narrowing her sharp little eyes and cooling her glowing face with an exquisite feather fan.

'I'm not an English girl,' said Arethusa brightly. Margherita raised her eyebrows.

Mrs Stubbs said, 'Oh?' and raised hers.

'I'm Anglo-Irish and there's a difference.' Arethusa wanted to be very clear about that.

'I should say there is,' said Mrs Stubbs, looking Arethusa up and down. The corners of her lips curled into a smile.

'Most English girls view us Americans with suspicion,' said Margherita and there was a regretful edge to her voice which Arethusa noticed and felt sorry for. If there was one thing she couldn't abide it was judgemental people.

'Only because they're threatened by you. You dress better, for a start,' said Arethusa. 'I guess your couturier is the famous Worth.'

Margherita's face brightened. 'How do you know?'

Arethusa laughed. 'Because all the most beautiful dresses are his creations. Not that I've ever been lucky enough to wear one.'

'I'll leave you girls to it,' said Mrs Stubbs, her eyes straying into the throng. She closed her fan and tapped Margherita's arm with it. 'Don't dawdle too long, my dear, I haven't brought you all the way from America to chat to the girls!'

As the formidable Mrs Stubbs moved away the two girls laughed. 'She's relentless!' said Margherita with a sigh. 'If she doesn't marry me off to a duke she'll consider the whole enterprise a terrible failure.'

'What's wrong with American men?' Arethusa asked.

'Mama wants a title.' She laughed again. 'And what Mama wants, Mama usually gets. Poor Papa is miles away in New York, signing the cheques.'

'He'll have to sign a very large one if you land yourself a duke. They don't come cheap, you know.'

Margherita frowned. 'You're exceedingly outspoken, Miss Deverill.'

'I have an older brother who tells me how the world works. He's outspoken too, but somehow it's acceptable in a man. Please call me Tussy. Everyone does.'

'I like you, Tussy. I think you and I could be friends.'

'I'd like that very much,' said Arethusa, who after a couple of months in London had not until this moment found a girl she liked enough to be her confidante. 'Do you know how I can meet those Minstrels?' she asked.

'Come with me,' said Margherita with a grin. 'This is where being American has its advantages. No one is surprised when we're strident!' And indeed, no one was.

The two women waited their turn, for the brothers were talking to a group of excited ladies, eager to find out how *they* could acquire a banjo. But they didn't have to wait long. Presently, Mr Crawford, who was escorting the Minstrels around the room, introducing them to the guests as if they were royalty, bowed to Arethusa and Margherita.

'Miss Stubbs and Miss Deverill,' said Margherita, extending her hand.

Arethusa felt as if her heart had been struck by Cupid's arrow. She stared at Jonas. He stared back at her and in that fleeting moment there passed between them an imperceptible quiver of energy that was not noticed by anyone in the vicinity, besides the two who had created it. He took her hand. She faltered a second, swallowed into his dark and alluring gaze, but a blink enabled her to focus and smile graciously as she had been brought up to do. It wasn't until he let go of her hand that she remembered to take a breath. 'Your music is so wonderfully original,' said Margherita, and Arethusa was grateful because she didn't think she was capable of saying a word. 'Really, I was moved and entertained in equal measure. Surely, you will play again?'

'Not tonight, Miss Stubbs,' said George Madison.

'I suspect banjo playing will be all the rage now that you have made it fashionable,' Margherita continued.

'We have the most finely crafted banjos from America, if you would like to purchase one,' George continued.

Arethusa knew she must speak. If she didn't speak, she would give herself away. 'I would very much like to play the banjo,' she said, then cleared her throat, for her voice had come out thin and reedy. 'Is it difficult to learn?'

'I find that even students who are not particularly talented learn to play to an acceptable standard,' said Jonas, without taking his brown eyes off Arethusa, as if he *couldn't* take them off.

'Will you be staying in London long?' Arethusa asked. The thought of this beautiful man slipping out of her world was suddenly unbearable.

'We leave for Manchester at the end of July,' said Jonas. Arethusa's mind raced as she contemplated the short amount of time they were to spend in London. She could think of nothing more to say. Her mind had gone blank and she stood like a stunned animal, eyes wide, cheeks aflame, feeling the full force of infatuation for the first time in her life.

'It's been a pleasure meeting you, Miss Stubbs, Miss Deverill ...' George Madison gave a bow, Jonas followed suit. Arethusa was suddenly short of breath. As the brothers were taken off and introduced to other guests, she put a hand on her stomach.

'I think I need some air,' she said, overcome by a wave of nausea.

'Are you all right?' Margherita asked anxiously.

'I think I'm going to faint.'

Margherita looked about in panic. She couldn't let Arethusa sink to the floor, not in the presence of royalty. She caught eyes with a tall, fair-haired man, who swiftly responded to her alarm. 'Might I be of assistance?' he said, putting his hand beneath Arethusa's elbow to steady her.

'My friend, Miss Deverill, is about to faint,' Margherita replied.

Rupert, who was standing close, heard the name Deverill and turned to see his sister, as pale as a lily and wilting like one too, sinking into the arms of the Marquess of Penrith. 'Good Lord!' he exclaimed, hastening to her side. 'Tussy, what the devil's come over you? Let's get you out of here at once,' he said, holding her round the waist.

Peregrine watched them leave the room. Then he turned back to Margherita. 'Lord Penrith,' he said, taking her hand and bringing it to his lips.

'Miss Stubbs,' she replied and gave him her most dazzling smile.

Chapter 17

Arethusa recovered in the conservatory leading off from the ballroom. There, in the cool, fragrant company of palm trees and flowers, she gradually defeated her nausea and managed to breathe calmly again. Rupert, lounging in one of the basket chairs, assumed she'd been overcome by the novelty of the two black men in their midst. 'I suppose they could be quite shocking to an unworldly girl like you,' he said, but Arethusa wasn't in the mood to be teased and ignored him. 'You were rescued by Peregrine,' he added, hoping to curry favour. 'I should think every girl in the ballroom would have liked to have been in your position at that moment.' He laughed, then shrugged. 'Every cloud has a silver lining.'

'I'm not shocked by the black men, Rupert,' said Arethusa crossly. 'I find them both charming and talented. It was a pleasure to meet them.'

'Perhaps it was Peregrine who caused you to faint,' he suggested.

'Peregrine came to my rescue *because* I was fainting. He was not the cause of it.'

'Then what caused it, I wonder?' He scratched his chin melodramatically and frowned.

'My silly corset,' she replied dismissively, putting a hand on her stomach again. 'It's much too tight.'

'And all that standing. You should sit down with the other old ladies.' He chuckled and Arethusa smiled reluctantly. 'Shall we return to the ballroom? There are quadrilles and polkas and waltzes to dance and I know how much you like dancing. I dare say your dance card is already full.'

'And what about you, Rupert? Are you going to continue to tease all those poor girls who feel faint in *your* company?' She grinned and Rupert could tell she was feeling better.

Arethusa returned to the ball. She searched for Jonas Madison in the crowd, but the Madison brothers were nowhere to be found. The Duchess must think them suitable for entertainment but not for dinner, she thought unhappily. They had gone.

That night Arethusa couldn't sleep. She lay staring at the ceiling where Jonas's dark eyes stared back at her. She pictured his handsome face, more handsome than any she had ever seen. In fact, handsome was a common word, she thought, considering the amount of handsome men she had met during her stay in London. No, Jonas was *beautiful*, and she hadn't met any beautiful men, ever. She recalled the way his lips curled when he smiled, the way his white teeth shone against his satiny brown skin, the way he had looked right into her. It was as if he had reached in and taken her heart. No one had done that before. No one had got near it. But Jonas, in the first moment of their meeting, had taken it. She put a hand to her forehead in despair. How was she ever going to see him again? She didn't care about the gentlemen who had proposed, they were insignificant now, chinless and as pink as plucked chickens. She didn't care about Ronald, either. Even Lord Penrith left her unmoved in spite of his title and estates and all the prestige that went with them. She cared for nothing and no one but Jonas.

However, Arethusa knew very well that Jonas was *more* than unsuitable, he was forbidden. There was nowhere in the world a woman like her and a man like him could even be acquaintances, let alone friends. It wasn't even worth contemplating, and yet, Arethusa couldn't stop herself. She was in love and the feeling was intoxicating. It made her rash; it made her brave.

The following two days were a struggle. Arethusa went through the motions as if her body knew very well what to do in the absence of her mind. She attended the usual social functions and smiled graciously, but everything looked less bright. It was as if London had lost its lustre. Her heart ached for Jonas. It was as if she were carrying a leaden weight in her chest. With every step it grew heavier. How it could trouble her so, having only met him once, was bewildering. But he dominated her every moment and without him the days were monotonous and bland.

Arethusa awoke on the third morning, feigning a headache. She didn't think she could push herself through another gruelling round of parties with such a melancholy heart and announced at breakfast that she would stay at home with Charlotte, in order to recover. Charlotte, who was quietly sipping tea at the end of the table, looked up in pleasant surprise. However, her hopes were swiftly dashed when a handwritten letter was delivered by a footman in the Sutcliffe family livery, embossed in gold with the Sutcliffe crest. Augusta, who had been busy feeding her Pekinese bacon from her plate, wiped her greasy fingers on a napkin then opened it with a trembling hand. It was from the Duchess of Sutcliffe, requesting the pleasure of Miss Arethusa to join Lady Alexandra that afternoon at 3 p.m. for a banjo lesson with Mr Madison himself.

Arethusa's heart spluttered back to life. She hoped Mr Madison was Mr Jonas and not Mr George. How disappointing would it be were he Mr George! The Duchess had written underneath that she would very much like the company of Mr Rupert Deverill for tea as well.

'Have you struck up a friendship with Lady Alexandra?' Augusta asked, surprised.

Arethusa was as surprised as she was. 'No,' she replied. 'Or not that I'm aware of.'

Charlotte put down her teacup and listened with interest.

Rupert grinned. 'I think it is *I* you must shower with gratitude,' he said, buttering a piece of toast.

'How so?' asked Augusta.

'Because Lady Alexandra has a liking for him,' said Arethusa with a smile. 'She blushes scarlet whenever she lays eyes on him.'

'And do *you* have a liking for *her*?' asked Augusta with mounting excitement.

'She's quite pretty, if one is attracted to mice,' he replied.

Charlotte looked horrified. Arethusa laughed. 'Oh Rupert! How mean you are!' she snorted.

'How very *clever* you are, Rupert,' said Augusta admiringly. 'So Lady Alexandra is using Tussy to get to Rupert. And Lord Penrith is interested in *you*, Tussy, perhaps?'

'Oh, Peregrine is not interested in *me*,' said Arethusa. Augusta looked disappointed. 'I would guess that he's interested in Margherita Stubbs and *she* is my friend. At the Sutcliffe ball the other night he danced with her three times and was barely out of her company.'

'Isn't she the American girl?' Augusta asked, her face darkening resentfully.

'Yes, she's very rich,' Rupert replied. 'Nothing speaks

louder to an aristocrat like Peregrine than money. Marriage isn't for fun, you know,' he added, grinning at his sister. 'It's jolly expensive being a duke.'

'And jolly dull being a duchess, I should imagine,' said Arethusa provocatively.

'Tussy!' Augusta duly gasped. 'You'd be very lucky to be a duchess. Well, I'm not convinced Lord Penrith has his eye on your American friend. I'm sure the Duke and Duchess would strongly disapprove. It's new money and new money is frightfully common. Didn't Mr Stubbs make his money with a hardware store?'

'He did, Augusta. He made his fortune selling hammers and nails in San Francisco. His was the only hardware store when the gold rush came.'

'Very lucky,' said Augusta tightly. 'But it does not make him a gentleman.'

'Everyone must start somewhere, surely,' said Arethusa. 'I bet our ancestor Barton Deverill was as common as muck before King Charles gave him a title and lands to boast about. Anyway, why is there so much concern about a person's pedigree? Can't we like people simply because they're nice people? Does a dukedom make a man a better human being than, say, George or Jonas Madison, who are far more accomplished but quite possibly descended from slaves?' It was a throwaway line and yet, as soon as she had uttered the word 'slave' she felt so nauseated by it that she wished she hadn't said it. She knew enough about American history to know that it was likely to be so, and the thought of their people's suffering sickened her to the core.

Augusta looked perplexed. 'You get those opinions from your mama, no doubt. I would keep them to yourself, if I were you.' She gave Charlotte a stern look. 'It is *your* job, Charlotte, to educate this child, is it not? Opinions like hers are not fit to be spoken aloud!'

'I'm not sure I've heard them before,' said Charlotte in her defence, a little offended by Augusta's reproving tone.

'Then let's ensure that we do not hear them again.'

Arethusa sighed loudly and put a hand to her head, well aware that if she was indisposed afternoon tea with the Duchess of Sutcliffe would be off and Augusta would be bitterly disappointed. But Augusta ignored her dramatics. 'Now, I think I must reply at once to this thrilling invitation. My dear, it will be an education to learn how to play the banjo and advantageous to you to do so with Lady Alexandra. Perhaps you will become friends. Goodness, wait until I write and tell your mama.'

After breakfast, Arethusa followed Charlotte up to her bedroom. It was the first time since arriving in London that Arethusa had seen her governess's room. With a high brass bed, floral wallpaper and thick curtains it was most definitely not a servant's room. Sunshine streamed in through the little dormer windows and below, the street was already busy with carriages and people. Charlotte gave Arethusa a quizzical look. It wasn't habitual for her charge to seek her out, at least, not since she had been a child. In those days the young Arethusa had been curious to learn and intrigued by this new person who had arrived at the castle especially for her. She had followed her around like a puppy. But since Arethusa had grown up, her pursuit of independence had led her away from the schoolroom, and shaking off her governess had become a sport as diverting as hunting and croquet. Charlotte wasn't as much of a fool as Arethusa thought she was; after all, isn't it also sporting to give the player a chance?

Arethusa flopped onto Charlotte's bed, which had been neatly made without so much as a crease. She reached for the book on the bedside table and opened it absent-mindedly, but her eyes didn't take in a single word. 'Have you ever been in love, Charlotte?' she asked casually.

Charlotte frowned. 'I think everyone of my age has been in love at least once in their life, don't you?'

'But have *you*?'

There was a short pause. Charlotte hesitated, unsure how to answer. 'Yes,' she said at last, turning her eyes to the window. Then she sighed and feigned distraction. 'It'll be a lovely day for the park. If you're feeling up to it the sunshine will do you good.'

'Who was he and why didn't you marry him?' Arethusa persisted, forgetting that she had pretended to be unwell. She put down the book and looked at Charlotte's serious face. 'Did he hurt you?' she asked.

'Oh really, Tussy. You ask too many questions,' Charlotte replied briskly.

'Isn't that what I'm supposed to do? You're here to teach me about the world. So, teach me about love. So far, discussions about marriage have never had anything to do with love.'

Charlotte sat on the edge of the bed and put her small hands in her lap. 'I did love a man once, Tussy,' she conceded. 'I loved him very much.'

Surprised by this intriguing piece of information, Arethusa arranged herself so that she was lying back against the pillows and settled down for what she hoped would be a long and enlightening conversation. 'What happened?' she asked.

Charlotte was amused. It was a long time since the girl had asked her about herself. 'He was called Tom,' she told her. 'He was the elder brother of my charge, who was a very spoilt girl, but then American girls are much more indulged than English ones.'

'You've never told me about your American charge,' she said.

'Because you've never asked,' Charlotte replied.

This caused Arethusa a certain amount of unease. Could she really have been so impolite as to never ask her governess about herself? 'For how long were you in America?' she said.

'I was in New York for five years.'

'With the same family?'

'Yes.'

'And this Tom, did he love you back?'

Charlotte lowered her eyes. 'He did.'

Arethusa grinned. 'Was he very handsome?'

Charlotte smiled wistfully. 'He was tall, with dark brown hair and hazel eyes. He was sensitive and kind, but funny too, once I got to know him. His sister was loud and opinionated and wrapped both parents around her little finger, but Tom was gentle and unassuming. He was just a very good person.'

'Was it love at first sight? Did you feel as if you had been struck in the heart?'

Charlotte laughed and her plain face ceased to be plain and lit up prettily. 'It wasn't at first sight, no. It was something that grew over time.'

'Is there such a thing as love at first sight?' Arethusa asked hopefully.

'I do believe so. I don't think poets make it up. They're inspired by truth and experience. I think one would be very lucky to fall in love like that. It's very romantic.'

'When did you realize you were in love?'

'I can't recall exactly. But I do recall the way he made me feel every time he looked at me.'

'How did he make you feel?'

'Oh, it's silly, really.'

'No, it isn't. I want to know.'

Charlotte looked at Arethusa's eager face. 'All right. He made me feel nervous and happy. I lost the desire to eat or sleep. I became full of energy and enthusiasm. When you are in love, Tussy, the world suddenly looks beautiful. Everything in it is rendered lovelier.' Tussy hadn't noticed the world looking lovelier. In fact, Jonas had made her feel anxious and fearful, not nervous and happy. 'You will find, Tussy, that when you are in love you will like who you are when you're with him.'

'Who were you when you were with Tom?'

Charlotte's eyes shone and she lowered her gaze bashfully, focusing on her fingers neatly knitted in her lap. 'Tom made me feel beautiful,' she replied softly. Arethusa frowned. Charlotte could never have been beautiful. 'That's the wonderful thing about love,' she continued as if reading Arethusa's thoughts. 'In Tom's eyes, I was beautiful.'

'Did he want to marry you?'

'He did, and I would have married him, but his parents had other ideas.'

'That's awful. Whom did he marry in the end?'

Charlotte's smile faded and she suddenly looked sad. 'An heiress from Austin, Texas.'

'It's all about money, isn't it!' said Arethusa crossly and Charlotte assumed she was outraged on her behalf.

'Money makes the world go around,' Charlotte replied and she shrugged in the way passive people do who have no option but to accept their fate.

'I think it's wrong,' ejected Arethusa. 'One should marry for love. What's the point in living if one spends one's entire life with a man one doesn't love, just to be comfortable and to breed children who will suffer the same dull fate when they come of age. It's an empty, repetitive cycle and it's mad.'

Again, Charlotte frowned at her charge. Here was Arethusa,

who had never before considered the heart or even questioned the idea of marrying for status and wealth, talking about love and the futility of living without it. She narrowed her eyes and wondered what had inspired this sudden awakening. 'It's the way our world works,' she said and she tried to keep the regret out of her voice. Arethusa had to accept her fate and it was Charlotte's job to ensure she did.

'But you must have been so terribly hurt,' said Arethusa with feeling. 'I mean, if you loved him very much, it must have been unbearable to have had to live without him.'

Charlotte's cheeks coloured. She had never heard Arethusa speak with such passion, indeed she had never spoken to anyone about Tom Burnett and now Arethusa's passion was bringing all the heartache and longing back in a torrent of memory. She put a hand on her forehead and sighed. 'It was a long time ago,' she said in a quiet voice.

'But does one ever heal? Can the heart be mended?' Arethusa thought of Jonas Madison and she felt a tightening in her chest. What if he wasn't there this afternoon and instead she had to endure a banjo lesson with his brother, what then? Would she ever see him again?

'Why all these questions, Tussy?' Charlotte asked, getting up. 'You should go for a ride in the park with Rupert. Get out into the sunshine. Really, my story happened a long time ago. I've forgotten all about it now.'

'But you never married,' said Arethusa. 'Was it because of Tom?'

'No, marriage is not for me.' There was an uncomfortable pause as Arethusa watched Charlotte force a smile in a vain attempt to reflect in her expression the sentiment in her words. 'I see you are quite well, Tussy. Why don't you go and ask Rupert if he wants to go out?'

'I'd like to go out with *you*, Charlotte,' Arethusa replied. Charlotte was astonished, but also a little suspicious. She did not allow herself to feel flattered or pleased in case this was a game of Arethusa's which would ultimately leave her feeling used and humiliated. 'Let's go for a walk in the park, just the two of us,' Arethusa continued, getting up. 'I'm frightfully bored of Rupert. I want to spend some time with *you*.'

Chapter 18

The hours seemed to drag by as Arethusa eagerly anticipated her banjo lesson with Jonas Madison. When, at last, it was time to get ready the maid helped her into one of the new dresses Augusta's tailor in Piccadilly had fashioned for her and curled her hair onto the top of her head in a stylish Psyche knot. The dress was the prettiest shade of blue, which complemented her skin and gave her face a pleasing glow, but nothing could outshine the glow that came from within. Augusta was so excited that Arethusa was going to be in such illustrious company that she lent her her very own suite of sapphires, the size of boiled sweets, which Stoke had gifted her on their first wedding anniversary. Arethusa gazed at her reflection in the mirror and even she, who had never been very inspired by jewellery, had to admit that they were exquisite. 'You will be the envy of them all,' said Charlotte, feeling happier and more intimate with her charge since their walk in the park.

'If they impress the Duchess and Lord Penrith, they will have done their job,' said Augusta with satisfaction.

Charlotte watched Arethusa's face with interest. Her cheeks were flushed and her eyes sparkled and really, she had never seen the girl look so lovely. Could it be, she wondered, that Arethusa had fallen in love with Lord Penrith?

With her heart drumming an agitated beat in her chest Arethusa climbed into the brougham and waved goodbye to Augusta and Charlotte. 'You don't need to be nervous,' said Rupert, settling languidly into the corner of the carriage and stretching out his legs. 'Lady Alexandra is a shy little thing and her mother is no different from Augusta, only her jewellery is more expensive and she is more self-regarding on account of the title she acquired upon her marriage. Otherwise they are both cut from the same cloth.'

'I'm not in the least nervous about *them*,' Arethusa replied, sitting with her back straight because it was impossible to slouch in a tight corset.

'I do believe you're trembling,' he added, running his lazy eyes over her. 'You're like a young horse in the starting block.'

'Are you going to make a play for Lady Alexandra?' Arethusa asked, hoping to divert the conversation away from herself.

'Only for my amusement.'

'Don't break her heart,' she said, remembering Charlotte and Tom. 'It's not kind to play with a woman's heart.'

'I'm not going to play with her. *You* are. You're going to learn how to play the banjo, and I'm going to entertain the Duchess and Peregrine and all the other old ladies present.' He folded his arms and turned his gaze to the city passing by his window. 'Do try not to faint, Tussy dear. Peregrine might not come to your rescue the second time round.'

'Nor would I expect him to,' Arethusa replied tartly. The one man she'd like to rescue her was the only man who couldn't.

At length the carriage drove through the black iron gates into the forecourt of the Duke of Sutcliffe's elegant townhouse in Belgravia. The horses drew up outside the big doors which were framed by sturdy pillars and an imposing triangular pediment. No sooner had the horses stopped than one of the doors opened and a pair of footmen in the family livery hurried out to escort the guests from the carriage. Arethusa took as deep a breath as her corset allowed and smiled cordially as she stepped down from the brougham. She silently prayed to the God she claimed never listened that Jonas Madison was the brother the Duchess had invited to teach her daughter to play the banjo. *Please, please*, she pleaded, *let it be Jonas.*

As soon as she entered the hall she heard the murmur of voices upstairs. With her heartbeat louder and more frantic than ever she lifted her skirts and followed the butler up the marble staircase. His slow ascent was infuriating. Rupert seemed in no hurry to reach the top and Arethusa had to concentrate on her pace so as not to look too keen. When at last they were shown into the drawing room, a large square room cluttered with elegant silk chairs, delicate side tables, a grand piano, black-and-white photographs in frames, potted palms and ferns, all dominated by a vast portrait of the Duchess in her youth which hung on brass chains above the ornate marble fireplace, Arethusa's eyes found Jonas's.

She caught her breath and her heart gave a sudden leap of relief and delight. There he stood, as beautiful as he had been at the ball, talking to his pupils, Lady Alexandra and Margherita Stubbs, while the Duchess, her son Peregrine and Mrs Stubbs sat on chairs at the opposite side of the room. Arethusa felt her face flood with a hot rush of blood and quickly averted her eyes and followed her brother across the floor to greet their hostess. While Peregrine jumped to his feet, the Duchess merely held out her hand, which Rupert duly took and made a low bow. She smiled at him warmly and introduced him to Margherita's mother, who was equally charmed. Peregrine needed no introduction. The two men's pleasure at seeing one another made the Duchess remark that if she didn't know any better she would have thought they were happier to see each other than they were to see the ladies. Rupert laughed in that easy, carefree way of his that could melt an ice cap and settled his gaze onto Lady Alexandra, who blossomed beneath it, like a sunflower in sunshine. 'Why, you are much mistaken, Your Grace. As charming as Peregrine is, it is Lady Alexandra who lights up the room.' And he proceeded to cross it to greet her.

Arethusa bobbed a curtsey to the Duchess and politely greeted Mrs Stubbs. Peregrine took her hand and gave a bow, smiling at her cheerfully with lips as full and pretty as a girl's. 'Now, no delay, my dear,' said the Duchess to Arethusa. 'You must join Alexandra and Margherita at once. Mr Madison must not be held up.' Arethusa, determined not to give herself away, walked across the floor towards the small group, trying very hard not to bounce. After greeting the girls and giving Mr Madison a formal nod, she sat on the empty chair. Jonas handed her a banjo. She took it and smiled. He held her smile for a second longer than was customary, then began to conduct the lesson.

The moment Jonas began to speak it was as if warm honey were being poured into Arethusa's heart. His voice was deep and soft and the accent like a melody. American English reminded her a little of the Irish and yet it was unlike anything she had ever heard before. Every time he looked at her, his eyes dark and mysterious and deeply intense, she felt a caress. It was as if he could see right into her, as if there was no one else in the room but the two of them. She sighed and thought how love's delightful clichés now applied to her. She hoped the other girls didn't notice.

She need not have worried.

Lady Alexandra was clearly not very interested in the banjo

or in Mr Madison. Her eyes kept wandering to the group at the opposite side of the drawing room, and whenever Rupert looked over, her cheeks caught fire and she hastily turned her attention back to her tutor. Margherita, on the other hand, was more attentive. She listened to the instruction, placed her fingers on the right strings and strummed as she was told to, and yet she too kept sliding her eyes to the small group who talked quietly among themselves. Arethusa, when she wasn't gazing at Jonas, noticed that the object of Margherita's desire was Peregrine, but Peregrine was more rapt with Rupert.

Arethusa realized very quickly that Margherita and her mother had been invited to tea in order for Margherita and Peregrine to get better acquainted. That was obvious. The Stubbses were very rich and Peregrine was very grand. They made a fine match. Rupert was there because Lady Alexandra had taken a shine to him, although Arethusa doubted that Rupert would be enough for the Duchess. But perhaps the Duchess was indulging her daughter. Would the Duchess encourage a friendship if she had no intention of allowing it to blossom? Therefore, Arethusa came to the swift conclusion that *she* had been invited simply as padding. She was of no interest to anyone, besides Jonas. She knew she was of interest to him. She had seen that look in Dermot's eyes and in Ronald's as well. She recognized infatuation when she saw it. Only, she had never felt it herself before. Now she did, she realized how very vulnerable it made her. How callous she had been with those poor men, she thought suddenly, as she strummed her first tune, quite to the astonishment of her two fellow pupils. One must not toy with people's hearts, she thought resolutely. They are tender when touched by love.

'You are a natural, Miss Deverill,' said Jonas, his smile broad and full of admiration.

'How did you learn so fast?' Lady Alexandra asked, a little put out that she hadn't managed more than a few hesitant chords.

'I'm not entirely sure,' Arethusa replied, but she knew that she was the only one of the three who really *wanted* to learn.

'I think you all have potential to play to a high standard, if you practise,' said Jonas. 'Some need more practice than others, but you will all get there if you want to.'

'Oh, I want to!' enthused Margherita, glancing at Peregrine.

'Me too,' said Arethusa, aware that, if Lady Alexandra did not want to continue, she might never see Jonas again. 'My brother is very keen for me to learn,' she said, looking directly at Lady Alexandra. 'He was so taken by the Madison brothers at the ball that it was *he* who suggested I take up the banjo. I think to be proficient at that banjo would make you the most accomplished lady in London.'

Lady Alexandra smiled. 'Then we must have more lessons,' she said firmly. 'Now, how do I learn to play a tune like Miss Deverill? And once I can play a tune, might I accompany it with a song? I'm told I have a lovely singing voice.'

Arethusa smiled with relief. 'Goodness, you are very fortunate, Lady Alexandra. There is nothing my brother likes more than a lovely singing voice. Sadly, I sound like a croaking frog.' She laughed at her own hard luck and knew that Lady Alexandra would like her more for it.

'I doubt that very much, Miss Deverill,' said Jonas and the tenderness in his voice caused her stomach to lurch.

'Then I will sing for him too,' said Lady Alexandra with a bashful smile. Arethusa was not sure that her brother would thank her for that. But it didn't matter. What mattered was seeing Jonas again. As he stood up to leave, she knew from the heaviness of his gaze, which lingered on hers for a heartbeat longer than convention dictated, that seeing her again mattered to him as well.

The following afternoon when Arethusa and Rupert arrived at the Sutcliffe mansion in Belgravia they found the Duchess was indisposed. The footman explained that only Lord Penrith, Lady Alexandra, Miss Margharita Stubbs and her mother, Mrs Stubbs, were in the drawing room with Mr Madison. Arethusa and Rupert were greeted by the sound of laughter that trickled into the hall with the *esprit* of a bubbling stream and caught each other's eye, silently questioning the unusual sound of high spirits coming from the room upstairs. They discovered, to their delight, that without the Duchess presiding over the occasion the atmosphere had an air of festivity, which hadn't been there before.

Mrs Stubbs had positioned herself in the middle of the sofa where the Duchess had sat the previous afternoon, sipping tea from the finest china cup and nibbling cake from the most exquisite china plate. She quivered with excitement, relishing having the Marquess of Penrith to herself – a marquess, no less, who would one day be a duke, and whom she hoped to very soon welcome into her family as the fiancé of her only daughter, Margherita. The excitement was almost too much and her cheeks glowed a vivid crimson as if they had received two healthy slaps. Squeezed into her corset and embellished with bright, ostentatious jewels, there was rather a lot more of Mrs Stubbs on view than polite London Society was accustomed to in a lady of her age. Her embonpoint was barely contained and ballooned out of the ruffles of her décolletage like a pair of soufflés that wobbled every time she laughed.

Perhaps Peregrine was making her laugh on purpose, for his own amusement. However, as soon as Arethusa and Rupert entered the room he got to his feet to welcome them with a look of relief.

After the usual pleasantries Arethusa seated herself between Lady Alexandra and Margherita (both girls more interested in the trio at the other end of the room than in their music lesson) and opposite the object of her most ardent desire, Jonas Madison. Her infatuation had only swelled overnight and she felt more in love with him than ever. Without the Duchess's incisive gaze upon her she felt braver and ready to take the odd risk.

'I practised last night when I got home,' she told Jonas, feeling a strange sensation in her belly as their eyes locked. 'I was so inspired.'

'It pleases me greatly to have inspired you,' Jonas replied.

'I couldn't practise,' added Margherita. 'Mama drags me out every evening. She's relentless.' Then her gaze strayed across the room. 'Perhaps now she will calm down a little and allow me to catch my breath.'

'I think she's where she wants to be now,' agreed Arethusa and she smiled as something Peregrine said made Mrs Stubbs burst into a fit of laughter again. Rupert looked up from beneath his dark eyebrows and caught Lady Alexandra's eye.

'I didn't practise either,' said Lady Alexandra, enlivening beneath Rupert's gaze. 'I suppose I must if I am to play and sing. And I don't want to let myself down. I'm not used to doing things badly.'

Jonas put the girls to work, teaching them how to strum and how to pluck, but only Arethusa had a real desire to learn. She listened, copied and concentrated and was thrilled by her progress. However, after an hour it became obvious that

Lady Alexandra's attention was waning and Jonas suggested they take a break. No sooner had he suggested it than Lady Alexandra and Margherita put down their instruments and hastened across the floor to join the men and Mrs Stubbs, who, being American, was less concerned about leaving a young lady alone with a man. It did not occur to her that Arethusa might harbour inappropriate feelings for her banjo teacher on account of his class and his colour. She was much more concerned about her own daughter appealing to Lord Penrith and doing everything in her power to promote their growing friendship.

While Lady Alexandra fluttered about Rupert like a butter-fly bedazzled in sunshine and Margherita diverted Peregrine in a more sultry and mature manner, Arethusa was left alone with Jonas.

'I don't want a rest,' she told him, gazing into his brown eyes steadily. 'I want you to teach me some more.'

'You're a rewarding pupil,' he said with a smile. 'I couldn't ask for more enthusiasm.'

'I learned piano as a child, but I never got beyond the most basic tunes, and I learned to sing, but I didn't enjoy that either. Now I realize that it wasn't me who was unmusical, but my teacher who was uninspiring. I am taking to the banjo like a fish to water because of you, Mr Madison. You're enthusing me and making me want to impress you. Had you taught me piano I'm sure I'd be a concert pianist by now, and had you taught me to sing I'd rival the nightingale. I heard you sing at the ball and lost my heart to your beautiful voice, and I wanted so very badly for music to be a part of my life again. Somehow my dearest wish has been answered. Here we are, you and I.' She slid her eyes to the other end of the room, saw that they were paying her not the slightest attention, and continued boldly. 'You are opening a door, Mr Madison, which I thought had been closed for ever, and now I'm looking out onto a new and exciting world. I'll learn the banjo and my life will no longer be so monotonous and dull because I will have this wonderful companion to accompany my voice and fill the empty hours with delight.'

'I don't know what to say,' he murmured, returning her uninhibited gaze with a frown. 'I've never met anyone like you in all my life.'

'And I've never met anyone like you.'

He grinned. 'Well, that I believe.'

She grinned too and positioned the banjo in preparation to play. 'I don't mean your colour, Mr Madison. I mean *you*.'

Jonas reached over and took her fingers in his. She caught her breath, electrified, and stared at him in surprise. But she did not take her fingers away. 'You have beautiful hands, Miss Deverill,' he said softly. She dropped her gaze to see how white hers looked in his brown ones. How well they fitted together. How natural it felt for his skin to touch hers. 'You'll find, if you bring your wrist down, like this' – he moved her wrist accordingly – 'that it will be easier to position your fingers over the strings. And don't grip the neck too tightly, unlike a guitar a banjo has a rather sensitive neck.'

Arethusa watched him closely. His face was serious, his eyes a little feverish.

He was still holding her wrist.

Arethusa's heart was so full and so light with happiness that she felt compelled to speak her mind. She allowed herself to sink into his rich mahogany irises. 'When one looks into a person's eyes, one sees past colour and class. One sees into the person's soul, which is not made of matter but of something finer, something indestructible. The eternal soul does not belong to this intolerant and prejudiced world, Mr Madison, only the body, which is mortal. When I look into your eyes, your soul is what I see. I only wish everyone saw the soul like I do.' She knew she sounded like her mother, but instead of thinking ill of Adeline, she was grateful to her, because right now she really believed it, as if a veil had been lifted, revealing only truth. To Arethusa nothing mattered but the soul that shone out of him like a light and connected with her own. At this very moment she believed she had never felt more at one with another person in her entire life. They were soulmates, twin souls, or whatever her mother meant when she spoke about those who connect on a level beyond the material. Arethusa had always scorned that kind of spiritual nonsense, but she was not laughing now.

'It's as if I've met you before, Miss Deverill,' said Jonas quietly, letting go of her wrist and casting his eyes briefly to Mrs Stubbs who was fanning herself with one hand and placing the other on Peregrine's arm, as if she were already his mother-in-law. He turned back to Arethusa and lowered his voice. 'It's as if we already know each other. Stop me if I'm being forward, but—'

'You're not being forward, Mr Madison,' Arethusa cut in quickly. 'It is I who am speaking out of turn.'

'If we both are, then it's not out of turn,' he added with a small smile.

Arethusa smiled back and she knew then that he had acknowledged their connection. They would only need to look at each other in future for that connection to be reinforced, for their mutual admiration to be confirmed. They might not get the chance to speak on their own again, but it didn't matter. They could communicate with their eyes. They only had one thing they wanted to say to each other anyhow and that needed no words.

Mrs Stubbs was now telling the girls to return to their lesson. 'Or the Duchess will reproach me for failing in my duty as chaperone!' she gushed. 'Really, you boys,' she added, looking at Peregrine and Rupert in turn, 'are a mighty distraction!'

Margherita and Lady Alexandra returned flushed and exhilarated from their break. They both glowed with infatuation and Arethusa wondered if she glowed too. Not that anyone besides Rupert would notice. He, of course, would comment on it on the way home, but he would not know its source. He would assume she had eyes for Peregrine and warn her that she didn't stand a chance against Margherita and her enormous wealth. But that suited her very well. It suited her very well indeed.

Chapter 19

I snap the diary shut. The blood rushes into my cheeks and I feel a sudden sinking sensation, as if my bed is no longer solid and I am losing my balance. I get up and walk unsteadily to the bathroom to fetch a glass of water. I take a deep breath, gulp down the water, then stare at my shocked face in the mirror. From the little I have read it is now obvious that my mother left for America because she fell in love with a black man. I could *never* have predicted that. The revelation has knocked me for six! I can only assume that somehow someone found out and there followed an unholy row. I don't see anything wrong with a relationship between two people of different races, but in some circles, even now, in the sixties, it would cause a scandal. I cannot imagine how scandalous it must have been at the end of the last century.

I want to read on but I'm afraid. On one hand I feel desperately sad for my mother. If she truly loved Jonas Madison she must have suffered. They must have *both* suffered. There was no earthly way they could have ever been together in those days, and it must have been agony for my mother to leave her home and her familiar world for a country far away – perhaps she followed him to America. I sense the next chapter of her diary is going to be full of distress and heartbreak. I'm not sure I can take it. On the other hand, I am extremely anxious. I feel duty-bound to share her story with Logan, but I'm not sure I can. My brother is not like me. He will hate to think of our mother having sexual relations with a man who was not our father. He will not want to think of her as a sexual creature at all. *Should* I share it? Does he need to know?

Wyatt slips into my mind then. I haven't given much thought to my husband over the last five days. The longer I am here the weaker he becomes. A mere dot on the horizon, getting smaller and smaller and fainter and fainter. Now he looms large. I definitely couldn't tell *him*. He is conventional and old-fashioned, even more so than Logan, and the revelation would appal him. I'm ashamed to admit that he will be shocked. He certainly wouldn't want it to get out. What other people think matters very much to Wyatt, and he assumes, quite wrongly of course, that everyone else is just like him. Thankfully, they are not.

As for my children, I *have* given thought to *them*, especially Rose. I know that she, in particular, will understand as I do, and, as a romantic, be enthralled by the love story. Who would have guessed that her grandmother had this secret past? I'm sure she'll be riveted, and saddened too, by the hopelessness of it. I wish she were here to share it with me. I long to tell her.

I wonder then about the banjo I gave to Temperance. It can only be the very one Mom learned to play with Jonas. She kept it all these years and I never knew about it. I wonder how often she took it out and played it. Or whether she just held it and thought of him.

I wonder, during her long marriage to my father, how often she thought of Jonas.

I return to bed and try to sleep, but I cannot. My mind is too agitated to rest. I cannot stop chewing on the flesh of this tragic tale. How devastating for her to love a man she couldn't have. How devastating for them both. And what became of Jonas? I know how her story ended, because I'm part of that ending. But I know nothing of him. If their affair was discovered, what happened to *him*?

But does it matter that she loved Jonas Madison? She eventually married my father and, as far as I know, was very happy. Perhaps Jonas married too and was happy as well. I suspect, however, that theirs was a love that accompanied them throughout the whole of their lives. I don't know why I know that. I just do.

I'm discovering that I knew my mother so very little. The woman I grew up with is not the same as the girl I'm reading about in her diary. Try as I might, I cannot reconcile the two. It's as if she arrived in America and put away her old self, never to revisit it. I find that unbearably sad. So, what made my mother change? Perhaps that's why I'm restless, because I know I'm about to find out. And it had to be something big. No one changes to that degree on account of a small ripple. It had to be an earthquake.

It occurs to me that perhaps I should skip to the end of the diary. Cut the suspense and just find out what happened. I have often wanted to do that while reading a novel. The story is so tense that I want to read the last page to put myself out of my misery. But I don't, because I know that the author hasn't written all those words for the reader to cut to the final paragraph. So I won't. Mom wanted me to read her diary and read it I will, in the right order, page by page.

I am relieved when dawn's gentle light dissolves the darkness and it is time to get up. I look at the clock on the mantelpiece and see that it is half past five. I haven't slept at all, I don't think. I realize there's no point lying in bed lamenting my lack of sleep. So I get up and dress, then creep out of the house and walk down to the beach. The sky is a pale, dusty pink and the sun has begun its leisurely rise. A flock of birds flies across it, silhouetted. There is something very beautiful about their silent flight. I don't know what they are. Cormac would know. As I begin to walk up the sand, with the wind in my hair and the briny tang of the ocean in my nostrils, my thoughts turn to Cormac. I understand my mother's infatuation. I know what it's like to be smitten – to be smitten by someone you can't have.

The waves wash up on the beach then retreat again. They swell and break and foam and their rhythm is comforting. They have done this for thousands of years. While the world has changed around them, they have remained the same. My mother must have paced this beach. She must have watched the same sea and listened to the same waves. I may not know the woman in the diary but I feel connected to her all the same. Perhaps that's what Mom wanted me to do. To understand who she was. To understand why she was the way she was. Why she changed. She could have kept her story secret. It would have died with her; but she didn't. She wanted me to know.

Perhaps she wanted to honour Jonas Madison in some way. Maybe she just wanted him to live on.

I want to see Cormac. I want to see him very badly, but I don't know how to. I don't even know where he lives. It's crazy. I'm a married woman and I'm hankering after a man I have only just met. What would Logan think? What would Wyatt say? How would my children react? Would they, like me, lament that they don't know their mother like they thought they did?

I know what my mother would do. She'd encourage me all the way. That's exactly what she'd do. She'd encourage me to follow my heart, because she wasn't able to follow hers.

I hurry up the beach, a growing sense of excitement charging my paces. I will ask one of the grooms, or the butler, where Cormac lives. Everyone knows everything about each other in this town, someone will know where he lives, for sure. But when I reach the house I find Kitty in the hall in her riding clothes. She is surprised to see me up at this hour. 'Well, look at the early bird!' she laughs. 'You're just like me. The first hours of the morning are the sweetest, I believe. Do you want to come out?'

I had not planned to go riding, but since she is offering, I accept. There is a wildness in me that I suddenly want to unleash. There's something about Kitty that tells me I can.

Up on the hills my anxiety evaporates. What does it matter whether my mother loved Jonas or not? The fact remains the same: she left Ireland never to return. If Jonas is the reason why, it's better than being pregnant with Dermot McLoughlin's baby, because bringing a child into the world like that would be heartbreaking. She would have had to give it up and I cannot imagine an agony such as that. Everything seems possible here, as if the only limitations in our lives are the ones we impose upon ourselves. I realize, as we gallop over the dewy grass, that I can make any life for myself that I choose. Mom couldn't, but I can. I think of Cormac and something in the wind encourages me to ask Kitty where he lives.

'Cormac?' she repeats. 'Not far from here. Come, we'll go and knock on his door. He's an early riser too.'

We set off at a gentle pace, allowing the horses to catch their breath after the gallop. With the sea on our right and the velvet green hills on our left, we meander along a well-trodden path, through long grasses and heather. The sun rises higher and floods the landscape with a soft, golden light, releasing into the warming air the scents of wild rosemary and thyme which remind me of my walk with Cormac. Then, like a schoolgirl who finds excuses to mention her boyfriend at every opportunity because the sound of his name is so sweet, I ask Kitty about him.

'Was Cormac devoted to his wife?'

'She was lovely and it was a great sadness when she died before her time, of cancer,' Kitty replies. 'She was a girl from Clonakilty, which isn't far from here. Very pretty, as one would expect. Cormac was quite a catch, you know.'

'Well, he's handsome now,' I say, trying to sound dispassionate.

'He was devilishly handsome when he was a young man, and quite the hero.' She laughs. 'He was brave to the point of being reckless. But that's Cormac. Everything he does, he does with passion.'

'He showed me his missing finger.'

'He was tortured by the Tans,' she tells me. 'He laughs about it because that's his way of coping, but I can tell you it was no laughing matter at the time. He had information that could have led to the deaths of a dozen good men.'

'He didn't divulge anything?'

'Not a word. He was black and blue when they rescued him.'

'How did they find him?'

'He was locked in a cabin in the hills, guarded by just a few men. One of those men was one of us.' I notice she used the word 'us'. I long to know more about the part she played in this war.

'We sheltered in a cabin yesterday,' I say. 'There seem to be lots of them in these hills.'

'Homes abandoned during the famine, and in the years that followed. Times were hard.' Kitty sighs, as if the resonance of pain is embedded in the earth and will always be there, as a constant reminder that freedom came at a price. 'They give the landscape a melancholy air, don't they?'

'Yes, but I like them. I don't know why, nostalgia perhaps for a bygone age.'

'Because they're full of romance, like Cormac's songs,' she adds.

'He does sing beautifully.'

'People like Cormac will never forget the struggle for independence and the suffering that came with it.'

'And you?' I ask.

She looks at me and I notice shadows beneath her eyes that I'm sure weren't there before. 'And me?' she says. 'I live a quiet life now, but I still hear the roar of my memories. They're all around me.'

I see a pretty white house ahead, nestled in the crescent of a cove down below the cliffs. 'Is that Cormac's house?' I ask hopefully.

'No, that's the O'Learys' house,' she replies. Her horse stops walking and mine copies and stops too. We gaze upon it. A silence falls over us, only the waves thunder and crash against the rocks, and I feel the need to break it, because it is heavy and uncomfortable.

'It's a lovely place to live,' I say.

She sighs again and tilts her head to one side. I sense longing in her sigh and wistfulness in the way she tilts her head. 'It *is* lovely,' she agrees. I think she is about to elaborate. I sense something happened here in her past and I'm sure she is going to tell me about it. But then she inhales sharply, moves her head briskly as if she has decided against it and now wants to leave. She turns her horse away. 'Come, I'll show you Cormac's.'

I follow her in silence, lost in thought. Once again she has given me a glimpse of her past, then closed the door.

At last we walk our horses down a farm track and come upon a modest white house with a grey slate roof. It is sheltered in the basin of the hill with a wide view of the ocean. Around the house are fields enclosed by those dry-stone walls Cormac was telling me about. I smile as I discover that he is also a farmer, as I suspected. There are sheep, donkeys and little birds everywhere, pecking at the seed he puts out for them.

We tie the horses to an old cart that lies discarded by the house and wander round to ring the bell. But of course, there is no bell, only our knuckles. Kitty uses hers to great effect. The door opens and Cormac is surprised to see us.

I'm embarrassed to call on him without invitation or prior warning, but he seems not to mind. He smiles with pleasure and opens the door wide. I get the feeling that people here are used to dropping in on each other like this. 'You're a farmer too,' I say as I step into a small hall with a low ceiling and tiled floor.

'As I said, Jack of all trades, master of none.' He looks at me and I feel dizzy beneath his gaze. His blue eyes seem to see through me, right into my heart, and I'm sure he knows what I'm hiding in there. I follow Kitty into the kitchen. There is a wooden table with spindle-back chairs, colourful rugs on the wooden floor, a bookcase cluttered with books and walls adorned with photographs and paintings. It is a cosy home, made all the more so by his dog Kite who presses her nose against my knees, asking to be petted. I stroke her and she gazes at me with large, shiny eyes and I wonder whether she knows how I feel about her master.

Kitty and Cormac chat with the ease of old, old friends. He 'wets' the tea, as they say here, and pours us all mugs of Barry's, which is an Irish brew. I take a chair and Kite sits beside me with her head on my lap as I stroke her. 'She'll never leave you alone now,' says Cormac.

'I'm glad,' I reply. 'She's very cute.'

Kitty is by the bookcase, browsing through the titles. She laughs. 'Do you have enough bird books?' she says, running her finger along the spines.

'There's always room for more,' he replies, putting the mugs on the table along with a wooden board of soda bread.

'You have a lovely house,' I say. 'It's very homey.'

'That has nothing to do with me,' he replies and I assume he's referring to his wife.

'It does have a woman's touch,' I agree.

'Thank the Lord for that. Decoration is not one of the many trades I'm Jack of.' His eyes twinkle at me then. I laugh, enjoying the joke that is ours alone.

We settle into an easy conversation while Kitty remains by the bookcase, pulling books off the shelves and opening them. I wonder whether she is deliberately leaving us to talk. After our chat in the cabin yesterday I feel a closeness to him. I feel that I can tell him anything and I want to tell him about Jonas, but Kitty is here so I keep it to myself, although it is a heavy weight I am longing to share.

Cormac and I chat away amiably and yet it feels like a charade. A show, perhaps, for Kitty. There's an intimacy in our eyes that I find almost too much to bear. It is as if we are suddenly seeing too much of each other; as if we are naked. I cannot hold his gaze for long and I slip mine away, to the dog, to the tea, to the bread, to the room, anything for a respite. It's not just the way his eyes penetrate mine, but the way mine penetrate his.

I'm drawn inside them as if there is a magnetic pull and I can't resist it. I want his eyes to swallow me whole but at the same time I'm afraid to let go. And all the while we are chatting, our eyes are having a decisive conversation of their own.

It is then that something gives. I know he knows and I can only assume that he knows I know. Our feelings are laid bare and we both turn away, embarrassed; our eyes have said too much.

'Kitty, your tea is getting cold,' he says, turning to her.

'Your bookcase says a lot about you,' she tells him gaily, pulling out the chair next to his and sitting down. 'Animals, birds especially, Irish history, no surprise there, and spy novels.'

He laughs and arches an eyebrow. 'I think you know me, Kitty, without having to go through my books.'

'I was hoping I'd find something astonishing.'

'Like what?'

'Oh, I don't know. Romance novels or something.'

'If you find any of those, they won't be mine.'

'Anyone who can play the accordion and sing like you do, Cormac, is a romantic.' She glances at me and smiles. I try to look nonchalant. The air feels thick and sticky. I wonder whether Cormac notices it too. Is Kitty being provocative on purpose? I wonder.

'Is it a difficult instrument to play?' I ask, thinking of my mother and the banjo.

His eyes look at me with intent. 'I could teach you how to play, if you like?' He holds my gaze in the same way I imagine Jonas held my mother's.

'What a good idea,' Kitty exclaims, before I can answer for myself.

'Who taught you?' I ask him.

'My da,' he replies. 'He was a musical man. He taught me to

play the guitar as well. Once you can play one, it's not hard to learn to play them all. The instrument I never learned was the piano. We never had one in the house. It wasn't big enough.'

'That's the only instrument I *can* play,' I tell him. 'My father insisted that I grew up accomplished.' I laugh at my father's old-fashioned ideals. 'He thought girls were only good for marriage. He was a little like the characters in Mom's diary. You know, girls have to play the piano, sing, paint, arrange flowers, dance and curtsey – then they must marry well.'

'Have you read more of the diary?' Kitty asks, and I wish I hadn't brought it up.

'Yes, I have,' I answer, because I cannot lie.

'And?' Kitty leans forward with her elbows on the table and narrows her eyes. I'm afraid to tell her, but I must. After all, it is her right. Arethusa was her aunt. I cannot keep her to myself.

I take a deep breath. 'I think I've found out why she left Ireland.'

'Oh?' Kitty raises her eyebrows.

'She fell in love with a black man, and he with her.'

I wouldn't imagine much could shock Kitty Deverill, but she gasps loudly and swears. 'Jesus, Mary and Joseph!'

Cormac is also surprised, but he's watching me carefully. I blush. The colour floods my cheeks because Cormac is looking at me with such a serious expression, as if he really cares about my feelings. 'At least she didn't leave because she was expecting Dermot McLoughlin's baby, which is what Eily Barry told me,' I say and laugh to show him that my feelings are fine. 'I can't imagine the romance went very far.'

'That would have been quite a scandal in those days,' says Cormac.

'I don't think it ever got out,' I say quickly. 'I've just got to the part where he plays the banjo at a ball and they meet and she is smitten.' I don't tell them that she had banjo lessons with him because Cormac has offered to teach me the accordion and the parallel would embarrass me. 'I imagined all sorts of scenarios, but I could never have predicted this.'

'My grandfather would have been outraged by his daughter falling in love with a black man,' says Kitty, shaking her head incredulously. 'He was very prejudiced, as most of them were in those days. He hated Catholics too.'

'Would Adeline have been appalled as well, do you think?' I ask.

Kitty is not sure. 'In her heart she judged all men as equal, whatever their colour or creed, but she was a woman of her time and she would have had to stand by her husband. I imagine, if there was a row, she would have taken Grandpa's side.'

'I couldn't sleep after reading about it. I just felt so sorry for them.' I stare into my empty mug.

Kitty agrees. 'It was an impossible situation. I feel sorry for them too.'

I look at her steadily. 'Do you think your father will be appalled?'

She smiles. 'You're speaking about a man who has had many surprises in his life. I think this will just be another.'

'When I finish it, I'll give the diary to you, Kitty. You and Uncle Bertie can read it in your own time. I'd rather you read her account of it than heard it from me. It's easier to understand her if you read her own words.'

Cormac drains his mug. He looks at me and there is that intent in his eyes again, it's unmistakable. 'You're not just here to find your mother's roots, Faye, but to see a bit of Ireland. How would you like a guided tour by the best guide in Co. Cork?'

'A guide too?' I quip, lightening the atmosphere and happy to change the subject.

'Brilliant idea,' enthuses Kitty. 'Cormac knows where all the elephants lie buried. There is no better guide than he.' She stands up. 'Come on, Faye, the horses will be getting restless and Robert will want us to join him for breakfast.'

I thank Cormac for the tea.

'I'll pick you up at eleven,' he says.

I make for the door, nonchalance in my step and in the way I depart without catching his eye, and yet I know I have reached a crossroads on my path. I have already put my foot on the road that leads into the unknown. There will be no turning back.

Chapter 20

Kitty has instilled a recklessness in me. I can't imagine where else it has come from. In only six days I am not the Faye Langton who left America, but someone else; I am a Deverill.

As the clock ticks with relentless momentum and eleven o'clock approaches I feel I am being propelled towards an inevitable destiny, one that I couldn't avoid even if I wanted to. It is written, somehow, on the planes of my subconscious, and my deepest desires are manifesting, almost without me being consciously aware of them. I am not fretful. I don't pace the floor in agitation. I am resigned, accepting of my fate, and Wyatt and the children are hidden in a fog which I have created to suit my ends. The guilt will come later, I don't doubt it. But now, as I listen for Cormac and anticipate his coming, I don't feel guilty at all. I just feel excited.

I change out of my riding clothes and put on a floral tea dress and short green cardigan. It is warm outside. Spring is colluding with me and the breeze that slips in through the window is sugar-scented. I tie my hair into a chignon, leaving a few wisps to hang loose about my face, and I wear little make-up. At home I never leave the house without a full face, but here I don't want to be painted. I want to be me, as I am, lines and all. With Cormac I don't feel I need to hide.

I check myself in the long mirror which is nailed to the inside of the wardrobe. I like what I see. I feel feminine and young. I'm not slim like Kitty, with her small waist, but I am womanly with my curves and I have always had an attractive décolletage. I glance down at my wedding ring and the diamond engagement ring that was once Wyatt's grandmother's, and I wish I could take them off. They are a part of Wyatt, watching me like piercing eyes stabbing into my conscience.

At last I hear the scrunch of wheels on gravel. I hastily leave my bedroom and skip down the stairs with a light, happy bounce. I am humming a tune as I run my fingers down the smooth wood of the banister. I am surprised to see Robert in the hall, looking through a pile of letters. I cease my humming and immediately subdue my bounce. When he sees me, his face softens but he does not smile. Robert is a serious man and does not smile easily. 'Where are you off to?' he asks.

'Cormac is going to give me a guided tour of the county,' I reply casually, as if Cormac is simply a regular guide.

Robert does not look surprised, or if he is, he doesn't show it. There is an impassiveness about his face that makes me wonder how much it is masking. 'Cormac certainly knows his way around better than most,' he says, looking at the letters again. 'I hope you have a good time.'

'I'm sure I will. Thank you,' I reply.

As I open the door, I'm sure I feel Robert's eyes upon my back, but perhaps it is the guilt, already creeping in.

Cormac is standing by the Jeep with his hands in his pockets. Kite is on the back seat, poking her nose out of the open window. Cormac smiles in that devilish way of his and the smile I give him in return seals my destiny. It leaves nothing concealed, nothing to conjecture. I have exposed my consent simply by being here, so happily and willingly, and my greeting is not as an acquaintance, but as an intimate friend. Our eyes have already stripped away any formality and politeness, and when we look at each other it is with obvious desire.

The tension in the air between us has grown stronger with the anticipation of what we must both know will happen.

He opens the passenger door for me and I climb in. I turn and stroke Kite's face. She wags her tail. She is used to me now. Cormac walks round to the other side. As he opens the door Kitty appears from the garden. She is carrying a pair of secateurs and gardening gloves. She waves and wishes us a good time, but unlike her husband her face is full of encouragement, collusion even, and I suspect she knows where we're headed and is not in the least disapproving of it.

Cormac glances at me and grins and I put my fingers to my lips and grin too. We are like a pair of thieves making our escape with loot that no one knows we have stolen. 'So where are we going?' I ask, because I have to break the tension somehow and release the nerves now building in my stomach.

'Surprise,' he replies. When I pull a face, he adds, 'If I tell you, Miss Deverill, it will ruin the fun. I have planned a full programme.'

I like the way he calls me 'Miss Deverill'. I know then that he does not want to use my married name. Neither of us wants to use that. Right now, in this Jeep, with Cormac, I am not a Clayton or a Langton – I am just me.

It is hot in the car with the sun streaming through the glass. I roll down my window and rest my elbow there, with my face in the wind. I feel carefree – and careless. 'Then I'll be patient,' I reply and I turn and smile at him and he glances at me and his lapis eyes smile back.

As he drives Cormac points out various landmarks. He knows the history of every old building, monument and hill – the War of Independence and the Civil War that came after weave like a ribbon of blood through all of them, and for Cormac and those who lived through it, the stain will never come out of the soil and stone. He tells me the history because he knows I am interested and, I realize, because he wants to remember. Brutal times they were, no question, but at the same time he must have really lived.

I soak it all up, enjoying listening to his sonorous Irish brogue and the fact that we are alone together and have the whole day ahead of us.

At length he turns off and drives slowly over a rough and neglected track that winds its way into the hills. I wonder where he's taking me. I notice a weathered sign saying 'Private Property', but that does not put Cormac off. There are holes in the ground where winter puddles have corroded the earth. Now they are dry and filled with long grass. As we turn a corner the ocean comes glittering into view, and in the distance I see a pile of rocks silhouetted against it, out of which rises a white lighthouse. It looks forlorn there, surrounded by an aura of foam, and I can't imagine how anyone can reach it except seabirds.

'Is that what you wanted to show me?' I ask.

'No,' he replies. '*This* is.'

At that point I turn my attention inland to see stone chimneys and gables ahead of us, peeping just above the trees. 'A ruined castle?' I ask with rising excitement.

'More of a stately home than a castle,' he says. 'Rosemore Court was built in the time of Cromwell and burned down during the Troubles. Home of the Carmoody family for over three hundred years but no one ever comes here now. It's been left to nature, which is slowly devouring it,' he says, pulling up.

I am thrilled to visit a ruin. I can imagine what Castle Deverill must have looked like after it was razed to the ground in the same way. This building is a shell. The walls are covered in moss and ivy and other creeping plants that have taken possession of it and will no doubt consume it. It may take decades, but one day there will be nothing left.

Cormac is pleased I am happy with his plan. 'I knew you'd like it,' he says.

'I love it,' I tell him, touched that he took the trouble to think about what would appeal to me. Flattered that he knew. 'I love ruins. We don't have anything this old in America.'

'Well, this isn't old by Irish standards. I can take you to some very ancient sites which date back thousands of years. But I thought you'd enjoy the romance of this.'

I step in beside him. 'You're right. It's beautiful.' We walk towards it. I am excited to be able to wander into the giant rooms, to imagine what it must have been like when fires burned in the grates and the family dined at a grand table, waited on by servants in red-and-gold livery. There is nothing left now but walls. No staircase, no marble floors, no distinction between upstairs and downstairs, just rows of windows that gaze blindly out to sea.

'Why do ruins pull at us so?' I ask, putting my hands on my hips and looking about in wonder.

'Nostalgia,' he replies.

'No, I think it's more than that. I think they remind us of our own mortality. That's why they make us feel sad. Once upon a time, generations of people inhabited this place yet now they are gone, all of them, as one day we will be gone. But during their lifetime they lived lives as real and full and vibrant as ours. They didn't imagine they'd ever die, just like we can't imagine we'll ever die. We think we're immortal.

They did too. But we're not. This ruin reminds us of that. It's like a skeleton lying neglected in an open tomb.'

'Time,' says Cormac. 'That's what it makes us think of. Time, and the lack of it.'

'How short our lives are,' I add as we amble into what might have been one of many drawing rooms. The chimney is still there, but the fireplace is long gone. I imagine there must have been grand portraits on the walls, rugs on the floors, sofas and chairs, perhaps big wolfhounds lying in front of the hearth. I go to the window, where the stone frame is still intact, and look out over the fields and trees. There must have been beautiful gardens once, I think, but they too have been reclaimed by the forest.

Cormac comes and stands beside me and we both look out onto the encroaching wood. 'We won't live for ever,' he says without looking at me. 'Our lives are but a blink on the eye of time. That's why we have to seize the day.' He glances at me and grins. 'I'm not just a Jack of all trades, but master of clichés as well.'

I laugh. 'Why is a cliché a cliché?'

'Because it's been overused.'

'Sure, but it's been overused because it's so absolutely accurate.'

'Then I'll give you another one,' he says and he's not grinning anymore. He looks at me with a serious expression that stills the air, and lowers his voice. 'I really like you, Faye.'

I look into his eyes, those eyes that seem to see right through me, and I let them suck me in. I don't resist. I stare into them and allow them to consume me, like the forest is consuming the ruin. 'I like you too, Cormac,' I reply.

His face softens, as if a warm, amber light has settled upon it. He puts a rough hand to my face and curls a stray piece of hair around my ear. That's a cliché too, but isn't love just one big cliché, after all? Then he bends his neck and kisses me. His lips are soft and warm, his unshaven chin prickly. I haven't been kissed by anyone in so very long. I can't recall the last time Wyatt kissed me, and before that, well, it's a lifetime ago; I can't remember the kisses of my youth. I'm fifty-eight years old and I feel as if I'm being kissed for the very first time. I barely dare breathe in case I ruin the moment. It is so sweet and so tender, I want to hold on to it. I want to feel like this for ever. I close my eyes and I have no age, no name, no wedding ring; I'm just a woman being kissed by a man and slowly falling in love.

He puts his arms around me and holds me close, and I put my hands against his cheeks and kiss him back.

How powerful a thing is a kiss? It dissolves barriers like sugar in water. With that kiss we are one. There is no longer awkwardness between us, no tension, no guessing or hoping or dissembling. We have acknowledged our desire and it is no longer in question. With that kiss I have also rediscovered a part of myself that was lost many moons ago. It is as if that part has been awakened and I find, to my delight and surprise, that it is as fresh and new as it always was.

Cormac unclips my hair and scrunches it in his fingers as it falls about my shoulders. 'You're a beautiful woman, Faye,' he says and there is a tenderness in his eyes that causes something to catch in my chest. I don't know how to respond. It's a long time since anyone told me I was beautiful. I've been a mother and a wife, a sister, a daughter and a friend, but I have not been a beautiful woman. I am too old to blush, but I feel my cheeks burning all the same. He kisses my smile and strokes my chin with his thumb. 'I've been wanting to kiss you,' he adds, arching an eyebrow.

'I've been wanting you to kiss me too,' I reply.

'I wasn't sure . . .'

I don't want my husband's name to tarnish the moment, so I add hastily, 'I'm glad you did.'

'It was this morning, when you and Kitty paid me a visit. Something changed in you. Something gave.' He looks at me intensely. 'It's still there, in your eyes.'

I frown. 'What is it?'

'A boldness.'

'A boldness?' I repeat.

'It wasn't there before.'

I laugh, incredulous. 'I wonder what it is.'

'It's the Deverill in you,' he says, grinning crookedly. 'That's what it is. And I think it's there to stay.' He becomes serious again. 'This is who you are, Faye.'

I think of Wyatt and Logan, my father and my mother, and I lift my chin in defiance. 'I feel different when I'm with you, Cormac,' I say. 'And I like this different me that you bring out.'

Indeed, it feels good to be bold. It feels good to be beautiful. In all the years I've been a submissive Clayton and an obedient Langton, I never realized that inside I had the power to be a bold Deverill too. It has only taken me six days to find it.

Now we wander around the ruins hand in hand. Kite senses our happiness and bounds about gleefully, while tactfully keeping her distance. The sun connives with the clouds to enhance the romance of our morning and shines down brightly, warming the earth and filling the air with the fertile scents of spring. I hear the twittering of birds like I have never heard them before. I feel the breeze on my skin, taste the brine on my tongue and see the vibrant green of spring's rebirth as if that kiss has sharpened my senses and awakened me to a new world. Or perhaps I am determinedly placing myself in the present moment because everything outside of it is now cast in doubt.

We are like teenagers. We steal kisses behind walls, we tease and cajole. We sit on the grass and watch rabbits graze and butterflies spread their wings in the sunshine. Then we lie on our backs and make shapes out of clouds. He sees a ship and I see a shoe, and we laugh at our childishness, while at the same time acknowledging that joy comes from the simple things, so we kiss again because there is nothing simpler than a kiss.

When we grow hungry we drive to a pub for lunch. The village Cormac takes me to is small and quaint, built into the curve of a cove, embraced by hills. The houses are white with grey-tiled roofs, a church's spire needles the sky, sailing boats bob on the water and window boxes are ablaze with flowers. Gulls wheel on the breeze and cows graze in the distant fields, and as if all that beauty isn't enough, the sun drenches the land with its dazzling radiance. I let Kite out and she immediately finds other dogs to play with. Cormac, confident that she can take care of herself, puts his hands in his pockets and walks towards the pub. There is a garden outside with tables and a few small groups of people eating lunch. We choose a table a discreet distance away. 'What'll you have and I'll go and bring it out?' he asks.

'I'd love a lime and soda,' I say and pick up the menu to browse. He saunters off towards the open door and I extract my eyes from the menu to watch him. He's a burly man with a slight stoop and his gait is nonchalant, as if he has all the time in the world, and I think how very different he is to the man I married. Where Wyatt is slim and athletic and very concerned about remaining so, Cormac doesn't care. I find his lack of vanity very attractive, very male. As I wait for him to return I consider the last few hours. I don't feel guilty at all; not yet. I feel excited.

Cormac returns with a lime and soda for me and a Guinness for himself. 'This is such a lovely place,' I tell him. My heart fills with gratitude that my mother led me here, to this enchanted place, and in so doing inspired me to find myself. How ironic it is that she left the Deverill part of her here, only for me to come and find it.

He grins. 'I knew you'd like it. I've got lots of plans for you.'

'Really?'

'Well, if this is day six of your stay, you have eight days left and I imagine you'll be wanting to fill them, won't you?'

I nod. 'I will, yes.'

'So, I've planned your itinerary.'

I laugh. 'You haven't really.'

'Well, I haven't written it down.' He taps his temple. 'But it's all in here. By the time you leave, you're going to have seen the very best Ireland has to offer.'

I look at him fondly. 'I already have,' I say.

We eat and talk and gaze at each other across the table, oblivious of the people who come and go around us. Kite lies under the table to sleep in the shade. Cormac asks me about my growing up and as I tell him he listens. He really listens. I'm not used to this kind of attention and I feel myself flowering beneath his focus. As I recount stories from my past he interrupts me, probing for more detail, questioning my motives, sympathizing with the choices I was sometimes forced to make because of convention, because of tradition but mostly because of my own lack of assertion.

'I feel strong when I'm with you,' I tell him.

'That's because I bring out the strength in you. Have you noticed how each person in your life brings out something different? A friend might make you feel diminished, another might empower you. You're not one-dimensional, Faye.

You're multi-dimensional. Bad choices leave you with the people who make you feel inadequate, good choices leave you with those who make you feel good.'

'You make me feel good. I felt good from the moment I met you.'

He takes my hand across the table. 'You make me feel good, too.'

I ask him about his wife. I feel I can ask him anything. He does not hesitate and he certainly doesn't look uncomfortable. I sense he wants to remember her. He tells me how they met when they were young and he smiles wistfully as he recalls the happy times. Then his face darkens as he tells me that they were unable to have children. 'We never found out which of us was infertile,' he says with a shrug. 'We didn't want to. We just accepted that it would never happen. When she died it was my greatest sadness; she left nothing of herself behind.' His eyes reveal his sorrow. It is deep and searing. I'm not jealous, I just feel desperately sorry for him. I want to make it better. I squeeze his hand. 'It's a long time ago now,' he says.

'And you never remarried?' I ask.

He shakes his head and I read in his silence that perhaps no one can ever fill her shoes.

After lunch we walk on the beach. The wind has picked up and purple-bellied clouds are scudding across the sky. The light is peachy, the sun mature as it wanes. We hold hands. It feels natural, as if we have known each other for a long time, not just six days. Cormac has lots to say. He is not a reticent man. He is deep in both thought and emotion, which is why he sings so beautifully, I think. He puts his soul into his music and his soul is a cavernous well of experience. And I, usually the listener in all my relationships, have much to say as well. Probably because Cormac wants to hear. He makes me feel interesting and intelligent. The only other person to ever make me feel either of those things is Temperance.

We pace the beach, up and down, while Kite runs in and out of the waves. We sit on the sand as the sun touches the horizon and the water is turned to copper. He kisses me again. And again. Then it is twilight and we must leave and this perfect day is ending.

'I want to spend every day with you,' he says, and 'before you leave' remains unspoken. I don't want to think about leaving either.

'You are my guide, so you must,' I reply with a smile, but behind my smile the thought of parting makes me melancholy.

'Indeed I am,' he says.

'I have no one to answer to here,' I add.

'You don't, but Ballinakelly is a small town, so it's best we be discreet. You never know . . .'

'I think Kitty will turn a blind eye.'

'You can be sure of that,' he says firmly. 'Kitty is a worldly woman. You'll get no finger-wagging from her.'

'You sound very certain.'

'I am,' he says and we walk back to the Jeep. 'But that husband of hers is another matter entirely. He's as morally upright as a priest.'

Kite jumps in the back and we climb into the front. Cormac starts the engine. I look out of the window at the darkening sky, and I think of Kitty and Jack O'Leary and the pieces of the puzzle begin to come together. I'd like to ask Cormac. I thought I could ask him anything. I don't think I can ask him that.

Chapter 21

Arethusa closed one eye and peeped through the slit between the door and its frame, just beneath the hinge. Her heart was racing now. She didn't know whether she was nervous about performing in front of the Duchess's friends, or about Jonas, who was there, supervising the recital as well as performing with his brother.

Margherita and Lady Alexandra stood in front of the marble fireplace, trying not to fidget. Margherita was wearing the most exquisite yellow dress by Worth, which accentuated her small waist and drew the eye to her milky-white shoulders and décolletage and the yellow diamond necklace that sparkled there. Lady Alexandra, not to be outdone by the girl who was more than likely to be her sister-in-law, was also wearing a gown by Worth, in the prettiest shade of dusty pink. Her diamonds were most certainly older than Margherita's, having been passed down the generations and worn by at least three duchesses, but the stones were noticeably smaller. The Duchess, on seeing Margherita's, had commented privately to her daughter that it wasn't suitable for a girl so young to wear stones so big, and besides, one didn't want to out-sparkle the eyes. But Arethusa, who cared little for jewellery, thought the Duchess was secretly very pleased, because the Stubbs jewellery would soon be gathered into the Sutcliffe family collection (and the wealth that came with it would no doubt pay for the maintenance of the family estates as well as Peregrine's shooting and hunting parties). Arethusa was not competitive with other women. She was secure enough in her own skin to feel she did not need the aid of the finest gowns and most expensive gems to enhance her. She only wanted to impress Jonas, and she knew, from having spent the last few weeks in his company during their banjo lessons, that he didn't care for lavish gowns either. He liked her for herself, his eyes had told her as much. However, Augusta had made sure that Arethusa shone as brightly as the other two. Her tailor had made up a stunning gown in the deepest purple and black, which gave her an enviable hourglass figure – perhaps a little too sensual in a girl so young, but it was impossible for Arethusa to look demure. She had a knowing in her eyes and a coquettishness in the way she used them, which were entirely unconscious. And the subtle padding of the bustle and the cheeky sweeping of her train only drew attention to the playful way she walked, which Augusta referred to as a bounce, but which was really more of a sashay. She stood behind the door and watched the guests through the open double doors of the ballroom at the other end of the landing. They had all arrived and were now taking their seats.

'Peregrine and Rupert are like a pair of thieves planning a robbery,' said Arethusa with a laugh. 'Really, they're standing by the door, obviously not wanting to be dutiful at all.'

Margherita became more agitated, as much as she could in such a tight corset. 'Perhaps they are lingering by the door because they want to see into here,' she said hopefully. 'Are they looking in our direction?'

'No,' said Arethusa bluntly, then added more gently, 'but I think you're right, they're hovering by the door to wish us luck as we walk in.' She did not believe that, but Margherita was so infatuated with Lord Penrith that it didn't seem fair to dampen her spirits, not before she was about to play the banjo for him.

Lady Alexandra, who blushed every time Rupert's name was mentioned and came out in a blotchy rash all over her neck and chest, was now scarlet in the face and as agitated as Margherita. 'Your brother has never heard me sing,' she said and Arethusa would have liked to tell her that he would not be in the least impressed by her fragile little voice, but again, she did not wish to be unkind.

'He'll be mightily impressed, I should think,' she lied. 'I'm glad you're singing and not me. I would empty the room after a single note.' Lady Alexandra smiled happily, delighted by the thought of Rupert being impressed and Arethusa singing badly. She lifted her chin and inhaled through her delicate nostrils, her sense of superiority curling her thin lips into a small smile.

It wasn't long before Jonas and his brother George entered the room. Arethusa stepped out from behind the door and grinned at Jonas, who smiled with equal encouragement on all three girls. 'Are you ready, ladies?' he asked. 'Your audience awaits and we're going to give them a great evening.'

'I'm so nervous,' cried Margherita. 'This is the first time I've performed in front of an audience.'

'Mama insists I play the piano for people all the time,' said Lady Alexandra grandly. 'But I admit I'm nervous about playing the banjo.'

George put up his hands. 'Ladies, you do not need to be nervous. You've practised and now you're perfect. Go out and conquer! Show them what you can do and be proud. Remember, no one else can play the banjo but you and the Prince of Wales!' George, who was more exuberant and comical than his brother, put them at ease by making them laugh, while Jonas gave them advice as any good teacher would.

'Just remember to breathe,' he said earnestly. He glanced at Arethusa, but only for a second. It was as if she burned his eyes. 'Now, pick up your banjos and let's wait on the landing for Her Grace to introduce us. I think they'll be ready now.'

The girls followed the Madison brothers out of the room and stood in a tight trio by the large double doors, banjos in one hand, fans in the other – Arethusa had looped the velvet strap of her black-beaded evening bag over her wrist and carried that as well. She could feel the body heat from the audience and smell the ladies' perfume in the thick, stuffy air. An expectant hush came over the room. Rupert and Peregrine stood together by the door and gave the girls encouraging looks. The girls waited anxiously as the Duchess took to the stage to welcome the Madison brothers once again to her home and to introduce three unlikely young performers. A murmur rippled over the guests as they all wondered who these young performers could be.

Arethusa caught Jonas's eye and held it. As hot as she was, this time he did not look away as if scalded but gazed at her with longing, as if realizing suddenly that tonight was the last time they would see each other, that tomorrow there would be no more lessons, that after this it would be over. Arethusa was not preoccupied with anything outside the present moment. She was here, with *him,* and she was about to show him how much she had practised and how effortlessly she had learned.

Had George Madison been her teacher, she would have been just as inept as her two companions.

She smiled at Jonas and between them there passed a silent communication, as had passed between them so many times already, during their lessons. It was hopeless, indeed it was already doomed, and yet they both held on to the fantasy, as so many ill-fated lovers had done before them, that in love nothing was impossible. The look they gave each other was one of unfailing hope.

Now the Duchess was announcing them and the sound of clapping was signalling their entry. Arethusa drew her gaze away and followed Lady Alexandra and Margherita Stubbs into the room. Behind her the Madison brothers walked, careful not to step on the train of her dress.

Margherita took her seat and stole a quick glance at Peregrine, who was taking his seat and beaming a smile of support, as a fiancé would do to his betrothed. It wouldn't be long, Arethusa thought, before their engagement was announced. Rupert, on the other hand, who was seated beside Peregrine, watched Lady Alexandra sit down and place the banjo on her knee. The young lady was too shy to look at him, but anxious to show him how beautifully she sang. Arethusa rather wished she hadn't lied about that. Rupert was no more interested in her singing voice than he was in any other part of her. She wasn't sure how that was going to work out, considering her brother had no intention of marrying at all, lady or no lady. However, he had entertained her during the three weeks of banjo lessons, which had worked to Arethusa's advantage, for it had allowed her time alone with Jonas to talk and to get to know him. In the brief conversations they had managed to snatch alone, Jonas had told her a little about his family. He been born in New Brunswick in Canada, and later moved to New York to pursue a career in music. As Arethusa had known, Jonas and George's ancestors were brought to America from the Caribbean on slave ships, the horrors of which she could barely imagine. He hadn't dwelt on the distant past, but on the luck that had given him success as a performer – and on the luck that had brought him here, to her. But now the lessons had finished there was no reason for either of them to come to the Sutcliffe home. She and Lady Alexandra were not natural friends, they were too different, and Rupert could see Peregrine at his club, as men of their sort did. As for Jonas, he and his brother would travel the country as planned. It was unlikely that their paths would ever cross again.

The three girls lifted their banjos and began to play, while Jonas and George watched proudly from the side of the stage. The atmosphere, which had been charged with expectation and a little dread, because it was quite possible that the girls were unable to play at all and would embarrass themselves as well as the Duchess, softened with relief and rising enjoyment. Arethusa didn't need to look at her hands as she changed chords, unlike Lady Alexandra and Margherita who had not practised with as much dedication as she had. Arethusa had poured her heart into her practice and it showed. As she outshone the other two with the fluid movement of her fingers and her exuberance (as well as some unladylike toe-tapping), she felt Jonas's eyes upon her and her determination to do better intensified. She ran her gaze over the glowing faces of the audience (it really was very hot in there) and felt a mounting sense of satisfaction. She might not be a lady like Alexandra, or as rich as Margherita Stubbs, but she could play the banjo better than the two of them put together. At the end of their piece they received a hearty clap. The Duchess looked pleased. None of them had played a wrong note, at least, not that anyone would have noticed.

The Madison Minstrels took over then, dancing and toe-tapping their way onto the stage, their voices rising into an exquisite harmony. They sang the upbeat 'American Jig', which made everyone smile, followed by 'Home, Sweet Home', which brought tears to a couple of old dowagers' eyes and a wistful mist in those of a few old men. Then they sang about slavery. This was unexpected and made many in the audience a little uneasy. It was not a subject the Duchess wanted raised in her drawing room, on a lovely evening such as this. *'Hark! Baby, hark, your mama is dying,'* their plaintive voices rang out. *'For saving her child from cruel master's blows. Oh! Cruel, cruel slavery! Hundreds are dying. Please, let my baby die – go.'* The Duchess's smile froze and looked less like a smile and more like a grimace. Two crimson stains spread onto her white cheeks like drops of blood on blotting paper. Arethusa was so moved by the lyrics, and the brothers' plaintive voices, that she did not notice the tension building in the room. She saw the raw pain in Jonas's eyes as he sang of his people's suffering and realised, in that moment, how very far he had come. How great the distance was between his ancestors' fate and his performance now, in the presence of the British aristocracy. She put a hand on her heart because she felt something snag there. She thought of those slave ships and the inhumane way his people had been treated and loved him all the more because of his courage. Surely, they had composed the song themselves. Those poignant images were undoubtedly reflections of their own family's history. Her attention was hijacked then by her brother's stare. It was insistent. When she tore her gaze from Jonas she noticed Rupert's face was grey and his jaw stiff with horror. Her gaze strayed over the shocked audience, whose faces were as white as Rupert's, and she was struck with terror. If Jonas and George displeased the Duchess, she could destroy their careers with a few carefully chosen words. Arethusa silently appealed to her brother to do something, but there was nothing he could do to halt the song. The Minstrels sang on, determined to enlighten their audience about their black American heritage. At last, Rupert whispered something to Peregrine, who leaned towards his mother and whispered something into her ear. As soon as the last note rang out and before they could launch into another rendition of something unsuitable, the Duchess was on her feet and inviting her daughter to sing. Lady Alexandra glanced at Rupert and managed a small, grateful smile, before taking the stool at the grand piano and composing herself for her song. The Madison brothers returned to their seats, unashamed by their faux pas, and waited expectantly for Lady Alexandra to begin.

Arethusa hoped she sang well. If she had a lovely voice no one would remember the song about slavery. The Duchess's daughter had the chance to lift the evening and end it on what they deemed to be a beautiful note rather than an ugly one. Arethusa felt desperate for Jonas. If word got out that they had offended the Duchess of Sutcliffe, they might never be invited to play anywhere again. She looked to her friend at the piano to put the evening right. But she couldn't imagine such a delicate, insipid girl, who only managed a few passable chords on the banjo, could either play or sing with any aplomb.

But she was wrong. The girl's hands turned into graceful doves as they flew up and down the keys. Arethusa was astonished, but then she remembered how very accomplished such English girls were, groomed to within an inch of their lives for the marriage market. Lady Alexandra took a breath and expelled the most delightful sound. Her voice was a flute, pure as clear water, tuneful as a canary's. She sang three songs, each one lovelier than the last. Arethusa's attention was diverted by Rupert lifting a hand to his eye and wiping away a tear. She then looked at the other faces in the room and her fears dissolved at the sight of their pink cheeks and glistening eyes. The Duchess was smiling in the proud, indulgent way a mother smiles on a beloved and talented daughter. Lady Alexandra certainly had the power to move an entire room with the tenderness and melancholy in her voice. Arethusa would never have guessed it.

While everyone was watching the performance, Arethusa looked at Jonas. His face was flushed and his eyes were glistening too, and he was looking right back at her. She realized then with a sudden searing feeling in her heart that they would never see each other again. That however much they hoped, hope was but a fragile beam of sunshine breaking through the thick cloud of convention. They were no match for society's rigid standards and prejudice. But Arethusa was not going to give up so easily. She had a gift for living in the moment, for choosing not to consider the consequences of her actions and for acting impulsively. She had a recklessness of spirit and a confidence that enabled her to get what she wanted, regardless of the obstacles. Certainly, there were more obstacles now than there had ever been before, but she wasn't thinking of them all, only the closest one, and she had already devised a way of overcoming it. She gave Jonas a barely perceptible smile, in the minutest curling of her lips, and then she turned away.

Once the recital was over Arethusa was relieved to find that no one was talking about the song of slavery but Lady Alexandra's angelic voice, which had moved them all to tears. Of course, the praise Lady Alexandra craved most was Rupert's. Aware of this he duly kissed her hand and told her that she had melted his heart, thus setting the girl's cheeks aflame. Arethusa felt sorry for her friend but wondered why on earth Rupert wouldn't want to marry her. She was one of the most eligible girls in the country. If the Duchess was encouraging their meetings, which she surely was, she and the Duke must indeed approve of the match. Arethusa watched Rupert, his head inclined, his twinkling brown eyes gazing into her puppyish ones, and wondered whether his apparent disinterest in marriage had been but a ruse and he intended to marry Lady Alexandra after all.

Meanwhile, the Duchess moved slowly around the room receiving compliments as if she herself had performed. Arethusa received many compliments too. She stood with Margherita who was still glowing from Peregrine's praise. 'I'll never be able to thank you,' Margherita said to Arethusa in the short moment they had together before other young men approached to compliment them.

'For what?' Arethusa asked.

'If it hadn't been for you I would never have been invited here.'

Arethusa frowned. 'Surely I had nothing to do with it.'

Margherita laughed. 'But of course you did. Alexandra wanted your brother so she invited you to take banjo lessons with her, knowing that Rupert would accompany you. But as you and she didn't really know each other, she invited me, knowing we were friends, thus she raised the odds of getting you into her mother's drawing room. Don't you see? It's all about Rupert.'

'I'm not sure Rupert is the marrying kind,' Arethusa said, doubting her words even as she said them. The way he was looking at Lady Alexandra suggested he was most certainly the marrying kind.

'If you hadn't fainted here in this very room, I might never have met Peregrine,' she added. Then her eyes narrowed and she grinned. 'You didn't do that on purpose, did you?'

Arethusa laughed. 'Of course not.'

'You didn't want Peregrine for yourself did you, dear Tussy? I'd hate to have—'

Arethusa stopped her. 'Peregrine is all yours, Margherita. My heart is elsewhere.'

Margherita arched her eyebrows. 'Oh? Who is he? Is he here?'

Arethusa shook her head and sighed. 'Mr Impossible, that's who he is. But while my heart is with him it can never be anywhere else.' She touched her friend's hand. 'I'm envious of you and Peregrine. You're a perfect match and you clearly like each other too. It appears to me that love has little to do with marriage, but sometimes, a lucky person like you manages to merge the two.'

Margherita's eyes filled with sympathy for her friend and gratitude for her own good fortune. 'I am very lucky,' she acknowledged. 'Peregrine is not only handsome but he's sensitive and kind as well.' Then she laughed indulgently, watching him and Rupert now talking together at the other end of the room. 'In marrying him I think I'll be marrying your brother as well. The pair of them are very close. But I suppose in that I can count myself lucky too. They are two of the most attractive men in London and I'll be getting both!'

At that moment Margherita was called away by her mother to be presented to the Dowager Duchess who wanted to meet her (and have an opinion about the American girl who was soon to enter her family) and Arethusa was left alone. She turned with the intention of finding her brother only to see Jonas making his way to her through the throng. His soft gaze fell upon her and with it the rest of the room receded into a blur. All that existed was him and the fragile ray of hope that illuminated the spot in which they stood. 'Your performance tonight was impressive, Miss Deverill,' he said softly. 'You have poise and grace and, well, something special that no one else has. Something unique to you.'

'If I do, you're the only person who sees it,' she replied, sinking further into his gaze. 'You're the only person I *want* to see it. The only person who matters.'

Once again her boldness took him by surprise and he was momentarily lost for words. He looked at her quizzically, as if he couldn't quite believe his own ears.

Arethusa knew now that she had declared herself but she did not avert her gaze. She held his with the brazen assurance of a girl who knows what she wants and is not afraid to reach for it.

He lowered his voice, aware of the other guests who mingled and chatted in his peripheral vision. 'I am leaving now for Manchester,' he said solemnly.

'I know, which is why I have a thank-you gift for you. Just a book of poetry I found that I thought you might like. Perhaps it will inspire you when you compose songs.' Arethusa pulled the strap off her wrist and opened her evening bag. He watched her lift out a miniature book, no bigger than the size of his palm, bound in green with gold letters that read: *The Little Book of Irish Poems*. It was innocuous enough. Something he could show to anyone without embarrassment. Something that would not compromise the giver.

'Thank you,' he replied softly. 'I'm touched.'

'And I will purchase the banjo,' she said, remembering suddenly that it did not belong to her.

'There is no need. It is my gift to you. I want you to have it.'

'I will treasure it.'

'And I will think of you practising.' He smiled, not the cordial smile of a teacher to his student, but the tender, intimate smile of a man who looks upon the woman he loves. 'I will just think of you,' he added, and Arethusa's chest expanded with happiness because he had now declared himself too.

'Music is a language of its own,' she said. 'One can say an awful lot without articulating a word. In fact, I would go as far as saying that music communicates more than words ever can. That sometimes words are inadequate, but music gets right to the heart of the matter. I want to play you something beautiful, Mr Madison. Something truly beautiful because what I feel in here' – she put a hand on her heart – 'is beautiful.'

'Miss Deverill, it has been a pleasure.' His change of tone alerted her to the approach of someone. She turned to see Augusta pushing her way through the crowd towards her like a stately galleon on the sea. Arethusa was furious to have been interrupted.

'My dear!' gushed Augusta, ignoring Jonas. 'You were marvellous. Everyone is saying so!'

Arethusa cut her off swiftly. 'Cousin Augusta, may I present my tutor, Jonas Madison. Mr Madison, this is my cousin, Mrs Deverill.'

Augusta had ignored him on purpose. It wasn't seemly for Arethusa to be talking to him alone. She gave him a lofty look but managed to greet him with politeness. If it hadn't been for the fact that Jonas had given the Prince of Wales a banjo lesson she might not have greeted him at all, Arethusa thought resentfully. 'You did a fine job teaching my young cousin how to play the banjo.' Augusta laughed dismissively, as if she didn't consider the banjo a proper instrument, but more of a novelty. 'We were all highly amused.' Then she gave him a stern look and Arethusa's stomach gave a lurch as she anticipated what her outspoken cousin was going to say. 'But if I were you I would perhaps take the song of slavery out of your repertoire. I don't know how it goes down in America, but we are a people of delicate tastes and find that sort of thing quite unsavoury.'

Before Jonas could answer, Arethusa jumped in. 'Cousin Augusta, Mr Madison has given me the banjo. Isn't that generous and kind of him?' she said.

Augusta's eyes widened and she blanched. It was clear from her expression that she was not pleased.

Jonas cut in, 'I am also going to give Lady Alexandra and Miss Stubbs their instruments too,' he reassured her. 'It's a pleasure to know that they might continue playing.'

Augusta laughed with relief that his gesture wasn't inappropriate after all, that he was going to give all three girls their banjos. If it was acceptable to the Duchess, it was acceptable to her. 'Yes, very generous and kind,' she agreed. 'Once the novelty has worn off, I'm sure it will look very pretty on the shelf.'

Jonas accepted his cue to leave without affront. 'It was very nice to meet you, Mrs Deverill, and an honour to teach *you*, Miss Deverill.'

Arethusa smiled at him and only *he* noticed the shadow of regret that lingered behind it. 'I can assure you, Mr Madison,' she said, aware that Augusta would no doubt chastise her for her boldness and write to her mother to report it. 'The novelty will *never* wear off.'

Jonas bowed and Arethusa watched him disappear into the crowd.

Chapter 22

The following morning Arethusa was sitting in the parlour with Charlotte and Rupert when she received a letter, brought to her on a silver tray by one of the footmen. She did not recognize the handwriting. Her heartbeat quickened as she studied it a moment, scared to open it in case it brought disappointment. She silently prayed that it was from Jonas. She had written her address in the poetry book she had given him the night before, but there was always a chance he hadn't seen it. Slowly she pulled the little white card out of the envelope and immediately looked for the name at the bottom. She caught her breath. It was signed, simply, *J.* There was no engraved gold lettering at the top, just the date, which he had written in his flamboyant hand. How like Jonas, she thought admiringly, to have beautiful handwriting.

'Who's it from?' asked Rupert, stretched out in the corner of the sofa, reading *The Times*.

Charlotte, most uncharacteristically, interrupted. 'One must never ask a lady such a question,' she reproved him.

'Says who?' Rupert retorted. 'Is it Ronald announcing his arrival? If he knew how many gentlemen howled outside your bedroom window like wolves, he'd be over on the next mail.'

'Oh really, Rupert! You're incorrigible.' Arethusa put the

card into its envelope without reading it. 'It's from a new friend, Jane Willoughby, inviting me to tea. But I shan't accept. I'm much too busy. Perhaps another time.' She put the envelope into the pocket of her skirt.

Charlotte, who had been embroidering, went back to her work.

'Do you mean Willoughby de Broke?' Rupert murmured.

'No, another Willoughby. Spelt differently, I think,' she answered vaguely. She wished she'd thought of a more common name, but she'd been caught off guard and had had to choose one in haste.

'Ah,' said Rupert. He lifted his eyes off the paper and grinned at her as if he knew the game she was playing. 'After all, there are lots of Willoughbys.'

'If you don't propose to Lady Alexandra, you're going to create a scandal,' said Arethusa, deliberately changing the subject. 'You've been toying with her for long enough. It's going to become awkward.'

Rupert sighed. 'I have no intention of marrying her,' he said firmly and Arethusa could see from the muscle moving in his jaw that he really did mean to hold his position.

'Why? She's eligible, sweet, and quite pretty—'

'She could be Helen of Troy and I still wouldn't marry her. I'm not for marrying.'

Arethusa glanced at Charlotte, whose mousy head was down as she focused on her embroidery and pretended not to listen. 'Margherita and Peregrine are soon to announce their engagement. I bet my life on it.'

'Oh, you never want to bet your life on anything, Tussy. One's life is precious. But luckily for you, I think you're right. Peregrine told me last night that he has already spoken to his parents and they have agreed that Margherita is a good match.'

'They love each other,' said Arethusa wistfully.

'I'm sure *she* loves him,' said Rupert and there was a bitterness in his voice that alerted his sister to something else at play: jealousy. It hadn't occurred to her that Rupert might have feelings for her American friend.

'Oh, Peregrine loves her back, I'm sure of it,' Arethusa replied.

'No, he doesn't,' Rupert said.

'How do you know?'

'Because it takes a man to know a man.'

Arethusa's spirits were dampened. 'Poor Margherita.' She sighed. 'She's marrying him because she believes he loves her. If he doesn't, she'll be devastated.'

'I'm not saying he doesn't like her. I just think you're endowing it with a romance it doesn't have.'

'Well, I'm sad to hear that, if it's true. Margherita is very happy.'

'Ignorance is bliss,' Rupert stated idly, folding the paper. 'I'm going to my club. How about a ride before luncheon?'

'Lovely,' Arethusa replied. 'I'll go and write to Ronald. It's been a few days since I last wrote.'

'And to your mama as well,' prompted Charlotte, looking up from her embroidery.

'Yes, and to mama,' said Arethusa, getting up. 'I will feel good about myself once I've written them. They're always such a duty.' But she left the room with a skip in her step because *one* letter was not going to be a duty at all. She put a hand in her pocket and felt Jonas's card as if it were a warm potato in her fingers.

Alone in her bedroom, she lay on her bed and read what he had written.

My dear Miss Deverill

It is with great pleasure that I read the book of poetry you were so kind to give me. I particularly enjoyed 'Believe Me, If All Those Endearing Young Charms'. Those Irish writers sure know how to pull at the heartstrings. I have never been to Ireland, but I am getting a strong sense of the country and its struggles through the words of some of its greatest poets. I found parallels with the struggles of my own people and was touched all the more because of them. Thank you for that gift. I shall be sad to leave London. It has made a deep impression on me.

Yours faithfully, J

Arethusa put the card to her burning cheek and closed her eyes. *My dear Miss Deverill*, she repeated happily. *My dear . . .* She imagined him sitting at a desk and writing those words. She wondered how long he had deliberated over what to write, and how much he had left unwritten. She knew his regret at leaving London was on account of her. After all, one wouldn't very well miss the drizzle and the smog! She pressed the card to her lips. The thought that she was kissing the very place he had touched made her body ache with desire.

Shortly she got off the bed and went to the desk to compose her reply.

Dear Mr Madison,

Thank you very much for your letter, which I received this morning. I'm so glad you found my address hidden within the poetry. It was the only way I could get it to you. They say water will always find its way downhill. With the same logic, I will always find a way to write to you. You have opened my eyes to the power of music. I was so deeply moved by the song

you sang about slavery. It has stayed with me, truly it has.
If I close my eyes, I can still hear you sing it. When I said
music has the ability to communicate more than words ever
can, I meant that at that very moment I wanted to play you
something. Something deep and tender, something magical,
because that is what I felt in my heart – what I feel. No
letters on a page, or words on the tongue, could ever do justice
to that. I hope you understand and forgive me for my lack of
restraint. I am sad you are leaving London because you have
made a deep impression on me.

Yours faithfully, A

She put down her pen with a shiver of excitement. Her letter
was audacious and improper. If Augusta or her mother ever
found out she'd be in terrible trouble. She'd be sent back to
Ballinakelly after a severe scolding. But they weren't going to
find out. How could they? No one would ever know.

After writing to Ronald and her mother she went downstairs and gave the letters to one of the footmen to post. As
Jonas was leaving for Manchester he would have to send her
his forwarding address in his next letter. She hoped he would
write soon.

'You look very pleased with yourself,' said Charlotte,
emerging from the parlour carrying her bag of embroidery.

'I have written my letters,' Arethusa replied with a smile.
'I feel very good about myself now. Let's go for a walk in the
park. I'm too restless to sit inside waiting for Rupert to come
back and I don't feel like calling on anyone. Let's go out, just
the two of us.' Charlotte smiled at the young woman who was
so clearly in love. She arranged her hat in the hall mirror and
picked up her parasol. As they left the house she wondered
which of Arethusa's suitors had won her heart.

A few days later news broke of Lord Penrith's engagement to Miss Margherita Stubbs. The newspapers were full of it, she being a wealthy American heiress and he being from one of England's leading aristocratic families. Rupert made a few catty remarks and then sulked. Arethusa was surprised that her usually sharp social antennae hadn't picked up his affection for Margherita. What was more extraordinary was that she hadn't seen them speak to each other for more than a few minutes, and when they had there had been no obvious chemistry between them. No blushing cheeks or gleaming eyes, just the usual politeness. If Arethusa's infatuation with Jonas was the yardstick with which she measured love, then Rupert's love for Margherita was sorely lacking.

A few days later Arethusa received another letter from Jonas. The footman brought the silver tray into the breakfast room and went straight to his mistress, who was sitting at the foot of the table with her Pekinese in its usual place on her knee. Augusta stretched out her pudgy hand and scooped them all up. She flicked through them one by one, then, seeing a small white envelope addressed to Arethusa, she held it out. 'This one is for you, dear, and it's not from your mama or Ronald. Though, I think it's time your mama wrote and as for Ronald, well, it's a relief to have a respite. If you're not intending to marry him, Tussy, you should let him know sooner rather than later. It's not kind to string him along.'

Arethusa took the letter and recognized the handwriting at once. She tried, without success, to maintain her composure. The more she tried not to blush, the redder she became. Rupert and Charlotte were both watching her closely. Stoke, who was at the other end of the table reading the newspaper, was not in the least interested. 'Must be from Jane Willoughby,' said Rupert breezily.

Charlotte opened her mouth to say something, then changed her mind and closed it.

Arethusa put the letter in her pocket.

'Aren't you going to read it, dear?' asked Augusta, opening hers. 'Oh, how kind, an invitation to dine from Lady Chadwell. Darling' – she raised her voice, but Stoke was so busy with his newspaper that he didn't hear it – 'an invitation from Lady Chadwell. Isn't that nice?'

'I think Tussy has a secret lover,' said Rupert, clearly bored and wanting a fight.

It had the required effect. Augusta's cheeks burned. 'I hope not!' she exclaimed hotly, looking at Arethusa with a steely, reproachful gaze. 'Nothing is going to be secret on *my* watch.'

'You're being very silly, Rupert,' said Arethusa dismissively. 'As if I'd have the opportunity to have a secret lover, even if I wanted to.'

'Then open it and read it to us. Give us some entertainment,' he said. 'If it's not from a secret lover, there's no need to hide it. Maybe it's an invitation to tea again from Jane Willoughby. Do you know Jane Willoughby, Augusta?'

Augusta frowned. 'No, who's Jane Willoughby? Do you mean Jane Willoughby de Broke?'

Rupert smiled, but it had a cruel twist to it. 'I think you'll find it's not Jane at all, but *James* Willoughby.'

Arethusa was incensed. 'You're just trying to bait me, Rupert. You've been in a sulk ever since Margherita got engaged to Peregrine.'

'Fine match,' said Stoke from behind his paper.

The four of them looked at him in surprise. 'It is a fine match, indeed,' Augusta agreed. 'Did you hear, darling, an invitation from Lady Chadwell?'

'You're just put out because she didn't fall in love with *you*,' Arethusa continued.

Rupert laughed joylessly. 'Margherita is not my type. She's brash and coarse,' he said witheringly. 'I don't warm to Americans.'

'And Lady Alexandra is like a mouse,' Arethusa added with a grin. 'Then I guess you're jealous.'

'Of whom?' he asked in a lofty voice.

'Of Margherita, of course, because she's taken away your playmate. Is that what this is all about? Peregrine?'

Rupert stood up abruptly. Stoke peered over the newspaper. 'Are you going out, old boy?' he asked.

'I'm not going to sit here and listen to my sister's prattle, if that's what you mean. Going out is the only alternative.'

Arethusa laughed. 'I think I've touched a nerve,' she said to Augusta and Charlotte.

'Then I'll come with you,' said Stoke, folding the paper. 'Excuse us, ladies.' The two men left the room.

Augusta opened the last envelope. It was large and stiff and very white. Inside was a grand invitation. Her face opened into an enormous smile. 'Well, isn't this exciting!' she exclaimed. 'The Castle Deverill Summer Ball. I always look forward to that Saturday night in August when we're at the castle for the month. It's the highlight of the summer. The highlight of *everyone's* summer. People are bored of the London season, which has just come to an end by then, and are delighted to flock to Co. Cork for a change of scene. It's got to be one of the most splendid events of the year.' She stared at the card for a long moment, lost in thought. Arethusa assumed she was already thinking about what she was going to wear, but then Augusta put the invitation on the table and surprised her. 'I think *we* should give a ball,' she said, her eyes glinting with competitiveness. 'Our own magnificent Deverill Rising ball.'

'What will the occasion be?' Arethusa asked.

'Does there need to be an occasion? Isn't it much grander to give a ball just for its own sake? What do you think, Charlotte? Really, you're so quiet, dear, one almost forgets you're here.'

Charlotte shuffled uncomfortably. 'I think a ball would be wonderful,' she said quietly, then added in a more confident voice, as if to convince Augusta that she was not so retiring, 'A Deverill Rising ball would be sure to outshine every other.'

This pleased Augusta. 'You're right, Charlotte. I like that. We will, indeed, outshine everyone else. But we must be original. We have to plan it very carefully. We must cause a sensation. The Ballinakelly Deverills do nothing by halves, so we must hold our end up. Tussy, you must help me, and you too, Charlotte. Oh! Wait until I tell Stoke. Of course, he'll try and talk me out of it, but now I've decided, nothing will stand in my way. Not even he who holds the purse strings!' She lifted her Pekinese to her face and kissed it on the nose. 'What do you think, Muffin? Do you think a Deverill Rising ball is a good idea?'

Arethusa fled to her bedroom as soon as she was able to get away. She threw herself onto her bed and read Jonas's letter with exhilaration and longing. Before, he had exercised restraint. This time he discarded it. Arethusa devoured his words hungrily, lingering on the sentences that revealed the full extent of his affection for her. He spoke of her talent, her beauty and her courage, for it took courage to write to him. Indeed, it took courage, or perhaps nerve, to even entertain the smallest idea of a friendship. It was clear that he did not entertain such an idea himself. He wrote of their impossible situation and promised to 'admire her, for always, from afar'.

*If only we lived in a world where two people like us could be
free to love each other. I would give my right arm to live in
such a world. But we do not. Everything is against us. There
is no escaping prejudice. Therefore, I hold your image in my
heart like a secret treasure, for myself alone, and knowing it
is there inspires me to higher ideals and aspirations. With
your sweet face smiling on me at every turn, I know I can be
the best possible version of myself. God shines down on all
of His creation with an indiscriminate light. You, my darling
Arethusa, are closer to God than most, for you see me only as
a man. For that alone you have my love.*

When Arethusa finished, her eyes were full of tears. Of course,
he was simply voicing the truth. How could they possibly be
together? The only option they had was to love one another
from afar. But Arethusa was not interested in the future, only
in the present moment. She did not want to think of what
was impossible, but to focus on what was possible. She disre-
garded consequence and only considered action for its own
sake. Wasn't it true that love had the power to burn through
every obstacle? That the only obstacles to success were the
limitations one put upon oneself?

Arethusa hid the letter beneath her mattress and went
downstairs. She found Charlotte hard at work on her embroidery in the parlour. She cut a lonely, almost imperceptible
figure there in the shadows with only the regular ticking of
the grandfather clock in the hall for company. 'Walk with me,
Charlotte,' she said in the doorway. 'I need some air.'

Charlotte looked up and smiled indulgently, as if to say she
knew why Arethusa was restless. After all, hadn't she been
there herself?

Once in the park, Arethusa found a bench and suggested

they sit down. She had something important to say to her. Charlotte looked anxious but swept her skirts beneath her and sat down. It was cool in the shade of the plane trees and the sound of children playing was faint like the chattering of birds. 'I'm in love,' Arethusa declared. She put a hand on her heart. 'I know it's mad, I've met him but eight times, however, my heart is what it is and I'm suffering.' She smiled at Charlotte, silently apologizing for all the times she'd passed her over. 'You're the only person I can talk to.'

Charlotte took her hand, pleased to be needed. 'Who is he?' she asked.

'I can't say. He's entirely unsuitable.'

'Oh.' Charlotte squeezed the hand in sympathy. 'Now I see why I'm the only person you can talk to,' she said softly.

'What am I to do?' Arethusa wailed, although the question was rhetorical. She knew exactly what she was to do. What was the *only* thing to do. Yet, she couldn't accept it.

'How unsuitable is he?'

'Very.'

'Is he promised to somebody else?'

'No.'

'Is he from a different world?'

'Absolutely. There is no resolution. Unless I run off with him, which you know is impossible.' Arethusa laughed at the thought. Her mother's horrified face popped into her mind along with her father's furious red one and the idea of eloping, which had never rooted itself, now blew away in the wind of reason. She shook her head and sighed helplessly. 'I suppose I should marry Ronald and be done with it.'

'Is there really no way you and this man can be together?' Charlotte's face was so eager to please that Arethusa's eyes welled with tears.

'Oh Charlotte, how sweet you are. You know how I feel, don't you? You know, because you loved Tom. Well, I know how you felt—'

Charlotte cut her off. 'Feel,' she said with emphasis.

Arethusa looked at her with compassion. 'You mean, it doesn't go away?'

'No, it never goes away.' Charlotte smiled sadly. 'It gets better. Time makes everything better in the end. One just has to surrender eventually and let time do its healing. But it never goes away entirely. There is a Tom-shaped hole in my heart and no one else will ever fill it.'

Arethusa put her arms around the woman who she believed was now too old to marry yet too young to give up on love, and felt very sad for her. 'I'm so sorry,' she whispered.

'I'm sorry too,' said Charlotte. 'I'm sorry you have to suffer as well. It's a horrid ache and there is no cure for it.'

Arethusa released her and laughed bitterly. 'What a *trio* we are, after all, Rupert is suffering too, although I'm not sure who is causing it.'

Charlotte frowned with both disapproval and bewilderment. 'He must propose to Lady Alexandra,' she said firmly. 'Or he will hurt her and insult her family. One doesn't want to insult a powerful family like the Sutcliffes.'

'I agree. However, I'm surprised the Duke and Duchess approve of Rupert. He's not going to inherit the title or the castle. In fact, he's not going to get much at all.'

'But Lady Alexandra is indulged. If she wants him badly enough her parents will no doubt support her. They are frightfully rich, after all. And don't forget, Lord Penrith is marrying a gold mine!'

They both laughed. 'And Rupert is very unhappy about it,' said Arethusa.

'I don't understand Rupert at all,' Charlotte confessed.

'Grandma does,' Arethusa told her. 'She said Rupert will never marry. That he'll be playing bridge with the Shrubs when he's an old man. Imagine! What a life!'

'Indeed. I think Rupert is one of those men who prefer the company of other men. Perhaps he'd be happier playing bridge at his club with Peregrine.'

'I think you're right.' Arethusa took Charlotte's hand and smiled at her with gratitude. 'You haven't given me any answers, and my situation remains unaltered, but you have made me feel much better. Thank you.'

Charlotte clasped her hand in both of hers as if it were a precious thing. 'A woman's lot is a hard one,' she told her gently. 'But if we can talk about it and share our problems, it will make the going easier, I promise.' Then she paused and took a breath. 'If there really is no possibility of this love of yours then I would accept Ronald's proposal.' She gave Arethusa a severe look, suddenly the governess again, rather than the friend. 'If there is any chance that you will do something silly, I would marry Ronald as soon as possible in order to save yourself from dishonour.'

Arethusa felt a chill about the heart. She knew Charlotte was right. That she should save herself from herself. But she also knew, given the opportunity and her wild and reckless nature, that there was a strong chance she would do something very silly indeed. After all, it wasn't restraint that was now taking hold of her, but quite the opposite. She was feeble against the overwhelming desire to engineer a meeting with Jonas.

Chapter 23

Arethusa was relieved when the London season came to an end at the beginning of August. Rupert had disgraced himself. The Deverill name was unmentionable in the Sutcliffe household and many doors which had been thrown open for both Rupert and his sister in London's finest avenues were now shut. On Arethusa's part, she too had caused lips to purse with disapproval having rebuffed some of the most eligible men who had plucked up the courage to propose to her. In short, London was not sorry to be rid of them. The only person who viewed their foray as a success was Augusta, who was so busy planning her ball and telling everyone about it that she did not hear the whispers or feel the many cold shoulders. Arethusa and Rupert left London under a cloud, but the sun still shone in Augusta's world.

Back at Castle Deverill they received a hero's welcome. Greville and Elizabeth threw a grand dinner party in their honour, inviting two hundred friends from all over the county to dine and dance. Among those friends were the Rowan-Hamptons. Ronald, being eager to secure an engagement, was the first through the door. Arethusa, who was under no illusions about what was expected of her, was ready to acquiesce. After all, she knew she could never marry Jonas. She also knew that running away with him was out of the question. Nor did she want to go off like fruit left too long in the bowl, as Augusta had said. If she didn't marry Ronald, she'd marry someone very like him. Therefore, she might as well accept her lot and hope that the odd letter from Jonas would be a small beacon of light in the dark monotony of her married life.

Ronald's happiness knew no bounds. He arrived pink in the face with anticipation, for in his pocket he carried a diamond and sapphire ring which had been given to him by his father especially for this very moment. He puffed out his chest with confidence and strode into the hall with a swagger, as if taking ownership of a Deverill gave him special status. He was relieved that Arethusa had survived the London season without being taken by anyone else, but he was also a touch complacent. After all, he believed his letters had kept him in her mind and, although adventurous and free-spirited, he was sure she appreciated his qualities and was fond of him because of what he represented: home, family and Ireland. There were not many in London who represented those.

Arethusa was a prize and he was about to win her. Ronald felt very pleased with himself. He remained at her side for the duration of the evening, attending her like an eager knight of olde with his lady, making sure her glass was full, that she wasn't too cold, or too hot even, and Arethusa thought that perhaps it wouldn't be so bad being looked after in this way, so long as he gave her breathing space from time to time for her windows of pleasure. Adeline's hand in the placement was revealed when they found themselves seated together at the dinner table. It was only after eating, when they wandered into the garden to sit alone beneath the stars, twinkling fittingly bright in a velvet sky, that Ronald bent to one knee and took her hand. Arethusa was unmoved by the charade. She thought of Jonas, of his beautiful face, still clear in her memory, and her whole body ached for him. Ronald's hand was warm and damp with sweat. The thought of it touching her intimately gave her a sudden shiver of revulsion. She looked down into his eyes that brimmed with affection, but they too failed to soften the hardening of her heart. Arethusa knew he was a good and kind man and would no doubt look after her as the Good Ones her grandmother spoke of could be relied upon to do. Her heart hardened towards her life and the unfairness of it and yet she did not pull her hand away.

'My darling Tussy,' he began, his face crumping into a sincere frown. 'I have loved you for years. You know that, of course. I have told you many times in my letters. There was a moment when I thought I had lost you to London, but I always knew your heart was in the right place. Home, family and Ireland matter to you as they matter to me and that is the kind of foundation upon which one can build a life together that is both satisfactory and pleasant. I'm asking you to make me the happiest man in the world tonight, by agreeing to marry me.' His eyes now sparkled with tears. 'My darling Tussy, will you do me the honour of becoming my wife?'

He slipped a hand into the inside pocket of his jacket and pulled out a little red box. Arethusa watched him open it with trembling fingers. There, glittering on a crimson cushion, was the diamond and sapphire ring. Arethusa had never been moved by material things and she wasn't moved now. The gems glittered but they promised a future that was hard and cold and restrained. She blinked and large tears rolled down her cheeks. Her lips quivered and she put a hand to her heart, which seemed to shrivel like a prune in anticipation of the loveless marriage that lay before it. Ronald, encouraged by what he saw as a sincere display of emotion, slipped the ring onto her finger, where it sat securely as if it had been made especially to her size. Then he stood up and pulled her against him. 'You have made me the happiest man alive,' he gushed, pressing his lips to hers in a kiss, which, although chaste, gave a moist preview of what was to come. 'I must now ask your father for your hand and then we can share our happy news with everyone. My darling,' he added, gazing into her eyes which appeared to shine brilliantly with affection for him. 'We will take the world by storm, the two of us. What a pair we shall be. And one day, when my father passes away, you will carry the title Lady Rowan-Hampton with great style. Sir Ronald and Lady Rowan-Hampton. Arethusa Rowan-Hampton, how does that sound? Like music to me, my darling. Come! Let us get back to the party. I need to get your father into the library before anyone sees the ring.'

It occurred to Arethusa as she followed him back inside that she hadn't actually said yes.

The following few days were a blur. She felt as if she were wading through porridge as people called to the castle to congratulate her and bouquets of flowers arrived wrapped in brightly coloured ribbons. Her heart bled for the man she loved and couldn't have. She nursed it by playing the banjo, deep into the night, on the window seat in her bedroom, but it served only to drive her sorrow deeper. The banjo was the only part of him she had kept. The only part she could touch, and the music connected her to him, wherever he was, and made her feel close in spite of the distance between them.

Everyone at Castle Deverill was oblivious of her pain. Hubert was relieved that the responsibility of taking care of his headstrong and unconventional daughter was no longer going to be his, while Adeline was happy that she had agreed to marry a kind and generous man who would take care of her – and make an honest woman of her. There would be no more dalliances into town or flirtations with the local men. Greville was of the opinion that girls like his granddaughter were rather like broodmares: only good for breeding; Arethusa was simply fulfilling her destiny and marrying a man from her stock, as was her duty. But Elizabeth smiled to herself because when a woman like Arethusa married a Good One, there would always be windows left ajar to allow in those deliciously wicked Handsome Knights.

'She'll tire of Ronald very quickly,' said Rupert to the Shrubs as they dealt the cards for a rubber of bridge.

'Tush!' chided Laurel. 'You're very cynical, Rupert. I think Ronald is the perfect match for her.'

'That's only because you don't really know Tussy very well,' he added with a knowing grin, which suggested he alone did.

'She's certainly free-spirited,' said Poppy, smiling fondly. 'Ronald will have his work cut out for him. But I think she'll settle down and make a very good wife.'

Rupert laughed. 'She's much too selfish to make a good wife,' he said, looking at his hand of cards and sensing an advantage. 'She'll make a challenging wife, a tiresome wife and most likely a demanding wife, but God forbid she makes a *bored* wife.' He looked at the three sisters from under his frown. 'Bored wives are trouble.'

Hazel shook her head. 'And what do you know of wives?' she asked.

'Enough to tell me that I don't want one,' he replied crisply.

'After your season in London I'm not sure there are any potential wives who want *you*,' said Poppy disapprovingly.

However, Rupert grinned at her and it was so full of charm and mischief that she couldn't help but smile. 'I did rather disgrace myself in London,' he said with a sigh. 'As did Tussy, of course. It's just as well that Ronald is gathering her up, but if I know Tussy, and I do, I predict dramas ahead. After all, Tussy is a round peg and convention is a square hole.'

Arethusa waited for a letter from Jonas but none came. She sensed that he had accepted the futility of their relationship and had given up corresponding. Perhaps he didn't want to encourage her when the very idea of it was hopeless. Arethusa knew that she should accept it too, but she could not. To look into a future without Jonas was like looking into a world devoid of joy. Music would sound uninspiring to her ears, dancing would feel joyless to her feet, even the changing seasons would be drab if there was no possibility of a word from the man she loved. Without Jonas, she'd be like a traveller without a compass, wandering without a sense of direction, without a sense of purpose. She only wanted to feel connected to him. It didn't matter that he lived on another continent, so long as he sent her the occasional word to reassure her that she was in his thoughts, and in his heart perhaps, then she could go on and the music wouldn't sound so flat and the dancing wouldn't feel so heavy. She could appreciate the seasons because the same sun would shine down on them both and she would know that he had not forgotten her.

The wedding was set for May of the following year. The ceremony would be held in the church of St Patrick in Ballinakelly with a reception at the castle afterwards. Adeline set about writing the guest list with the help of Augusta, who had arrived with Stoke and two of their sons for their usual August sojourn, while the Shrubs had much to say about the dress and what it should look like. Charlotte helped Adeline plan Arethusa's trousseau, though inside her heart was heavy. She knew that her employment would end with Arethusa's marriage and she would have to go out into the world and find another position.

Nothing, she feared, would compare to Castle Deverill and Arethusa, of whom she was so terribly fond.

Arethusa feigned interest in her wedding. It seemed that was all any of the women in her family could talk about, even though the Deverill Summer Ball was approaching and there was a lot to organize. Besides Charlotte, only her grandmother sensed her lack of enthusiasm, winking at her across the dining-room table and occasionally making comments under her breath while she sat beside the fire in the library, knitting. 'My dear,' she said one evening, while Arethusa sat at her feet holding the ball of wool and staring into it forlornly. 'You're only a prisoner of Fate if you *think* you are.' Arethusa looked back at her and frowned. Elizabeth smiled and continued to knit.

'What did you say, Grandma?'

'You heard me well enough, Tussy,' she replied. 'I'm speaking of the power of thought to create your reality. Dreams come true, you know, if you dream hard enough.'

'Do you know what I dream?' Arethusa asked.

'Your dreams are no different to everyone else's. We all want to be happy, don't we?'

'Do I look miserable to you?' Arethusa lowered her voice.

Elizabeth put her knitting on her lap and ran a hand down her granddaughter's hair. 'Only to me, because I was once just like you. Where did you think you got your nature from? Not Adeline, she's much too otherworldly, and certainly not from Hubert, who is much too conventional. No, you're just like me. That wild, impulsive and reckless thread weaves through my side of the family. Greville didn't tame me, he just thought he did.' She chuckled like one of her hens. 'I played a clever game, as must you. We might be the weaker sex, but there's no reason why we can't be the sharper one.'

Arethusa stared at her grandmother. She was so articulate. Her thoughts so clearly communicated. Suddenly, Elizabeth didn't look dotty at all, in fact she looked cunning. Either she was totally mad, or incredibly calculating and shrewd. Arethusa narrowed her eyes. 'Grandma, are you an actress, playing the part of a dotty old lady, or are you really a dotty old lady?'

Elizabeth lifted her chin and resumed her knitting. 'I don't know what you mean, Tussy,' she replied severely, but Arethusa could see a secretive smile hovering about her lips.

The next day dawned bright and optimistic. The sun dazzled in a royal-blue sky, infusing the hills and valleys of Co. Cork with its late-summer radiance. The wind that came off the sea was warm and playful. Arethusa had dreamed of Jonas. She had been in his arms and he had been kissing her. She had awoken surprised to find herself alone and had closed her eyes and tried to bring the dream back, but slowly it had faded and the feeling of being wrapped in his love had faded with it. She got up and called for her maid. The young Eily appeared, eager to please. 'Take this note and give it to Dermot McLoughlin at once.' Eily looked down at the envelope and frowned. 'And if you open it I shall know and you will never work in Ballinakelly again. Do you understand?'

Eily gave a curtsey. 'I do, miss.'

'Good. Now go at once and if anyone asks where you're going, tell them I have sent you to deliver an important letter to Mrs Poppy.'

Arethusa watched the maid put the envelope in the pocket of her skirt and leave the room. She thought of Jonas, of the impossibility of any kind of relationship, and then she thought of Dermot, the only consolation in what was otherwise a bleak and unhappy future. She would seek her windows of pleasure while she could, in the only way she could. If she didn't, she knew she would go mad. As long as she was cunning, like her grandmother, she could survive the boredom of being Lady Rowan-Hampton. And in the meantime, she would dream, because sometimes dreams came true if one dreamed hard enough.

Eily hurried across the fields towards Ballinakelly, Arethusa's letter smouldering like a burning coal in her pocket. She longed to know what was in it. What Miss Arethusa had written to Dermot McLoughlin. Eily had heard rumours that the two of them met in secret, the town was awash with gossip, but that was fervently denied by those loyal to the Deverills. There were many who weren't loyal. Men who talked of independence from the British, men willing to fight for it. But Eily was young and she didn't understand the snippets of conversation she picked up at the dinner table while the men in her family voiced their resentment at the ruling Anglo-Irish class who lived lavishly while *they* had barely enough to feed their families. She was much more interested in the gossip and here, in her pocket, was a letter from Miss Arethusa herself to Dermot McLoughlin, either confirming or refuting an improper relationship. It was irresistible. Yet the envelope was sealed. If she opened it, Arethusa would surely find out and she would be finished. She'd never get another job. She couldn't afford that. She stopped walking and pulled the envelope out of her pocket and looked at it closely. She held it up to the light but the paper was too thick. She tried peeling it open but the gum was too strong. She was so frustrated she nearly ripped it open in spite of knowing the consequences, but eventually she accepted it couldn't be done and put it back in her pocket and walked on briskly.

When Eily reached the foundry Dermot was outside,

smoking a cigarette and talking to a couple of grubby-looking men in caps and tatty jackets who she knew as she knew all the locals. When Dermot saw her, he broke off the conversation. 'What are you doing here at this time of the morning, Eily Goggin? Shouldn't you be tending to your mistress?'

Eily's position at the castle gave her a certain confidence and she scowled at him. 'I need a word with you, in private.' She glared at his friends.

'Talk later,' Dermot said to them, dropping his cigarette on the ground and stamping it out with his boot. 'Come on then, Miss Goggin. What do you want with the likes of me?'

She looked up and down the street to make sure they weren't being watched. 'I've got a letter for you. From Miss Deverill.'

He scratched his beard. 'From Miss Deverill? She gave you a letter, for me?' He was incredulous.

'Indeed she did.' She pulled it out and handed it to him. He too looked shiftily up and down the street, then slipped it into his pocket.

'She must trust you to give you a letter like this,' he said, looking Eily up and down, this time with more respect.

'She trusts me with everything,' said Eily proudly. 'She knows I'm safe so she tells me all her secrets.'

'Does she now?' said Dermot.

'She doesn't want to marry Mr Rowan-Hampton,' she told him confidentially. 'But she has to do her duty. Indeed, she says marriage is like a public hanging.' Eily grinned, baring a crooked and incomplete set of teeth. 'I don't think Miss Arethusa will make a very good wife.'

Dermot shook his head. 'She'd be a good wife to the right man.'

'Is that you, Mr McLoughlin? Are you the right man?'

He looked at her steadily, as if weighing up whether or not she could be trusted. 'You're too young to be asking those sorts of questions, Miss Goggin. But seeing as she confides in you, I'll tell you the truth. If she wasn't a Deverill I'd make her a McLoughlin, sure I would.' Eily's eyes widened. 'Now you go back to the castle before anyone sees you here.'

Eily walked back across the fields, deliberating whether or not she would be able to restrain herself from sharing what Dermot McLoughlin had told her. It would be a challenge, but then Eily enjoyed knowing something that others didn't. She enjoyed the sense of power. With seven older siblings to contend with, power was something she had precious little of.

Arethusa headed off to the woods outside Ballinakelly in the late afternoon. Already the shadows were lengthening as the mid-August sun travelled ever lower across the sky, sinking slowly towards the western horizon. The air was sweet with the scents of heather and brine, the wind cold, as if it had caught a chill somewhere over the sea. She loved this time of year, when the scents of summer rose up from the ground and the light was mellow and soft, the colour of a mature peach. She loved the twittering sound of small corncrakes in the gorse and the sight of large grey crows circling above with their wings outstretched, scanning the earth for prey. The beauty of nature soothed her aching heart yet still she felt a melancholy in the depths of her soul. She hoped to find comfort in Dermot. She hoped to lose herself in him, or perhaps to find her old self there, in his arms where she had been reckless, brazen and brave. This mournful person who pined for a man she could never have was not someone she wanted to be, and yet, she couldn't help herself. She was a prisoner of love and there seemed little hope of rescue.

Dermot was waiting for her in the trees, smoking. When

Arethusa saw him she was suddenly choked with emotion. Her vision blurred and her chest grew tight. A ball of tension lodged itself in her throat and she couldn't speak. She ran to him and took his face in her hands and kissed him passionately. Dermot pulled her into the shadows, unsure of this new, vulnerable Arethusa. She did not tease him, as she usually did as a prelude to their lovemaking, but touched him with tenderness, her hands trembling, her eyes shining with unhappiness and longing. He didn't question her but drew her into his arms and held her tightly, sure that he could comfort her. Sure that he was the *only* man who could.

They lay on the forest floor, on the soft mossy ground among the long grasses and ferns, and Arethusa forgot herself in arms that were at once dependable and familiar. She pushed Jonas out of her mind and concentrated on the taste and smell of the man who would have to do as a substitute. She took her pleasure, but not in her usual selfish way. Dermot meant more to her now. He was the only possible window of pleasure available to her and she was grateful for his affection and respectful of his love, for love her he did; and she needed to feel loved. Now she knew what it was like to yearn for someone she could never have she treated his heart with more care.

When they were satiated they lay entangled in the grass. The setting sun dropped golden shafts of light through the holes in the canopy of leaves, illuminating the harvest dust and the midges and small flies that coasted across them. It was quiet, but for the sound of birds and the rustle of small animals in the undergrowth. Arethusa felt peaceful and recharged. She felt herself again, as if Dermot had reminded her of who she was and had, in making love to her, perhaps given her back a little of herself.

'You're different,' he said, pressing his cheek to her forehead and tightening his arms around her. 'What's London done with the Tussy I know and love, eh?' But he wasn't teasing, his tone was concerned and Arethusa was reassured by it.

At the mention of London she felt her heart grow heavy again with melancholy. 'I must marry Ronald,' she said dully. 'I have to marry someone and Ronald is the best choice I have. At least I get to stay in Ireland. At least I won't be far from home – or from you.'

'You'll always have me, Tussy.'

'Will I?'

'Sure you will. I'll always be here. I'm not going anywhere.' Arethusa's eyes filled with tears. 'Your heart is sick,' he said, frowning at her. 'I can feel it.'

'Sick hearts heal,' she replied, but she knew they didn't. Charlotte had told her as much.

'Run away with me, Tussy. We could go anywhere you wish. Anywhere at all.'

She propped herself up on her elbow and ran a finger down his nose. 'And what would we live on?'

'I'm a blacksmith. Everyone has need of a blacksmith.'

She smiled indulgently. 'Oh Dermot. What a romantic you are. We can't run away together. You know that. Besides, I don't ever want to leave my home. I love Ballinakelly. I love Castle Deverill. I love Ireland.'

'And you love *me*,' he said firmly. 'I know you do. I can see it in your eyes. You're sick with longing.'

Of course, he spoke the truth, but it wasn't *him* she was longing for. Immediately she felt bad and wished to make it up to him. 'If I marry Ronald I'll be able to see you,' she replied, hanging on to this small consolation as if she were lost at sea clinging on to a piece of driftwood. 'We'll be able to meet. We'll find a way.'

'You'll have to give him an heir,' he said. 'And a spare, just in case.'

'I'll do my duty. I'll play the part. He's a good man. He's kind, he'll look after me.'

Dermot's expression hardened. 'He'll stifle the life out of you. He'll want to tame you, Tussy. He'll want to change you. He'll want you to be an obedient wife.'

'I'm much too independent to allow him to do that,' she said, but his comment made her uneasy. She knew he was right. Ronald would want to change her as any conventional, traditionally minded husband would. He was like her father. Her heart sank as she contemplated Ronald. It was true, she was marrying her father. 'The only way I will survive is if I can see you,' she said and bent down to kiss him. 'You will always be here for me, won't you, Dermot?' she said.

'Indeed I will,' he replied and Arethusa felt a little ashamed that she could not give him her heart, only her body. Her heart would always be Jonas's.

Chapter 24

The Deverill Summer Ball was a much anticipated event on the social calendar. Friends travelled from England especially to be there, while all the grand houses in the county were invited and the ladies came in their finest gowns and jewellery to show their English sisters that there was plenty of style across the water. The castle, possibly the most beautiful in the whole of Ireland, looked magnificent lit up with flares and adorned with flowers. In the old days Elizabeth had presided over the arrangements and done a fine job of it, for she was a woman of flair and good taste, but nowadays she was old and distrait, and she preferred to feed her hens and wander around the gardens enjoying the sound of everyone else doing the toil. Therefore, Adeline had taken over the running of the operation, and an operation it certainly was. For this momentous occasion almost everyone in Ballinakelly was employed, as waiters, maids, extra gardeners, footmen and kitchen staff. An orchestra had to be hired from Dublin, a chef was shipped all the way from London. Flowers were grown in great quantities in the castle greenhouses, vegetables picked from the walled garden and Greville's finest wines brought up from the cellars to sustain the three hundred guests. The preparations began weeks in advance with the taking down and cleaning of all the chandeliers and the polishing of silver. Expectations were high because of the reputation the ball had acquired over the years of being the most opulent of the summer.

This year Adeline felt she had surpassed herself. The ball was going to be magnificent, as it always was, but thanks to Augusta it was going to have an added element of surprise which she knew would thrill her guests, especially the Anglo-Irish ones. Adeline rarely sought Augusta for advice. Her English cousin was competitive and opinionated and thrust advice upon people without being invited. But this time Augusta had made a suggestion, sharing a piece of information, and it was invaluable. Of course, she wouldn't have shared it had she been able to use it for her own lavish ball, to be held at Deverill Rising in the autumn, but Adeline was grateful. It gave her a headache having to find new ways of entertaining her guests every year. When Elizabeth had arranged them they had had costume balls and Venetian masked balls, hired dancers from Paris and musicians from Vienna. There had been no limit to the expense and the Deverills could be counted upon to be habitually overindulgent. But Adeline didn't think it was right to be quite so wasteful now. Unlike her mother-in-law, she was conscious of the poverty that seethed all around Castle Deverill, leaving them in splendid yet uneasy isolation like a bountiful island in a barren wasteland. Yet, she was married to a man who, like his father, chose not to concern himself with the needy masses. Greville and Elizabeth were determined that their lives should continue in the way they always had, that traditions should be upheld (they saw no reason why they should change their way of life), and that meant a luxurious ball. If Adeline declared that perhaps it wasn't tactful, Hubert replied that, on account of the ball, every man in Ballinakelly would be employed and well fed. Wasn't that something to be commended?

Adeline did her duty and no one complained, not even Arethusa, who would usually be the first to protest against the shameless and indelicate display of wealth. Arethusa was distracted. Adeline knew she was anxious about marriage. But weren't all women anxious about that? The wedding night was a terrifying blot on a woman's future landscape and yet, Adeline was certain Ronald would be kind. He might not be the most dashing of men, but he was from the same Anglo-Irish world and there was a lot to be said for that. He would give Arethusa security, comfort and a way of life that was familiar. He would respect her and honour her and hopefully tame her. Children and the responsibilities required of a wife would anchor her to the home, which was what Arethusa needed. Adeline still shuddered when she remembered the green lichen on the back of her daughter's dress.

As for her affection for Ronald, Arethusa did not appear wildly enthusiastic about her marriage. Yet, Augusta had told Adeline that the girl had turned down numerous proposals from the most eligible men. Even the Marquess of Penrith had apparently been within her reach, but she had turned him down too. Therefore, Adeline could only conclude that she was, after all, attached to Ronald. The girl's melancholy was not unusual. She was about to leave her home and embark on a new life (although not far away); it was natural that she should feel anxious.

The morning of the ball Arethusa awoke to a new attitude. Dermot had given her hope. There surely would be windows of pleasure within her marriage. She didn't have to change if she didn't want to. She could play a part as her grandmother played a part and be the good wife and mother Ronald wanted her to be. Only Dermot would know the real Arethusa. With him she could be herself. She had also come to the sad but inevitable conclusion that Jonas must be forgotten. As hard as that was to accept, she knew in her heart that she could not go on living like this, pining like a dog, or it would destroy her. She had to focus her attention on her present life and not gaze back into the past. She would put the banjo away, like a secret treasure buried in the ground, and live no more in longing.

Everyone noticed the change in Arethusa's mood when she came down for breakfast. There was colour in her cheeks and she was no longer subdued. Only Charlotte sensed the resolution she had made, for she too had once been compelled to make it, but not the reasons behind it. She knew not of Arethusa's tryst with Dermot McLoughlin or Lady Deverill's advice to find windows of pleasure in the monotony of a dutiful married life. Adeline assumed she was excited about the ball and was glad that something had managed to distract her from her fear of marriage. Rupert, who had inherited his perceptive nature from his mother, also noticed that his sister's mood had lifted, but unlike Charlotte *he* knew all about Dermot McLoughlin and had seen Arethusa the day before, setting off across the garden with a determined stride, from the seat at his bedroom window where he had a very good view of the lawn.

When Arethusa entered, the entire family was already in the dining room and the talk was of Adeline's surprise. 'Fireworks,' said Bertie, who wasn't very interested in the surprise but was playing along for the game.

'We always have fireworks,' said Hubert. He looked at his wife, holding her china teacup in front of a secretive smile, and hoped it wasn't something spiritual. Adeline was inclined to hold séance evenings with her sisters where they supposedly contacted the dead. Hubert thought it a load of old rubbish but indulged her for it was quite harmless. However, it wouldn't do for the Deverill Ball; it most certainly wouldn't.

Arethusa took the chair beside Bertie's wife Maud and sat down. The footman poured her a cup of tea. Maud waited until she had finished chewing her mouthful of toast and then spoke. 'The surprise will be in the entertainment,' she said, dabbing the corners of her mouth with a napkin. 'I bet Adeline has shipped over the best thespians in London to perform a short play.'

'Or a dancing troupe,' said Arethusa, watching her mother closely. 'Russian ballet dancers perhaps?'

'Or a circus act,' Elizabeth trilled from the end of the table, shovelling a large piece of porter cake onto her fork. 'I'd like trapeze artists and an elephant, from India. That would be original, now, wouldn't it? I don't believe anyone has ever hired an elephant from India for their ball.'

Rupert grinned at his grandmother. 'We could put *you* on the elephant, Grandma, and parade you around the garden. Now that would be both stately *and* original.'

Elizabeth chortled but her mouth was too full of cake to reply.

'Or musicians,' interjected Archibald, one of Augusta and Stoke's sons, who was a bumptious young man of twenty-five whose plump, boyish face was constantly flushed from the effort of compensating for his diminutive size with an overconfident personality. At five feet nine he was only just taller than his mother (and two whole heads taller than his poor father). He was proud, however, of his thick blond hair, which he swept off his forehead and set with a lotion, and his gunmetal-blue eyes, which distracted the ladies from his stature. 'I'll bet it's musicians,' he continued cheerfully. 'Something splendidly original. Am I not right, Adeline?'

Adeline continued to smile mysteriously and said nothing. Augusta slyly winked at her son to encourage him along the right path. Archibald, with his mother's help and eager to be right, continued, 'You have invited the Wandering Minstrels themselves!' Adeline's eyes flickered and her smile faltered. 'I'm right! Ha!' he crowed, waving a stubby finger at her.

'You are not right,' said Adeline calmly.

'But close. I can tell by the look on your face that I am close.'

Arethusa's mind turned to the Madison Minstrels, but she held firmly to her resolution and pushed Jonas out of her head.

Archibald's more sensible brother, William, who was tall and well-built as was most becoming in a man, leaned back in his chair as the footman refilled his teacup. 'If we guess the surprise, it will no longer be one,' he said.

'Hear, hear!' Greville agreed with a chortle. 'Now, we must get out of Adeline's way—'

'Before we're made to help,' Rupert interrupted with a smile at his mother.

Elizabeth rose from the table. 'I must check the hens have not been upset by the arrival of the elephant.' And no one was sure whether she really believed there was an elephant or was simply running with the joke.

Arethusa could not get out of helping, like the men in her family, and her grandmother, of course, whose helping days were over. Arethusa, Maud, Augusta and Charlotte awaited instructions from Adeline. The Shrubs arrived in a flurry of excitement like a trio of twittering birds. Soon the castle was full of people and Arethusa busy with the duties her mother asked her to perform. There was no time to see Dermot today.

It was early afternoon, just before she was due to retire to her room to bathe and dress for the ball, when she saw Jonas. She was hurrying down the stairs to the kitchen to pass on a message to the chef when she was stopped, suddenly, in her tracks. There he was, standing in the corridor with his brother, talking to Mr O'Driscoll, the master of the house, as if it were the most natural thing in the world. She froze and stared at him in astonishment. She couldn't believe her eyes. It couldn't be Jonas Madison? Surely, it couldn't! But it was.

The colour drained from her face. Her corset seemed to constrict. Her breath quickened. She gripped the banisters and put a hand to her chest where her heart was now pounding hard against her ribcage. She stared at him as a wave of nausea knocked her off balance. It was then that Jonas raised his eyes. Although his face registered surprise, he was not as shocked to see *her*. From the look he gave her, it was as if he had been expecting to.

'Miss Arethusa,' exclaimed Mr O'Driscoll in a panic. Mr O'Driscoll was a big, burly man with a thick neck, wide shoulders and a barrel chest. He hurried up the stairs to catch her as she lost her footing and began to fall.

'I'm quite all right,' she protested weakly, but he lifted her into his arms and carried her down the stairs. Her eyes searched for Jonas but all she saw were flustered housemaids and Mrs Harrington the housekeeper, fussing over her as if she were made of porcelain. 'Really, I just felt a little dizzy. I'm well now. Thank you,' she said, anxiously trying to see past them. But Mrs Harrington insisted she come into her office and sit down while one of the housemaids scampered off to get her a glass of water and another to make her a cup of tea. Arethusa was desperate to see Jonas, but it was impossible to leave Mrs Harrington's office without being impolite, or without giving herself away. Of course, she now realized that Jonas and George were her mother's surprise, put forward by Augusta. She couldn't believe her good fortune. It was an incredibly good idea of her mother's. The Madison brothers were a sensation. They had been all over the British press when they had performed in London and taught the Prince of Wales to play the banjo. Everyone would be very impressed by this exotic pair of entertainers. But Arethusa's head now throbbed with ways she could contrive to get Jonas on his own. She knew the castle grounds better than anyone. If she could just lure him into one of the greenhouses . . .

By the time she managed to extricate herself Jonas and George had gone. It didn't matter. She knew they were in the castle, somewhere, and she was determined to find them. Her excitement mounted as she made her way back up the servants' stairs while the housemaids whispered that it had been the sight of the two exotic men from America that had caused her to faint.

She was crossing the hall when she bumped into her mother. 'Darling, you must start getting ready. I need you to be dressed and on parade by half past six.'

'I know what the surprise is,' said Arethusa, grinning broadly.

Adeline sighed but her smile was indulgent. 'I suppose you've been downstairs, have you, Tussy?'

'I saw them in the corridor. The Madison brothers. I think they are a very good choice, Mama.'

'I take no credit. Augusta suggested it. They're going to sing five songs and dance as well.'

'They're wonderful dancers,' said Arethusa enthusiastically. 'Where are they? I'd very much like to say hello. Then I'll go and dress, I promise.'

'Very well, but make it quick. They're in the ballroom, rehearsing.'

Arethusa hurried off to the ballroom. The place was full

of servants, bustling about putting the finishing touches to the room. Arethusa didn't notice the vast displays of flowers, heaped into stone urns and cascading from tall structures to look like floral waterfalls, or the candles arranged on every surface ready to blaze through the summer night. She didn't even smell the heady scents of lily and rose. All she noticed was Jonas on the stage which had been erected at the far end of the room, and he eclipsed everything around him.

'So, *you* are Mama's surprise,' she said, standing before him at last. He turned and smiled at her, and in his smile she saw the same tenderness she had seen the night she played for the Duchess's friends.

'How lovely to see you again, Miss Deverill,' he said and Arethusa realized that words were superfluous. It didn't matter what they said. They could have recited a recipe for lemon cake for all she cared and the result would have been the same: words, syllables, sounds that meant nothing. The light in their eyes communicated everything they wanted to say.

It would have been polite for George to have greeted her as well, but he hung back, toying with his instrument and flicking through a dog-eared music score, as if tactfully leaving them alone to talk.

'I hoped I would see you here.' Jonas spoke in a low voice, his eyes flicking momentarily about the room to make sure they were not overheard.

'I never thought I'd see you again,' Arethusa replied. 'Only this morning I had resolved not to think of you anymore. Yet here you are . . .'

'It is as if Fate intervened.'

'Yes. A clear message not to give up,' she said firmly.

'But you know it's impossible, Miss Deverill.'

'Tussy. Call me Tussy,' she said, angry suddenly that Fate

should bring him to her home only for him to tell her their love was impossible. 'Nothing is impossible if you want it enough,' she said, fighting the ache in her throat.

Jonas smiled, this time sadly. 'I admire your courage, Tussy. But I know the world better than you do and there is no place for us in it.'

'The world is a big place. There has to be somewhere,' she insisted, the ache intensifying with the onset of tears. 'There has to be—'

'Tussy.' It was Charlotte, appearing in the frame of the big double doors at the far end of the ballroom behind her.

Arethusa stiffened her jaw and blinked back her tears. 'I look forward to watching you perform,' she said tightly, pulling back her shoulders and assuming an appropriately formal air. Then she added, 'I hope we get the chance to speak later because I'd like to tell you how I've been practising the banjo. Music is a language that speaks to everybody, no matter where they come from. When I play, I believe in miracles.'

Charlotte accompanied Arethusa to her bedroom and helped her prepare for the ball. The governess noticed that she was very pink in the face and that her eyes were strangely burning, and worried she might be coming down with a fever. 'I feel very well,' Arethusa told her crisply when Charlotte voiced her concern. 'I've just been on my feet all day running around for Mama. I'm sure a bath will restore me.'

The servants filled her tub with hot water brought up in big cans from the kitchens and Arethusa lay back and closed her eyes. She sighed heavily. She should be thrilled that Jonas was in the castle. Having thought she would never see him again, this extraordinary twist of fate had brought him right into her home. And yet, she wasn't thrilled. She had suffered and just begun to get over her suffering. She'd made a resolution not to think about him and, after her tryst with Dermot, she had finally accepted her lot. Now he was here, the pain which had begun to settle was being dredged up all over again to hurt her anew, and the longing and pining would resume, more intense than before. Jonas was right, of course, there was no place on earth that would accept them as a couple. It embittered her to think that the world wasn't big enough for them, that prejudice would follow them wherever they went.

Eily helped her into one of the ball dresses Augusta had had made at her London tailor's. It was bright blue silk, trimmed with yellow-gold, and had a bustle, which, much to Augusta's disapproval, accentuated the bounce in her walk. Arethusa had not allowed Eily to do her hair; the young maid was clumsy and had no gift for styling. Instead, she borrowed Becky, her mother's briskly efficient maid, who crimped it with a hot iron and put it up, adorning it with ribbons and blue flowers from the garden. Her grandmother had lent her a suite of sapphires, which had been passed down the generations on her side of the family. 'You're not a child anymore,' she said to Arethusa. 'You've been presented at Court and you're engaged to be married. You should now sparkle like a lady.' Elizabeth scrunched up her nose and added under her breath, 'And sizzle like a Deverill.'

Arethusa could only think of Jonas and how she was going to contrive to see him. She found out from O'Flynn that he and his brother were staying in the Inn at Ballinakelly. She'd rather hoped her mother might have arranged for them to stay in the stable block, or even in the castle attic. There were plenty of rooms. But she had not thought to do so. They were due to leave the following day at dawn. This did not give her much time.

Arethusa stood on the lawn with her family, greeting guests

as they arrived. While she remained stuck there, doing her duty, her anxiety intensified. Every moment away from Jonas was a moment lost. What if she didn't get to see him alone after all? What if it was impossible to arrange? Tonight was perhaps the last time she would ever lay eyes on him. After tonight there would be no other opportunity. He would go back to America or continue touring the world, and she would have to get on with the life she was born to lead. That was the way it was. That was the way the world worked.

Arethusa was overwhelmed by her desire to see him. Desperate to tell him how she felt. To tell him plainly and candidly. To lay bare her heart without restraint. She yearned to hold him, to kiss him, to feel the solidity of his body against her hands and to emboss it on her memory so that she would carry it inside her always, for as long as she lived. But what if the opportunity to tell him slipped through her fingers? She knew it would never come round again.

As the guests arrived Arethusa greeted them with serenity and grace, extending her gloved hand, smiling with charm and remembering everyone's name, yet inside, her stomach was tightening with panic. When Ronald arrived (he was one of the first) her panic deepened; she'd forgotten all about Ronald. 'My darling Tussy,' he said, taking in the milky-white skin of her décolletage and the pretty curve of her neck as if they already belonged to him. 'You look beautiful tonight, like a goddess. You outshine all the other ladies, you really do.'

Trying not to look surprised, she allowed him to take her hand. 'Thank you, Ronald.'

'And I, the luckiest man in the world to have secured my future with you.' The word 'future' had a sharp edge to it and Arethusa felt grazed. 'I wish it were May and we were already married. The waiting is excruciating.' He smiled sympathetically, taking it for granted that she felt the same frustration. He patted her hand. 'But we must both be patient.'

Arethusa would have laughed had she not been so desperately unhappy. 'I can be patient,' she replied tersely.

'That's my girl,' he said, putting her hand to his lips and kissing it. 'I will return to you once you have finished doing your duty.' Arethusa could only nod in agreement. Where was Jonas?

She finally saw him when the Madison Minstrels performed for the guests after dinner in the ballroom. She was escorted in by Ronald, who had barely left her side all evening for he had been seated beside her at the dinner table. In the golden glow of hundreds of candles, she watched them sing their songs and dance lightly across the stage as they had done at the Duchess of Sutcliffe's ball and she felt a searing sense of impending loss. Here he was, so close, and yet she couldn't speak to him, let alone touch him. Was this what her future was going to be like? Stuck to Ronald's side and unable to breathe?

Arethusa looked around her at the faces of the guests, who beamed with pleasure at the novelty of these two black entertainers from America, and knew that her mother would be pleased. Her evening was a tremendous success. There would be dancing and fireworks and everyone would leave at dawn, declaring the Deverill Summer Ball the finest in the county, but what of her? For her it would be more memorable than any other on account of her loss.

When the brothers had finished their performance the orchestra picked up their instruments and began to play. The dancing commenced. Arethusa did not want to dance, but she had no choice. Her dance card was full and she could not escape her duty, nor could she offend the gentlemen who had engaged her. Sick with frustration she gripped Ronald's arm. 'I think I'm going to faint,' she declared, rolling her eyes. Alarmed, Ronald escorted her out of the ballroom and into the garden. 'You need some air,' he said, putting an arm around her waist.

'I need to lie down,' she replied. 'I will retire to my room for a while, Ronald, if you don't mind. I feel very sick.'

Ronald knew he could not accompany her there. 'Shall I fetch your mother, or Charlotte?'

'No, don't ruin the evening for them. I will be well again shortly, if I go now and lie down. Thank you for your concern.' She gazed at him gratefully. 'You really are very sweet, Ronald.'

He smiled back and puffed out his chest. 'If we were anywhere else I would insist upon finding someone to escort you, but as this is your home I trust you will find your way to your bedroom on your own.'

'Your concern is very touching,' she said, already moving towards the door. 'Please enjoy yourself. The Deverill Summer Ball comes only once a year and I insist that you have fun.' He followed her to the hall and waited at the bottom of the stairs like a loyal dog as she made her way up. Only when she had disappeared did he return to the ballroom to explain her absence to anyone who asked.

Arethusa was heading down the corridor, wondering how to engineer a meeting with Jonas, when she saw Rupert walking out of the shadows towards her. So intent was she on her mission it did not occur to her to ask him what *he* was doing there, in the middle of the party. 'Rupert!' She took his hands and squeezed them. 'I need your help.'

Rupert grinned. 'Not running away from Ronald, are you?' he asked.

'For tonight only,' she replied, but she did not smile.

'Then what can I do for you?'

'I need to speak to Jonas Madison before he leaves.'

Rupert looked surprised. 'Jonas Madison? Really?'

'I need to speak to him urgently.'

'Well then, if it's urgent, let's go and find him at once, Tussy. I assume he'll be tucked away behind the green baize door eating our leftovers.'

'No, I can't come with you. I told Ronald I was going to lie down.'

He arched an eyebrow. 'Ah, another fainting fit, I presume?'

'The first one was genuine,' she retorted.

'Where shall I tell him to meet you then?'

Arethusa wanted to cry with relief. 'Oh Rupert, would you?' She squeezed his hands again. 'I'm so grateful to you.'

'Gratitude doesn't become you, Tussy. Gratitude makes me uneasy.' He looked at her worriedly. 'I won't waste my breath cautioning you.'

'Tell him to meet me in the vegetable garden.'

Rupert cocked his head. 'The vegetable garden?'

'No one will find us there.'

'But if they do, you will be ruined.'

She caught her breath. 'It is worth the risk.'

'Tussy—'

'Then I will accept my lot. I promise. I'll marry Ronald and go quietly. You'll never hear another squeak out of me. I'll do my duty and conform.'

Rupert sighed. 'Very well. But something tells me you never will. Some people can never change, however hard they try.' He shrugged. 'You'd better leave by the back and for God's sake keep to the shadows. It's a full moon tonight and you'll be lit up like an effigy on St Patrick's Day.'

As Arethusa hurried on down the corridor she was

surprised to see Peregrine slipping out of one of the bedrooms. On seeing her his face first registered surprise, then alarm. But when Arethusa smiled at him, absorbed in concealing her own guilty mission, his face softened and he did the only thing he could do to distract her from asking what he was doing up there, at this time of the night: ask her about herself. 'What brings you up here, Tussy?' he said.

'I'm feeling a little faint and in need of a lie-down.' Then she added naively, 'I've just bumped into Rupert. If you hurry, you'll catch him up.'

Chapter 25

Arethusa paced the ground in agitation. The train of her dress soaked up the dew and her pale silk shoes darkened with moisture, but she didn't care if her dress got dirty and her shoes were ruined. She'd sacrifice everything she had for this rendezvous with Jonas. Hands on hips, strides fretful and impatient, she kept her eye on the gate in the old wall that surrounded the vegetable garden, expecting him to appear at any moment; hoping with all her heart that he would.

The moon lit up the two magnificent greenhouses which rose out of the long grasses like a pair of stately galleons on a dark sea. Their blancmange-shaped domes reflected the silvery light and glowed like sails fully spread. The garden was quiet, the neat rows of vegetables still, only the nocturnal creatures crept about in the shadows for the moonlight cast the landscape in a luminosity that exposed them to predators as surely as sunlight.

Arethusa was reckless. She was expert at living in the present and not considering the consequences of her actions, and tonight she was more reckless than ever. Nothing existed but this garden, on this night. She determinedly shut out the past and the future and concentrated with all her endeavour on this very hour, as if nothing was real outside of it.

The sudden screech of a barn owl drew her attention. She stopped pacing. Then the garden gate opened slowly and Jonas stepped cautiously into the moonlight.

They stared at each other for a second and if, in that brief moment, they felt a twinge of doubt, it was swiftly swept away in the rush of passion that swelled in their hearts and propelled them forwards. Arethusa ran to him. There was no time for coyness or games. She had declared herself weeks ago, in the blushes that burned her cheeks and the words that scalded the paper. Jonas strode towards her, his pace quickening with each step, until they stood face to face, alone at last. Arethusa did not hesitate. She threw her arms about his neck and pressed herself against him as only a woman who has been intimate with a lover can. She felt him embrace her fiercely, wrapping her in his arms as if he intended never to release her. This was not the man who told her there was no place on earth they could go, but a man who loved her so intensely he didn't care. In this isolated moment his ardour matched hers absolutely. Their lips came together in a kiss that was both passionate and tender and Arethusa realized that her whole life had, up until this very second, been but half a life. Now it was complete.

Shortly, she led him to the furthest greenhouse where they could be sure they wouldn't be found. It was pleasantly warm inside, the air damp and earthy and close. Jonas took her hand and they walked down the avenues between the plants, stopping every few paces to kiss, not wanting to waste a moment of the only time in their lives they knew they'd be at liberty to love each other freely. 'I have been unable to think of anything else but you,' said Jonas, cupping her face and caressing her cheeks with his thumbs.

Arethusa gazed into his rich brown eyes and felt a reassuring sense of familiarity, as if she belonged in their reflection, as if she had always belonged there. 'I have tried everything to distract myself from you,' she told him. 'But you are behind everything I do.'

'You have more courage than me. I admire you for that. I would never have dared—'

'But it is courage that has brough you here, is it not?,' she interrupted, not wanting him to articulate his fears. 'If I have shown myself to be brave, it is only because you have made me so. I love you, Jonas. I love the man you are.' She laughed softly and lowered her eyes. 'I never believed in love at first sight but you've shown me that it's possible. I know now why poems are written. Why poets write about stars and sunsets and the dance of light on summer leaves, because of love. I never saw it before, but now I see love everywhere and that's because of you.'

'How romantic you are, Tussy,' he laughed and his face glowed with affection.

'I didn't think I was romantic. You've made me so.'

'I am honoured that I have not only taught you to play the banjo, but taught you about love as well.'

Suddenly the sky cracked with a loud bang. They both turned their eyes to the glass ceiling. 'Fireworks,' said Arethusa, although she couldn't see them.

Jonas's face flashed with concern. 'Surely, you will be missed,' he said.

'I told Ronald I felt unwell. Then I retired to my room, locked the door, and left through the adjoining sitting room.'

'Who is Ronald?' Jonas asked and his eyes betrayed his hurt, even though he was in no position to lay claim to her.

'My fiancé,' she replied flatly.

'Of course,' he groaned. It was inevitable that a girl like Arethusa would be betrothed.

'I am getting married next spring.' She must have looked wretched because he pulled her to him and held her tightly against his chest. She heard his heart beating hard beneath his shirt and squeezed her eyes shut. 'I know we can't be together, Jonas,' she said in a resigned voice. 'I live in the same world as you do and know that there is no place in it for us. I hoped, indeed I dreamed, but I must not wish for things I cannot have because they will only make me miserable. You are here now and I am blessed with this opportunity to speak with you alone and to tell you what is in my heart. I know the chance will never come again.'

'I must let you return to the ball or you will be compromised. You and I are not from the same world, Tussy, not at all. I am not welcome in yours.' Jonas took her face in her hands and kissed her again. 'Come, let me escort you as far as the garden gate and then you must return to the castle before you are missed.'

Arethusa felt as if something had sucked the air out of the greenhouse. She could barely breathe for panic. 'No!' she whispered, grabbing his jacket. 'You cannot leave me. Please, don't ever leave me, Jonas. My life will not be worth living. Surely, we can find a way . . .' She clutched his lapels with both hands, her knuckles turning white. 'Please.'

'My darling, your life is here. With me there is only prejudice, isolation and exile. It cannot be done.'

She tightened her grip, suddenly overcome with a terrible urgency. 'Then love me, Jonas. Just once. Then I can live my life, do my duty, and carry the memory of you, like a beautiful jewel that belongs only to you and me. I think I can endure my future without you if I have that.'

Jonas held her gaze. 'What are you saying, Tussy?'

'I'm asking you to make love to me,' she whispered.

He shook his head. 'Tussy, you have lost your mind. We cannot. I will not put you in danger, put us *both* in danger, for a moment of rashness . . .'

Her eyes shone with tears. She lightly brushed his lips with hers. 'Don't make me beg . . .' She pressed herself against him again and she knew, from the heat radiating from his body, that he would be unable to refuse.

Arethusa crept into the sitting room adjoining her bedroom, closed the door behind her and leaned against it with a sigh of relief. She had made it back without being caught.

A slice of silver moonlight poured through the large window and partially illuminated the room. Arethusa's gaze was drawn to it. She stiffened. Something told her she wasn't alone. Her eyes darted from the window seat to the mantelpiece and then settled onto the sofa where a woman sat quietly in the dark, watching her.

Arethusa gasped and put a hand to her breast. 'Charlotte! You gave me such a fright! What are you doing here?'

'I think I should ask you the same question, Tussy.' Charlotte's voice was stern. It was years since Arethusa had heard her use that tone.

'I needed air, so I went for a walk,' she told her crisply.

'Don't lie to me, Tussy.'

Arethusa looked suitably offended. 'I told Ronald I felt faint and needed to lie down. Then I sneaked out of the back of the castle and went for a walk.'

Charlotte stood up and stepped into the moonlight. 'I've had to cover for you.' She wrung her hands, clearly upset. 'I've had to lie for you. Ronald has been very worried about you, but I persuaded him not to upset your mama and came up here myself. Your bedroom door was locked, so I came in this way. When you weren't here, I worried. But I know you, Tussy. You've been up to no good and I thoroughly disapprove.'

Arethusa clicked her tongue impatiently. 'You're wrong and besides, with whom am I supposed to have been up to no good?'

'The man you love but cannot have. You told me about him yourself.'

'He is not here,' she said softly. Charlotte took a deep breath and Arethusa sensed she was willing to be convinced. Arethusa thought of the man she loved, and the trauma of having said goodbye to him made her eyes well with tears. She decided to put those tears to good use. 'I don't love Ronald, Charlotte,' she said and her chin wobbled with emotion. 'I don't want to marry him. But I must. Is it so wrong to feel overwhelmed by my future and in need of some time alone, in the garden?' She walked to the window and gazed out onto the silvery grounds below. She wondered where Jonas was now. 'The garden is so beautiful tonight, with the full moon and the stars. It's the only place I feel fully myself.'

Charlotte stood beside her and looked at her apologetically. 'I have no choice but to believe you, Tussy. I don't want to accuse you of impropriety if you really have been walking alone in the garden.'

'I wouldn't lie to you, Charlotte. Haven't I already told you my greatest secret and you have told me yours.'

Charlotte sighed again and cocked her head. Arethusa knew she had won. 'You should have let me know,' said the governess gently. 'Then I could have covered for you without the anxiety.'

'I'm sorry. I saw Rupert on my way upstairs and told him. I didn't think it necessary to tell anyone else and besides, I didn't want to be stopped. I needed to get away. Ronald's attention is stifling. I hope he'll give me more space when we're married.'

Charlotte smiled. 'He'll give you children and then settle into marriage in the way all men seem to do. Putting themselves and *their* needs first.'

'I should like never to marry,' said Arethusa bitterly. 'I feel my life is ending.'

'In a way it is, Tussy,' said Charlotte. 'The life you've lived up until now is ending and a new one is beginning. Life is like a book. You're simply about to start another chapter.' Charlotte gazed forlornly out of the window. 'As am I.'

'What will become of *you*?' Arethusa asked.

'I shall find another employment elsewhere. Another family, another young girl for me to tutor and guide.' She smiled resignedly. 'But I will miss you, Tussy. I will miss Castle Deverill and everyone in it.'

Arethusa rejoined the ball and only Ronald knew for how long she had been gone. However, with Charlotte explaining how poor Arethusa had fallen asleep and that she had not wanted to wake her, Ronald was satisfied. No one would ever know what had taken place in the vegetable garden. No one would know how Arethusa was suffering and how much it cost her to dissemble. She would never see Jonas again. It was over. But he had left her with a memory she would treasure and with the knowledge that he loved her, and that would have to be enough.

Chapter 26

Ballinakelly, 1961

I have been in Ballinakelly only seven days and I am in bed with a man who is not my husband. I can see the rain pouring down outside the windows. It sounds like gravel being thrown against the glass. The sky is bruised and below it the waves rise restlessly in a dull grey sea. There are no boats on the water today, only seabirds who seem not to notice the inclement weather. It is late afternoon and I am in Cormac's bed. We have made love. I lie in his arms, my head on his chest, and he runs his hand up and down my spine. We listen to the rain, watch the tormented sea and talk. Inside our cocoon it is cosy and tranquil; no one can touch us here.

I have read enough novels about infidelity to know that what I am feeling now is pretty much universal: making love to Cormac feels right; more than it ever felt with Wyatt. I should feel guilty, but I don't. I should feel sheepish, but I don't. I should feel afraid, but I don't. I feel as if, with each caress, he has peeled away the tired old Faye and awakened a fresh new Faye beneath. I'm like a hydrangea blooming in the spring. I know that when I see my reflection in the mirror I will look younger too. I have never been more willing and ready for change.

'If the extent of your guided tour is this bedroom, I will be totally satisfied,' I tell him happily.

He laughs and I hear it loud and gravelly in his chest. 'You mean you don't want to see the lighthouse or Blarney Castle or the Cathedral of St Peter and Paul's?'

'I want to stay here with you.'

He pushes me playfully and lies on top of me, pinning my wrists above my head. 'Are you telling me that you want me to make love to you again?'

'Yes.' I look him straight in the eye. 'I want you to do nothing but make love to me.'

He smiles, pleased. 'I'm not the young man I used to be. You'll have to let me catch my breath.' He laughs and there is real abandon in it.

'I'm not the young woman I used to be, either,' I say, 'but I'm happy as I am now, here with you.'

'You're finding the Deverill spirit,' he says, sharing my pleasure.

'What's that?'

'There's a wild and reckless streak in that family.'

'My mother clearly had it.'

'Kitty has it,' he adds.

'Then I want the Deverill spirit in me.'

He kisses me and I feel him becoming aroused again. 'Then you'd better remain in Ireland, hadn't you? You won't find the Deverill spirit anywhere else but here.'

We both know I cannot stay in Ireland, but I laugh and make light of it. 'I'll find it with you, Cormac.'

'Sure, you will.' He kisses me again. 'Now what were you saying?'

We remain in bed until sunset. I rather wish I was staying in the hotel, then it wouldn't matter what time I returned, but I'm Kitty's guest, therefore I must get back to the White House before dinner. How I would like to stay in Cormac's bed and luxuriate in his arms all night. 'Tomorrow I'm going to teach you how to play the accordion,' he says, watching me dress.

'Surely that was just a ruse to get me here. Now I'm here, you don't have to.'

He grins. 'Sure, it was a ruse, but it wasn't *just* a ruse. I'd like to teach you.'

'All right.' I think of my mother learning to play the banjo with Jonas and smile at the parallel. 'I'm not sure we'll be able to pull the wool over Kitty's eyes. She's much too clever.'

'You don't have to worry about Kitty Deverill.'

'I know, she's worldly. I can tell.'

'She's more than worldly, she's lived many lives. Perhaps she'll tell you about them one day.'

I shrug on my cardigan and slip into my shoes. 'What do you mean, she's lived many lives?'

'Ask her.'

'No, you tell me.'

'It's not mine to tell.'

'Are you suggesting she's had an affair?'

'Just ask her.' He grins and I know I'll get nothing out of him.

'I can count on her support then,' I say instead.

'Indeed, you can.'

'Robert is a different matter,' I add and pull a face.

'That's not a surprise.'

'He's an odd choice for her.'

'From your point of view, but you don't know either of them.'

'He's so serious and she's so vivacious and warm.'

'I can't say I know him well. The likes of him don't mix with the likes of us.'

I frown. 'But Kitty does.'

'Kitty's different. Kitty's classless. Now come here. I'm not driving you back until you've paid me in kind for my hospitality. You've been here all day and you owe me.'

I laugh and climb onto the bed. He holds me tightly. How well we fit together. 'Is this how all the women pay you for their rides?' My comment is loaded.

He looks at me. 'Just you, Faye,' he says. 'There are no other women.'

I smile happily. That's the answer I wanted.

Cormac drops me back at the White House and I find Kitty in the sitting room with her sister Elspeth, side by side on the sofa. From the tray of empty teacups and cake I can see that they've been here for some time. 'Ah, you're back,' Kitty says. 'I have a message for you from Wyatt.'

The mention of Wyatt punctures my good mood. I wonder how he has found me, seeing as I never left my details with his secretary. I suppose there aren't many hotels in Ballinakelly and, as I'm the local novelty, everyone knows where I'm staying. 'What did he want?'

'To know how you're getting on. I told him you're well and enjoying Ireland.'

'Thank you.'

Kitty gives me a sympathetic look. The look of someone who knows where I've been and what I've been up to and how unwelcome the mention of my husband will be.

'I hear you're seeing the sights,' says Elspeth. Kitty watches me from the sofa. Her expression is inscrutable but I sense her collusion.

'Cormac O'Farrell has been very kind and shown me

around,' I say. It's better to hide in plain sight than to bla-
tantly lie. I hope I have managed to give nothing away in my
demeanour.

'Oh, Cormac, he's quite a character,' says Elspeth. She
laughs and glances at her sister. 'He must be thrilled you're
giving him something to do!'

I'm affronted on Cormac's behalf. As far as I know he's a
man who keeps himself busy. I can't jump to his defence without exposing my feelings for him, but Kitty can. 'Cormac's
one of those men who does a bit of everything,' she says.
'He's never wanted to be conventional or tied down. His life
may be unusual but it's happy. I don't know anyone as contented as him.'

I smile at her gratefully. 'I don't know him,' I say with a
shrug. 'But he seems contented to me. He's good company. I'm
lucky to have found him. After all, I haven't come all this way
just to find out about my mother, but also to see the country
of her birth. He's an enthusiastic guide.'

Elspeth gives me a teasing look. 'Do be careful, Faye,
Cormac's quite a ladies' man and you're a married woman a
long way from home.' She laughs because she does not realize
how close she has come to the truth.

'Don't worry, Elspeth,' I say. 'I'm very capable of looking
after myself.'

Kitty smiles knowingly. 'There's nothing wrong with a
healthy flirt,' she says, but her sister's face snaps into a disapproving frown.

'Oh Kitty! Shame on you!' she exclaims. 'Peter would not
consider any type of flirting healthy.' She looks at me seriously.
'Don't listen to my sister, Faye. She's talking nonsense. Robert
wouldn't approve of a healthy flirt either and I'm sure Wyatt is
the same. No man wants to be made to look a fool.'

I watch Kitty. Her face does not change. She gives nothing away. Although Cormac did not specifically say she had an affair, he didn't deny it. If she did, it would certainly explain her readiness to collude. 'Is Wyatt going to call me back?' I ask her.

'No, he said not to worry. He just wanted to make sure you're okay.'

'Did you tell him who you are?'

'I did. I told him you have a very large family here. He sounded surprised.'

'Like me, he believed Mom's relations had all died.'

'Isn't that extraordinary,' says Elspeth incredulously. 'To turn your back on your home and your family and spend the rest of your life denying they even exist. What makes a person do that?'

I catch Kitty's eye. 'Hurt,' Kitty says simply. 'Aunt Tussy was very hurt.'

'Why?' Elspeth asks and I know Kitty will not tell her. She won't want anyone to know Arethusa's story before her father knows. If Elspeth is appalled at the thought of harmless flirting, she will be horrified by Arethusa falling in love with a black man – I almost want to tell her just to see her face.

'Faye is reading the diary, aren't you, Faye?' says Kitty.

'I am, but it's long and detailed and I haven't had much time lately.'

The corners of Kitty's mouth twitch and I am glad to see that she is not such an accomplished actress after all. 'It's a big county and there's much to see,' she says.

'I will read some more tonight,' I reply. But I don't want to know what happens next. I'm beginning to get the measure of my mother and I fear her infatuation with Jonas Madison did not stop at healthy flirting.

Kitty and Robert have asked Peter and Elspeth for dinner, and another couple who live the other side of Bandon called Purdy and Petula Padmore. I laugh when Petula tells me her children's names, Patrick, Paul and Patricia, all begin with the same letter. How very confusing it must be. Purdy is the shape of a toad, with a round belly, a shiny red face and expressive, bulbous eyes the colour of blue topaz. His wife is pretty in a masculine way with short black hair and an angular face. She is so thin it is as if she has been rolled on. Both are exuberant characters and very funny. Even Robert laughs at their jokes. They are a team, bouncing their witty repartee off each other and keeping us all entertained. I warm to them immediately.

The Padmores are very curious about me and ask all sorts of questions about my mother and my reasons for being here. Neither thinks it odd that I'm here without my husband, although Elspeth is uncomfortable with it. She says that, in all the years she and Peter have been married, she has never spent a night away from him.

'Good Lord!' cries Petula. 'The horror of spending every night of my life with Purdy.'

Purdy laughs and his face shines with mirth. 'My dear, as lovely as you are, and you are, indeed, quite lovely, I do need a break from your loveliness from time to time. A brief interlude renders it all the *more* lovely when I come back to it.'

'This is the first time I've travelled abroad without Wyatt,' I say. 'But I'm really enjoying some time on my own.'

'Of course you are, my dear,' says Petula. 'A woman only truly knows who she is when she's not measuring herself against a man.'

'Very true,' Kitty agrees.

'And Wyatt will appreciate you all the more when you return,' says Purdy.

Elspeth glances at Peter. 'I have no desire to know myself any more than I do already.'

Peter smiles at her approvingly. 'Everyone is different, my darling,' he says diplomatically.

Robert, who never says much, adds, 'I think independence is a good thing as long as one knows where one's loyalties lie.'

'You see, Robert, how good you are for Kitty. My sister had to marry a man who allowed her her freedom,' says Elspeth and I sense naivety in her words, but she continues carelessly, 'Kitty has always been a free spirit.' I wonder whether her free spirit has got her into trouble in the past. Elspeth smiles at Robert – the smile of someone who knows nothing. 'But you tamed her, didn't you, Robert.'

Kitty puts her lips to her wine glass and maintains an even expression. Robert looks a little uncomfortable, or perhaps I am imagining it. What I've seen of him so far, he never looks very at ease with himself.

'I think we're very lucky to be able to choose the people we marry,' I say, deflecting the subject from Kitty and Robert. 'I've been reading my mother's diary and at the turn of the century people didn't seem to have much choice. Or rather, love didn't count for much.'

'Oh, we are so lucky,' Petula agrees. 'I'm sure I wouldn't have been allowed to marry Purdy if I had lived in those days.'

'What tosh!' retorts Purdy. 'I was straight out of the hanky drawer!'

We all laugh at that. 'What's the hanky drawer?' I ask.

'The *top* drawer,' says Petula, smiling at him with affection. 'You were, darling, straight out of the hanky drawer, but you didn't have any money, nor did you have a great house.'

He smiles slyly. 'Then *I* would have been allowed to marry *you* because you had both.'

'I would have run away with you all the same,' says Petula.

'Where would you have gone?' Kitty asks, enjoy-ing the game.

'America,' says Purdy. 'Everyone who eloped went to America.'

I think of my mother who also ran off to America and wonder, suddenly, whether I'm going to discover that she eloped. How has that not occurred to me? 'But you would have come back?' I ask, feeling a prickly apprehension creep over me.

'Dust always settles eventually,' Purdy replies. 'Of course I would have come back. Home is home, and if Ireland is one's home, well, there's no other place like it.'

I look at Kitty and I know she's thinking the same as me. Why didn't the dust settle for Arethusa?

That night after everyone has left, I read Mother's diary. Purdy has got me wondering. It's all very well running off to America, but what's odd is never coming back. Not ever. That's quite extraordinary, considering Mom's family ties and the depth of her roots. I say goodnight to Kitty and Robert and head to my room. As I look out over the glittering sea, for now the clouds have moved away and the moon has scattered diamonds over the water, I wonder what Cormac is doing. Is he lying in bed, wondering what I am doing? We have agreed to meet tomorrow. He is picking me up at ten.

I lean against the pillows and open Mom's little book. I open it to the page where last I left off and turn it to the hand-held mirror on my lap. It's not the easiest way to read a book, but I have mastered it now. I get so engrossed in the story that I forget the time.

Chapter 27

Castle Deverill
The Past

Everyone agreed that the Deverill Summer Ball was the most successful ever. Greville was entirely satisfied that traditions had been upheld and Elizabeth was delighted that so many people had congratulated her on a wonderful evening, when she had done nothing but dress and turn up. Hubert was relieved that the Madison Minstrels had been his wife's choice of entertainment, bearing in mind the alternative. The guests had clapped loudly, though he didn't think they would have been quite so enthusiastic had it not been for their association with the Prince of Wales. Society is fickle, he thought, and easily led. In his opinion the brothers' dancing and singing was rather second-rate. Stoke had enjoyed himself immensely. Due to his fine bones (Elizabeth said he was like a cockatoo) he was light on his feet and showed up all the other gentlemen during the quadrille. Augusta was delighted the ball was such a success and told everyone that the Madison Minstrels had been *her* idea. She was in a position to be gracious because she felt secure that her own Deverill Rising ball in October would be superior. She had hired a small, very elite ballet company from Russia. Apparently, they had danced on the stage at the Yusupov Palace in St Petersburg, in the presence of the Tsar and Tsarina themselves. She would make sure that *that* little gem of information would somehow slip out on the night. Bertie, who was handsome and genial, had enjoyed himself enormously and even though he was married to one of London's most celebrated beauties, he had not been able to refrain from flirting with the pretty young ladies. Maud had noticed and minded, but it was early in their marriage and she was too young and insecure to make a fuss. She had already learned that turning cold on him brought him to heel like a bashful puppy. As for Rupert, he had also flirted with the pretty young ladies but, as usual, had not been inspired by any of them.

As the days shortened and the dazzling summer light mellowed to an early autumn gold, Arethusa kept her word to Rupert. She didn't pine for Jonas; she let him go. Neither did she seek out windows of pleasure and head off into Ballinakelly in search of Dermot McLoughlin. With a great application of will she forced herself into the present and committed herself fully to the life she was destined to live. There was no point dreaming the impossible for that only brought unhappiness and Arethusa was weary of being unhappy. She dedicated her time to helping her mother plan her wedding and to being an attentive and enthusiastic fiancée to Ronald. Having reconciled herself to the fact that she would never see Jonas again, she gave herself to her intended. He would be hers and she would be his, whether she liked it or not, so it was better to like it. And while she played the part of liking it, she genuinely began to do so.

Augusta's ball in October became the most talked about ball of the year. The Prince and Princess of Wales attended, which gave it the glitter Augusta craved, and the Russian dancers were a triumph, performing a scene from *Swan Lake* with the grace and lightness of fairies. Although Rupert had offended more mothers than he could count, he was forgiven due to his charm and because he was the Marquess of Penrith's closest friend and no one could resist *that* connection. Arethusa was also forgiven for having made a fool out of the most eligible gentlemen in London because she was safely engaged to Ronald Rowan-Hampton. The two of them redeemed themselves at Augusta's ball by being gracious and cheerful and, in a society where good manners were highly prized, being gracious and cheerful counted for a lot.

Now Arethusa no longer saw Ronald as the obstacle to her happiness, but the only and unavoidable source of it, she began to look at him with different eyes. The fact that she had once laughed at him appalled her for she wanted to respect him and look up to him. His character reflected on her and if he was considered a fool, so was she. Therefore, she was pleased that he was known as one of the finest horsemen in Ireland and the more people spoke of his accomplishments in the saddle the more she was able to admire him. She observed him as they moved around the room at Augusta's ball. He was adept at finding exactly the right thing to say to everyone and both women and men clearly enjoyed his company. He was genial and left people feeling good about themselves, which is the key to any successful relationship.

And who was Arethusa when she was with Ronald? How did he make *her* feel? The Arethusa Ronald brought out was not passionate, reckless, rebellious or wild. Those qualities that Dermot McLoughlin knew so well had no place in her new life. Nor was she a young girl in love, for that was the Arethusa Jonas knew and *she* was now gone for ever. With Ronald

Arethusa was everything her parents wanted her to be. She was demure, compliant and gracious, obedient, decorous and poised. Indeed, she felt clever because Ronald did not have a brilliant mind. She felt witty, because Ronald was not funny. She felt beautiful, because Ronald never ceased to tell her so, and she felt cherished, because Ronald was attentive and kind.

The better she got to know him the more she realized that they had a great deal in common. They shared their opinions on God and religion, their love of Ireland and the importance of family. And even though Ronald, like Arethusa's father and grandfather, did not bother himself with concerns for the poor, she was sure she could educate him.

Arethusa was determined to make life without Jonas work. She believed she was making real progress and beginning to like the person she was when she was with Ronald. Then she missed her menses for the third month.

Arethusa had barely troubled herself over the first two – she had missed the odd menses in the past and was often late, but to miss it three times gave her cause for worry. She did not think she was pregnant. Women who were pregnant suffered from morning sickness, everyone knew that, and she hadn't felt a moment's nausea. She had heard that unhappiness or strain could cause a woman to miss her menses, but since she had let Jonas go she did not believe she had been unhappy. To the contrary, she was beginning to find happiness with Ronald. What perturbed her more than the possibility of being pregnant was that perhaps she was fooling herself that she was happy and all her hard work was simply a dressing over a wound that was deeper than she realized.

She decided to confide in Charlotte.

'My God!' Charlotte gasped, sinking onto the window seat in Arethusa's bedroom and putting a hand to her chest.

'That can only mean one thing.' She looked at Arethusa with terrified eyes.

Arethusa sighed huffily. 'You don't need to be dramatic, Charlotte. I'm not pregnant.'

'Is there any possibility, Tussy?'

Arethusa hesitated for a second before she replied. 'Of course not! What are you suggesting?' But that moment's hesitation put fear into Charlotte's heart.

Charlotte began to mentally count the months. Then she stood up and took Arethusa's hands. 'Tussy, it's three months since the ball. I won't be cross, but you have to be honest with me. When you went for a walk around the garden, were you in fact meeting a lover?' Arethusa's mouth opened to protest. 'Tussy, if you are pregnant you won't be able to hide it much longer.' Her voice was firm now and Arethusa blinked at her apprehensively.

She sat down on the window seat and put her hands in her lap. Charlotte sat beside her and waited for her to speak. Arethusa was now beginning to feel fear in her own heart. 'I do have a lover,' she said. When Charlotte's face crumpled with despair, she added crossly, 'My life is just duty, duty, duty. I needed something for myself, Charlotte.'

Charlotte was white. She looked as if she was about to cry. 'You could have had any amount of things for yourself, but not that.'

'I have missed my menses before.'

Charlotte shook her head. 'Don't be naive, Tussy. You know how these things work. Goodness, I've educated you myself. I should have done a better job of it. If you are indeed pregnant, you will be ruined.'

Arethusa began to pick her nails. She thought of all the times Dermot McLoughlin had made love to her and never once had her body let her down. 'I am not pregnant, Charlotte. I can't be.'

'If you have had intercourse with a man, Tussy, you can be.'

She'd had intercourse with *two*, in the space of a few days!

Arethusa stood up and began pacing the floor. 'I must see a doctor.'

'I will call for Dr Johnson. You must pretend you are sick. If it is, indeed, something else, we don't want him to know we ever considered pregnancy.'

Arethusa looked at Charlotte and frowned. 'If I am pregnant, what do I do?'

Charlotte looked at Arethusa and sighed. 'Pray,' she replied.

Chapter 28

Ballinakelly, 1961

It is three in the morning when I am struck with the shocking truth. Mother was most certainly pregnant. But that is not all. She would not have known whether she was carrying Dermot McLoughlin's baby, or Jonas Madison's.

I shut the book, not daring to read on, and lean back against the pillows with a sinking feeling. This has knocked me for six. Truly, it has. Mother had a wild and reckless streak that would be outrageous today, but to behave like that in the last century was simply foolhardy. Now I know why she fell out with her parents. They must have despaired of her. She was about to marry a suitable man who would look after her. Her future was settled. Then this! My heart swells with compassion; everything was going so well.

I have an urgent need to share this with Cormac. But I must wait until morning. I know I'm not going to be able to sleep. I'm going to turn this over and over in my head and drive myself crazy. I recall my mother's will. She has left a third of her wealth to an anonymous person. Well, it seems very obvious to me now that this anonymous person must be her illegitimate child. But who is he – or she? I'll have to share this with my brother. Logan will be furious. We'll have to find this stranger and inform them that their birth mother has died and left them a considerable amount of money. Do they even know they are Arethusa Deverill's child? If not, that will really set the cat among the pigeons. I assume she gave birth in America, but what became of the child after that? I have a vision of an orphanage, a miserable childhood, a life in penury while Logan and I were brought up in a world of privilege and comfort. I feel wretched. This is now getting complicated, and serious.

What has become clear, however, is why my mother wanted *me* to read the diary rather than Logan. If she had left it to my brother he would have probably thrown it into the fire in a fit of temper. But she knew *I*, the dutiful, acquiescent daughter, would follow her instructions to the letter and persuade Logan to carry out her wishes. I'm doing exactly as she planned. I'm reading her story, in her own words, in order to better understand her, so that when I discover that I have a half-sibling I am compassionate. Had she simply stated in her will that a third of her wealth must go to her illegitimate child both Logan and I would have been angry and horrified. This way, I'm not; I'm saddened. I feel sorry for her for getting into trouble. But I also understand her motives for sleeping with both men. I don't condemn her; I empathize with her, which is exactly what she wanted me to do.

The following morning Kitty is not at breakfast. She is out riding. I have breakfast in the dining room with Robert. We talk a little but mostly he reads the newspaper. I'm relieved I don't have to make conversation with him. I find him difficult to talk to. I wonder whether he was a more animated man when he was younger. Or perhaps she needed a solid presence to temper her capricious nature. I finish my breakfast in haste and retreat to my bedroom to wait for Cormac. I'm longing to see him. I stand at the window and gaze out onto the drive. When his Jeep appears at the gate my heart gives a leap. I grab Mom's diary and hurry down the stairs to meet him. I'm relieved Robert is not in the hall this time to give me a disapproving look. I barely give Wyatt a thought. While I'm here, so far from home, Wyatt is not a concern. Nor are my children. They are old enough to look after themselves. For the first time in my life I am looking after *me*.

I climb into the Jeep. Cormac and I exchange a knowing look, acknowledging our intimacy and the need to conceal it until we are out in the lane. As soon as the car turns the corner, he stops on the kerb, pulls me to him and kisses me. 'I've missed you,' he says.

'And I've missed you too,' I reply.

'Shall we go and make up for lost time?' he asks and there's that irresistible twinkle in his eye.

'I think we'd better,' I answer with a smile. 'As a tour guide you do want to keep your client happy, don't you?' He laughs and I run my fingers down the creases in his cheek.

'And if my client would like to have a music lesson, I might be able to fit it in to our very busy schedule.'

'I'd love that.'

'That's grand. Today's all arranged then.' He pulls out into the lane. 'So, did you get to read the diary last night?'

'I did and I need to talk to you about it.'

'Oh? It was bad, was it?'

I sigh. I don't know where to begin. I decide to cut to the chase. I tell him what I read and then I take a deep breath and add, 'Mom got pregnant but she doesn't know whether it's Dermot McLoughlin's baby or Jonas Madison's.'

Cormac whistles. 'Well, that's quite a revelation. Have you told Kitty?'

'No. I wanted to tell you first. I didn't think reading her diary would have any impact on me, but it does. You see, she has left a third of her wealth to an anonymous person.'

'And the other two thirds?'

'To me and my brother Logan.'

He nods. 'So, you're thinking that this third person is her illegitimate child.'

'That makes sense, doesn't it?'

'It does. The fact that it's an equal share gives that person the same status as her two other children.'

'I can understand why she wanted me to read the diary and not Logan. He is quick to temper and quite inflexible. This way she gets to explain herself before she drops the bombshell.'

'You have to read on,' he says.

'I know, which is why I brought the diary with me. I don't want to read it alone.'

'What are you afraid of?'

'I don't know.' I glance at him anxiously.

He arches an eyebrow. 'Don't take on your mother's guilt, Faye.'

'What do you mean?'

'If she gave the child up for adoption, or put it in an orphan-age, it's got nothing to do with you. Remember the time she lived in. She couldn't have kept an illegitimate child, certainly not if she turned her back on her family. She wouldn't have had the financial support to raise it on her own.'

'What if I have to track the child down? What if he or she doesn't even know they're her child? This is suddenly turning into a real nightmare.'

'Then we'll read it together and find out what happened. When you have all the pieces of the puzzle in place, I'll help you work out what to do.'

'Thank you.' I take his hand over the gear stick.

He squeezes it. 'You can handle this, Faye.'

'I know *I* can. But I'm not sure about my brother. I wouldn't know where to begin.'

Cormac grins and turns into the lane that leads down to his cottage. 'I'd suggest you begin at the beginning.'

I pull a face. 'That's not helpful, Cormac. You don't know Logan. He'll be appalled, horrified . . .'

'Very well. Then I'll give you a real piece of advice. It's not *your* problem how he handles it. It's your problem how *you* handle it.'

'That's better,' I say.

'I'll give you another piece of advice.'

'Go on.'

'I don't think you should concern yourself with anyone else but you and me.' I laugh because he's got a mischievous look on his face. A mischievous look that promises a whole day in bed. 'Let's spend some time in the present before we delve into the past.'

Chapter 29

Castle Deverill
The Past

Arethusa leaned over the side of the bed and vomited into the chamber pot. Dr Johnson took off his glasses and turned to Charlotte, who was standing by the window looking on worriedly. 'I'm afraid I am going to have to tell her mother,' he said. Charlotte put a hand to her breast and sighed heavily. Dr Johnson was a tall, dignified Englishman, with curly greying hair swept off an intelligent face and a thick moustache covering his top lip like a thatch. He had been the Deverills' doctor for over forty years and had brought Arethusa and her siblings into the world. Charlotte did not imagine he had ever anticipated *this*. He regarded his patient with pity. It was regretful that the girl had got herself into trouble and he didn't look forward to breaking the news to her mother.

'Is there nothing that can be done?' Charlotte asked as Arethusa heaved herself back onto the bed with a moan; the news that she was, indeed, pregnant, had shocked her to such a degree, she had thrown up.

'Carrying a child is not a disease, Miss Hope. It's usually a blessing. In this case it is a misfortune.' He looked at Arethusa who was lying on her back with her eyes closed, as if shutting out the world would make it all go away. 'Tussy is three months pregnant. There's nothing much to see at present, but it won't be long before she is unable to hide it and then what are you going to do?'

'I just want to protect her from dishonour and scandal.'

'With respect, Miss Hope, that is not your job. It is her parents'. Now, I suggest rest and fresh air. I will go and talk to Mrs Deverill now.'

The doctor left the room. Charlotte, in a fever of worry, rushed to Arethusa's side. She perched on the edge of the bed and put a hot hand to the girl's forehead. She didn't know what to say. There were no words to reassure her and nothing she could do to get her out of this mess. 'I've been a fool,' Arethusa groaned, opening her eyes. Charlotte couldn't bear to look into them. 'But if I could go back in time, I'd do it again. I love him, Charlotte.' Tears ran down her temples and into her hair. 'I love him so much it hurts.'

Charlotte, who knew very well what that felt like, stroked her cheek tenderly. 'I know you love him, and there's no cure for that.'

Arethusa put a hand on her stomach and smiled feebly. 'I'm carrying his baby,' she said, eyes brightening a little. 'I've got a part of him inside me. What if he knew? What if we got a message to him?'

Charlotte withdrew her hand. 'Tussy, you can't keep the child!'

'Why not? What else am I going to do with it?'

'There are ways of dealing with this kind of thing. You're not the first to be pregnant out of wedlock and you won't be the last. You disappear for a while, have the baby, give it to an orphanage where a nice family will be found to look after it, and then you return to your life.'

Arethusa laughed mirthlessly. 'Oh Charlotte, that's very naive of you. Ronald won't have me once he finds out I'm damaged goods, and if you think I'm going to give my baby away, you don't know me at all.' Her face hardened and Charlotte recoiled. 'This child is half of the man I love. I'm not going to give it away. I don't care what Mama and Papa say or what anyone says, for that matter. I'm going to keep it.'

Charlotte sighed again. 'I think you'll find you have to do what your parents tell you, because you have no independent means and no support outside of the family. You depend on them, so you'll have to do as you're told.'

Arethusa rolled onto her side. 'Please leave me alone, Charlotte.'

'Tussy, I'm just being realistic.'

'You're being cruel.'

'Tussy! It's my duty as your governess to tell you the truth.'

'It's your duty as my friend to shield me from it.' She shrugged off the hand that tried to pacify her. 'Now leave me alone. I don't want to talk anymore.'

Charlotte got up reluctantly and left the room.

Arethusa curled up on the bed and cried into the pillow. Her future was now uncertain. She had thrown it away for an hour with Jonas Madison – or Demot McLoughlin, the child could be either of theirs. And yet, in spite of her tears and the fear of what her parents would say, she felt Fate had somehow rescued her from a secure but lacklustre path. She didn't love Ronald. She had tried to love him and had, at least, succeeded in liking him, but perhaps the monotony of being married to him would have eventually deadened her senses. The predictability of a life which was simply a continuation of the one she had up until this moment lived would most certainly have turned her mad with boredom. She knew not where she was headed now, but there was something invigorating about the possibilities. Whatever happened, it would be new and different. Praying that the child was Jonas's, because she so *wanted* it to be his (her past liaisons with Dermot had never led to *this*), she thought that if she could get word to him he would *have* to marry her. They would have to find a place where they could belong, a place where they were accepted. Surely, they couldn't be the first white woman and black man to have fallen in love?

As she lay working out her future it seemed to grow less bleak. Arethusa had a gift for making the best of every situation, and a situation as dire as this one simply made her more determined to survive it. She was strong-willed and courageous. She would face whatever came to her with fortitude and her usual optimism. She knew her parents would be furious. She'd get no sympathy from her father, and her mother would support her husband, as she always did, so she'd get little sympathy from her either. Charlotte would support her, of course, but her governess had no power or influence. Rupert would roll his eyes, call her a 'bloody idiot', but he'd help her. She was certain she could count on him. But besides her brother, she was alone.

Arethusa must have drifted off to sleep because she was awakened by the sound of the door opening and of her mother saying her name. Arethusa opened her eyes, alert at once to the unfamiliar tone of Adeline's voice, which had an uncharacteristically hard edge to it. She pushed herself up into a sitting position. Adeline stood in the middle of the room with her hands folded in front of her dress. Her face was a picture of disappointment and despair. Arethusa blinked at her but said nothing.

Adeline was lost for words. She shook her head and drew her lips into a thin, unhappy line. She watched her daughter from beneath a tight frown and struggled to put her jumbled thoughts into a coherent order. 'Tussy, how could you? I am in despair,' she said at last. 'I cannot comprehend how a well-educated, intelligent young woman such as yourself could be so unbelievably foolish, not to mention immoral. I can only assume that you were seduced, or coerced, because I don't believe my own daughter would throw away her virtue willingly and without a thought for the consequences.' She caught her breath. Arethusa watched her resignedly, neither attempting to explain her position nor defend it. 'Have you no idea how the world works?' her mother continued. 'Hasn't Charlotte educated you at all? What possessed you to do it, when you know very well the value of a girl's reputation? And who is the man?' Adeline put a hand to her mouth to stifle a sob. 'If your father ever finds out he'll put a gun to him, God save us all!'

Arethusa swung her legs off the bed and sat stiffly on the edge of the mattress. 'I love him,' she said flatly. 'I know I shouldn't have allowed him to . . . but I wanted something for myself before I entered into marriage with Ronald and resigned myself to a life of duty and boredom.'

Adeline's eyes widened with disbelief. 'A life of duty and boredom? Is that what marriage is to you? No one forced Ronald upon you, Tussy. You could have had anyone. From what I understand from Augusta London rolled out the most eligible and charming men for you and you chose not one of them.' She shook her head in exasperation. 'I can only presume that the man you claim to love is not suitable for marriage.'

Arethusa nodded. 'He's not,' she replied.

'Who is he?'

'I can't say.'

'My dear, I insist that you do.'

'I won't ever betray him.'

'I'm afraid it's gone well beyond betrayal, Tussy. You'll marry him whether he's a cobbler's son or a Catholic.'

At the mention of marriage, Arethusa saw a faint glimmer of light. 'He's neither, Mama.' She looked at her mother boldly. 'He's black.'

Adeline gasped. It was as if she had been struck between the eyes. She stared at her daughter in horror. 'Black?' she choked.

'Black,' said Arethusa firmly.

Adeline shook her head, wanting desperately to *un*hear what her daughter had just said. 'He's not one of those entertainers? What were they called? The Madison Minstrels?' She staggered to the armchair and sank into it.

'Jonas Madison,' Arethusa declared.

'The man who taught you to play the banjo?' Adeline said in a thin voice.

'That's the one.' Arethusa got up and crossed the room to sit on the floor beside her mother. She gazed up at her with pleading eyes. 'I love him, Mama, and he loves me. What does it matter that he's black or that he makes a living playing the banjo. He taught the Prince of Wales.'

Adeline had gone very white. 'He taught the Prince of Wales! You think that makes the slightest difference? Tussy, you're deluded. You can never marry him. Not in a million moons can you marry him.'

'You've always told me that God sees neither class nor colour,' she said, hoping to appeal to the spiritual side of her mother which she had always scorned. 'You consider all men equal.'

'And they are equal, in the eyes of God, but not in the

eyes of society. We have to live by society's rules. We have no choice. I'm sure he's a good person, a kind person. I'm sure he's got all the qualities one would want in a man, but he has none of the qualities one would need in a husband. Tussy, what were you thinking?' Her mother had gone very weak. She lifted a lifeless hand to her forehead and took a deep, shuddering breath. 'What part of you thought it was ever possible?'

'My heart,' Arethusa replied, putting a hand there for emphasis.

'Darling, you cannot keep the baby. We will have to pretend that you are sick and postpone the wedding. Then you will have to disappear for a while—'

Arethusa interrupted her. 'I'm not going to give up my child,' she protested crossly. 'Don't even try to persuade me.'

Adeline frowned. 'Do you want to ruin your life, Tussy?'

'I'd rather ruin *my* life than the life of my child.'

'This is no time to be romantic. The child will be black, Tussy. Make no mistake. You cannot bring up a black child. Have you gone quite mad? You cannot bring up any child on your own, let alone one of colour.'

'Then I will write to Jonas and tell him that he must marry me.'

Adeline looked doubtful. 'Has he said he will?'

Arethusa hesitated. 'No, it was never discussed.'

'Then he's got more sense than you.'

'But if I tell him I'm carrying his child, he'll have to marry me.'

'No, he won't. He'll run a mile. If he really loves you he will walk away from you.'

Arethusa lowered her eyes. 'He already has,' she said in a small voice.

Adeline sat up. 'I am going to have to discuss this with

your father. But while I do, I want you to go for a walk in the garden and think about what I have said. Your future can still be saved. The wedding can be postponed and we can draw a line under this. We can pretend it never happened.'

Arethusa lifted her chin defiantly. 'I can walk all you want me to, but I won't change my mind.'

'Oh, I think you will,' her mother retorted fiercely. 'When you consider the options. There really are only two. You either do as I ask, or you are out in the cold on your own.' Adeline fixed her with a hard stare. 'I love you, Tussy. God knows how much I love you. Which is why I will not let you ruin your life.'

'If you love me, then you can understand how I love my own child, even though it is not yet born.'

Adeline pushed herself up from the armchair and made to leave. 'Tussy my darling,' she said as she opened the door. 'You don't even know what love is.'

Arethusa did as her mother asked and went for a walk around the garden. She wished Rupert were at home to advise her, but he was staying with Peregrine in Cumbria, even though the invitation was for grouse shooting and Rupert detested killing living things. She strode across the damp lawn, shoulders hunched against the wind, and wondered how she could get a message to Jonas. Surely, if he knew she was carrying his child, he would come and save her. But then, with a sinking heart, she remembered Dermot. There was a chance, of course, that the child was his. If she managed to persuade Jonas to run off with her and then the baby turned out to be white, what then? She couldn't risk it. She'd have to wait until the birth.

The wind had blown orange and yellow leaves into little piles around the edge of the lawn. Arethusa marched over them, kicking them out of her way crossly. She felt walls closing in around her – castle walls – and was suddenly suffo-cated. She wished she could leave and not have to answer to her parents, or to anyone else. She resented their control. How she wished she were a man, then she could do as she pleased, but as a woman she was never going to be master of her own destiny, but another person's property, subject always to some-body else's will. She stomped resentfully over the wet grass where decaying apples and plums from a bountiful autumn harvest lay where they had fallen, ravaged by wasps. She did not change her mind.

When she went back inside, her father was waiting for her with her mother in their private sitting room. Arethusa knew he was going to be angry and braced herself for a tirade of abuse. However, she had never seen him quite so furious before. She felt the tension in the room the moment she walked into it and closed the door softly behind her. Hubert was pacing the floor, shoulders stooped, as if defeated by the weight of the problem now facing him. For a while he said nothing, he just grew redder in the face and more agitated. He inhaled like a bull, nostrils dilated, puffed out his cheeks and dabbed his forehead with a handkerchief. At last he stopped in front of the fireplace, where turf logs spat and smoked in the grate, and spoke.

'Never in my life have I been so bitterly disappointed, Arethusa.' Arethusa glanced at her mother who stood by the window, fiddling nervously with her fingers. 'I'm appalled that a girl with your education and upbringing should behave like a common harlot.' He raised his voice, emphasizing the word 'harlot' with disdain, which made Arethusa flinch. 'Have you no shame?' Arethusa knew he did not expect or wish her to reply. She remained very still and stiff and waited for it to be over. Hubert began to pace again. 'But you will not bring the family into disrepute,' he said, dabbing his forehead with the handkerchief again. 'You will not inflict scandal upon us. No one else must know about this but the three of us. It must remain between these four walls, do you understand?' He looked at her directly. She nodded. It wasn't the time to mention that Charlotte also knew. 'Now this is what you will do.' He repeated what her mother had told her in the bedroom. But Arethusa was not going to give up her child, whatever the cost.

'I won't do it,' she said when he had finished. Her father stared at her in astonishment. Had she turned into a frog before his very eyes he would not have looked more startled.

'What did you say?'

'I said, I won't do it.'

Hubert looked at his wife, who looked back at him help-lessly. 'Good God, girl! You simply don't have a choice in the matter.'

Arethusa stood up. 'I do,' she said, surprised by her own lack of fear. 'The child I'm carrying belongs to me. I will not give it away. It is not an object one can disregard. It's a human being and it will need its mother.'

'What do *you* know about motherhood!' he bellowed.

'I know that it's not natural for a mother to give away her child. I will not do it.'

Hubert's face had gone puce. It looked as if it might pop. 'By Jove you will, even if I have to rip it from your arms and do it myself!' His voice boomed, sending a spray of spittle into the air. 'You will marry Ronald if it's the last thing you do, although you don't deserve him, or anyone else for that matter. You are soiled goods.' He took a breath and wiped his mouth. 'I should disown you, for the disrespect you have shown me.

But I'm offering you a way out. I suggest you take it before I change my mind.'

Arethusa clenched her fists and stood defiantly in front of her father whom she had never before disobeyed. 'I don't want to marry Ronald. I never did,' she said. 'I want to marry Jonas and have his child.'

Hubert looked as if he was about to strike her. 'Get out!' he raged, pointing to the door. 'Get out and don't come back until you are ready to do as you're told. Have you forgotten who you are? I will not be challenged, do you understand?'

When Arethusa left the room her legs almost buckled beneath her. She realized she had lost control of her bladder. She held on to the banisters for support and heaved herself slowly up the stairs. She had never been spoken to like that in her life. She understood her father's rage, what she had done was unforgivable, but still she couldn't believe he could call his daughter a harlot. When she reached her bedroom she flung herself onto the bed and buried her face in the pillow. The tears she shed were not of unhappiness but of fury. How dare they tell her what to do with her baby!

Eily found her there when she came to turn down her bed before supper. 'I'm unwell,' Arethusa told her. 'And I'm not hungry.'

'Shall I bring you something on a tray? You can't go to bed on an empty stomach, Miss Arethusa.'

'I can and I will. I want to be alone.'

Eily left the room wondering what had happened. One of the footmen had heard a commotion in the sitting room and Mr Deverill raising his voice in anger. She didn't believe Miss Arethusa was unwell and her sharp little antennae turned to consider all the possibilities.

Concerned that Arethusa had not appeared for dinner,

Charlotte went to her room. She found her packing a suitcase. 'Tussy! What are you doing?' she asked in alarm.

'I'm leaving,' Arethusa stated.

'Where are you going?'

'To London.'

'On your own?'

'What does it look like?' she snapped.

'But where are you going to stay?'

Arethusa threw a garment into the suitcase. 'I'll go to Augusta's. She'll have me, for a while, at least.'

'But what about the baby?'

'What about it?'

'You're going to start showing very soon. You won't be able to hide it. Are you sure London is the right place to be?'

'I have to go somewhere.' Arethusa sat on the bed and began to cry. 'And I have nowhere else to go. I can't stay here. Papa is going to disown me and Mama is going to stand by him, so I'll get no support from her. I'm out in the cold on my own.' Then she added melodramatically, 'It's just me and my child.'

'What will you do for money?'

'I will appeal to Rupert, or Aunt Poppy.'

'You're going to tell them?'

'I have to.'

'I think you're being rash, Tussy. Let's talk about it. Why not wait a few days? For your father to calm down. For everyone to calm down.'

Arethusa looked at Charlotte with red-rimmed eyes. 'They won't change their minds, Charlotte, and I won't change mine. I will not let them take my baby away. It is the only part of the man I love that I'm able to have.' She wiped her eyes with the back of her hand and sniffed. 'Perhaps it's Fate, after all. I was never meant to marry Ronald. I'd be condemned to a dull and repetitive life. I'm meant for bigger things.'

Charlotte sighed deeply, put her hands on her hips and narrowed her eyes ponderously. 'If you really have decided that you want to keep the baby, then you will have to have it where no one knows you. In secret. London is not the place for that.'

'Then where do you suggest?'

'America,' said Charlotte with a shrug.

'America? That's very far away.'

'I have connections in America,' said Charlotte.

Arethusa's face lit up. 'You do?'

'Of course I do. I used to work there.'

'Do you think you can help me?'

'I think I can.'

Arethusa leapt to her feet and ran to her governess. She took her hands and squeezed them. 'Will you come with me? We could go together, just the two of us. We could start a new life in a new country. It will be an adventure. You were going to be looking for a new job after the wedding anyway. You were going to have to start again. So, start again, in America, and take me with you.'

'I will come with you on one condition,' said Charlotte.

'What condition?' Arethusa looked at her suspiciously.

'That you tell your parents where you're going. Don't burn your bridges. You need them. You don't realize now that you need them, but you do.'

Arethusa pursed her lips. 'I don't know,' she said, unconvinced.

'At least give them the chance to put out the olive branch. Promise me you'll write to them when you get to America and tell them where you are.'

'All right, I will,' Arethusa agreed. 'I will tell them I am leaving. I'll say goodbye.'

'Then I will arrange our passages and our entry into the country.' She looked at Arethusa with compassion. 'Your parents will be devastated,' she said.

'No, they won't,' Arethusa replied. 'I have appalled and disappointed them in equal measure. I don't think they will ever get over it.'

Chapter 30

When Arethusa broke the news to her parents that she was going to America she did it in a calm and mature manner that surprised them. She requested an audience in the sitting room and waited for them to sit down, Hubert in the armchair by the fire, Adeline stiffly on the edge of the sofa. Arethusa noticed how pale and fragile her mother looked and how her father's face had gone the colour of bull's blood. Arethusa stood in the middle of the room. She took a deep breath and eyed them steadily and with confidence. She knew any sign of weakness would be seized upon and used to their advantage. She then proceeded to tell them that she had no intention of giving up her child and would therefore travel to America to have it there, where no one knew her. 'I assure you there will be no scandal,' she informed them gravely. 'I will not sully the good Deverill name, I promise.'

Hubert stared at her with a mixture of disbelief and disdain. 'Do you have any idea what it's like to raise a child without the support of a husband, Arethusa?' he asked.

'I am soon going to find out,' she replied coolly.

'It's one thing to raise a child on your own but a *black* child . . . Good God, girl, you're more of a fool than I thought you were.'

'Darling,' Adeline interrupted in a softer tone, appealing to her daughter with supplication rather than fury. 'This is madness. You will be an outcast. No one will want to know you. What future will you have? Please think hard about what you're intending to do. I beg of you, don't throw your life away when you've only just begun to live it.'

'A black child, I ask you!' Hubert muttered crossly.

'Black or white, it's a child, Father. Equal in the eyes of God,' said Arethusa.

Hubert could not argue with that. 'And who the devil is going to pay for this elaborate trip?' Hubert asked, outraged by her insolence. 'Because you won't get a penny from me. Not a penny!'

'I will find the means.' Arethusa did not want to tell them that she was going to ask Aunt Poppy and Rupert for money.

'You know you can't just wander into America, Tussy,' said Adeline, hoping that the practicalities of the venture would deter her.

'Charlotte has connections and is going to come with me. I won't be on my own. Charlotte will look after me.' Adeline looked surprised.

'And who the devil's going to pay for Charlotte, I ask you?' Hubert exclaimed.

'Charlotte is coming as my friend.'

'She's a bloody fool too. The pair of you are bloody fools!'

'Perhaps I am a fool,' said Tussy, lifting her chin. 'But God will look kindly on me for not abandoning my child just because you think it's the wrong colour!'

'Don't bring God into this, my girl!' Hubert shouted. 'You've never believed in God before, now's not the time to start just because it suits you.'

'I am doing the right thing as a human being. What you're

asking me to do is wrong.' She folded her arms. 'I stand by my decision.'

Hubert stood up. 'Then we have no more to discuss,' he said in a quiet voice, and there was a finality in his tone, as well as a sense of defeat. Adeline's mouth opened as if she was about to say something, but then it closed, as if she suddenly thought better of it. 'Come, my dear,' said Hubert to his wife. 'Arethusa has made her choice and there's nothing more to be said.' He turned to Arethusa. 'As far as I'm concerned you are no longer my daughter. No daughter of mine would treat her parents with such contempt. You are free to do whatever you choose. The parental ties have been severed. On your head be it.'

Adeline's face went grey. She looked at Arethusa and her eyes were laden with disappointment and pain. 'I am at a loss for words,' she said sadly. 'But as your father said, you have made your choice. We have done all we can. I only hope that in time you will understand that our demands came from a good place.' She put a tremulous hand on her breast. 'We've only ever had your best interests at heart.'

With that they left the room.

Arethusa sank into the sofa and lost her gaze in the half-distance, too traumatized even to think. Every part of her was numb. She felt only a terrible emptiness.

She was leaving; there was no going back.

That afternoon Charlotte accompanied Arethusa in the pony and trap to Poppy's house. 'I'm not meant to tell anyone,' she told her aunt as they sat side by side on the sofa in the small sitting room in her cottage. 'But I don't consider *you* anyone.'

'What's happened, Tussy? You look as if your whole world has fallen apart.' Poppy smiled, because she didn't imagine it had.

Arethusa's eyes filled with tears. 'I have got myself into

trouble, Aunt Poppy,' she said, tightening the muscles in her face to stop herself crying. 'I'm leaving for America, with Charlotte, and I won't be coming back.'

Poppy was horrified. 'What kind of trouble?' she asked, but her eyes dropped to Arethusa's belly.

'I'm pregnant,' Arethusa stated and watched her aunt struggle to comprehend it.

'My darling girl . . .' Poppy took Arethusa's hand. 'My darling, darling girl. How . . .?'

'That's all I'm going to say about it,' Arethusa cut in, throat constricting with emotion because there was so much she couldn't say. 'But as you can imagine Mama and Papa are furious with me. Naturally, they want me to give up the child.'

'That would be the most sensible thing,' said Poppy, her eyes full of compassion. 'You're not the first girl to get pregnant out of wedlock. There are ways of dealing with this problem. It does not have to ruin your life.'

'But I won't give it up,' said Arethusa. 'So, I have no option but to leave.'

Poppy frowned. 'Oh, Tussy. Are you sure that's wise? Perhaps you've been too hasty in arriving at that decision. Have you given it enough thought? I mean, it's all very romantic, but the practicalities of raising a child alone . . .'

'I haven't come here to be persuaded, Aunt Poppy. Believe me, Mama and Papa have tried. I've come here to ask you for help.'

Poppy sighed resignedly. 'Well, I was about to ask how you're going to manage.'

'I will pay you back as soon as I can.'

'My dear, that won't be necessary.'

Arethusa began to cry with relief. Poppy pulled her into her arms and pressed her cheek against her hair. 'Don't cry, my dear. It's going to be all right. You'll manage. You're a strong and courageous girl. I dare say you'll work something out.' Arethusa clung to her. She didn't really feel very strong at all. The only thing keeping her going was the thought of writing to Jonas once the baby was born and telling him that she had given him a son. That was a fantasy she replayed over and over in the hope that it would come true. Once his child was born there would be no denying her. They'd *have* to marry.

Poppy turned to the governess who was sitting in a wicker chair, sipping her tea quietly by the window, trying to look inconspicuous. 'Now, Charlotte, tell me your plan. Who will vouch for Tussy once she arrives in New York and where are you going to stay?'

'I have it all worked out,' Charlotte replied confidently. 'I have written to a dear friend of mine, the Reverend Brian Holmes, who I'm hoping will vouch for her. We are going to stay in New Jersey. I have a friend who can put us up.'

'But you will need money,' said Poppy. 'I don't have much, but my late husband did not leave me penniless. I have enough to give you a small allowance which will keep the wolf from the door.'

'How will I ever thank you?' said Arethusa with a sniff. 'You're the only person who understands.'

Poppy took her face in her hands and wiped away her tears. 'I longed for a child, Tussy, but Henry died before I conceived. Were I in your situation, nothing in the world would make me give away my child. Nothing.' She smiled wistfully. 'I understand your parents' anger, Tussy. Anger is usually born out of fear and they fear for you and your future. Your father is a traditional man with traditional values. He is also a proud man.'

'He has disowned me,' said Arethusa.

Poppy sighed heavily. 'I thought as much. But it won't be for ever. In time he will come to terms with it and forgive you.'

'I don't think *I* will ever be able to forgive *him*, Aunt Poppy,' said Arethusa, straightening her shoulders and raising her chin. 'And I won't ever forgive Mama for siding with him.'

Rupert returned from Cumbria the day before Arethusa was due to leave for America. It was a drizzling and cold November day, but the two of them went for a walk up the beach all the same, and Arethusa told him the whole story. Rupert was not at all surprised that she was pregnant, but he *was* surprised that the father of her child was Jonas Madison. 'What is it with you, Tussy?' he said, raising his voice over the crashing waves and wind. 'It's as if you have a death wish. You choose not just an unsuitable man, but the *most* unsuitable man you can find. And then you get pregnant? Isn't that wildly irresponsible, even for you?'

'This isn't a joke, Rupert,' Arethusa snapped.

'The pleasures of the flesh are very seductive, I agree, but you really should have restrained yourself.'

'I know that now,' she replied with a sigh. 'But perhaps it's a good thing I'm not going to marry Ronald. One has to be grateful for small mercies.'

'You could have married anyone, Tussy,' said Rupert sensibly. 'If you didn't like Ronald, why didn't you say?'

'Because it's what Mama and Papa wanted and I was doing my duty.'

'They would have been just as happy with someone else.'

'I fell in love with Jonas. I didn't want anyone else. But I couldn't marry Jonas so I accepted Ronald. He was just as tolerable as all the other possible husbands. And I do *like* him, you know. I like him very much. As far as I can see, marriage has nothing to do with love. Ronald is a good man.' She dropped her gaze onto the sand in front of her. 'I would have been content with him.'

'But you're heading out to America where you're going to give birth to this child and raise it on your own.'

'That's right.'

'Enlighten me as to why?'

'Because I'm not going to give up my child, Rupert. Surely you can understand that. You who know me better than anyone.'

'And you'll never marry.'

'I'm going to marry Jonas,' Arethusa retorted defiantly.

'No, you're not,' said Rupert. He stopped walking and looked at his sister with surprising tenderness. 'Because he already has a wife.'

Arethusa stared at him. 'Jonas has a wife?'

Suddenly the beach and the ocean, even Rupert and his arms, which were reaching out to hold her, fell away. She closed her eyes and swayed as an inky black mist appeared behind them. 'Jonas has a wife?' she repeated feebly.

Rupert held her wilting body against him. 'You didn't know?' he asked gently. She shook her head, too devastated to speak. 'Oh Tussy!' he groaned. 'What a mess.'

'He told you he was married?'

'I was being polite. I wasn't remotely interested. If I had known how you felt I would have been *very* interested.'

'He was married and he made love to me all the same?'

Arethusa's fantasy of Jonas hurrying to her bedside after she had given birth to his child was swiftly crushed, along with her belief in love. Now she had lost everything: her home, her family and her future. She had nothing but a child growing inside her to remind her of her naivety. 'Don't leave,' he said. 'Do as Papa commands. Ask his forgiveness. You have a chance to put all this right.'

She pulled away and looked up at him miserably. 'Nothing can be put right now, Rupert. Papa has said things to me that he can never take back, and I have seen his prejudice, which I can never *unsee*. I don't belong here anymore.'

'The fact that Jonas has a wife does not mean he doesn't love *you*,' said Rupert kindly. 'Perhaps if he had loved his wife you would not have got into trouble.' Arethusa shrugged, defeated by so many odds against her. 'There was never any chance for you both. You must have known that, Tussy.'

'I knew it and I gave myself to him all the same because I believed he loved me. Because *I* loved *him*,' she replied flatly.

'The wife is irrelevant, as so many wives are,' said Rupert, trying to cajole her out of her misery with a smile.

'What does it matter now? I will never love anyone else. Jonas will always have the key to my heart and there is only one key.' She put a hand on her belly then looked up at Rupert with the determined gaze of a woman who always finds the silver lining, however grey the cloud. 'But he left a part of himself inside me and no one can ever take *that* away from me. No one.'

Besides Hubert and Adeline, Rupert and Poppy, no one knew why Arethusa left suddenly for America. They knew there had been a row, the servants could talk of nothing else but raised voices and a furious-looking Mr Deverill, but the reasons behind her departure were nebulous. Adeline explained to Ronald, as kindly as she could, that Arethusa had changed her mind about marrying him and gone to stay with friends in

America. Ronald was both devastated and furious, for he had been seriously humiliated. He was hurt that she hadn't had the courage to tell him herself and declared that it would take him a lifetime to recover from the heartbreak. Hubert declared that he would never articulate Arethusa's name again as long as he lived and the Deverills rallied around him, casting the blame at Arethusa's feet and assuming that it was *she* who had turned her back on her family because she wanted a more exciting life in America. Only Poppy and Rupert knew the truth and they would never divulge it to anyone.

Arethusa and Charlotte crossed the Atlantic aboard the *Teutonic* in the second week of November. The seas were rough, the winds high and yet Arethusa walked incessantly up and down the promenade deck, dragging poor Charlotte with her. The governess wrapped her coat tightly about her and tried not to complain about feeling seasick. The crossing was due to last ten days, and although arduous for steerage passengers, it was luxurious for first-class passengers like Arethusa and Charlotte, for whom Rupert had bought tickets at a cost of twenty-five pounds each.

When Arethusa wasn't pacing the promenade deck she was in the sitting room in their suite playing the banjo and singing for the child growing inside her who would never know its father. After a few days Charlotte's nausea was such that she had to retreat to the bedroom and lie groaning in her bed. Arethusa, who didn't suffer from either morning sickness or seasickness, grew impatient listening to Charlotte's moaning and went to find company in the first-class lounge. Mostly occupied by women, the lounge was a wood-panelled sitting room with velvet-covered armchairs and sofas, a grand

wooden fireplace where an electric fire gave out warmth as
well as an inviting glow, and little tables and chairs arranged
in small groups where passengers took tea, played cards, and
idled away the hours in lazy conversation. It was there that she
was invited to make up a four at the bridge table with a lady
she had met the night before, when Charlotte had retired early
to bed. The lady was a grand American in her early sixties,
with lustrous brown hair pinned up with a glittering diamond
brooch and large, empathetic eyes the colour of molasses. Her
name was Gertrude Davenport and she was accompanied by
her son, Cyrus, and a man in his thirties who was travelling
alone called Edward Clayton.

Gertrude and Cyrus were both good company, but
Arethusa liked Edward especially, for he was a challenge.
He was confident, assertive and handsome, with a proud,
patrician face, light hazel eyes and fair hair, swept off his
forehead and curling just above the collar. He was direct,
which appealed to Arethusa because she, too, was unafraid
to speak her mind. Gertrude Davenport told Arethusa that
she was returning to America having been to Ireland to
find her roots, for her family were originally from Galway.
Cyrus, dutifully, had agreed to accompany her. 'He's a good
son,' she said with an indulgent smile. 'I would not have
been able to come had he not agreed to accompany me. You
see, my husband passed away many years ago and Cyrus is
all I have.' She glanced then at Edward Clayton, who was
talking to her son and out of earshot. 'Mr Clayton has also
been in Ireland for the same reason,' she told Arethusa. 'We
Americans like to know where we come from. He lost his
wife a few years back and has since thrown himself into his
work. It has been a tonic for him to take the sea air and walk
in the Irish hills.'

Arethusa now searched for the shadow of grief in Edward's eyes but found none. She wondered, as she partnered him at bridge, whether he had children. He looked a good many years older than Bertie. She wondered whether he had it in mind to marry again. Arethusa, regardless of the child growing inside her, which was still small enough to go unnoticed, decided to use her entire arsenal of charm and allure, because if she couldn't have Jonas, she'd have to find someone else and Edward Clayton, as far as she could tell, was a man worth having.

During their rubber of bridge, Arethusa explained that Charlotte, her chaperone, was taken ill and confined to their suite. 'We're on our way to New York to visit friends,' she told them casually. 'I've never been to New York and I'm very excited to see it. They say the buildings are as tall as giants!'

'Taller,' said Mrs Davenport with a laugh. 'But we're not from New York, we're from Chicago. You must come and see Chicago. It's a magnificent city. We'd be glad to entertain you.' She turned her soft brown gaze onto Edward Clayton. 'You're from Boston, aren't you, Mr Clayton?'

'I am indeed, Mrs Davenport,' he replied.

'I have not been to Boston, but my husband used to travel there for business and I know it's a very historic city, and pretty too.'

'Indeed it is, the Common and the Public Garden are especially beautiful in summertime. Even more lovely than Central Park,' said Edward. 'But what is more beautiful is the Emerald Necklace, designed by the landscape architect, Frederick Law Olmsted, which is a series of interconnecting parks and waterways. Besides its beauty, Boston is, quite frankly, the centre of higher learning in the United States. We have Harvard, of course, but more recently Radcliffe and

Wellesley, which are all-women colleges. A novel idea. I could go on, but I don't want to bore you.'

Arethusa looked at Edward and smiled. 'You are clearly very proud of your city. I should like to see all those things,' she declared. 'Boston is a place I'd very much like to visit.'

Over the course of the voyage, Edward and Arethusa spent a great deal of time together. It suited Arethusa that Charlotte was indisposed and that Mrs Davenport did not feel the need to step into her shoes; after all, Arethusa was not her responsibility and perhaps, Arethusa thought, young women were more at liberty in America. Whatever the case, Edward and Arethusa were able to walk up and down the promenade without the tedious company of a chaperone. The more time she spent with Edward Clayton the more she grew to like him. Love was never going to blossom again; it had already done so. Arethusa felt like one of those orchids that only flower once in their lifetime. But marriage had little to do with love. She knew that. It was about partnership, respect and security. It wasn't long before Arethusa's arsenal of charm and allure had achieved the desired result. Edward was in love with her, she was certain of it. She had seen that spark in the eyes of Dermot McLoughlin, Ronald Rowan-Hampton and Jonas Madison. It was as unmistakable as fire.

As soon as Charlotte was feeling better, Arethusa introduced her to the Davenports and Edward Clayton. It took the governess only a few minutes to notice what was happening between Arethusa and Edward. The moment they were alone in their suite she rounded on her charge with exasperation. 'What kind of game are you playing, Tussy?' she exclaimed. 'That young man is in love with you!'

'I know!' said Arethusa. 'Isn't it thrilling?'

'You can't do this to him. It's not fair.'

'Do what to him, Charlotte? *I'm* not doing anything.'

'You're toying with his heart. Surely you of all people should know how cruel that is.'

'I'm not toying with his heart. I like him too.'

Charlotte stared at Arethusa as if she had morphed into someone very different from the broken-hearted girl who had begged her to accompany her to America. 'Well, you do have a fickle heart!' she exclaimed disapprovingly.

'I don't love him, Charlotte. I *like* him.'

'But what about the baby?'

Arethusa's smile vanished and she bit her lip. 'I know, it's a problem.' She began to pace the floor, hands on hips.

'It's more than a problem, Tussy. It's an obstacle you simply cannot overcome.'

Arethusa stopped pacing. 'I'm going to tell him,' she declared.

Charlotte was appalled. 'You can't tell him.'

'It's a gamble, I agree.'

'Think again, Tussy. If you tell him, you will never see him again. No man, however in love he may be, will accept another man's child. Perhaps if you were a widow, but even then ...' She shook her head and sucked the air through her teeth. 'You can't risk it.'

'I will write him a letter once we dock and explain myself.'

'I wouldn't waste your ink.'

'I have a feeling Edward Clayton is not like other men.'

'He's exactly like other men, Tussy. *You're* not like other women!'

Arethusa went to the dressing table and sat down before it. She stared at her reflection in the mirror. 'The only way to get out of this mess, Charlotte, is to marry. Rupert said I never will. *You* don't think I will either. Mama and Papa consider me as driftwood washed up on the beach, "soiled goods". But I'm going to prove you all wrong. Not everyone is old-fashioned and conventional like Papa. I predict that Edward is going to ask me to marry him, and that when I tell him about my child he will marry me regardless. He has a look in his eye. I've seen it before.'

'Where have you seen it before?' asked Charlotte wearily.

Arethusa leaned closer to the mirror. 'Here,' she replied. 'In mine.'

On the final evening of the voyage, Arethusa and Edward walked up the promenade. The moon was high, the stars twinkled above them and the sea was calm, like a silk gown spread out before them, studded with diamonds. The beauty made Arethusa think of Jonas and her heart bled a little from the tear in it that would never heal. 'I should like to marry you, Miss Deverill,' said Edward, drawing her swiftly out of her thoughts. Arethusa had not expected him to propose so soon. She stopped walking and frowned up at him, lost for words. Registering her surprise, he added with an awkwardness that was foreign to his nature, 'I am not a sentimental man, Miss Deverill, so please forgive me. I find you both beautiful and fascinating, but I think you know that.' He smiled down at her and Arethusa saw a tenderness in it that startled her. She put a hand on her stomach. 'You're sure of yourself, Miss Deverill, and I like that,' he continued. 'I admire a woman who knows her mind and isn't afraid to speak it. You remind me of myself.' Arethusa put her hands on the railings and cast her gaze across the ocean. Until this moment, she hadn't realized how much she liked him. 'I hope that you will consider my proposal and will forgive me for being so forward. I'm aware that you barely know me, but I can offer you a comfortable and interesting life in the heart of politics and Society. I think you will grow to love me. We will grow to love each other.' He took her hand off the railing and sandwiched it between his own. 'What I admire in you most, Arethusa, if I may be so bold, is that you are a woman equal to me in spirit. There are few women in my world to whom I can give that compliment.'

Arethusa put her other hand on top of his and looked at him sadly. His expression turned at once to disappointment, anticipating rejection. 'Edward, I'm flattered by your proposal,' she said, realizing that the only way forward was with honesty. 'It is both unexpected and welcome. However, you don't know anything about me and, as you are a man who respects directness, and I am a woman who is both direct and candid, I have to tell you about my circumstances so that you may consider whether *you* want to marry *me*.'

Now it was Edward's turn to look surprised. Arethusa let go of his hand and put hers once more on the railings. 'I am on my way to New York because I have been disowned by my father for falling pregnant out of wedlock. The man I loved is unsuitable.' She sighed heavily, knowing now as she articulated the story that Charlotte was right. Edward would never marry her. 'He already has a wife,' she added flatly. She did not reveal that he was black; she didn't have to. She could tell by the air that changed between them that he was already lost to her.

There was a long silence. Arethusa stared out to sea, Edward stood stiffly beside her, his profile inscrutable. Neither spoke for what felt like a very long time. The ship sliced through the waves, which were black and cold and timeless, and neither noticed the stars strewn over them by a bright and buoyant moon. Arethusa thought of the child inside her and her heart warmed at the thought of the part of Jonas she was able to keep for herself. What did it matter if she never married again? She'd have her baby. She'd never be alone. They'd muddle along somehow. And once again, Arethusa pushed away the future, as was her great talent, and focused on the present moment.

Edward withdrew from the railings. He looked at her with a sad and troubled expression and bowed. 'Goodnight, Miss Deverill,' he said in a voice that was drenched with disappointment.

'Goodnight, Mr Clayton,' she replied. She gave him an acquiescent smile, then watched him walk through the door into the lounge.

She remained a while with the cold air on her face. As she inhaled, her breath caught in her chest and she was overcome by a sudden swell of self-pity. It took her by surprise, like a creature leaping out of the darkness and landing on her chest, claws bared, and left her reeling with confusion. In spite of her bravado the truth was that she needed a man and Edward would have been her salvation. Alone on the deck where no one could witness her lack of restraint, she cried into the wind.

Charlotte was not surprised when Arethusa told her. 'You were right, Charlotte,' she said in a small voice when she returned to their suite. 'No one will want to marry me with another man's child in my belly. I will have to wait until the baby is born and pretend that I am a widow.'

'I hate to be right,' Charlotte replied. 'I only want your happiness, Tussy.'

Arethusa looked at her with shiny eyes. 'Why do you stay by my side, Charlotte? Why do you put up with me? I have been a fool. An utter fool. I've been self-indulgent and selfish. I don't listen to advice. I always think I know better, which I don't. I clearly don't. As Papa would say, I'm soiled goods. Yet, here you are. You could be anywhere, but you're here . . .'

Her shoulders began to shake. 'If I didn't have you, Charlotte, I don't know what would become of me.'

The governess's heart inflated with tenderness. 'I'm with you, my darling Tussy, because you're very dear to me,' she said, drawing the young woman who would always be a child to her into her arms. 'You're very dear to me indeed.'

Arethusa did not sleep. For the first time in her life she felt a real sense of hopelessness. Every time she closed her eyes she felt as if she were falling into a big black hole from which she would never find her way out. The most distressing thing was the acknowledgement of the part *she* had played in her destiny. The pain she was suffering now was completely self-inflicted; she could not blame anyone but herself.

The following morning while they prepared to disembark there came a knock on the door of their suite. Charlotte went to open it. Arethusa heard a deep voice, which she recognized at once as belonging to Edward Clayton. 'Please come in,' said Charlotte, stepping aside.

Edward entered, looking grim. It did not appear that he had slept much either. Arethusa was startled. She had not expected to see him again. 'Hello, Mr Clayton,' she said, folding her hands in front of her.

Charlotte disappeared into the bedroom and closed the door behind her.

'I have done nothing all night but think of you,' he said, his face as sombre as a grave.

'Oh,' murmured Arethusa. 'I'm sorry for that.'

'No, it is I who must apologize for leaving you on the deck yesterday evening. It was very rude of me.'

'I quite understood,' she said, reading regret in his expression and feeling a small flicker of hope ignite in her heart.

'The fact is I have fallen in love with you, Arethusa.'

The flicker at once grew into a flame.

'I have fallen in love with you and I cannot leave this ship knowing that I will never see you again.' He looked at her with uncertainty. 'I must be candid and direct with you too, as you have been with me,' he continued. 'I was married to Geraldine for nine years before she died and, in spite of our desire to have children, we were not blessed. Perhaps I will never be blessed with children of my own. I have a sense that you are as bold as I am.' He hesitated and looked at her steadily and there was a steely quality to his gaze that reminded Arethusa of his sang froid at the bridge table. 'What I'm trying to say is, I would like to marry you in haste and pass off the child as my own. Would that be acceptable to you?'

Arethusa was astonished. 'You really are audacious!' she exclaimed.

'We are both audacious, I suppose,' he replied, a smile creeping onto his face, mirroring hers. 'So, Miss Deverill, how might you answer me now?'

'Yes,' she said happily. 'It would be an honour to be your wife.'

Chapter 31

Ballinakelly, 1961

'But the baby is going to be black!' I gasp and stare at Cormac in horror. 'What is Daddy going to do when he realizes that she hasn't told him the whole truth. I can't bear it!'

Cormac gets off the bed and stretches. We have read the diary together and are both in need of a break. I take the diary and the hand mirror and follow him down to the kitchen and watch him put the kettle on the stove. 'Your mam was a brave girl, no mistake,' he says.

'A gambler,' I add, thinking of the risks she took time and time again.

'But the baby could be Dermot McLoughlin's. Don't forget that,' he reminds me.

'Unlikely, considering she never got pregnant with him before.'

'Perhaps he was firing blanks,' says Cormac with a grin.

'What has become of him, of Dermot McLoughlin?'

'He's an old man now. In his eighties. He still lives in Ballinakelly. He married, had children, grandchildren, the usual stuff. Didn't always fire blanks.'

'I never knew my father was so exceptional,' I say, taking

a chair at the table and sitting down. 'I knew him as fiercely traditional, dogmatic and autocratic. He worshipped my mother. They were a team, the two of them. They agreed on everything. They were both ambitious, my father was Governor of Massachusetts, and tirelessly social. They knew everyone. Now I know why they were as thick as thieves, because their marriage was built on a secret.'

Cormac pours the water into the teapot and comes to the table. 'They appear to be cut from the same cloth,' he agrees.

'I suspect my mother pretended she was Catholic. Another lie. And if Daddy knew that her father had disowned her, they must have fabricated her history together. We grew up believing she was from a poor Irish family and left Ireland in search of a better life in America. We never questioned it. On reflection, a man like my father would never have married someone like that. He was as aware of social status as everyone else. And she wouldn't have been travelling first-class if she had been poor.' I shake my head and laugh at our naivety. 'We never thought to ask. Mom didn't talk about the past, period.'

I open the diary and hold it up to the mirror. Before I begin to read, I am suddenly struck by an extraordinary thought. I put the book down and stare at Cormac. 'Oh my God!' I gasp, putting a hand to my mouth.

'What?' says Cormac.

'Oh my God!' I repeat. 'I think I've worked it out.'

'Well, come on then. Don't keep it to yourself.'

'Temperance!'

Cormac frowns. 'Who is Temperance?'

'Our maid. She came to work for us at fourteen. She's only a couple of years older than Logan.'

We stare at each other.

'Oh my God!' I exclaim for the third time and stand up. I cannot remain seated with my blood pumping so fast around my body. 'It makes perfect sense. That is why Mom has left a third of her wealth to an anonymous person. I had to read the whole story before that person was revealed so that I understood. Mom was never going to give her child away so the only option was to take her in as a maid, as soon as she was able to. God knows what the child did for the first fourteen years of her life. But that would explain it.' I am short of breath, excited by the drama. 'That's why Tempie can play the banjo! Her father is Jonas Madison.' My head is swimming with memories. Of Temperance and my mother, so close and intimate and affectionate. 'Tempie is Mom's child!'

I sit down and hold the diary to the mirror, heart pounding against my bones, blood pulsating in my temples. I can barely contain my thoughts. Cormac sits down too and calmly pours the tea. 'Well, read on then. What does she say? Are you right, Inspector Langton?'

I ignore his joke and feverishly scan the sentences for the entry where the baby is born. I cannot restrain myself any longer. I don't have the patience to read the details of their hasty wedding, or how they remained in New York to have the baby in order to avoid my father's family getting too close. I flick through the pages until I finally arrive at the crucial point. Even though I know what happened I almost can't read it. I don't want to be right. It's not that I fear Temperance is my half-sister; I fear my father's reaction to her birth. Because I want so very badly for Arethusa and Edward to love one another. They are my parents, after all. I want Jonas to disappear and that means I want his baby to disappear too.

I read aloud:

*Labour seems to be eternal. Hour upon hour of unspeakable
pain as my baby fights its way into the light. And then he is
in my arms. A bonny pink-and-white boy, squealing with fury
at the shock of leaving the comfort of my womb for the chaos of
this world. And my heart bleeds again for I will have no part of
Jonas to accompany me through my life. Nothing to remember
him by. It is as if he never existed. I cry with sorrow but also
with relief because Edward and I can pass this child off as our
own and no one will ever know. God has forgiven me for my
sins. I have been given another chance. And what shall we call
him? I ask my husband. He looks into the little face and smiles.
'Logan,' he says, 'after my mother's father. Because we met
in the Irish Sea and I want to honour the two most important
women in my life. You, my dear wife, and Mother.'*

*'Logan,' I repeat and I feel like a new day is dawning.
'I like it very much.' I blink away the tears, and in so doing
I put away the past. I look only to my future now. I'm
Arethusa Clayton and God knows, I'm going to make the
best of it.*

I tear my eyes off the page. That is the end. That is all
she wrote.

I stare at Cormac and I can feel the blood draining out of
my face. 'Logan is Dermot McLoughlin's son,' I say, barely
able to take it in. For once Cormac is lost for words. He shakes
his head and reaches for my hand. He knows this is a massive
shock for me. We sit in silence, staring at each other. It is as if
the world has just crashed around us and we are the only two
people left alive.

Now I understand why my mother wanted *me* to read the
diary. *I* am the one who will have to tell Logan the truth about
his parentage. *I* am the one who will have to drop this bomb

into his world and shatter it. I understand also why she didn't include any dates, because I would have done the math and worked it out before she had had time to tell me her story. She wanted me to know her heart before I learned that my brother is really my *half*-brother.

I squeeze Cormac's hand and I squeeze it hard. It is a while before I can speak. Shock has stolen my voice. 'I don't know how I'm going to tell Logan,' I choke.

Cormac has no words of advice. 'I don't know either, Faye,' he says, gazing at me with compassion. 'What are you going to tell Kitty?'

'I'm going to give her the diary to read for herself.'

'You see,' he says, arching an eyebrow. 'That's why your mother gave you the diary, because it was impossible for her to *tell* you the whole story when she was alive. She couldn't have begun. You had to *read* it slowly and deliberately to fully understand her. Kitty and Lord Deverill must do the same.'

'I suspect, even though she is not Mom's daughter, that the anonymous person is Temperance,' I say. 'It is too much of a coincidence that her father played the banjo, don't you think? I mean, who else could it be?' And yet, as I try to fit together the pieces of Mom's life, I see the flaws in my argument. Temperance has already been accounted for in the will. Mom has left her the use of a house and two hundred thousand dollars. Would she also leave her a third of her wealth?

'I think you're right,' Cormac agrees. 'Your mother was able to keep a part of Jonas, after all.'

'Mom really loved Tempie.' I sigh heavily, wondering whether or not I am right. 'When I return to Boston, I'll ask Tempie for her story. I'd like to know how she found Mom and why. I'd like to know what happened to Jonas. If they ever met again.'

At the mention of returning to America my heart sinks with dread. I don't want to leave Ireland; I don't want to leave Cormac. I look at him across the table, that gentle face I have come to love. I withdraw my gaze, not wanting him to know what I am thinking. Not wanting him to sense my neediness and to be put off by it. I turn my thoughts once again to Mother. One part of the story still fails to make sense. 'Even when Mom was married she didn't come home,' I say, still unable to fully understand how she couldn't find it in her heart to forgive. 'She burned her bridges and turned her back on her family. But did her family turn their back on her?'

'How do you mean?'

'I can understand her father's wrath, but I find it hard to understand Adeline's. I know she had to support her husband and what Arethusa had done was pretty unforgivable in their eyes. Yet, she was her mother. I can't imagine, in the same circumstances, never seeing my daughter again. It would destroy me.'

'Yet, Arethusa wants her ashes scattered here,' says Cormac.

'She waited until she was dead to come home.' I shake my head, baffled. 'That is just so sad.' Then Eily Barry pops into my head and I feel a tug somewhere just below my ribs. It's the same feeling that brought me to Ireland in the first place. I dwell on the old woman for a moment and recall her mumbling something about a secret: 'If I don't go gaga I'll take it to my grave.' I wonder now what that secret was. I sense it is important. 'I want to go and see Nora Maloney's grandmother again,' I tell Cormac. 'I don't know why. I'm just listening to my intuition. Something's telling me I need to speak to her.'

'Adeline Deverill would approve of that,' says Cormac with a nod.

'She would,' I agree with a smile. 'Mom would think it a

load of nonsense. Do you think it's okay if I just turn up at her door?'

Cormac grins crookedly. 'This is Ireland, Faye. You can just turn up all you like.' He stands up. 'Let's take her a bottle of brandy,' he adds. 'If you want something from her, it's best you give her something in return.'

Cormac drives me into Ballinakelly with Kite in her usual place on the back seat. I feel safe and contented in his company, as if we are old, old friends. As if we have been together for a very long time. 'Thank you, Cormac,' I say, looking across at him and feeling my heart filling with gratitude and fondness. 'I couldn't have read that bit of the diary on my own.'

'I'm glad you didn't have to,' he replies and his lapis eyes smile back at me.

'You're very special,' I add. I'm embarrassed to tell him how I feel, yet I want him to know.

'You're special too, Faye,' he replies. 'Special to me.' And then we settle into an intimate and easy silence, content at being special to one another.

Eily Barry is surprised to see me. I give her the brandy and she remembers who I am at once. She does not mistake me for Adeline Deverill this time but looks at me with a clear and curious gaze. 'You're Miss Arethusa's daughter,' she says and I confirm that I am. 'What do you want to know?'

Nora's father is at work, only Nora's mother is home and she wets the tea while Cormac and I talk to the old woman. 'Mrs Barry,' I begin. 'You are the only person who can shed light on my mother's departure to America and her family's violent reaction to it.' I'm not sure what I've come for, but I'm hoping my intuition is right and that she will give me what I need. 'It is

Adeline Deverill's reaction I'm interested in. As a mother, I find it very hard to understand that she simply let her daughter go.'

The old woman stares at me like a little bird, small blue eyes shiny and unblinking. 'I am not long for this world and I'm ready to go,' she says in a voice so quiet I have to lean in to hear her. 'Mrs Deverill, God rest her, made me swear on the Protestant Bible that I would take their secret to the grave and before God, I haven't told a Christian, not one living Christian. Jesus and his Blessed Mother are a witness to that.'

'What did you swear you'd take to the grave, Mrs Barry?' I hold her gaze. I'm afraid if I let it go, I will lose her, or she will lose herself and forget what she was about to tell me.

'It was not long after Miss Arethusa had departed for America that I was on the landing outside Mrs Deverill's sitting room. She was in there with Mrs Shaw, that being her sister Poppy, and they were talking, Lord have mercy on them. We below stairs were addled and consumed by Miss Arethusa's leaving and Mr Deverill losing his mind in fury, Lord have mercy on him and all the holy souls. Since I was a small girleen, I loved news, so, I cocked my ear at the door, God forgive me. Didn't I hear Mrs Deverill telling Mrs Shaw that she would support Miss Arethusa and the baby, but that Mrs Shaw had to pretend the money was coming from her, otherwise Mrs Deverill feared Miss Arethusa would not accept it and end up in the gutter or worse.' She raised her eyes to Heaven. 'God forgive me for breaking my vow,' she whispered. 'Almighty Jesus, didn't Mrs Deverill open the door of a sudden and I tumbled into the room. She cornered me and made me swear that I would never tell another soul what I had heard. You see . . .' The old woman leaned towards me and narrowed her eyes, a sly look upon her face. 'Don't I know I am right about the childeen. And Jesus himself knows I'm right. Dermot McLoughlin's baby. But I never told a soul. Not a soul. Until now.'

'You're right to have told me,' I say and watch her relax. 'A mother's love is unconditional,' I add, thinking of Adeline supporting her daughter in secret.

''Tis indeed, girleen,' she agrees. 'Blood is thicker than water. But what happened to the poor little childeen? I never went to bed any night without saying a prayer for that little childeen and indeed poor old Miss Arethusa too.'

'He is my brother,' I whisper, because I know that Eily Barry can keep a secret and I am overwhelmed with gratitude for her sharing it with me.

'May God bless him and protect him from all harm,' she says and her hand, like a chicken's claw, clutches my forearm. 'His father is a good and decent man,' she adds. 'And a God-fearing man at that. Better that he lives out his days in peace and ignorance and they can all come together in the Kingdom of Heaven. Life is hard enough and we should never go half-way to meet trouble. Let the secret stay in the ground with the dead, and never see the light of day.'

I wish Logan could live out his days in peace and ignorance, but I know he cannot.

I spend the day with Cormac. We take Kite for a walk in the hills. We hold hands. It feels natural, as if we have walked like this and held hands like this for years. And yet our love is new and fresh and exciting. The love of young people who feel the blissful expansion in their hearts for the very first time. Birds play about the heather and gorse, sunlight sprinkles the water with glitter, the breeze is soft and warm and scented. I am happy.

We discuss my mother's life. It feels good to talk about it.

The more we process the choices she made and their consequences the better I feel about it all. I know it will take time for me to come to terms with the fact that Logan is not my father's son. Even though Mother didn't include dates in her diary I could have worked out for myself the year her illegitimate child was born and come to the conclusion that it was Logan, but I'm glad I didn't. I never suspected it, not for a moment. I never felt the need to do any math.

We picnic on the beach, a simple basket of soda bread and cheese. We are alone. Only the seabirds witness us lying together on the sand while the noise of the waves drowns out the sweet nothings we whisper to each other. We laugh – no one has ever made me laugh like Cormac does – and we doze. The day is long when one has nothing to do but idle the hours away in the eternal Now.

When Cormac drops me back at the White House in the late afternoon I go in search of Kitty. She is in the garden, on her knees by the border, pulling out ground elder and nettles. 'I have finished Mother's diary,' I tell her.

She looks up and shades her eyes from the sun with her arm. Her hand is full of weeds. 'And?'

'You must read it for yourself,' I tell her. 'It's too complicated to tell you.'

'I'm intrigued,' she says.

'You're *meant* to read it as I was. It's what she wanted.'

'Then I will. May I give it to Papa after I've read it?'

'Of course. I'll put it on the hall table.'

She looks at her watch. 'Wyatt telephoned again this afternoon.' She registers my lack of enthusiasm. 'He didn't sound very pleased to miss you again. I told him you're out all day, sightseeing. Anyway, he's going to telephone again this evening at seven.'

'All right, thank you,' I say.

Kitty pushes herself up. She is agile for a woman of her age. 'Did you have a nice day with Cormac?'

Her gaze is penetrating. I know she knows what is going on between us. She's no fool. I also know she is not judgemental. There's something in her expression that tells me she understands and I remember Cormac insinuating that Kitty had a secret friendship of her own. I long to know about it. I long to share my love for Cormac. 'I had a lovely day,' I reply. 'We picnicked on the beach. Took Kite for a walk in the hills. I'm falling more in love with Ireland every day that I'm here,' I gush and I know my face is aglow and giving me away. But I don't care.

'You'd better not tell that to Wyatt,' she says with a smile, linking arms with me and walking towards the house.

'I don't want to leave,' I tell Kitty suddenly. 'I want to stay here for ever.'

'I know you do,' she says.

'Do you?' I ask, glancing at her.

'I do, because there was a time in my life when I had the opportunity to leave Ireland with the man I loved. But I didn't.'

'Because you couldn't tear yourself away?'

'I love Ireland, Faye. It's in the marrow of my bones. It runs in the blood of my veins. Nothing, not even the greatest love, could tear me from it.'

'Is that why you fought for independence?'

'I fought for independence because I believed in it. Because the man I loved believed in it, and because I craved adventure. Your mother was a Deverill, Faye, like I am. We're not good at abiding by the rules. Elspeth and my other sister, Victoria, are paragons of virtue. Somehow the Deverill spirit never penetrated their hearts. But it penetrated mine, and Aunt Tussy's.' She looks at me searchingly. 'I think it's penetrating your heart too.' When I don't reply, because I'm embarrassed to admit to my adultery, she smiles. 'Am I right?'

I avoid answering directly. 'I feel different, Kitty.'

'That is because you're happy,' she says.

As I walk into the house, anticipating my husband's telephone call, I wonder whether Wyatt will notice.

Wyatt telephones just before supper. I have only been away for eight days and yet his voice already sounds strangely unfamiliar. The line crackles and he shouts down it. 'Faye? Is that you?' he asks. It has an instant effect. The person I have been for the last week swiftly retreats like the head of a tortoise into its shell. The demanding tone of his voice sucks me back into my marriage and I become the person I used to be. The person I no longer want to be.

'Yes, it's me, darling. How are you?' There is a long delay.

'All very well here,' he replies. 'I've been trying to get hold of you, but you're always out.'

'I've been seeing the sights of Co. Cork. It's beautiful,' I tell him. There is another long delay. It is awkward and unnatural to speak like this. I find talking to him unrewarding. It pulls me down and makes me irritable. I want the call to be over. I want to forget that I am married.

'We're all missing you here,' he says after another long pause. He must be missing me very much to articulate it. The way we left each other was quite hostile. I didn't think he'd miss me at all. To hear him say it sounds very out of character. But then I have never been away like this before. Perhaps, in my absence, he is beginning to appreciate me.

I ask him about the children. I don't want him asking me about Ireland. I don't want to share it. So I keep it to myself. It is *my* treasure and I am guarding it fiercely. The call is expensive, being long distance. We don't speak for long.

'Have you found your mother's roots?' he asks.

'Yes, I have found her family. Turns out she has lots of relations. I'll tell you about it when I see you.'

'Good. I'm curious to know.'

'I'd better go,' I say, which is unusual for me. When Wyatt telephones me it is *he* who always chooses when to hang up.

'Oh, right, sure. You go. I'll call you again in a few days' time.'

I want to tell him not to bother. But I can't. 'Sure,' I reply instead. 'Speak to you soon and send my love to the kids.'

We hang up and it is a relief.

Wyatt's call has made me feel out of sorts. As if I've been all shaken up and my insides have landed in the wrong place. I go upstairs to have a bath before supper. I lie in the warm water and think of Cormac. I recall our walk over the hills, the sensation of his hand in mine, the feeling of his lips kissing me, of his beard scratching my skin, of the solidity of his body as we lie together on the sand, the intimacy of falling asleep in the sun, the gentle rise and fall of his chest against my ear as he breathes, the sound of happiness, all around me, everywhere, and the sense of tranquillity returns. Wyatt retreats. America retreats. I'm in Ireland and Cormac is beneath the same sky, beside the same sea, and tomorrow we shall be together again.

Chapter 32

I sit on a stool in Cormac's kitchen with the dawn light tumbling in through the windows and Kite at my feet watching her master, who is sitting on a chair behind me, his hands on mine as he guides my fingers over the keys. The accordian is strapped over my shoulders, pressed securely against my chest and resting on my knees. It's a heavy, strange-looking instrument. Part bellows, part keyboard. I laugh because I know I am never going to make this thing sound like it's supposed to.

'I don't understand how you manage to get it to sing,' I say, leaning back against him and nuzzling my face beneath his chin. 'It's an impossible instrument.'

He covers my hands with his and nuzzles me back. 'You're going to get a note out of this if it takes us all day, Faye Deverill!'

'You won't last all day, Cormac O'Farrell, and neither will I.'

'I'm a patient man.'

'And I will exhaust your patience as well as my own. I didn't realize it would be so hard.'

'You can't give up now. You've only just begun and I'm

determined to get a few notes out of you. Just a few. Look at the hope in Kite's eyes. You don't want to disappoint her, do you? She's waiting for a song.'

'For one of *your* songs. If I sing she'll howl with pain and leave the room.'

'I'm sure she's heard worse.'

'Not in this kitchen.'

'Come on. Listen and concentrate.' He pats my hands and they respond, finding the position they were in and waiting to be guided once more.

I think of my mother and how easy it must have been to fall in love with Jonas as he showed her where to put her fingers and how to strum the chords. It is an intimate and peaceful relationship between teacher and pupil. But I have little patience to learn. I don't really want to know how to play this thing. I'd rather listen to Cormac sing those old Irish ballads about the war, because when he does, his eyes mist and his voice falters and those old hurts resurface to cut him again like bones unearthed from a river bed. He moves me and I feel his wistfulness as if I too were up on those hills, fighting for freedom, for a country I loved so dearly.

'I want to you to play for me,' I tell him. His hands stop guiding my fingers and caress my wrists instead, and I can tell that he doesn't care whether or not I learn to play a note, that he just wants to be close to me.

'On one condition,' he says. 'That you sing with me.'

'And if Kite starts to howl?'

'She'll be joining in, that's all.' He lifts the straps off my shoulders. 'It'll be a compliment.'

And so Cormac sings for me and me alone and I don't take my eyes off his face, but watch transfixed as my heart swells with love until it not only fills the cavity of my chest but my whole being and eventually the entire room. I feel I have enough love to light up the world.

I wipe away a tear and feel such immense gratitude for this wonderful man who has stepped into my life at this late stage. I thought I was too old for this kind of magic to ever happen to me, or too unworthy. But he's gazing into my eyes and singing just for me and a voice in my head tells me that I deserve him, that it's right, that it's simply meant to be.

We sing 'Danny Boy' together, because that is my favourite. Kite doesn't howl, but cocks her head and wags her tail as if she is finding our duet amusing. My voice is nothing special but it is not bad either. With Cormac's rich voice to guide me I lose my inhibitions and let myself go as if I am Ella Fitzgerald herself. And as we fill the kitchen with music I don't think of home, or Wyatt or my children. In that blessed moment I exist only here, in Cormac's house, and nothing exists outside of it.

And yet time is running out. Soon I will have to go back to America. I turn the other way and hope that by ignoring it it will never happen. It takes Kitty two days to read the diary. While she is distracted, I spend the time with Cormac. We walk on the hills, we picnic on the beach, we make love and talk and the hours pass slowly as if the universe is colluding to give our love time to take root.

The children surface in my mind every now and then and I push them out because they and only they have the power to make me feel guilty, and I can't bear it. I know I have a right to be happy – I don't feel bad about loving another man, I should, of course I should, but I don't – however, it goes against the grain to feel happiness at the expense of my children. My love for them is unconditional and my sense of duty as a mother is unwavering, even though they are grown-up and need me less. I know I have to go back, for *them*, and I have to stay married to my husband, for *them*. While I am here I can ignore them, but as my departure date shifts into focus, the reality of my situation begins to shift into focus too and the pink haze of blissful romance starts to evaporate. I am a mother before I am a wife. I am a lover last and that cannot be helped.

Then Kitty tells me she has finished the diary and we walk around the garden to discuss it. It is evening, the shadows are long, creeping over the lawn which has recently been mown. I can smell the viburnum and wild woodbine, they saturate the air with their sweet perfume, and the light twittering of birds is gentle as they settle down in the branches of the horse chestnut trees to roost. It is a peaceful evening. The light is golden and filled with promise for the long summer days stretch out before us and autumn is a long way away.

Kitty is moved. When she speaks her voice is soft and her eyes are full of gentleness. She holds the diary to her chest as we stroll, as if it belongs there, against her heart. 'When I was little my grandmother rarely mentioned Aunt Tussy,' she tells me. 'I never really thought about it – children are so consumed with themselves, aren't they – but now I understand why. I also understand why she was so close to *me*. I was the daughter she had lost, and with me she could be herself, rather than the other half of a marriage where she had to agree with and be subordinate to her husband. I shared my secrets with her and she never judged me, ever. We were like conspirators. Just the two of us, on a little island, keeping everyone else out at sea. Tussy changed her, I suspect. The Adeline I knew was very different to Tussy's mother. As a grandmother she was unshockable. I could tell her everything, and I did. We cleaved to each other because *I* had such an uneasy relationship with my own mother and *she* had lost her daughter. I see it all now, very clearly. And it moves me, Faye. It really moves me. I would have liked to talk to her about Tussy. I think she would have liked to talk about her, but my grandfather forbade it, so her name was never mentioned. It pains me to think how much that must have hurt Grandma and how much she must have hidden that hurt.'

'Rupert knew,' I add. 'He was good at keeping secrets.'

'I adored Uncle Rupert. He was charming, funny, irreverent – and troubled. He was homosexual. I realize from having read the diary that his great love was Peregrine, Lord Penrith. But that was never going to bring him lasting happiness. He died in the Great War. It broke Grandma's heart. It broke all our hearts.'

'That's so sad. I would love to have met Rupert,' I say, feeling genuinely sorry. After reading my mother's diary it is as if I know all the characters in it. 'What happened to Poppy?'

'She died before I was born. Of pneumonia.'

I am shocked at that news. 'Would Mother have known? Who would have told her?'

Kitty shrugs. 'I don't know. You didn't find any letters when you were clearing out her things?'

'Nothing. Do you think she knew about Rupert dying in the war?' I am bewildered as to how my mother could have cut ties with all the people she loved and known nothing of what became of them.

'Possibly not. It just depends whether Grandma had an address for her.'

'From the little I know I would say she didn't.'

We walk down the well-trodden path to the beach. The long grasses sway in the breeze and the sound of the sea gets louder as we approach. Spring is beautiful everywhere, but here, in this quiet corner of Ireland's western coast, it is especially so. It tugs at my heart and with every gentle tug I feel myself being pulled into the earth, as if I have roots and they are taking nourishment from the soil and feeding my soul. Little by little I am beginning to feel a sense of belonging.

'Are you going to tell your brother?' Kitty asks.

'I wish I didn't have to, but I do.' I glance at her. 'She was too cowardly to tell him herself.'

'I don't blame her. I doubt it's going to be well received.'

'No, Logan will be devastated. He takes great pride in being a Clayton.'

'Your father must have been a very good man,' she says. 'It takes a big character to do what he did.'

'And a devious one too,' I add wryly.

Kitty is unruffled by deviousness. 'Sometimes it's better to be devious. Papa had a child with one of the maids. It's a long story, but I raised him.'

'JP,' I say. 'Alana told me.'

'Yes, JP. When Papa finally and very publicly recognized him as his own son, Mama did not take it well and she left him. The fact that they are together now still baffles me. But the point is, telling the truth isn't always the best option. Do you have to tell Logan who his father is?'

'I think Mama wants me to. That's why she gave me the diary.'

'Not necessarily. She gave you the diary so you would know where she came from and why she hid it. She also gave it to you so you would understand why she wants to come back and be buried here. I have another idea too . . .' She glances at me and I can see her mind working behind her narrowed eyes.

'And what's that?'

'I think she is ready to forgive.'

I frown. 'She's dead, so how can she?'

Kitty smiles in the knowing way that Temperance smiles

when she is talking about the afterlife. 'No, she isn't, Faye. She's very much alive in spirit, and she is ready to forgive. Why else would she want her remains brought home? If her heart was still hardened towards her family she would have wanted them to stay in America. No, I think she's ready to forgive and that is why she wants to come home. And she wanted you to come home too. That's why she gave the diary to you. She wants you and Logan to both come home, but I suspect when your brother learns that he is a McLoughlin, he won't want to.'

'Maybe,' I reply ponderously. 'Certainly, by keeping her past secret, she denied us *this*.' I spread my arms wide and embrace the land and sea and sky.

'But in coming here you have discovered who you are and where you come from. It's never too late, Faye. You're still young.'

'Never too late for what?' I ask.

'To be a Deverill.' I know she is indirectly encouraging me to follow my heart with respect to Cormac. 'Adeline is your grandmother too. For her there was nothing more important than family and home. I see her hand in this, Faye. In your coming here. Don't underestimate the things they can do on the other side. I don't expect you to understand, but you're her granddaughter, as is Martha, who was Bridie's other child and JP's twin, who was adopted in America and grew up knowing nothing about where she came from. With a little help from Adeline, Martha found her way home too.'

I laugh. She sounds like Temperance again. I'm about to make a quip to show how sceptical I am about those things, but then I remember my dream. It was Adeline at the mantelpiece. And then I recall little Aisling, JP's daughter, in the tower, who claimed to see a woman who looked just like me – Adeline, perhaps? Are these just coincidences or is there something in it?

Kitty is very sure of herself. She speaks about the paranormal as if it is as ordinary as making tea. 'Mother hated anything to do with spirituality and metaphysics,' I say to deflect my own cynicism. 'She thought it all nonsense. I now know why, because her own mother was very into it. I'm sure it put her off.'

'You have the same gift, Faye, only you're afraid to use it.'

'I really don't,' I reply, laughing uncomfortably.

Kitty smiles again knowingly. 'Yes, you do.' But she is tactful enough to change the subject.

Kitty gives the diary to Uncle Bertie. He is grateful and says he will read it immediately. Judging by the scandals of his own life, I don't think it will shock him as much as it had shocked me. I spend a lot of time thinking about Logan and wondering how I am going to tell him. I wish he too would just read her diary, but somehow, I don't think he is interested enough in Mother's life to bother finding a mirror and making his way through all those pages of handwriting. He wouldn't have the patience. I don't imagine he reads anything but the newspaper. Therefore, I will not be able to avoid having to tell him myself. That is a curse my mother has left behind.

I spend as much time with Cormac as I can and we grow even closer. I am used to him now. I can't imagine leaving. I don't want to think about it, but the day of my departure is near and I cannot ignore it. I have pretended to be a Deverill for nearly two weeks. But I am a Langton too. I must not forget that. I'm married, unhappily, but married none the less. I must return to my family. I will persuade Logan to bring the ashes with me and lay them in view of Castle Deverill as Mother has requested. I will see Cormac again. And yet ... it is not enough.

The Thursday before I leave is the Corpus Christi Procession. The walls of the town have been whitewashed, the windows cleaned. The route of the procession has been tidied of anything unsightly. Statues and large holy pictures have been put on display in the shop windows of the Catholic shops, set against backgrounds of crepe paper or lace, and candles burn day and night, illuminating eerily the sombre faces of the icons. Bunting criss-crosses the streets and a flag is displayed at the upstairs window of every house. Cormac tells me that the flags are all home-made, except those bought by the grander people which are copies of the yellow papal flag depicting the Keys of the Kingdom. There are plastic flowers on little outside altars in front of pictures of Jesus. Apparently, they're collected during the year, being given free with boxes of Persil and Rinso, which are products to wash clothes with. I find the whole thing intriguing and ask Kitty if she will take me. I cannot very well go with Cormac.

The day of the Procession Kitty and I head into town in her car. Robert, as usual, declines to come. It is a Catholic tradition and he is not Catholic. Kitty's excuse is that *I* am. However, I sense that she is excited to go, whatever the reason. She enjoys anything that allows her to mingle with the local people. She is wearing a pretty green dress and cardigan. Her hair is pinned up and her grey eyes shine with excitement. There is a youthfulness about her that belies her age. A bounce in her step that makes me think of my mother, whose bounce so irritated Augusta. Her enthusiasm is infectious and I find myself bouncing too.

The sky is mottled with cotton clouds. Every now and then the sun shines through and pours its radiance on the lush green hills and grey-slate roofs of Ballinakelly. The women smile and nod at Kitty and the men doff their caps. There is deference for this family who have presided over them for three hundred years. Yet, Kitty is not a woman who requires people to look up to her. She considers herself no different. And yet she *is* different. She has a magnificence that sets her apart irrespective of her family name.

We very quickly find Jack and Emer O'Leary. They are with Alana and her children. Emer greets me with her gentle warmth and I feel we have a silent understanding, being both American from Irish descent (the tribal instinct in human beings is very strong), and she was once an outsider too. She is very kind to me and takes trouble explaining the order of the day. Of course, there are such processions in my own country, but I have never been to one. I'm looking around, at the hundreds of people preparing to process, the girls in white dresses, the women in black mantillas, those who were Children of Mary in blue cloaks and the nuns from the convent in black and white, and I search the faces for Cormac's. I know he is here and my heart accelerates at the thought of seeing him.

Jack O'Leary and Kitty talk together in the tight, self-conscious way they did that night at Ma Murphy's when Cormac sang. While I am listening to Emer I can sense the tension between them. I ask Emer more questions and point at things to divert her gaze away from her husband. I do it automatically, as if I am conspiring with Kitty by default. I know nothing about her history with Jack, or indeed, whether she has a history at all. But I sense that this tangible thing between them is something that Emer should not see.

The people arrange themselves into groups. They all seem to know where they have to stand and in what order the groups must be. The priest positions himself beneath a canopy, holding the host in a gold monstrance. He is surrounded by other men of the clergy and stewards carrying banners and I feel they are about to begin. We go to the back, where the public are congregating, and it is there that I see Cormac. He catches my eye and winks.

We step in together and walk side by side as the Procession begins to move slowly through the town. He greets everyone, with a nod or a smile, and I realize that Cormac's geniality is infectious. He's one of those rare human beings that light up from within and people are drawn to him. He makes them feel good. He makes me feel good too.

'I want you to stay,' he says suddenly. He looks down at me and his face is solemn. Those lapis eyes aren't twinkling now. They're gazing at me tenderly; and they are vulnerable.

I don't know what to say. We are in the middle of a crowd. There is noise and movement all around us. Yet, we are strangely still. 'I want to stay,' I reply, but the word 'want' confirms the fact that I can't.

I also want to take his hand. I want to wrap my arms around him and hold him close and tell him I love him. But I am married. I have a husband, children, a home, a long way from here, and I will have to return. In four days' time I will have to leave. The certainty suddenly hits me and I feel like I've walked into a brick wall. There's a terrible finality about it that steals my breath. A certainty that sucks the blood from my face and debilitates me. I cannot walk on.

We stop and let the town move past us like a river around two rocks.

Then we are alone, just the two of us, with the singing fading as the Procession continues on up the street.

'I want you to stay, Faye, and I've never said that to anyone before apart from my wife.' He shakes his head dolefully and raises his eyes to the sky, as if he's revealing too much of himself and doesn't want me to see. 'I don't think I can let you go.'

His voice cracks.

I can feel the sting of oncoming tears and hold my eyes open to curtail them. 'I don't want you to let me go,' I reply.

'Then stay.' He looks at me now. Directly. 'Stay.'

I turn to see Kitty striding towards us. Her face is anxious. 'Why do you choose now to ask me?' I say, frustrated that we will now have to part and the situation is not resolved. 'This isn't the place.'

'I couldn't help myself,' he replies. 'I looked at you. I thought of you leaving. I had to speak my mind.'

Kitty reaches us. Her eyes dart from me to Cormac and back again. 'Are you all right, Faye?' she asks.

'I felt a little dizzy,' I reply, but she knows. Of course she knows. She can read the situation clearly, as if it were written.

'Come, let's go home.'

'No, I don't want to go home. Let's walk slowly. I'm sure I'll feel better in a moment.'

Cormac puts his hands in his pockets. 'I'll leave you both,' he says. I sense him giving Kitty a long stare and wonder what it is telling her.

I watch him stride up the street. Then I drop my shoulders and give Kitty a long stare of my own.

'You've fallen in love, haven't you,' she says and it's not a question. It's simply a statement of fact.

'I have,' I reply and I allow the tears to come.

'Oh, Faye!' she sighs. 'I saw it happening. I knew it would come to this.'

'He wants me to stay,' I tell her.

'Of course he does. He's in love with you too. And he's not a man who takes love lightly, either.'

'But I'm married.'

'Yes.' The tone of her voice is doubtful. She knows my marriage is not a happy one.

'I will return with Mom's ashes,' I tell her, my spirits lifting a little. 'I will come back to lay her to rest and I'll see Cormac again.'

'You will. But you will not be alone. You'll bring your brother with you, won't you?'

'If he agrees to come,' I say.

She pulls a face. 'It will be hard to see Cormac if you come with your brother.'

She is right. 'I don't know what to do,' I say in desperation. 'I have my children to think about. I'm married and I'm a mother. Believe me, I've agonized over this. But I have no choice. I'm not the sort of woman who can build her happiness on the unhappiness of everyone else. I'm not an island. I have four people to think about. How can my happiness be more important than theirs?' I close my eyes, anticipating the fall-out. 'What would my children think if I told them I wasn't coming home?'

Kitty stops walking and settles her grey eyes onto mine. They are soft and compassionate, but they are also the eyes of a woman who has the courage I lack. 'Look, Faye. I was once where you are now,' she says and I sense the door to her past finally opening. 'I had the opportunity to run off with the man I loved and start a new life in America. I was married. I loved my husband, but I loved this man more.'

'Jack,' I say slowly, not taking my eyes off hers. 'Jack O'Leary.'

She smiles sadly and nods. 'I loved Jack more, Faye. I loved him with all my soul. I always have. Since we were children. But I didn't go with him. I chose to stay here with Robert. I broke Jack's heart and with it, I broke my own. It was probably the biggest mistake of my life. He went, met Emer and married her. I will always love him, but I will never have him. You, Faye, have the chance to do what I couldn't do. One could say it's selfish, but for how long do you have to put the wants of others above your own? Life is short. Don't you deserve a little happiness for yourself?'

'I have never thought about leaving Wyatt,' I say truthfully. 'When Cormac and I . . .' I hesitate. I don't want it to sound sordid. 'I haven't thought further than the moment. It was never meant to be something that lasted beyond these two weeks.'

'But now you can't live without him.'

'I don't think I can.'

'It's your choice, Faye. How do you want to live the rest of your life?'

She leaves me with that thought and we quicken our pace to catch up with the Procession. I find Cormac. It's easy to spot him for he is a head taller than everyone else. I smile, and in it I hide the terrible dilemma that only I can resolve. He smiles apologetically. 'All right?' he asks.

'Fine,' I reply.

The priest is giving a sermon. I stand beside Cormac. Slowly and subtly so I won't draw attention, I put my hand next to his and touch his little finger with my own. It is a small movement, but big in significance. It tells him that I love him and that love will always find a way.

As the priest rattles on, I think about Wyatt. I realize that, as my time in Ireland runs out, I have to think of home. I have to think of where I want my home to be. If I stay here, I don't think I will break Wyatt's heart. Perhaps I'm clutching at straws. I don't want to hurt him. If he doesn't love me, I can't hurt him, right? But who am I to measure his love? Who am I to say whether or not I will break his heart? I do know, however, that I will damage his pride. That's a certainty. Wyatt cares very much what people think. I also have my children to consider. They are grown-up now, but they will mind terribly if I leave their father. I think of my own father and how appalled he'd be. But then I remember Logan and the secret he and my parents kept. The secret that cemented their marriage and went with them to their graves. Perhaps my father wouldn't have been so appalled after all. As for my mother, I know now that she would tell me to follow my heart.

As the day ends the women return to their houses to prepare their families' tea and the men head to the pubs for a bottle of stout. Kitty knows I am not coming back to the White House with her but going to leave with Cormac. She puts a hand on my arm. 'Think hard, Faye,' she says quietly. Then her gaze is diverted by Jack, who is walking down the pavement with his family, his back to us, his arm around his wife's waist as he guides her through the crowd, and Kitty's shoulders drop. 'Don't live in regret like me, Faye,' she says and her face is so pained my heart goes out to her. 'Life gives but few chances, you must take care to seize them when they come. They don't often come round again.'

Cormac and I drive to his house where Kite is waiting patiently to be taken for a walk. The light is fading, the wind picking up and the ocean serene beneath a flamingo-pink sky. We head to the beach. The setting sun has turned the sand to orange and the waves glitter and sparkle with a thousand jumping stars. Inspired by beauty and love I feel my chest grow tight with melancholy. Cormac takes my hand. His is big and rough and warm. Mine feels comfortable there, as if in his palm my hand has found home.

We walk without speaking. Kite runs in and out of the water. It feels natural to be walking together with his dog and I think of my family back at home and then of the parallel life I'm living here, like I'm somebody else entirely. I don't feel like Faye Langton anymore. I don't feel like Faye Clayton either. Perhaps I don't even feel like a Deverill. I just feel like Faye. Cormac's Faye. I know that is the person I want to be. The person Cormac sees every time he looks at me.

My eyes fill with tears. He perceives my sorrow and stops to embrace me. We stand there, holding on to one another while the seagulls circle above us and the wind blows through the long grasses and heather, as they always will regardless of the two of us and the choices we will make, and I press my head to his chest and long for a sense of permanence.

He kisses my temple then holds my face in his hands and looks at me tenderly. 'In four days' time you'll go back to America. Back to your husband and your children. Back to your brother and your mother's ashes. You'll have time to think about what you want to do. Then you'll come back to lay your mother to rest and make your choice. I want you to stay because I love you. I want you to stay because *you* love *me*. What we have is special, Faye, and rare. Few ever find it. Most settle for something less and life isn't all that bad. But we've found something more and life could be grand, really grand.' He kisses my lips, his hands still warm upon my cheeks. 'I don't want you to think about it now. I want to enjoy these final days with you, because if they are, indeed, the last, I want to commit them to memory so I have something to chew on in my old age, like a dog with the remains of a juicy bone.' I laugh and the tears spill. He wipes them away with his thumbs. 'You're a juicy bone, Faye.' He smiles and his eyes shine too. 'The juiciest I think I've ever had.'

Chapter 33

I don't say goodbye to Cormac. The day of my departure we make love, take Kite for a walk and have lunch in a pub. We do all the things we usually do, pretending that I am not leaving, that we have days and days stretching out ahead of us. Then he drops me off at the White House and I walk inside without looking back. I don't want my last memory of him to be, through tears, him sitting at the wheel of the Jeep.

In the evening Kitty drives me to the airport and I embrace her fiercely. In Kitty I have found a sister and I don't want to leave her either. 'We're always here,' she says. 'When you come back with your mother's ashes, there'll be a Faye-shaped space waiting for you to step right back into.'

I board the plane, put my head back against the head rest and close my eyes. How different I am from the woman who arrived two weeks ago. How much has happened in such a short time to change me so profoundly. The only thing holding me together is the knowledge that I will be returning soon with Mother's ashes. I will see Cormac then. I don't need to make any decisions right now. I sigh wearily, as if I am carrying a weight too heavy for my small build.

I will see Cormac again, I keep telling myself, over and over again. *I will see Cormac again.*

Yet, there are a few hurdles to jump before then. I must tell Logan about his birth. I must tell him about Mother's past. I must speak to Temperance and I must decide what I am going to do about my future. Can I find the courage to do something for myself?

The plane lands at Boston Airport and I disembark. I do not expect to see Wyatt in arrivals, but he is there and he is looking unusually pleased to see me. I feel as if I've just emerged from my parallel world and am Faye Langton once again, stepping back into my old life.

Wyatt smiles. He has missed me, I can tell. Forgotten is his disapproval at my leaving and travelling to Ireland on my own. Forgotten is his resentment at my uncharacteristic determination to have my way. 'You look well,' he says, taking me in as if I look new. He is handsome, debonair, smooth, and my heart aches for Cormac's rugged face and weathered Irish charm. 'Ireland has done you good,' he adds, as if he's now getting back a better version of his wife, one who won't be demanding to leave again. One who simply won't demand. 'I want to hear all about it.'

He kisses my cheek and it feels alien against my skin, which is so used to the scratchy feeling of Cormac's beard. He takes my bag and we walk through the airport to the car park. He keeps staring at me and grinning like a boy. 'What is it?' I ask. I'm not used to his playfulness. He hasn't been playful for thirty years.

'You look different,' he says. 'Ireland's taken years off you. You look well, Faye. Really well.'

'Thank you.' I'm flattered. Wyatt hasn't noticed me in such a long time. I feel guilty accepting his compliment, guilty for enjoying it, as if I'm betraying Cormac in taking pleasure from Wyatt.

We climb into the car and head home. After asking about the children, I tell him about the Deverills and he listens intently. Wyatt usually listens to me with half an ear, the other half is on his golf or his work, but now he listens with both and takes it all in. 'To think you're an English aristocrat,' he exclaims, impressed. 'Who'd have thought your mother was the grand-daughter of Lord Deverill of Ballinakelly.' I know he is going to boast to his friends at the golf club and I cringe because his shallowness diminishes him. I start to tell him about Mother. I intended to tell Logan first, but I find myself fulfilling my duty as a wife. Isn't it right that I confide in Wyatt first? Ask his opinion? It's what I've always done, after all. How quickly I slip into my old skin. Like Aesop's Saggy Baggy Elephant, it feels unpleasant, as if it is full of small stones.

As I suspected Wyatt is appalled that my mother had a relationship with a black man. He gasps in horror and screws up his face with disgust. 'Well, I'll be damned!' he exclaims, banging the steering wheel. 'Talk about skeletons in cup-boards. That's one mighty big skeleton! I don't think you should share that information with anyone besides Logan,' he says, and I know he's not *suggesting* I don't tell anyone besides Logan, he's *telling* me not to, because Wyatt is controlling and he's used to controlling me. He doesn't want anything to tarnish the family's reputation. I am uncomfortable with his prejudice. I am about to tell him that I suspect Temperance is Jonas Madison's daughter, but I stop myself. I want to protect Tempie from his contempt.

'She really loved him, Wyatt,' I say in my mother's defence. 'She didn't see his colour.'

'I suppose you should be grateful she didn't run off with him.' When I don't reply immediately he looks at me in panic. 'She didn't, did she?'

I'm furious with Wyatt for his lack of compassion. His lack of heart. So, I shut down. I simply switch off the transmit button and withhold the rest of the story. It gives me a surprising sense of empowerment. I will not share any more. He will not know about the pregnancy, or Dermot McLoughlin, or the gamble Mom took in agreeing to marry Ted Clayton, not knowing whether her baby would come out black or white. He won't know that Logan is really Dermot McLoughlin's son. He'll never know. I will only tell Logan.

'So, what happened? Did she run off with him?' he demands, eager for yet fearful of more scandalous details.

'No, she didn't,' I say in a flat voice. 'She fell out with her parents and came to America to start a new life.'

'What happened to the black guy?'

'I don't know. I don't think she ever saw him again.'

Wyatt is torn between relief and disappointment. So I tell him about Castle Deverill and its history, about Uncle Bertie and JP, and Kitty. Wyatt is very interested in the Deverills. He likes the idea of a family castle and a long history going back to King Charles II. The more I tell him the happier he is with me. I feel like the unpopular kid at school who has suddenly made friends with the coolest kid in class, and my dad is really pleased with me.

I am relieved to be home. Wyatt takes my case upstairs and I shower. I let the warm water wash off the plane and the weariness and I close my eyes and think of Cormac. His gentle face floats into my mind and I hold him there, caressing each beloved feature with my attention. I'm brought abruptly back to reality by the door of the shower opening suddenly. It is Wyatt. I stare at him in alarm. He's grinning. I haven't seen that look on his face in years and my skin prickles with dread. He wants to make love.

'Darling, I'm really tired,' I protest. But Wyatt doesn't care about tired, or headaches, or not being in the mood. He has always taken his pleasure when he wants it. He hasn't wanted it for years. Why does he want it now?

'Come on, Faye! I haven't seen you for two weeks. We haven't slept together in a long time. Let's just plant a quick flag.' I think of the pioneers crossing America and staking their claims. Wyatt wants to do just that. He wants to reaffirm his claim on *me*. Does he perhaps, deep down inside, sense that I now belong to someone else?

He runs his eyes over my naked body and I feel ashamed. I'm no longer a young woman and Wyatt hasn't seen me naked in a very long time. Cormac made me feel beautiful. He loved all my flaws so that they no longer felt like flaws; Cormac loved me just the way I was. Wyatt is a man who demands perfection and I know that in his eyes I don't shape up too well. I slip past him and wrap myself in a towel. He reaches for me but I shake him off. 'Wyatt, I said I'm tired.'

He looks at me with a wounded expression. 'Don't I at least get a hug?'

I know where hugs usually end up, but I don't want to be mean. I know I need to hide Cormac behind a veneer of normalcy. I let him embrace me and gingerly pat his back, hoping it will be over quickly, that it won't lead to sex. I don't feel easy in his arms. My heart aches for Cormac's. I feel like I'm being unfaithful to him and it sickens me.

Wyatt holds me in a tight embrace. 'There, that's better,' he says. 'I am your husband, after all.'

'I know,' I reply, feeling guilty. 'It's just been a long flight.'

'You're home now,' he says. 'You won't be going away again.'

Once more the tone of control. I feel the claustrophobic sense of walls closing in around me. Of limitations, prohibitions and obstacles that have kept me in my place all my life. My instinct is to accept them, to jump back, to be obedient, but something takes over, something deep inside me that refuses to be suppressed. 'I'll be heading back to Ireland to scatter Mom's ashes,' I tell him firmly.

'Logan can do that,' he replies, dismissing my plan as if it isn't important, as if scattering my mother's ashes is something anyone can do.

'Logan and I will do it together,' I say and I feel my jaw clench with determination. 'If you think I'm leaving my brother to put our mother to rest on his own, think again!'

I know, as I say those words, that I don't sound like me. I sound like a Deverill.

Wyatt steps back and stares at me in confusion. 'I don't like that tone,' he says.

'I don't know what you're talking about,' I reply sharply, sharper than I intended.

'You've changed, Faye. I don't know what you've been up to in Ireland, but I suggest you snap out of it. You're home now and I won't be spoken to like that.'

I purse my lips and walk into the bedroom to dress. I can feel his eyes up on me and wish he would leave me alone. Why, when he's spent the last thirty years rushing to the office or the golf course, does he now linger in my bedroom?

'After calling the children, I'm going to go and see Logan,' I tell him, slipping into my shoes. 'I need to talk to him.'

Wyatt is uncertain how to deal with this new, strong Faye who has come back tossing her mane like a headstrong mare. He runs a hand through his hair and sighs. 'Sure,' he mumbles.

'Then I must set up a meeting with Mr Wilks. There are certain things in the will that I have to deal with now I've been to Ireland.' I look at him steadily. 'Mom's ashes will be

scattered in Ireland and I will be the one to do it. I'm sure
Logan will want to come too. But if he doesn't, I'm going. I
just want to make that clear.'

Wyatt puts his hands in his trouser pockets. 'I suppose your
mom is only going to die once,' he says.

I have an awful feeling that, for Logan, she's going to die
all over again.

I lie on the bed and pull the telephone onto my lap and call
the children. I speak to Edwina first, who asks me about
Ireland but isn't really interested in hearing the details. It's
early morning for her and I can sense her impatience to get to
work. She tells me she will call me later, she has lots of news.
She's working on a new and exciting project and she wants to
tell me about it. How typical of Edwina to only think about
herself. But I smile, because I know and love her in spite of
her faults, and I'm happy that nothing has changed this side of
the Atlantic. Happy to be here, in Boston, with a clear conscience because I am home and she is none the wiser. Then
I call Walter. He's never been very communicative on the
telephone. He is sweet and asks me how it all went. I tell him
I met lots of his grandmother's relations and that his great-
uncle is a lord, but he's not interested in titles like his father,
and he doesn't really care about his grandmother's relations.
He's a Deverill, but he doesn't know what that means. He's
happy being a Langton.

Then I call Rose and it is like rubbing balm into my heart.
Just hearing her voice stops the aching and fills me with
gratitude for the fact that I am here. That I haven't left her
father, that I haven't disappointed her or made her unhappy.
I'd do anything for Rose. Anything. I tell her about Kitty

and the castle. I tell her about Mom's diary and that she left Ireland because she fell in love with the wrong man and came to America for a fresh start. I don't tell her about Jonas and I don't tell her about Cormac and I don't tell her about the baby. I protect her from the truth. She is fascinated and wants to meet her Deverill cousins. She loves castles and would adore to visit. She does not tell me about herself, she does not cut me off with the excuse of having something better to do. She says she's going to come up and spend the weekend with us as soon as she can get away, because she wants to see me. 'I missed you, Mom,' she confesses. 'I know I don't see you very much, but you're always on the end of a telephone and I suppose I got used to that. I felt your absence. I'm glad you're home.' And because of Rose, I'm glad I'm home too.

I meet Logan in the park. It feels strange to be in Boston. It's almost as if I've never left, and yet I feel different. There's a power in me that wasn't there before. I no longer feel small.

It's spring. The park is green. Birds clamour in the branches and sunshine streams through the leaves, covering the grass in a soft, dappled light. We sit on a bench. I hand him Mom's diary. 'You can either make your way through this – it's mirror writing, a little clumsy to read, but not impossible – or I can tell you what's in it.'

Logan, like Wyatt, is taken aback by my tone. He looks at me with an expression of surprise. I wonder, do I sound so very different? He takes the diary and opens it in the middle. 'She really wrote all this in mirror writing?' he asks, gazing into the neat but illegible lines of script. I know he doesn't want to plough through it.

'Leonardo da Vinci wrote in mirror writing too,' I tell him.

'Mom must have been a genius then,' he quips.

'It's a fascinating read.'

He sighs. 'I'm sure it is. But I'm busy. Just give me the abridged version.'

'Okay, the reason Mom wants her ashes scattered in view of Castle Deverill is because that was her home. Her grandfather was Lord Deverill of Ballinakelly, a title given to his ancestor Barton in the mid–seventeenth century by King Charles II . . .' I tell him about the Deverills, which amazes him as much as it did me, and then I tell him about Arethusa. 'She was wild and, I'm afraid to say, rather louche. She was having an affair with a local boy called Dermot McLoughlin, who was the son of the blacksmith, but she then went to London . . .' I tell him about the London season, her brother Rupert and the parties. Then I tell him about Jonas. He leans forward with his elbows on his knees and shakes his head in disbelief as I recount Mom's love story.

'Jesus! No wonder she kept her history to herself,' he muses, unable to reconcile his impeccably behaved mother with the rebellious, lusty girl she once was. He does not like to hear that she had lovers. He does not want to think about our mother having sex at all. 'It's in the past,' he says, wanting it to remain there. 'Her private life has got nothing to do with us. We shouldn't even know about this.' He frowns. 'Why do we need to know about it? Why did she want you to read her diary? I don't get it.'

I continue telling him her story. When I reach the point where she leaves on the boat for America, uncertain whether the child she is carrying is Jonas's or Dermot's, I stop.

'So, whose was it? Please don't tell me there's a black kid out there who's our half-sibling!'

I take a deep breath. I don't want to tell him. I don't want to shatter his world. But I have to. Mom left me no choice. 'Logan, the baby was *you*.'

It takes a moment for my words to settle. They remain spinning around his head for a good while before they slow down, form a coherent line and make sense. He stares at me. His face is twisted with horror and disbelief. He blinks. I know what he's thinking. That he's heard wrong. That I'm joking. Surely, he thinks, there must be some mistake.

'You're Dermot McLoughlin's child,' I explain, drowning in compassion. He looks so hurt, so shocked. Yet, there's nothing I can say to make it better. 'Dad and Mom decided to bring you up as a Clayton,' I continue. 'They kept the secret all their lives. They never told a soul. But it's in the diary. She wants you to know. She wanted *me* to tell you.' How I wish she had had the courage to tell him herself.

Logan stands up. He cannot believe it. He puts his hands behind his head and paces up and down the path. I remain on the bench, my heart going out to him, this tall, strong man who now looks as vulnerable as a boy.

'Who else knows about this?' he asks after a long while.

'No one. Only you and me,' I reply. I don't want to tell him that Kitty and Uncle Bertie both know too, because they have read the diary. Sometimes it's better not to tell the whole truth. Just part of it.

Logan sits down and holds me steady in the grip of his stare. 'No one must know about this, ever. Do you understand? Not Wyatt, not anybody.' His face is red like a berry and his mouth is distorted. He no longer looks like Logan, but an ugly version of him. He shakes his head. 'I will never forgive Mother for this,' he says in a deep, deliberate voice. 'Never.'

'Would you rather she had told you herself?' I ask.

'I'd rather not have been told at all.' He drops his gaze to the ground. 'I'm going to forget you ever told me, Faye. Do you understand? I'm going to ignore it.'

'All right, if that makes it easier—'

He cuts me off. 'Nothing will make it easier, Faye.' He stands up. 'I need some time alone.'

I get up too. 'Sure. I will arrange to meet with Mr Wilks. There's that third part of her wealth that she's left to an anonymous person. I've been to Ireland. He can tell us who it is now.'

'She should have discussed all this with us before she died,' he says in a quiet and angry voice. 'Not left mines to explode beneath our feet once she had gone.'

'I'm so sorry, Logan.'

'Don't be sorry, Faye. Just keep this to yourself. That means not telling Wyatt.'

'I won't tell him.'

'You tell him everything.'

'Not any more,' I reply. He nods. As far as we are both concerned, Logan is still a Clayton.

I telephone the attorney's office and make an appointment for Logan and me to meet him the following week. I keep my promise to my brother and tell Wyatt nothing. Wyatt has no intention of divulging Mother's affair with Jonas Madison, but he tells everyone about her aristocratic family. I bump into the wife of one of his golfing buddies at the bakery and she comes straight up to me, a radiant smile on her prettily painted face, and declares that she always knew Arethusa had blue blood because of her fine features and imperious bearing.

'Wyatt says the castle is one of the most beautiful in the whole of Ireland and that if your mother had been a boy she'd have inherited it and the title.' Her eyes widen and she adds, 'Then Logan would be a lord!' That's just ridiculous. I silently curse Wyatt for showing off. I'm glad I kept the details of my visit to myself. I hastily pay for the bread and hurry out of the store. She calls after me. 'We must do dinner. We haven't seen you in much too long!' I have no intention of having dinner with her and her bland bore of a husband. But that evening Wyatt announces that we are invited to their house for a small gathering of friends – and by small, I know he means at least ten couples – and he has accepted. He always accepts on my behalf without consulting me. I never minded before. I mind now. But I don't want to fight on my first day home. I smile and say how nice. Then I tell him I want to go to Nantucket for the weekend. I don't tell him it's because I need to talk to Temperance.

Wyatt loves Nantucket. He loves playing golf with Logan and he loves the society there. He thinks it is very superior, being made up of grand old Bostonian families who claim to have arrived on the *Mayflower*. When Mother was alive the beach house was home, but now it belongs to Logan and his wife Lucy. I'm not sure Logan is going to want to see me, but I telephone him all the same and to my surprise he acts as if nothing unusual has happened. He has erased our meeting in the park and the conversation we had. 'Of course you must come,' he says in a jovial tone of voice. 'We're filling the house with friends this weekend, so what's two more.'

I realize he is trying to drown out the revelation of his past with the noise of entertainment. I suppose he believes that if he surrounds himself with people and keeps himself busy, the horror of what I told him will recede until it becomes nothing more than a niggle in the back of his mind. I don't feel like being with lots of people, but I know Wyatt will be thrilled, and I do need to see Temperance. It is a small sacrifice to pay. I will try not to look around the house that was once my home and lament the changes they have made.

I miss Cormac. I miss the things about him that make him unique. The loping way he walks, the slight stoop in his shoulders, the gentle expression in his eyes, the crooked way he smiles, the gravelly sound of his laughter, his big rough hands, tanned forearms and ragged fingernails. I want to be the woman he sees when he looks at me, when *only he* looks at me. I want to blossom again beneath his gaze, when we are naked and alone and making love is not only an expression of our love but an effort to be close, and it is never close enough because as tightly as we press ourselves against each other our bones are always in the way. I ache for him with all my soul. I have no desire to eat and sleeping is restless and tormented. And all the while I have this nervous churning in my stomach and sickness in my heart and I know that it is grief. Grief I cannot share with anyone.

We head off to Nantucket for the weekend. Lucy has indeed altered the house. It no longer smells of home. I compliment her changes, but she has stolen its essence. It is just a house and the ghosts of memories linger awkwardly in the shadows, feeling out of place and unwanted, and as much as I try to summon them, they do not come.

Logan is the life and soul of the party. He laughs too hard, drinks too much and speaks too loudly. Lucy thinks nothing of it. She just assumes he's having a wonderful time, entertaining all his guests. And they are nice people, I cannot deny that. I switch to my default setting and blend in with the other women, and I force myself into my old skin so that no one is aware of the change in me. The change Cormac has made in me. They are only aware of how well I look. Wyatt is attentive and I don't know whether his appreciation of me is due to the glow of love that radiates out of me or the fact that I am descended from English aristocrats (he tells everyone!). But I fool him as well. I am really sick in my heart and desperate to return to Cormac, and every time Wyatt touches me I cringe. There was a time, not so long ago, when I craved his attention. Now I shrink from it he gives me more.

At last I am alone with Temperance. I visit her in the house my mother has bequeathed her for her lifetime. It is a white clapboard house a short distance from the main one, where my father used to put up the servants. It is spacious, with large windows overlooking the garden. Big bushes of hydrangeas are planted all around it so that it looks like a white gull in a nest of blue. I sit on the small veranda, just like we used to when I was a child seeking her company. Just like we used to at the big house when Mom was dying and we shared that precious time in the early mornings while she was sleeping. I come to her now to talk about my mother's secrets.

'Tempie,' I say, looking across at her and noticing how she has aged. Her black hair is streaked with grey and her skin, always so plump and youthful, has begun to line. 'Mom left me her diary in her will and a request that I go to Ireland.' Temperance smiles knowingly and I stop. I narrow my eyes. 'You know about her past in Ireland, don't you?'

She nods. 'I know everything,' she says. Her eyes are wells of information. Deep, compassionate, secretive.

My heart begins to accelerate. 'You know about Jonas Madison . . .'

She nods again. 'He was my father.'

So, I was right. 'He taught you to play the banjo.'

'He did, and he taught your mother too.'

'Please tell me how you came to work for her?'

Temperance lifts her chin and smiles. She has been waiting to tell me. I can tell, she has been biding her time, knowing I would eventually come to her and ask this very question. 'The first I heard of Arethusa Deverill was when I was eight years old and my father was dying.'

'Was he ill?' I ask.

'No, he wasn't ill. He was stabbed by a white man who felt my father was getting above himself.'

'That's terrible!'

'He had been travelling around Europe and had acquired a reputation for himself. He was a success. There were many that didn't like a black man to be a success in a white world.' She looks at me sadly. 'There are many that still don't.'

'Where did the stabbing happen? In New York?'

'My father made his name as an entertainer in New York, but he was from the South. From South Carolina. My father was stabbed on his way home one night from a rehearsal. It was a busy street but no one saw nothing. They all had their eyes closed that night. As he lay dying in hospital, he whispered to me. "Temperance," he said, holding my hand. "There's a little book of poetry I need you to find. It was given to me by an Englishwoman called Arethusa Deverill. There are some letters too, with the book. Keep them safe. They're very special to me. Don't worry your mamma about it. It's between you and me. Just you and me, you understand?" So, I found the book and those letters and I kept them safe, just like he told me to. I didn't read them because at that time I didn't know how important they were, and how important they would become for *me*. Mamma died six years later. She just gave up on life, I suppose. Her heart

stopped ticking and I was left alone in the world. I was fourteen years old.'

'What did you do?'

'I turned to my uncle George. He was all I had left. Since
my father died Uncle George had fallen on hard times and
only had eyes for the bottle. He lost his mind in a pool of
moonshine and in the end, you could say he drowned in it.
I asked him about Arethusa Deverill and he told me that my
father had received letters from her right up until he died.
Well, I had to find out for myself. I untied the letters which
were bound in a bundle and read them. Every one. My heart
bled to think of my mamma grieving for a man who loved
another woman. The last letter she wrote him was dated
1898 She was married to Mr Clayton and was going to live
in New York.'

'So, you tracked her down?'

She shrugs. 'I had nowhere to go. No one to turn to. I
found Miss Arethusa and I told her who I was and I gave her
the poetry book and the letters. You should have seen the look
on her face. It was like I was the Second Coming. Then I told
her that my father had died. She didn't take it too good. She
sank into a chair and went as white as snow and that's when
I knew she had loved my father more than she loved anyone.'
Temperance shakes her head and looks at me with sheep's eyes.
'I wanted to hate her, Miss Faye. I wanted to hate this woman
who had stolen my daddy's heart from my mamma, but I
couldn't. She took my hands in hers and said I was a blessing.
That Fate had brought me to her. That I was the part of Jonas
she was able to hold on to and her eyes filled with tears and she
asked me to stay. You were a little suckling of two and Logan,
why, he was nine, a couple of years younger than me. I took
the job with both hands and reached out to the only part of

my father that *I* could hold on to, and that was your mamma. I didn't hate her after that. I loved her, and I still do.'

'You were the only one, besides my father, who knew Mother's history,' I say, marvelling at her ability to keep secrets.

'I swore I would never tell, so I never did. She told me everything.'

'She left me her diary and a request that we scatter her ashes in Ireland.'

'She wanted you and Logan to know the truth, Miss Faye. She wanted Logan to know where he came from. She didn't want him to go through life denying his people as she had denied hers. All her life she missed her home. She missed Ireland and her family. But she was too proud to go back. The only way she could return was in death. Now it's up to you to see that she is laid to rest at Castle Deverill. She must be reunited with her past.'

'Logan is in denial,' I tell her gravely. 'It's come as an awful shock.'

'He just needs time,' she says wisely.

'I don't think he'll ever accept it.'

'He has the right to do whatever he chooses,' she says. 'He's a proud man, just like his mother.' In which case, I am not optimistic.

'There is something else I want to know. Whatever happened to Charlotte?'

Temperance smiles. 'Dear Miss Charlotte. She was your mamma's most devoted friend, Miss Faye. Don't you remember Miss Charlotte?'

I frown. 'I don't remember a Charlotte at all.'

'Well, you knew her as Aunt Lottie.'

'Aunt Lottie was Charlotte?' I exclaim, astonished. Of course I remember the gentle spinster with the long earnest face and soft voice. When I was a child she was always around the house, following my mother from room to room like a shadow.

'Mom used to visit her in that old folks' home.' I don't think my mother ever missed a day.

'That wasn't an old folks' home, Miss Faye. That was a hospital. She got sick in her mind. In the end she didn't recognize your mamma no more, but Miss Faye, she continued to visit her because *she* recognized *her*. She was loyal, your mamma. As loyal as a dog. You see, Miss Lottie was the only part of home your mamma could hold on to.' She chuckled wistfully and shook her head. 'We were all clinging to each other in those days, Miss Faye, clutching at remnants of those we had lost.'

Temperance pushes herself up from the chair. 'Come,' she says. 'I think it's time I gave you the little book of poetry and the letters your mother wrote to my daddy.'

'But, Tempie, they are yours,' I say, following her into the cool darkness of the house.

'I have the banjo,' she replies, white teeth gleaming. 'That's all I need to remind me of him. My daddy is in here.' She puts her long fingers on her heart. 'With your mamma and mine. An unlikely trio, but I don't think they're gon' mind where they are.'

Chapter 34

Logan and I follow Mr Wilks into the boardroom of his sumptuous office. It is raining outside. The light that enters the big sash windows is muted and lacking in enthusiasm, as if, like us, it has no wish to attend the meeting. There is a fireplace with a dark and empty grate and on either side are bookcases stuffed full of encyclopaedias and large, expensively bound books on law. The mahogany table is oval and highly polished and on it is a jug of water with three crystal glasses, a pile of notepads and a glass of sharpened pencils. It has an air of formality and smells of furniture polish and aged wood. Mr Wilks stands at the head and puts a blue folder on the table. He offers me the green velvet chair to his left and I sit down. Logan sits opposite me on Mr Wilks's right. His face is thin and drawn as if the shock of being told he is not his father's son has sucked the juice out of it. It has certainly sucked the juice out of his spirit. He has deflated like a punctured hot-air balloon. There is little small talk. It is not the time for pleasantries. We might as well get straight to the point.

Mr Wilks opens the folder and pulls out the copy of the will. He holds it in his small hands and looks from me to Logan and back to Logan again. 'As you know your mother requested that you travel to Ireland before the identity of the third beneficiary is revealed.'

'Yes, I've just returned,' I begin. Mr Wilks turns to me and arches an eyebrow with interest. I am about to elaborate but Logan cuts me off briskly.

'Who is it?' he demands. He does not want to waste time. He wants to leave as quickly as he can.

Mr Wilks sighs. I can tell Logan's impatience aggravates him. Mr Wilks does not like being rushed. 'Very well,' he says. 'I will read what your mother wrote.' He perches his spectacles on the end of his nose and lifts his chin. He licks his forefinger and slowly turns the page. He is not going to be rushed. 'Ah, here it is.' He inhales through his nose then begins. 'The third part of Arethusa Clayton's remaining wealth is to be used to set up a home for single mothers in Ballinakelly, Co. Cork, the Republic of Ireland. She has written as an add-on: *Now that Logan knows the true circumstances of his birth, with his permission, I would like the home to be named after him. The Logan Home for Single Mothers. May it be a sanctuary for women who are not as fortunate as I was.*' Mr Wilks looks at Logan whose face is flushing with embarrassment and anger. Only I can see the hurt in his eyes, an open wound behind the fury, because I know him so well. Mr Wilks continues. 'She has requested that you, Faye, supervise the project and see that her wish is carried out.'

I glance at my brother. He does not want anyone to know the truth about his birth. He certainly won't want the centre to be named after him. I know he is wishing that it would all go away. Mr Wilks takes a white envelope out of the folder. 'Finally, she wrote a letter to you both, to be opened on this occasion. Mr Clayton . . .'

Logan leans back in his chair and folds his arms. 'I don't

want to have anything more to do with this ridiculous charade,' he says and he draws his lips into a thin, defiant line.

'Mrs Langton, perhaps you would like to read it then.'

I take the envelope and pull out the letter. The sight of my
mother's handwriting causes my heart to snag. Her diaries
were written in an unfamiliar hand. This letter vibrates with
her energy and I can feel her as if she is right beside me. I
can almost smell her tuberose perfume. I clear my throat. I
cannot look at my brother. It is unbearable to see him like this,
diminished and in pain.

My darling Logan and Faye,

*I hope that you have scattered my ashes at Castle Deverill
and returned me to my beloved home. I hope by now
my remains are in the long grasses overlooking the castle,
spreading in the wind that blows in off the ocean and sinking
into the soil with the soft rain that turns the island so green.
I should never have left, but if I hadn't I would not have met
Ted or enjoyed so many happy years with him. I would not
have had you, Faye, and raised you and Logan together. I
have been blessed in so many ways. All the negativity in my
life is due to my own foolish choices and my stubbornness. I
know that now. My heart was hardened by my own vengeful
pride. I was never able to forgive my father for demanding
that I give away my child, or my mother for standing by him.
But anger is a destructive emotion that eats away at the soul.
I spent years denying that anger, pretending I wasn't hurting,
making a lot of noise to convince myself that I wasn't full of
regret. But old age has made me look back over my life and
the choices I made and I have learned one thing too late: love
is all that matters.*

My dear, dear Logan. I didn't have the courage to tell

you about your birth when I was alive. I can only apologize that you have had to find out about it now, in this way, and I apologize to Faye, too, for having had to tell you. I am a coward. I thought I was strong and brave and nonconformist, but in my deepest depths I am afraid. I love you and can't bear to face your anger and your pain and ultimately, perhaps, your condemnation. Maybe that is what I fear the most: your rejection. Know that I fought very hard to keep you, Logan, and in keeping you I lost everything I loved. You were worth it. If I have done one thing right in my life, it is fighting for you. I ask of you one thing, don't waste your energy feeling angry and betrayed like I did. You are Ted's son in everything except your blood. He was the father who loved you, raised you and nurtured you. You have never been anything other than a Clayton. However, if you wish to find Dermot McLoughlin, I'm sure he would be willing to meet you. I never told him about you, but he loved me. He was kind and funny and patient, and in my own way, I believe I loved him back. He represented Ireland, home and freedom. No one else has ever represented that. When I needed him, he was there.

My beloved Faye, I know I haven't been the easiest mother. I have always been selfish and temperamental – if you have met any of my relations in Ireland, I'm sure they will tell you! However, I realize that a lot of my drama was symptomatic of the hurt in my heart, which, like a stone, was always evident to remind me of the vast part of myself that I had lost. How much one learns about oneself as one grows old. I suppose the ego melts away, the end is near, one has time to review the past, to see it for what it was and oneself with some detachment and hopefully a little hard-earned wisdom. I have learned too late for me to make amends, but perhaps, by returning home in death, if there is life after as Mama so

strongly believed, my family will know that I am, in my own
way, asking to be forgiven and forgiving them in turn.

　　I thank you both for your love and for your understanding.
I hope you now know what it is to be a Deverill. A Deverill's
castle is his kingdom. I thank you for returning me to mine.

　　　　　　　　　　　　　　　　　　　　　　Your mother.

I am barely able to read the last lines for the tears in my eyes.
I wipe them away and fold the letter and put it back in the
envelope. Logan is still sitting with his arms crossed, a hard
and unforgiving look on his face. We sit in silence for what
seems like a very long time. Mr Wilks is a patient man, a
man who likes to do things slowly; he is not at all concerned
about the silence or the length of it. At last Logan speaks. His
voice is thin, as if the ballast has gone from it and all that is
left is the sound of one who feels very alone. 'You can take
her to Ireland,' he says. 'But I'm not coming with you. I want
nothing to do with this home for single mothers and over my
dead body will it be named after me. I won't have anything
to do with it. Do you understand?'

　　I nod.

　　Mr Wilks turns to me. 'May I make a suggestion. You could
call it the Arethusa Deverill Home for Single Mothers.'

　　'Yes, that would be appropriate,' I say. 'I don't think
she'll mind.'

　　'She won't mind, because she's dead,' Logan snaps and I
ignore the nasty tone in his voice because he is hurting.

　　'Logan, I totally understand why you don't want it named
after you,' I tell him. 'It's fine by me.' I want him to know how
much I feel for him, but I suppose he considers *me* part of the
conspiracy, even though I only learned about his parentage
recently and was also upset. But I'm a true Clayton and he isn't.

There's nothing I can do about that. I stare at his features and try to find Dermot McLoughlin in them, even though I don't know what Dermot McLoughlin looks like.

Logan stands up. He puts his hands on his hips. 'There's nothing more, is there?' he asks.

Mr Wilks shakes his head. 'No, we've covered everything, Mr Clayton.'

'Good.' Logan does not have to ask Mr Wilks to be discreet. Mr Wilks takes his job very seriously and has probably never allowed a secret to slip out in all the years he has worked here.

The two men shake hands. I sense that Logan will not be contesting the will. He is like a lone boat on the sea, adrift, with no wind to fill his sails. There's nothing I can say or do to comfort him. 'You keep this,' I say, giving him the letter.

'I don't want it,' he replies.

'You don't want it now, but you may like to read it later. You've got a lot to digest.'

'I'm not going to think about it ever again. I'm not going to think of Mother, either.'

'That's your choice. But please, take the letter. Put it away. Maybe you'll never read it. But maybe one day, when you're old and wise and looking back over your life, you may take it out and see things differently.'

Reluctantly he takes it and slips it into the inside pocket of his jacket. We leave together, but neither of us says another word.

When I get home I have time alone to reflect before Wyatt arrives. He has been on the golf course all day. It seems to me that he does most of his business on the golf course. I turn my mind to Cormac. I wonder whether he is thinking of me and missing me too. I cannot wait to go back. I long to hold Cormac with every fibre of my body. And I have the perfect excuse. It is my duty to take the ashes to Ballinakelly and to begin exploring the possibility of carrying out Mother's wishes in building a home for single mothers there. Wyatt will just have to understand. And if he doesn't, does it matter? Do I care? I shiver with excitement. I can go straight away and I can go alone. Logan does not want to come with me. No amount of persuasion will change his mind. I know my brother. Wyatt will have no option but to agree. Again I think of Cormac and the image of his face gives me strength. I'm going to make plans to go back to Ballinakelly, and I'm going to do it *now*.

Wyatt returns home in a good mood. He is carrying a bouquet of flowers. He hasn't brought me flowers in a very long time. I don't deserve them. How can I deserve flowers if my heart and mind are with another man? He kisses my cheek and gives them to me with a smile. 'No particular reason. Just because you're beautiful,' he says and I feel a pang of guilt. They are my favourite. White roses, lilies and peonies. I want to tell him about my plan to return to Ireland to scatter my mother's ashes, but I know it will ruin the moment. I put the flowers in a vase and wait until supper.

Wyatt's face falls. 'You've only just come back!' he exclaims.

'I know, but it's my duty to lay Mom to rest.'

'There's no urgency,' he says indignantly. 'I mean, she's not going to go anywhere, is she?'

I ignore his insensitive comment. 'She has also given money for a home for single mothers to be built in her name in Ballinakelly.'

'Why would she do that?'

I shrug. 'Because she's philanthropic?'

'If she was so philanthropic, you'd have thought she'd have done it while she was alive.' He wipes his mouth on a napkin.

'I don't understand these people who leave their generosity until they're dead. Much better to give with warm hands.'

'It's complicated, Wyatt,' I say, but I have no intention of explaining.

'And why give money to a place she hated?'

'Who says she hated it?'

'If she'd loved it so much she would have gone back.'

'She *is* going back. I'm taking her.'

'Why wait until you're dead?' That horrid word again. Dead. Wyatt says it with such irreverence. It's as if he's forgetting he's speaking about my mother.

'Logan doesn't want to come with me,' I tell him.

'That's no surprise. He doesn't want her to be buried in Ireland, period. At least one of you has some sense.'

'Wyatt, it means a lot to me that I do as she asked and take her remains home.' His insensitivity is grating. I can't believe he was this insensitive before I went to Ireland. How did I put up with it? Was I so conditioned that I didn't notice?

He picks up his wine glass and swigs it. Then he looks at me over the rim and holds my gaze. 'All right, if it means so much to you. Go to Ireland.'

'Thank you.' The relief is overwhelming. I feel awash with gratitude.

Then Wyatt snatches it back. 'If Logan isn't going to go with you,' he says. 'I'll go.'

I try not to show my shock. Cormac crashes into my head on a wave of panic. How will I see him if my husband is with me? I don't want Wyatt in Ireland! I don't want him to have anything to do with the Deverills. If he comes with me I will not be able to be myself. 'That's a great idea,' I croak and he grins broadly, pleased because he thinks he has made me happy. He arrogantly mistakes my flushing face for pleasure.

He doesn't realize he is stealing my joy. I feel sick. Ballinakelly is the only place that belongs exclusively to me. If Wyatt comes it will no longer be mine.

There is nothing I can do. Wyatt takes over as he always does. He chooses the dates. He telephones Robert Trench and asks if we can stay with them. He buys the flights and arranges the car to drive us to the airport. I should be excited but I'm not. I'm dreading the whole trip. I'm dreading the agony of seeing Cormac and not being able to hold him. I don't know whether I'll have the strength to hide the way I feel.

I telephone Kitty while Wyatt is at the office. Being a long distance and very expensive call, I make it brief. I tell her about the home for single mothers and she says she will discuss it with her father and JP. She is delighted by the idea and wants to be involved. 'You can't very well organize it on your own,' she says.

'How is Cormac?' I ask. There is no time to be subtle, to beat about the bush. I want to talk about him. I want to know that our connection is unbroken. My throat tightens. Hearing Kitty's voice brings him home to me and I am struck with an urgent and desperate longing. There is a lengthy silence, then Kitty replies. She doesn't beat about the bush either. Her voice is serious. She's been here before. She doesn't want me to make the mistake that she made.

'You have a choice, Faye,' she says and the line crackles. She sounds very far away suddenly. 'When you come back, you have to decide whether you're going to leave or whether you're going to stay. You only get one chance. Don't throw it away.'

My eyes blur. My heart contracts into a small and timid thing. Cormac is like a tiny pinprick of light glimmering through the darkness, beckoning me to come. I put down the receiver and remain in the chair, numb with indecision. I look out of the window of our Boston apartment, hoping to find an answer there. My eyes settle on the brownstone buildings across the street; they are so close I can see two people in their sitting room, arguing. The noise of traffic is intrusive. It is constant and unrelenting. The wail of a siren pierces the air and I think of the silent hills of Ballinakelly and the soft rain that makes them so green, and the ache in my soul snatches my breath and leaves me feeling desolate and alone and so very, very dissatisfied.

Wyatt is excited about travelling to Ireland. He thinks he is doing me an enormous favour by coming with me. He thinks he's being supportive and generous with his time. He wants praise and gratitude and I have to muster all my strength to give them without exposing my resentment. I telephone Logan with the details of our trip in case he changes his mind, but I know he won't. It might take him the rest of his life to come to terms with the truth about his parentage, or he might never accept it. That is a choice only he can make. We both have choices and neither is easy.

The weekend before we leave Rose comes to stay with her husband and children. Frank, her husband, is the son-in-law I dreamed of. He runs the marketing team for a big global retailer and is charming, attentive to Rose and the kids, and kind. They fit together like a pot and its lid. The three children are under ten, all of them well-behaved and polite. How typical of Rose to bring up her young family with patience and love, allowing them to be themselves, not trying to push them into being mini versions of their parents, like so many parents do. On the Sunday morning Frank takes the kids out for an ice cream and Rose and I are given the time to walk around the park and talk.

'You've been very distracted all weekend,' she says as

we wander along the path in the sunshine. 'What's going on, Mom?'

'Well, I am a little distracted,' I confess. 'Logan doesn't want to come and lay Grandma to rest, which is upsetting.'

'Why won't he go?'

I suddenly feel the urge to confide in my daughter. I haven't told a soul about Dermot McLoughlin, but I've wanted to share Ireland with Rose right from the moment I arrived. 'Let's go and sit down,' I suggest. She gives me a look. She knows I'm going to confide in her and she's ready to listen.

We take a bench in the shade and sit side by side. 'What I'm going to tell you now must remain between us,' I tell her seriously. She nods. I know Rose can keep a secret (unlike her sister who likes to be the first to know everything and the first to share it). 'Your grandmother left Ireland because she was pregnant.' Rose stares at me in astonishment. 'She met your grandfather on the crossing to America and when he asked her to marry him, she told him that she was carrying another man's child. Your grandfather was a brave and daring man, for he wasn't put off but married her all the same and brought the child up as his own. That child is Uncle Logan.'

There is a long silence as Rose gazes at me with her eyes wide and her mouth agape. She cannot believe what I have just told her. I realize that's why Mom wanted me to read her diary. She wanted me to read her story slowly, with time to digest it. I have just dropped it into Rose's lap with no scene setting and she is duly horrified.

I put a hand on hers. 'Let me tell you from the beginning.' Rose listens without saying a word as I tell her Arethusa's story. I include Jonas because I don't ever want her to think I lied to her. I tell her the whole story, unabridged, and her eyes grow wider and her cheeks flush a little and yet, I don't see any trace of disgust in her eyes. I see only compassion and understanding. When I finish I breathe a heavy sigh. 'That's the truth, so now you know.'

'Oh Mom, what a story! Poor Grandma, to have lost her home and the man she loved. And you, to discover that your brother is only your half-brother and that your mother was disowned by her family.' She shakes her head and frowns. 'And Uncle Logan. No wonder he doesn't want to go to Ireland. He must be furious with Grandma. And hurt. He must be so hurt.' She puts a hand on her chest. 'How will he ever get over it?'

'Only time will help him do that,' I say. 'Maybe he'll never get over it.'

Rose looks at me steadily. 'You know, I knew something was wrong the moment I heard your voice on the phone. You sounded so different. I said to Frank, "Something has happened over there and I don't know what it is, but I hope she'll tell me." And you have.'

'I know I can trust you, and to be honest, I had to tell someone. I was good to burst, holding it all in.'

'Haven't you told Daddy?'

'No, I don't think Daddy would understand.'

Rose nods. She knows her father. 'Better keep it between us then.'

'That's what I think.'

She smiles. 'Thank you, Mom, for trusting me.' She puts her arms around me and I hold her tightly. I hold her tightly because I love her so much and I'm so afraid of hurting her. Cormac is on my mind and in my heart and ticking like a bomb about to go off and hurt not just Rose, but everyone I love.

Wyatt and I fly to Ireland. I feel anxious because I know Ireland won't be the same with Wyatt in it. He will taint it; my secret treasure will become his and I don't want him to have it.

I hope Kitty has warned Cormac that my husband is coming with me. I bite my nails as I watch Boston shrink in the little round window of the plane and I wish that Wyatt was shrinking with it, but he is beside me, reading the newspaper, ignorant of the turmoil he has generated inside me. Ignorant of the weighing scales I'm using to decide my future, which are, at the moment, falling very heavily in Cormac's favour. The more I resent my husband, the more he wants me. If he had wanted me like this over the last twenty years, I would never have fallen in love with Cormac. There would never have been a void for him to fill. But now he has filled it, it is no longer a void. Cormac has made me complete. Wyatt is in the way.

I do not sleep on the plane. I read my book but don't turn the page. So much has happened in the last month that I have an awful lot to think about. I wish I could still my mind, but I can't, no matter how hard I try. I wonder if my mother is watching me. I hope that she is. I close my eyes and allow the tears to trickle down the edges of my face. I'm a little girl again, missing my mother. Wyatt sleeps beside me, oblivious.

At last the velvet green fields of Ireland come into view. I press my nose to the glass and gaze out with elation. In spite of Wyatt sitting beside me, sharing my view, commenting on how small the city looks, I am mesmerized by the soothing sight of this land which has inveigled its way so unexpectedly into my heart. It feels like home. I yield to the comforting sense of belonging and some of my anxiety evaporates.

To my surprise Kitty herself is in the arrivals hall. I run to her in delight and we embrace. I don't need to tell her how I feel, she understands. She squeezes me and I soak up her empathy. I want to cry with relief, because she is silently sharing my burden and making it lighter.

I have forgotten how similar Kitty and I look, so it takes me by surprise when Wyatt stares at her in amazement and comments on it. 'Wow!' he exclaims. 'You two could be sisters.' He looks from her to me and back again.

'Faye is like a sister to me,' says Kitty and she shakes his hand and smiles warmly. She settles her grey eyes onto him and I know that she is sizing him up and taking him in and knowing exactly what sort of man he is before he has shown anything of himself. I wonder whether he's what she expected him to be.

After a brief chat we head out to the car park. It is a blustery summer's day. Fat white clouds amble across the sky like sheep, shepherded by a gusty, impatient wind. Wyatt sits in the front seat and I in the middle of the back seat, so the three of us can talk. I see the country anew through Wyatt's eyes. He makes the same comments I made to Cormac when I arrived. Oh Cormac! We're under the same sky, our feet are on the same soil, we're breathing the same air. I'm injected with excitement, although I don't know how I'm going to manage to see him with Wyatt at my side. I don't think Robert plays golf.

I did not expect Robert and Wyatt to get along. Robert is quiet, pensive and literary. He writes books, he reads books and he doesn't seem to do much else. His stiff leg prohibits him from doing anything physical. Wyatt, on the other hand, is arrogant, loud and athletic. He loves all games that involve a ball. He watches them and he plays them and I don't think he has ever read a book. Yet, to my surprise the two men discuss politics. Wyatt is very interested in politics. He used to talk with my father late into the night over a Bourbon on the rocks. They used to sit on the veranda with Logan and I'd hear their voices from my bedroom window upstairs. Robert, it transpires, follows American politics and is very well-informed. I wonder why he never discussed them with me? Did he assume that, being a woman, my opinion was not worth hearing?

Kitty is my ally and my co-conspirator. We leave the men at the lunch table and go for a ride. Wyatt wants to come too. He likes the idea of riding, but Kitty puts him off. Robert watches her warily, as if he knows she is deliberately creating a diversion. Wyatt suspects nothing. We leave the house and head off to the stables where the groom has already saddled up our horses. Then we set off into the hills. Wyatt remains in the house with Robert and in leaving him behind I feel an exhilarating sense of liberty. My hair flies out behind me, the wind blows against my face and the speed of the horse galloping over the long grasses fills me with excitement. I know where we are going and I know Cormac is expecting me.

I am overwhelmed with gratitude towards Kitty. As Cormac's whitewashed cottage comes into view I realize that she is helping *me* because she failed to help herself when she had the chance. She is living vicariously through me. My pleasure is her pleasure. My pain is hers as well. She knows which way the scales should fall. If I were her, I would run into Cormac's arms and never let him go.

We trot up to the front door. Cormac is standing in the sunshine, waiting for me. His smile is tentative, his hands are on his hips, his hair curls beneath his cap. His face is darkened by his beard. He takes the reins and I dismount. We don't speak. I wind my arms around his neck and press my lips to his. I forget that Wyatt is at the White House. In Cormac's embrace I forget that I am married at all. Kitty takes my horse. 'I'll be back in an hour,' she says.

Cormac looks down at me and his eyes brim with longing. 'Stay,' he says. I press my forehead against his and close my eyes. I put my hands to his face and run my thumbs across his cheeks. He covers my hands with his. 'Stay.'

Chapter 35

That afternoon Kitty and Robert accompany us to the castle. Wyatt is impressed by the size and grandeur of it. He sweeps his eyes over the magnificent stone walls and the fairy-tale towers and turrets that pierce the sky, and he cannot believe how my mother was able to walk away from it for ever. How she was able to turn her back on her past when it was so prestigious. I do not enlighten him. He only knows that she fell in love with Jonas Madison. He doesn't need to know that there was a baby and that that baby was Logan.

We are met by JP and Alana and the six of us have tea on the terrace in the sunshine. Wyatt is welcomed warmly but I watch him with mounting unease. He doesn't fit in here at Castle Deverill. It's not something anyone else would notice. It's a feeling that is mine alone. Wyatt looks smaller here, like a lion without his mane or a tiger without his teeth. Ireland diminishes him and yet it empowers *me*. I belong here, and with my sense of belonging comes a new vigour. It is as if the Deverill in me has been awoken after decades of sleep and is looking at Wyatt with new, more worldly eyes.

After tea we wander around the gardens. JP walks ahead with Wyatt and tells him the family history, how the castle was built, burned down and rebuilt by Kitty's cousin Celia. Wyatt is transfixed. He relishes the fact that it's my history too. I have grown in his eyes because I come from this magnificent castle and have a three-hundred-year history and an aristocratic lineage. Yet, he is diminished in mine, because he cares. We wander through the vegetable gardens where the magnificent greenhouses float like glass galleons on a sea of green, where Arethusa met Jonas for the last time and gave herself to him in the hope that she would never forget. JP leads us through the garden that he planted in memory of his late mother. There is a pretty wooden bench set beneath an arch of pale pink roses. It is a wistful, tranquil place, among the bees and butterflies, but all Wyatt wants to know is how she ascended from the daughter of the castle's cook to the wealthy Countess di Marcantonio, and I wonder whether he has always been so unsentimental, or whether I am noticing now because my eyes have been opened and my heart has been touched. He is a materialistic man only interested in the value of things; I wonder what my value has been.

That evening we have dinner at the castle. Uncle Bertie and Aunt Maud are there along with Kitty's sister Elspeth and her husband Peter. It is a small family gathering. I talk quietly with Uncle Bertie while Aunt Maud sits on the sofa with Wyatt and asks him about himself, which delights him for Aunt Maud is still a beautiful woman and he brightens in the mesmeric glare of her attention. Uncle Bertie takes me into a far corner. We sit on chairs placed next to each other. 'I want to thank you for letting me read Tussy's diary,' he says. 'It saddened me very much.'

'It saddened me too,' I agree. 'Because in leaving her home and family Mom lost so much.'

'That was her choice, Faye,' he says. 'She could have come back at any time. We would have received her with open arms. No, my dear, what saddened me was the effect her departure and consequent exile must have had on my parents. They never spoke of her, but I never thought to ask. I'm saddened by the secrets. It doesn't surprise me that Rupert knew all about it. Tussy and he were very close. I was a little older. But family is about sharing, the good times and the bad. It's about pulling together when things go wrong and sticking together and seeing them through. I know that now. My own life has taught me about the importance of family. You only get one. How little I knew Tussy. That saddens me too, because through her diary I have come to know her better. Thank you, Faye, for letting me share it. You can't imagine what it means to know the truth. I will no longer ask myself the question for now I know the answer.' He looks at me and his eyes are full of concern. 'Tell me, how has your brother taken it?'

I shake my head. 'He doesn't want to know.'

'I don't blame him. It's very tough accepting that something which has seemed solid and certain all his life is in fact a lie. I'm sure he is both angry and wounded.'

'It's a terrible shock.'

'I've had a few shocks of my own in my life, but one does get over them, in the end.'

'I don't think Logan will. I think he'll pretend I never told him and bury his head in the sand. No one knows but us. I haven't told Wyatt. I didn't want to let Logan down. It's his secret to tell if ever he wants to share it.' I wince inwardly at the lie, because of course I've told Rose. But Uncle Bertie doesn't need to know that.

'I'm touched that your mother should want to build a home for single mothers. That's the Tussy I know. The girl who defied her governess and sneaked into town to give to the poor. She and her aunt Poppy were great philanthropists.'

'She took up many causes in America too,' I tell him proudly. 'She always had compassion for those in need.'

'I gather it will be called the Arethusa Deverill Home for Single Mothers.'

'Yes, but she would have preferred it to be called the Logan Home.'

'Arethusa Deverill is appropriate too.' He gently pats my hand. 'And how good of you to bring her ashes home.'

'It's where she wants to be,' I say and watch the sheen on his eyes intensify with emotion.

'Tonight we shall decide when and where to do it. I think a little ceremony on the hill above the castle would be appropriate. What do you think?'

I feel moved. My own eyes begin to shine. 'That is what she wanted,' I reply.

'Let's bring the rest of the family into the conversation, shall we? I dare say they will all want to be involved.' And indeed they do. It is decided that we will scatter her ashes the day after tomorrow, and that we will inform the people of Ballinakelly so that anyone who knew her when she was a girl can come and pay their respects.

A couple of days later we assemble on the hill above Castle Deverill with the priest, a thin old man with a stoop who looks like a bulrush. To the right we can see the ocean, to our left bright green fields, and ahead, in a blaze of sunlight, glows the castle. It stands dutifully like an ancient coastguard keeping watch over the flotilla of clouds that sail rapidly inland on an easterly wind. In my hands I hold the urn that contains Mom's ashes. Wyatt is beside me, hands on hips, gazing at the castle. It looks even more impressive from up here. I remember seeing it for the first time from this hill, with Cormac. I remember how it loomed out of the mist and snatched my breath. Now it is snatching Wyatt's.

Uncle Bertie and Aunt Maud hold hands. Their affection

for each other is touching. The way he looks at her for reassurance, the way she gives it with an indulgent smile that softens the sharp edges of her face. JP and Alana stand together and JP has his arm around her, sheltering her from the wind. How handsome he is with his straight shoulders and thick auburn hair. I can see Kitty in his profile and in the strength of his jaw. Then there is Elspeth who is sweet and plain and her stiff husband Peter, and Robert, who puts his hands in his pockets and says nothing, the three of them are like lesser stars to Kitty's brilliance. Kitty goes to stand beside her father, she knows how much this moment means to him, and she gives him a gentle, compassionate smile.

Some of the older servants are here. Those who knew Arethusa when she was young. Eily Barry is too old and unwell to make it, but there is a small group of her contempories who stand a little apart. I catch their eyes and they look away nervously. But once I have averted my gaze, I can feel them turning back again. They are curious about this foreign Deverill who has brought her mother home.

We are about to begin when we see a group of men and women in black making their way slowly towards us. There are about eight of them, walking in a huddle along the path that snakes through the long grasses. Uncle Bertie squints, but it is not until they are almost upon us that he recognizes them. He lets go of Maud's hand and walks over to me. Then he lowers his voice and says, 'That's Dermot McLoughlin and family.'

I'm astonished. I watch them approach with curiosity. An old man with a stick, an elderly woman in a black mantilla leaning on a younger man for support and five others, both middle-aged and young. I recognize Dermot immediately. I always thought that Logan looked like Mother, but now

Dermot's features surface in his face and I can see that he is also like his father. He has his height, the shape of his head and his colouring. Dermot is a handsome man, even in his eighties, and I realize now that my brother's good looks are his.

'You are very welcome,' says Uncle Bertie in a manner that shows he has spent all his life being polite and gracious, like a king to his subjects.

Dermot and I find each other and our eyes lock. His eyes are Logan's. I do not look away. He stares at me quite deliberately, but he will not find Arethusa in my face. Then I realize that he is not looking for Arethusa; he is looking for himself.

It is then that I know he knows. He knows about the pregnancy and he thinks his child might be me.

The priest asks everyone to gather round. I drop my eyes to the ground where yellow and pink flowers flourish in the long grass. We form a semicircle. The priest announces that he's going to say only a few words, and then says many. When he is finished Uncle Bertie opens a book he has brought with him and reads a poem. While he is reading I can feel Dermot's eyes upon me. They are hot and enquiring.

> Let Fate do her worst, there are relics of joy,
> Bright dreams of the past, which she cannot destroy,
> Which come in the night-time of sorrow and care,
> And bring back the features that joy used to wear.
> Long, long be my heart with such memories fill'd,
> Like the vase in which roses have once been distill'd.
> You may break, you may ruin the vase if you will,
> But the scent of the roses will hang 'round it still.

I wonder what Dermot thought of Arethusa's running away to America. Did he mourn her? Did he feel betrayed and cast aside?

What impact did her leaving have upon *his* life? He later married and had children, half-brothers and sisters of my own brother who stand with him now, and I wish that Logan were here to meet them. I wish he could embrace our mother's past and accept his own. I'm not sure, however, that *I* could. Then I wonder how Dermot knows. Perhaps he has always known, as Eily knew. Or maybe Eily isn't so good at keeping secrets, after all.

Uncle Bertie reaches for the urn and I hand it to him. He opens it and turns away from the wind. Then he shakes it and the ashes are released. They are carried on the gale and his words go with them:

> *Do not stand at my grave and weep;*
> *I am not there. I do not sleep.*
> *I am a thousand winds that blow.*
> *I am the diamond glints on snow.*
> *I am the sunlight on ripened grain,*
> *I am the gentle autumn rain.*
>
> *When you awaken in the morning's hush,*
> *I am the swift uplifting rush*
> *Of quiet birds in circled flight.*
> *I am the soft stars that shine at night.*
> *Do not stand at my grave and cry;*
> *I am not there, I did not die.*

It is only when I feel Wyatt's hand taking mine that I realize I am quietly crying. At last my mother is set free, in the place where she grew up. In the place where she left the larger part of her heart. If Kitty is right and she lives on in spirit, I hope she is happy that I have carried out her wishes. She did want forgiveness after all, and *she* was ready to forgive as well.

Wyatt's hand feels awkward and contrived and a little embar-rassing. He hasn't taken my hand in years, I don't feel it belongs there. I wish he wasn't being so sweet. It would make me feel less guilty if he were being thoughtless or unkind. It would make it easier for me to justify the feelings I have for Cormac.

We remain standing as the last of the ashes fall softly into the earth. I glance at Kitty. Her lips are curled into a know-ing smile. It is small, barely perceptible, but it is a smile that conveys her unwavering, undoubting belief in the eternal nature of the soul. She, like our grandmother Adeline, does not believe in death. I wish I shared their conviction. I want to believe my mother is here, watching over me, and that one day, when it is my turn to go, I will join her on the other side of the veil.

The priest finishes the service with the Celtic blessing. '*May the road rise up to meet you. May the wind be always at your back. May the sun shine warm upon your face, the rains fall soft upon your fields and until we meet again, may God hold you in the palm of His hand.*'

I let go of Wyatt's hand so that I can thank the priest and Uncle Bertie for such a lovely service. Uncle Bertie's eyes are moist. 'She is home,' he says and I feel the warm flood of tears well in my eyes all over again. It is then that I see Dermot McLoughlin walking slowly towards us. He is a blur and I blink to clear my vision. He shakes Uncle Bertie's hand, but neither says a word. He turns and settles his dark, misty eyes onto mine. I can tell he is struggling to find the right words. He is shaking his head and his face is flushing with emotion. He sandwiches my hand in his and I struggle to find any words at all. 'Your mother was very special to me,' he says at last.

'I know,' I reply. 'She wrote very affectionately about you in her diary.'

He raises his eyebrows and nods in pleasant surprise. He is looking at me intensely and I sense he is searching for traces of himself in my features. I want to tell him that it is not I but Logan who was born nine months after their last meeting. But I can't. I can't betray my brother.

I realize that he is still holding my hand between his two rough ones. I don't know whether he is holding on to me because I am a part of the woman he loved, or because he thinks I am a part of them both. Uncle Bertie has not left my side. I am grateful for his support. At length Kitty joins us and diverts Dermot's attention by asking him smoothly about his children and grandchildren. The tension is defused. He releases my hand and shifts his gaze to his family, who are waiting for him so that they can leave. I doubt they have any affection for Arethusa Deverill.

I watch Dermot make his way slowly down the path in the bosom of his family, a fragile old man who was once my mother's vigorous young lover. He gets smaller and smaller until he is out of sight. I would have liked to talk to him about his past. I'd like to have told him about Logan. I sense a thirst in him that only the truth can quench, but I am not the person to divulge it. It saddens me to watch him go because I feel I have left so much unsaid that should be spoken.

I turn away and join *my* family. JP has an excited look upon his face. It is the face of someone who can barely contain good news. 'What's going on?' I ask suspiciously.

Uncle Bertie takes my hands. 'Faye, JP and I are concocting a plan.'

I frown. They look like a pair of excited schoolboys. 'What sort of plan?'

'How would you feel if the Arethusa Deverill Home for Single Mothers was built on Deverill land?'

'Really? You have land you can spare?'

JP nods. 'Just on the edge of Ballinakelly. We've been look-ing to develop it. We'd like to honour your mother's wish and build her home there.'

'It's also a way for us, as a family, to give something back to the community,' Uncle Bertie adds. 'Tussy was always concerned about those in need. I don't believe we did as much as we could. This would enable us to make up for our ineptitude.'

I am so happy that they are supporting me. I had no idea how I was even going to begin to set up her home, but with my uncle and JP by my side I know I can pull it off. 'I'm overwhelmed,' I exclaim. 'Really, I can't thank you enough. Mom would be so happy.'

I catch Wyatt's eye and he smiles approvingly. He's the sort of person who thinks it is only men who are capable of getting things done. I know he is also smiling with relief that I am not going to embark on this project alone. Perhaps he is thinking that, if the family are involved, I won't have to come back.

But I *will* come back, to lay the foundation stone. I wouldn't miss that for the world. I smile at Wyatt, but beneath my smile is sorrow, because once I loved him and now I don't. Whatever magic we had is gone. I turn my eyes to the ocean. America is very far away. There is a strong reluctance in me to leave. My feet are firmly planted on Irish soil and I don't want to lift them. I want to stay. Wyatt takes my hand again. 'Come,' he says. 'You've done your duty. She's been laid to rest. Life can go back to normal.'

But can it? For Logan, it never will, and for me? I don't want it to.

Chapter 36

Kitty persuades Robert to take us to Ma Murphy's for supper. Robert is reluctant to go. He seems just as out of place in Ballinakelly as Wyatt does. But after a long discussion and Kitty's gentle coaxing, he relents. If it wasn't for Wyatt I know he wouldn't come, but because he has an ally, he breaks his habit of staying at home and joins us.

I have not spoken to Cormac since I left him two days ago. I am grateful to Kitty for giving us that precious time together, but I was left longing for more, resenting my husband for coming to Ireland with me and agonizing over what to do about it. I have been with Wyatt for thirty-seven years. For the greater part of my life. I am conditioned to our dynamic, used to our routines and accustomed to the person I am when I'm with him, even if I don't like that person very much; it is my life. The only life I know. We share our home, our past and our children and grandchildren. I love Cormac. I want to be with him. But I am afraid. The people-pleaser in me worries about what everyone would think were I to leave my husband. It is very hard to change the habits of a lifetime. It is very hard to change the person that I am; it is just hard.

Cormac is at Ma Murphy's when we arrive. He is the first person I see, as if he has sat there on purpose, in the direct line of my vision. He is on a stool at the bar, sharing a joke with the barmaid. He turns, beer glass in hand, and looks at me gravely as I enter with Wyatt, Kitty and Robert. He is not alone. The whole room goes quiet. It must be the first time that Robert has been here. I don't think they are all staring at me and they are certainly familiar with Kitty. It is Robert. Or perhaps it is Wyatt. Or is it *us*? Is my affair with Cormac a badly kept secret? I think of Dermot McLoughlin and wonder whether the people of Ballinakelly are just bad at keeping secrets.

We sit at a table in the corner, Kitty and I with our backs to the wall. Wyatt and Robert are probably happy not to be able to see the locals who are staring at them as if they are Martians. The barmaid tears herself away from Cormac and comes to take our order for drinks. The menu for supper is written on a blackboard on the wall. I pretend to read it, but I read Cormac's face instead. It says one word: *Stay.*

We order food, Robert chooses a bottle of white wine. Wyatt asks for a whiskey and Robert recommends Jameson's, which is a good Irish brand. I try not to look at Cormac. I try to listen to the conversation at the table. Only Kitty knows how hard it is. She has been where I am now and, I'm beginning to realize, she enjoys a bit of drama. She is willing me to succeed where she failed.

I am managing to keep my emotions under control when Cormac picks up his accordion. Without any introduction he begins to play. Ma Murphy's goes quiet and everyone stops what they're doing to listen. They are used to Cormac's plaintive voice and the tears it induces. I feel my face flush and my eyes sting as he begins to sing.

When my love and I parted the wind blew cold
When my love and I parted, our love untold

How my heart kept crying love come with me
But I turned my face from her and faced the sea
When my love and I parted we shed no tears
Though we knew before us lay weary years
For a bird was singing upon a tree
And a gleam of sunlight lay on the sea

Parting is bitter and weeping vain
And all true lovers will meet again
And no fate can sever my love and me
For her heart is the river and mine the sea

I get the feeling that everyone in Ma Murphy's, besides Wyatt and perhaps Robert, knows this song is for me.

Then Kitty whispers in my ear. '"For *his* heart is the river and mine the sea", that's the original lyric.' I frown. I don't understand what she means. She smiles. 'He's changed it so he can sing it for you.' Now I'm certain they all know and my blush deepens. *Stay.* That's all I can hear, repeated in my head over the sound of the music. *Stay.*

The next few days pass in mounting anguish. We go to Mass, we visit the sights and all the while Wyatt is with me, but Cormac is in my head and in my heart and I am torn between duty, the vows I made before God, and love.

I send a telegram to Logan to let him know that Mom's ashes have been scattered. I don't suppose he cares very much, but I want him to be in the loop. He is her son, after all. Although he is probably wishing he wasn't right now.

I don't discuss Cormac with Kitty. I know her mind, but only I can make up mine.

The final morning of our stay she asks me to ride with her. We set off into the hills and she asks whether I want to see

Cormac one last time. She can give us another hour, she says. I tell her I don't. I'm hurting enough. I cannot bear the agony of parting. I cannot bear the agony of an hour saying goodbye. I cannot bear to hear him say that word: *Stay*.

Wyatt notices how unhappy I am and tries to make me feel better. He suggests asking the Learmonts for dinner as soon as we get back. Jenny Learmont is a good friend of mine and Roddy Learmont is a golfing buddy of Wyatt's. But my heart sinks at the thought of returning to the same old routine, the same old people, the same old *me*. My life in Boston seems shallow now and without joy. I feel I have awoken from a sleep and realized that the life I have been living is only a dream and now that I am fully conscious that dream can no longer satisfy me. *And no fate can sever my love and me/For his heart is the river and mine the sea.* How will I go on without him?

As I pack I tell myself that I'll come back. That I *have* to come back on account of the home we're going to build in my mother's name. But can a love affair last when there are long gaps between meeting and a distance so great I need to spend a whole night on a plane to get here? Is it possible to sustain it under such circumstances? And all the while that voice in my head which brings tears to my eyes and a tightness in my chest: *Stay*.

Robert takes my suitcase downstairs, Wyatt carries his own. We stand in the hall, ready to say our goodbyes. I feel desperate, like a cornered animal with nowhere to run. I am surprised when Cormac's Jeep appears outside the house and parks on the gravel. I look out of the window in alarm, then at Kitty in confusion. 'I'm afraid I can't take you,' she explains, feigning disappointment. 'I have a charity meeting this evening. But Cormac O'Farrell is a good driver and will make sure you get to the airport safely.'

I frown. Wyatt, oblivious of the game she's playing, thanks her and shakes Robert's hand. 'It's been real fun,' he says. 'Thank you for your hospitality. If you ever come State side you must allow us to entertain you. Perhaps a week in Nantucket.'

Kitty embraces me. I feel feverish, as if I'm coming down with something. I want to ask her what she thinks she's doing, but I don't need to. I know what she's doing. I know the game she's playing. Except it isn't a game. It's my life and she seems to understand me better than I understand myself. 'Goodbye, Faye,' she says. 'And remember you're always welcome here. You're family, after all.'

Cormac greets me as if he barely knows me. Wyatt treats him like he would treat any taxi driver, dismissively. Wyatt doesn't think he has to be polite to those he considers working class. Whether it's waiters or hotel staff, he says they are there to provide a service, not to befriend. He lets Cormac put the suitcases in the back of the Jeep then opens the back door for me. I climb in and sit next to the window, directly behind the driver's seat. I look out at Kitty in desperation. She stares at me, her face serious. She's not playing a game, she's trying to make it easy for me. But she's just making it harder.

Wyatt gets in beside me and Cormac turns on the ignition. I can smell Kite. I can also smell Cormac. I think of all the times I've sat in the front seat of this vehicle. The amount of times we've reached for each other's hand across the gear stick. The lingering looks, the laughter, the teasing and the fun. Now it is vibrating with sadness and I want to put my hand into the gap between Cormac's seat and the door and touch him. He is so close. I can see his greying hair curling beneath his cap and the curve of his shoulders. That word resonating all around him as if his thoughts are manifesting into sounds and letters: *Stay.*

It is a long and agonizing drive to the airport. Cormac says very little. Wyatt exchanges a few pleasantries and then we fall into silence. I think of Cormac's history. His involvement in the War of Independence, his capture, his torture and his escape and I feel sad for Wyatt because he misses so much by being prejudiced. He views Cormac as a taxi driver, not as a man. If he could only ask the man about himself he'd discover that he's not just a man, but a hero. My eyes fill with tears and I turn to the green hills passing swiftly by my window. He's *my* hero.

Wyatt reaches for my hand. It sits limply in his as he tries to squeeze it back to life. He knows I'm sad to leave Ireland, but he doesn't know I'm sad to leave Cormac. He pulls a sympathetic smile, but Wyatt has never been very good at sympathy. He finds it awkward to show emotion and has little empathy. He's doing his best. I wonder *why* he's doing his best.

I catch Cormac's eye in the rear-view mirror. His gaze takes me by surprise. I look away and let go of Wyatt's hand guiltily. I cannot bear to see the pain in Cormac's eyes. Those lapis eyes which are usually twinkling with mirth. I cannot bear to see them sad. I wish he would play the radio. The silence is insufferable.

I sense Cormac is angry with me. He wants me to stay, but I can't. He wants me to be strong, but I'm not. I bite the skin around my thumbnail and wish I was more like Kitty. But even Kitty shied at the final hurdle. Am I going to regret my cowardice for the rest of my life? Am I going to be like Kitty, loving from afar, lamenting the choice I made, wishing I had done things differently? That is no way to live. That is not life; that's loss.

We arrive at the airport and Cormac stops the Jeep at the kerb. He hesitates before he climbs out. Perhaps hoping that

Wyatt will get out first so he'll have a moment alone with me. But *I* open the door and step out before either of them. When Cormac walks round to the boot, I am standing there with Wyatt. He avoids my eyes and lifts out the suitcases.

'Thank you,' says Wyatt, not even remembering Cormac's name. 'Come on, Faye. We're in good time.' He sets off towards the doors into the airport.

I look at Cormac. But there is nothing to say. He looks at me.

Stay.

I turn and follow my husband into the airport.

We check in and head to passport control. If Wyatt notices my tears, he ignores them. We stand in line in silence. Together but miles apart. What are we to each other now? Husband and wife are two words and in our case they have little meaning. Labels, that's all they are, thin, dispassionate words that can be peeled off like stickers. Do I want to spend the rest of my life being the submissive wife to a husband who doesn't really *see* me? He sees the label, that's all.

My children's faces float then into my mind and hover there, causing me to falter. What will they think if I leave their father? How will they judge me? Will I lose them? Will they ever forgive me? Will they be forced to take sides? Will I hurt them irrevocably and regret it for the rest of my life? But I hear Rose's voice, as clear as if she were standing beside me, whispering into my ear, 'Thank you, Mom, for trusting me.' And I know I have to trust them. I have to trust them to love me enough to understand; I just have to trust them to love me.

'Wyatt,' I say. He looks at me. He chooses not to see my distress. His eyes are weary, with a glint of impatience. We are on our way home now. I don't think there will be any more hand holding. Could it be that he sensed I was drifting away? 'I'm not coming with you.' Those words give me a strange feeling of empowerment and I lift my chin.

Wyatt stares at me as if I've gone crazy. 'What are you talking about?'

'I'm not coming.'

'What do you mean, you're not coming?' His eyes flicker to the other people in the line. He puts a hand on my upper arm and moves me briskly to the side. 'What's going on, Faye?' he asks, lowering his voice.

'I don't want to be married to you anymore. I'm sorry.'

'Christ, Faye!'

'I'm in love with another man.'

'Who? Who are you in love with?' He is so stunned, he can barely get the words out.

'Cormac O'Farrell.'

'Cormac who?'

'The man who drove us to the airport.'

'The taxi driver?' He spits out the words in disgust.

'He's a musician too,' I add.

'And you think you're in love with him?' His face is now crimson.

'I *know* I am.'

'When did this happen?'

'When I came here the first time.'

'You're out of your mind, Faye. Don't be stupid. You need to remember who you are.'

'I know who I am,' I reply. 'I'm a Clayton and a Deverill. I don't want to be a Langton anymore.' I put my hand on his arm. 'I'm sorry, Wyatt. This is the first and only time in my life I'm going to be totally selfish.'

Wyatt is aghast. 'You'll come to your senses and realize

you've made the biggest mistake of your life!' he hisses. Even in his anger he is aware of strangers listening. 'You do know that, don't you? You'll wake up from this ridiculous infatuation you have with Ireland and you'll come running home, begging for forgiveness. He's a taxi driver, Faye. A taxi driver. Christ!'

I walk away. I don't look back, but I can feel his bewilderment and his fury as if they have feet and are following me out of the airport.

I am swept out of the building on a wave of exhilaration. I cannot run fast enough. I don't expect to see the Jeep, but it is still there. Cormac is inside, staring out of the window in desolation.

I open the passenger door and climb in.

He looks at me in amazement. 'Faye?'

I smile through my tears. 'Ask me again,' I say.

He looks at me askance. Then he gets it. 'Stay.'

I nod. 'Yes.' I wipe my face with the back of my hand. 'Yes, Cormac, I'll stay.'

Chapter 37

More than a year has passed. Autumn has come around again, ushering in shorter days and blustery gales. The air is warm and damp, mist clings to the valleys and the woodlands are set aflame with yellow and orange and red. I stand with Uncle Bertie, JP and Kitty on the land they have given for the Arethusa Deverill Home for Single Mothers. The rest of the family are here too: Aunt Maud, Elspeth and Peter, Alana, Robert and their children. Kitty and Robert's daughter Florence has flown over from England with Celia, Kitty's cousin, and her husband Boysie. The townspeople have all turned out to celebrate this moment of laying the foundation stone. I notice Dermot McLoughlin among them. He knows why Mom has given this home to the town, he just doesn't know who his child is. He must surely know by now that it is not me. I am not old enough to be his child.

It was Mother's wish that the home be called after Logan. I am sad that I am unable to fulfil her wish in the way that she wanted me to. I'm sure she intended for Logan to meet his father and in so doing reconcile them both with their past. I sense it is all part of her coming home. The scattering of her ashes, the laying of the foundation stone and the meeting between Dermot and Logan – it's all about forgiveness and love, and yet, Logan is not here and he does not wish his parentage to be made public.

As for me, I am almost divorced and living 'in sin' with Cormac. I don't wish to remarry and neither does Cormac. We like things just the way they are. We are happy. I see him with Kite, standing beside Celia and Boysie, and he grins at me, that slightly lopsided, bashful grin that I love so much.

Uncle Bertie takes out a piece of paper. He's written a speech and Aunt Maud has told me it brought tears to her eyes – if it brought tears to *her* frosty old eyes I think there'll be a river of tears from the rest of us. He clears his throat and sweeps his gaze over the expectant crowd. There is silence.

A murmur of voices interrupts Uncle Bertie's big moment and the sudden movement to our right averts our attention. I see a group of people striding across the field purposefully. I squint in the sunlight. I recognize that walk. I look harder. To my astonishment it is Logan. He has come with his wife Lucy, their children and *mine*. Then I spot Temperance, walking beside Rose. Yes, my eyes are not deceiving me. It is my darling Tempie, come all the way from America!

None of them told me they were coming. I wonder if they are here to hinder the proceedings or to help.

I whisper to Uncle Bertie, 'That's my family,' and my heart is gripped with anxiety.

None of us know what to expect. My children were not happy with my decision to divorce their father and stay here with Cormac, but they accepted it, and Rose, especially, has been typically supportive, calling me from time to time, sharing her news. But none of them has shown any willingness to come here and meet him. Yet, here they are. A formidable group, marching over the grass with intention.

The crowd parts and Logan walks through it. He is wearing a long dark coat and fedora hat and I notice he has aged at last. Peter Pan no longer looks eternally young. The trauma of the last year has stolen his magic. I can see that he has wrestled with his soul and that he is now weary of the fight. He is mortal after all, just like the rest of us.

He stands before me. His dark eyes are Dermot's. He doesn't greet me. He looks at me with a clear, unwavering gaze and says loudly for everyone to hear, 'I want the home to be called the Logan Home, as Mother intended.' I don't know what to say. I am too moved to speak. I put my hand on my chest and feel a sudden wave of emotion rise inside me. 'It's what Mom wanted and Mom always got what she wanted,' he adds with a wry grin.

I smile. 'Oh Logan,' I manage and my vision is misted with tears.

He looks at Uncle Bertie. 'Don't let me stop you. Please, carry on.'

Uncle Bertie clears his throat again. 'We stand here today, on Deverill land, to honour my sister Arethusa Deverill, who left Ireland in the autumn of 1894 and returned in death in the summer of 1961, where she now remains, over-looking the home she loved. Tussy, as she was affectionately known, departed as a single woman of eighteen, carrying a child. She left because she refused to give her baby up. Many girls and young women do not have the means to hold on to their children. Their suffering was in my sister's mind when she wrote her will shortly before she died. She asked specifically that a home be built in Ballinakelly for those who fall pregnant like she did and lack the support to enable them to be delivered safely of their babies and to keep them. Society is rigid, judgemental and unforgiving. As, all too often, family can be. As we lay this stone today I want to reach out to my sister, wherever she may be in spirit, and ask that she forgive us, her family, for letting her go. We never tried to find her, we never tried to help her and we never told her we loved her. Why? Because she brought an illegitimate child into the world. If that is a crime then I too am guilty of it.' There is a murmur of amusement and JP looks at his feet and grins. 'Love for one's children, legitimate or not, is the wind that fills our sails and propels us on. Without that wind I know that I, for one, would be adrift in a cold, unfriendly sea. In the laying of this stone I ask that we all forgive where forgiveness is due and love with all our hearts because life is short, much too short, and we must make the most of every moment of being together. In remembering Tussy I hold my family close and urge you all to do the same.' I catch the eyes of my children, one by one, and Temperance, whose gaze I hold for a little longer, and they return my gaze with affection and delight because their turning up today has been the surprise they wanted it to be. Rose is smiling triumphantly and I know that it was she who engineered their coming, and perhaps Logan's too. I smile back at her, aware that my face is wet with tears and my breath is catching in my throat with the sudden onset of sobbing. How typical of Rose, then, to slip through the crowd to take my hand. She holds it tightly and doesn't let it go.

Uncle Bertie folds up his speech. 'I hope that this home will be a refuge for many women in need. I am proud to announce the laying of the first stone of the *Logan* Home for Single

Mothers.' He turns to my brother and extends his hand. Logan takes it. Then my brother pulls my uncle into his embrace. Uncle Bertie chuckles, embarrassed. Being very British he is not used to hugging. I laugh and embrace my brother too. I feel, in a way, that we have all come home.

Hesitant at first, and then with determination, Dermot McLoughlin makes his way through the crowd. Logan sees him. Does he recognize himself in the old man's face? Does he work out who he is from the look of resolve and curiosity in Dermot's eyes? Does he sense sorrow, regret or longing in his gait? I don't know. All I know is that the two men meet. They take each other's hand and they talk. I suppose that's all Mom wanted them to do.

And me? I am enfolded into the bosom of my family. My old one and my new one, as Cormac and Kite come up to be introduced. They finally meet. I suppose that is all *I* wanted them to do.

Last night I dreamed I was at Castle Deverill again. I wander into the great hall where there is a baronial fireplace. Flames crackle and flicker and throw dancing shadows across the walls. Everything is majestic, as if I am in a royal palace. There are paintings in gilt frames, Persian rugs on the flagstone floor, a grand staircase that leads me up into dark corridors, enticing me deeper and deeper into the castle, and I run now, because I know that I am close.

Candlelight illuminates the darkness. I reach a gap in the wall and take the narrow staircase there. This is the core of the castle, the oldest wing, the only section to survive the fire. I climb the uneven wooden steps, each worn into a gentle hollow from centuries of treading feet. I place mine into those hollows and slowly ascend. My heart accelerates but I am not afraid. I know what to expect. I know who will be waiting for me. I am impatient to see my grandmother. At the top there is a sturdy old door. It is blackened with age and smoke and the iron hinges and studs are from another age, when men wore plumed hats and boots and carried swords at their hips. I put my fingers on the latch and gently lift it. The door opens without protest. It is used to my coming.

To my surprise there are two people standing with their backs to me, looking into the fire. One is slim with thick red hair falling in waves down to her waist, the other has long dark hair, a small waist and curved hips, and there is something coquettish in the way that she is standing, as if she cannot contain her excitement and is longing to turn round. They hesitate a moment, to heighten the drama, then they turn, like a pair of delighted children at a surprise party. I gasp, astonished. Adeline and Arethusa are together, their smiles full of gratitude and joy. I feel their happiness. I feel their forgiveness; and I feel their love. It radiates out of them in a bright white light and embraces me.

I realize then that in bringing my mother's mortal remains home I have enabled her to return home in spirit. To return home to her family, where she has always belonged.

My gaze drifts to the mantelpiece behind them. There, in the dust, are JP's daughter Aisling's fingerprints, just where she left them.

I wake to see Cormac sleeping soundly beside me. The dawn light is already breaking through the curtains and chasing away the night's shadows. The familiar sound of the sea triggers a rush of joy. I am here. I am home. I am where I am meant to be. Where Mother and perhaps Adeline always wanted me to be.

I turn on my side and gaze at him. My heart floods with gratitude.

He asked me to stay; I am happy that I did.

Acknowledgements

I intended the Deverill Chronicles to be a trilogy and planned it as such. However, I meant to include Arethusa Deverill's story in book two, but didn't have the space to do it justice. Therefore, the trilogy was always unfinished business. I have now written her story and the trilogy has become a quartet! I won't say that's the end of the Deverills . . . I do have another idea, but right now I'm writing a very different novel. Who knows, at a later date I might revisit Castle Deverill.

There are a lot of people I wish to thank: Tim Kelly, my dear Irish friend, who helped me with my research for the trilogy, has once again been invaluable. We have had a lot of fun with this book and I thank him so much for his time and enthusiasm. Robert and Nancy Phifer from Boston have also been wonderful. We've known each other a very long time, having met when I was on book tour in the USA eons ago. I'm always grateful for their readiness to help and the swiftness of their email replies, and I treasure their friendship.

A heartfelt thank you to my dynamic friend and agent, Sheila Crowley, and her brilliant team at Curtis Brown: Abbie Greaves, Alice Lutyens, Luke Speed, Enrichetta Frezzato, Katie McGowan, Claire Nozieres and Callum Mollison.

Thank you to my publisher, Simon & Schuster, who

have published me for so long they are like family now: Ian Chapman, Suzanne Baboneau and their excellent team: Gill Richardson, Dawn Burnett, Rich Vliestra, Laura Hough, Dominic Brendon, Sian Wilson, Rebecca Farrell and Sara-Jade Virtue.

I also want to thank my parents Charlie and Patty Palmer-Tomkinson, my mother-in-law April Sebag-Montefiore, my husband Sebag and our children, Lily and Sasha.

The
TEMPTATION
of
GRACIE

England, March 2010

The muffle of cloud that had settled over Badley Compton Harbour was so dense that the little fishing boats tethered to buoys in the middle of the bay had completely vanished. So too had the pretty white cottages which were stacked in rows up the hillside and the crown of green at the top where Ruby Red cows grazed on sweet grass and clover, and small birds played about the hedgerows. It was all gone now, as if it had never been.

Gracie Burton sat at the mirror of the salon, her short hair wrapped in tin foil, her diminutive body draped in a black gown, and gazed at the fog through the big glass window. She swept her eyes over the shimmering pavements and glistening stone wall to where one would normally see the sea, then turned back to the photograph in the magazine on her lap where a Tuscan castle glowed like amber beneath a bright Italian sun. She was seized by a deep and urgent craving. She had read the article several times already, but she read it again now, and it was as if she were growing a small sun inside her that was all her own.

Set high on top of the undulating Tuscan hills, with an uninterrupted view of the breathtaking Italian countryside all the way to the sea, Castello Montefosco is a rare jewel. Built by the Montefosco family in the twelfth century it can boast a long list of prestigious guests including Leonardo da Vinci and various popes. The widowed Count Tancredi Bassanelli, whose mother was a Montefosco, has now opened the doors of his beautiful home to paying guests, who will have the privilege of learning how to cook authentic Italian food under the expert eye of his octogenarian cook, Mamma Bernadetta. Don't expect to see much of the count, he is a private man, but you will enjoy the outrageous beauty of the gardens and terraces, the magnificence of his ancestral home full of treasures and the cookery lessons with the eccentric and talented Mamma Bernadetta.

Gracie let her eyes linger on the photograph. The castle was everything an Italian *castello* should be: harmoniously pro-portioned with a crenulated roof, tall shuttered windows set beneath half-moon pediments, sandstone faded to a pale grey-yellow by centuries of burning summer sun and bitter winter winds. It dominated the crest of the hill like a grand old king, rising majestically out of the cluster of medieval houses that had grown up around it in a forest of stone. Gracie closed her eyes and inhaled. She could already smell the wild thyme and rosemary, the honeysuckle and jasmine, the luxurious gardenia, dewy grass and aromatic pine. She could hear the gentle chirruping of crickets and see the velvet sky twinkling with a thousand stars like a vast canopy of diamonds spread out over the Tuscan hills. Her chest flooded with longing, a longing that she hadn't felt in years, deep in her heart. It frightened her, this feeling, because she had forgotten what to do with it. She had forgotten what it felt like to be young, to be in love, to be reckless, adventurous and brave. She had forgotten how to live. She had stuffed herself into a shell and remained there, hidden and safe, for decades. Now this photograph had forced her out like a cork from a bottle and all the fizz was coming with it and she didn't know what to do, except to go to Tuscany, as soon as possible.

She looked at her reflection and the fizz died away a little. She was sixty-eight, and although relatively well-preserved, she was still old. *Where had the years gone?* she asked herself. Not that she had ever been beautiful, so mourning the loss of her looks was never going to be her misfortune. However, there is a loveliness about a young woman simply because she is young, and that quality in Gracie had withered a long time ago.

She ran a rough hand down her cheek. Time had sucked the juice out of her skin but the elements had also played a part during her daily dog walks up and down the beach in all weathers. Her nose, she noticed, hadn't changed. It still dominated her face with its aquiline curve, giving her the look of a bird, an old bird now, a strange bird then, never a beautiful bird. Her eyes had always been special, though. Everyone used to say so and she had clung to that compliment when as a girl she had yearned to be pretty. They were large and grey-green, the irises encircled by a darker shade of grey, which had given her a feral look that people had once found compelling. Her eyes were less noticeable now, she thought, on account of her wrinkled face. Time had stolen the one thing that had set her apart. She hadn't cared how she looked since she was a young woman, but she cared now, suddenly, very much.

'You all right, dear?' said Judy, who cut her hair and gave it a colour rinse every now and then. Young and fashionable, Judy had a pierced nose, a tattoo and a ring on every vividly manicured finger. 'Won't be long,' she added. 'Would you like another cup of tea?'

'Thank you,' Gracie replied, still gazing at her reflection. She feared she'd look a hundred if she didn't tint her hair brown. She glanced down at her hands, the rough hands of a potter and gardener; the coarse hands of a woman who had never bothered with creams or manicures. The article drew her gaze again and she stared at it and allowed it to swallow her whole.

'Oh, that looks lovely,' said Judy, returning a few moments later and putting the mug of tea on the little shelf in front of the mirror. 'Where is it? Spain?'

'Italy,' said Gracie.

'Lovely,' the girl repeated.

Gracie sighed with longing. 'Yes, it is. Would you mind if I borrowed the magazine?' she asked.

'You can take it. It's out of date now anyway. I think it's the February issue.' Judy knew that Mrs Burton never went anywhere and she gave her a sympathetic smile. 'Doesn't cost anything to dream, does it, dear?' she said.

Gracie returned home to her small whitewashed cottage that looked out over the harbour. The two rescue mongrels she had bought after her husband died eight years before greeted her enthusiastically. 'You'll be wanting a walk, I suspect,' she said, putting the magazine on the hall table and bending down to give them a pat. She changed into boots and squashed her freshly coiffed hair beneath a woolly hat. A moment later she was making her way down the foggy road in the direction of the beach, the two dogs trotting excitedly beside her.

Gracie Burton had lived in Badley Compton for just over forty years. Ted, her late husband, had taken her to the Lake District for the occasional holiday, but like her he had preferred to remain at home. They hadn't had much money, but even if they had, they wouldn't have indulged in extravagant cruises or expensive trips abroad. Ted, who had been twenty years older than Gracie and a freelance journalist by trade, had liked his golf, his evenings in the pub and his books. Gracie liked books too. She travelled the world vicariously through the pages of the stories she read, but until now she hadn't been inspired to go anywhere. As she strode down the pavement she smiled, a nervous and excited smile, for she had decided, quite spontaneously and extremely uncharacteristically, that she was going to go to Italy. For a woman as cautious and unadventurous as Gracie Burton, this decision was extraordinary.

Gracie was by nature a solitary woman. She didn't crave company but she knew that if she allowed herself to withdraw completely from the community she might disappear altogether, and Ted had made her promise, on his deathbed, that she would make an effort to reach out to people. Consequently, she had allowed herself to be drawn into the Badley Compton Ladies' Book Club rather like a small stone that gets carried downriver by much bigger ones. It had started as a book club, but evolved into an anything-we-can-do-to-be-busy club, and was organised by the self-proclaimed queen of Badley Compton, Flappy Scott-Booth, whose husband was very rich, and attended by a flurry of four eager women, who, like attentive ladies-in-waiting, agreed with everything their queen said.

Gracie, the fifth and lowest in the pecking order, found herself doing all the menial tasks in the arrangement of charity events, bridge nights, coffee mornings, the annual town fête as well as book club lunches and other small get-togethers. She wondered, while her mind drifted, how on earth she had allowed herself to be so zealously gathered up and taken for granted. But she didn't complain. She was patient and accepting, working quietly and diligently while the limelight shone on the other more enthusiastic ladies. Gracie relished her dog walking, because, for those precious hours alone on the beach, she was entirely in her own company.

This sudden notion of going to Italy had only just seeded itself in Gracie's mind when she casually mentioned it to Harry Pratt, who liked to sit on the bench near the bus stop and watch the coming and going of boats in the harbour. She came across him on her way back from her walk and asked if he was all right. After all, there was nothing to see but cloud. He enjoyed the tranquillity of it, he replied, for he was reminded of his flying days when he had been in the RAF during the war. He'd often flown into thick fog over Dover, he explained. Gracie was so excited at the thought of the adventure ahead that she told him. Harry Pratt stared at her in astonishment, for not only did Gracie rarely talk about herself, but she barely ever left Badley Compton. She was as much a feature of the town as the bench he was sitting on. 'Good Lord,' Harry exclaimed, bright blue eyes gleaming. 'What the devil do you want to go to Italy for?'

'I'm going to learn to cook Italian food.' Gracie beamed such a wide smile that Harry wondered whether she was on something. It made her look like a young girl and Harry blinked in wonder at the sudden transformation.

'And you have to go all the way to Italy for that, do you?' he asked.

'That's the fun of it,' she replied, before walking off with an unusual bounce in her step.

Harry Pratt had to share the news and share it at once. No sooner had Gracie disappeared down the road than the old man hurried into Café Délice opposite the bus stop, which was always full of people he knew. He pushed open the door and was greeted by a noseful of warm, sugar-scented air and a number of expectant faces looking up from their coffee and croissants. Big Mary Timpson was behind the counter hovering over the feast of sticky buns, pastries and gateaux displayed enticingly behind glass. 'Good afternoon, Harry,' she said, and her Devon drawl curled softly around her words like icing around a cake. Fat and cheerful with plump, rosy cheeks, a ponytail of platinum-blonde hair and a perky candy-cane-striped apron stretching over her voluminous bosom, Big Mary Timpson had time to talk to everyone, and time to listen too. Since she had opened fifteen years before, Café Délice had been the hub of town gossip.

Harry Pratt took off his cap and ran a rough hand through thinning grey hair. He swept his twinkling eyes over the faces and was spoilt for choice. He knew every single one. 'Double espresso with whipped cream for you, Harry?' Big Mary asked, taking down a pink cup and saucer from the shelf behind her.

'And a slice of apple tart,' he added and pulled out a stool. He sat between two small tables, not wanting to commit to either one, and decided to share his news with the entire café. 'Did you know that Gracie is going to Italy?' he said. He directed his question at Big Mary, but his gaze darted from face to face, delighting in their surprise.

'Gracie? Gracie Burton? *Our* Gracie? What do you mean, going to Italy?' Big Mary gasped, forgetting about the coffee and putting her hands on her wide hips. '*Really* going to Italy?'

'She's going to learn to cook Italian food,' Harry announced gleefully.

'Why?' Big Mary asked after a long pause.

Harry grinned raffishly. 'For fun,' he said and he didn't elaborate, not only because he didn't have many more details to share, but because the idea of Gracie Burton going to Italy for fun was so completely extraordinary, unbelievable even, that Harry wanted to savour it – as well as the effect it was having on everyone in the café.

It was exactly five minutes before the news leaked further. John Hitchens, who had been in the café having tea with his son and granddaughter, told his friend Pete Murray, who was on his way to the newsagent's, who in turn shared the gossip with Jagadeesh behind the counter as he paid for cigarettes and a National Lottery ticket. When John arrived home he informed his wife, Mabel, who hurried to the telephone to tell Flappy, hoping that no one had got to her first. Flappy liked to be in the know about everything and Mabel liked to be in Flappy's good books. *It would be a mutually beneficial telephone call*, she thought excitedly. 'Please, please, please . . .' she mumbled to herself as she clamped the telephone to her ear and waited for Flappy to pick up. A good seven rings later – Flappy always answered *after* seven to give the impression that she was busy – the queen of Badley Compton's pompous voice resonated down the line.

'Darnley Manor, Mrs Scott-Booth speaking.'

'Flappy, it's me, Mabel. I have news,' Mabel hissed urgently.

'Do tell,' said Flappy in a tone that suggested she was interested but not too eager.

'Gracie's going to Italy,' Mabel blurted breathlessly. Then she waited for the shriek of delight, followed by, 'Goodness, Mabel, who told you?' or, 'How good of you, Mabel, to let me know.'

Instead there was a long pause. Flappy inhaled through her nostrils to control her surprise. How could Gracie be going to Italy and she not know about it? Gracie was the only 'doer' in the group, if *she* went away there'd be no one to do all the tedious organising of Flappy's many events. Flappy was so affronted she could barely speak, but speak she did because she was a master at keeping up appearances. 'Yes, I know, isn't it extraordinary!' she said at last in a tight voice.

Mabel was deflated. 'You know already?' she asked, put out.

'But of course I know, my dear. I'm always the first to know everything in this town.'

Mabel rallied a little at the prospect of further details. 'Then you'll know more than me,' she said. 'When is she going?'

There was another pause, then Flappy said, 'How about *you* tell me what *you've* heard and I'll fill in any gaps.' Mabel was too admiring of Flappy to notice the flaw in that suggestion and hastened to tell her what John had heard in the café. She waited keenly for something more from Flappy, but Flappy was not forthcoming.

'We must hear it from the horse's mouth,' Flappy declared, her mind whirring with ideas. Gracie was notoriously secretive, but if she had told Harry Pratt of her plan then she wasn't intending to keep it secret. Harry was famously loose-tongued. 'I will give an impromptu soirée tonight,' she announced impulsively. 'Kenneth is away and I have the house to myself. Yes, I'll summon the ladies and cook a splendid dinner.'

'What will the soirée be for?' Mabel asked eagerly, because she loved an occasion and Flappy's soirées were *always* an occasion. The last one had been in celebration of the money they had managed to raise to repair the church roof and Flappy had hired a string quartet from Exeter to play especially for them. But there wasn't enough time to put on that level of entertainment tonight. Flappy went silent for a moment as her busy mind made space for a new idea.

'But for Gracie, of course. If she's told Harry Pratt, she'll know the whole town will have heard by now. We'll have pasta and Prosecco and *parlare Italiano* . . .' Flappy sighed contentedly. 'Yes, it will be fun to *parlare* the *bella lingua*. After all, I've spent so many holidays in *Firenze*, *Roma* and *La Costa Amalfitana*, *Italiano* is second nature to me.'

Mabel wasn't in the least surprised that Flappy was fluent in Italian. She always said a very hearty *'bonjour'* to the French teacher who taught at the primary school and liked Big Mary's cakes, and just from the way Flappy said *'bonjour'* Mabel could tell that she was fluent in French too. *There is no end to Flappy's talents*, Mabel thought admiringly.

'Be a dear and summon the ladies, Mabel,' Flappy commanded. 'I will call Gracie myself.' She hung up and hastened across the hall to the library to find the Italian dictionary so that she could flash a few well-chosen phrases at the dinner table.

Gracie was sitting in an armchair beside the fire, drinking a cup of tea and gazing longingly at the photograph of the castle, when the telephone rang. She wrenched her thoughts away from the Tuscan countryside and lifted the receiver. 'Hello?' she said.

'Good, you're home,' said Flappy officiously.

'Flappy!' Gracie exclaimed and put down her mug.

'Now, I know it's short notice, but your presence is required at Darnley this evening.'

'This evening?' Gracie repeated. She'd rather been hoping to stay in and warm herself with the thought of that hot Italian sun in the blissful silence of her pottery room.

'This evening, at seven-thirty to be precise. I'm having a

small, informal get-together and it's imperative that you're here.' There was a determined tone to Flappy's voice which Gracie immediately recognised. A tone that suggested she would not accept any excuse Gracie might give in order to avoid going out on this damp and foggy evening. Besides, Flappy knew very well that Gracie had no reason to decline; it wasn't as if she had anything else to do.

'How lovely,' Gracie replied weakly, feeling decidedly *un*lovely about it. Italy beckoned. She was already there. But tonight she would be firmly embedded in Devon – her pottery and her planning would have to wait until the morrow.

'Good,' said Flappy, then she added cheerfully, '*Ciao*.'

Gracie frowned. She had never heard Flappy say '*Ciao*' before.

Flappy's husband Kenneth had made his money in a chain of fast food restaurants that became popular in the 1970s. He sold it for millions in 1983 and promptly retired, buying the big house in Badley Compton and building a golf course for which the people of Badley Compton were enormously grateful. It had been Flappy's idea to join their names together when they married, but no one in Badley Compton knew that. For all they were aware the Scott-Booths were an old English family with a house in the Algarve and plenty of money to spend on holidays in the Caribbean where they invited their four children and ten grandchildren for Christmas every year.

Darnley was a pretty white house with a grey slate roof that boasted fourteen bedrooms, an indoor swimming pool and an outdoor tennis court. The gardens were open to the public for three weeks in June (when Flappy could be spotted floating around the borders in a big straw hat and summer dress wielding a pair of secateurs with which she lopped off the occasional dead rose). Tonight Karen, the girl who came to cook, managed to disappear in time for Flappy to put on an apron and start stirring the Napoli sauce before any of her guests arrived for dinner. The first to appear was Mabel Hitchens, who made it her business to arrive before anyone else. She had brought Sally Hancock with her in her small green Golf and the two of them were more excited than ever, ringing the doorbell three times with impatience.

Flappy let them in, wooden spoon in one hand, glass of prosecco in the other, looking elegant and serene in an ivory silk blouse, floaty black trousers and pearls, her shoulder-length blonde hair immaculately coloured and blow-dried. At sixty-six she was still strikingly beautiful and aware of it. 'Buona sera,' she said, closing the door behind them. 'What a bella evening this is going to be. Come, you must have some prosecco. I've been slaving in the kitchen all afternoon so I took the liberty of helping myself to a teeny tiny glass before you arrived.'

The two women followed Flappy's willowy figure across the black-and-white chequerboard floor to the spacious kitchen, which was warmed by a large Aga and scented with the savoury smells of fried onions and garlic. Both Mabel and Sally had dressed up for the occasion because Flappy's interpretation of the word 'informal' was notoriously understated. Always chic with a Continental air and a permanent suntan, Flappy wore silk and cashmere and lots of gold jewellery even when she had no plans to see anyone. She detested denim and never wore boots. She abhorred trainers even on the young, and her shoes were dainty with a low, discreet heel. She professed that it was vulgar to show off one's wealth (and came down very heavily on the modern celebrity who flaunted theirs) but managed to let the other women know by allowing the odd detail to slip out in conversation that her clothes were expensive designer items bought on Net-a-Porter and delivered to her door, then waving her manicured fingers in the air and adding breezily, 'I don't care for that sort of thing but Kenneth expects it, you know.'

As the two women stepped into the kitchen Flappy caught sight of Sally's sparkly gold stilettos and gave a little sniff. Anything sparkly besides diamonds was enormously vulgar to Flappy. But this small act of rebellion was as far as Sally would dare go. Being on the wrong side of Flappy Scott-Booth was an experience none of the women wanted to risk. Eileen Bagshott had been foolish enough to call a meeting at *her* house and worse, to *chair* it, an act of outright rebellion which had resulted in the end of her membership of the Badley Compton Ladies' Book Club as well as invitations to Darnley. Eileen was now a sorry figure sitting in the shadows in the back row at church on Sundays, and had to practically beg for tickets to concerts in the town hall. So, besides her stilettos, Sally, who had written unashamedly trashy romantic novels for thirty years under the pseudonym Charity Chance, wore burgundy trousers (a touch on the tight side), a pink blouse and her red hair swept into what she believed to be a modern take on the 1960s beehive. Her leather trousers and glittery tops were reserved for dinners at home with her family.

Unlike Sally, Mabel would have rather died than induce Flappy to think ill of her. She was a nervous, conventional creature and eager to please. Mabel wore a busy floral blouse fixed at the throat with a pastiche diamond brooch, navy-blue slacks and gold buckled pumps on her small feet – a high street version of Flappy, worn with less flair. Her hair was shoulder-length, grey-brown and too thin to copy Flappy's billowing bob. If it hadn't been for the glasses that exaggerated the size of Mabel's watery grey eyes, which had an unsettling habit of staring, she would have looked decidedly unremarkable. Now they stared at

Flappy who had gone to such trouble to lay the table beautifully. Really, Mabel thought it remarkable how Flappy had thrown together a soirée at the very last minute, and for a moment she forgot about Gracie going to Italy and gazed in wonder at the clusters of candles, flower displays and starched blue-and-white Provençal tablecloth with matching napkins. 'I don't know how you do it,' she murmured, propelling Flappy, already on a pedestal, to even greater heights.

'*Fa niente,*' said Flappy, taking credit for Karen's good taste and hard work and feeling very pleased with her Italian, which sounded flawless to her ignorant ear. She handed them crystal flutes of prosecco and then swept into the hall to answer the door. A few moments later Esther Hancock and Madge Armitage, who had spent the previous couple of hours reading the book club choice in case Flappy asked them about it, hurried into the kitchen, bursting in their enthusiasm to talk about Gracie.

Flappy had taken care to invite Gracie half an hour later than the other women so that they'd have time to discuss her decision to go to Italy before she arrived. Once Flappy was satisfied that the women had witnessed her cooking apron and the few professional-looking sweeps of the wooden spoon around the tomato sauce, she hung the apron on the back of the door and led her guests into the drawing room where Karen had lit the fire and scented candles. The four women had spent many evenings in Flappy's cream-and-taupe-coloured drawing room and yet they hovered about the chairs until she invited them to sit down.

'We need to talk about Gracie,' said Flappy in her slow, well-articulated voice, and the other women listened respectfully. 'I've been thinking about her ever since I heard the news. I believe *I* was the first. I've decided that the worry is *not* about

Gracie going to a foreign country on her own, even though she hasn't gone anywhere on her own for as long as I've known her, and really, as her friends, we must discourage her, it's about her running away. What is she running from? What has happened to induce her to take such drastic measures?' Flappy looked at each lady individually, fixing them with her topaz-blue eyes and silently asking them to think carefully and not all reply at once.

'How clever you are, Flappy. Running away had never crossed my mind,' gushed Mabel, enjoying the taste of prosecco but trying not to gulp it. 'I just assumed she wanted a holiday.'

'No, she's never wanted a holiday. She's running from *something*,' Flappy persisted. 'And we must find out what it is.'

'She must want to run away very much to venture so far from home,' said Esther, who had the deep, gravelly voice of a man and the ruddy, weathered skin of someone who has spent most of her life on horseback. 'She could run to Land's End, but to run to Italy ... That's very far.'

'Boredom?' Sally suggested with a grin that might have won support had the others not been so nervous of Flappy.

Flappy put her head on one side and gave Sally a look as if she were a teacher ticking off a student who had said something unkind. 'Just because *you* might think her routine a little dull does not mean to say that it *is* dull, Sally,' she said. 'Gracie is comfortable in that routine and she's very happy to be given things to do for the book club. There's nothing boring about being busy, *I* know *that* better than anyone! Gracie is not a woman who wants to be adventurous and social like us.' Sally took a swig of prosecco and noticed that none of the others were willing to catch her eye.

'I wonder what her daughter thinks,' said Mabel, knowing that the mention of Gracie's daughter would please Flappy, who enjoyed criticising the girl for not taking trouble with her mother when Flappy's four children and ten grandchildren made such a fuss of *her*.

True to form Flappy inhaled through dilated nostrils and shook her head gravely. 'That girl should be ashamed of herself. She hasn't been down to see her mother for over six months. If my memory serves me right, which it usually does, I believe her last visit was in August. However busy her life is in London, she should spare a thought for her poor mama who is alone in that house with only her dogs for company. I know what comfort children can be. I can't imagine being ignored like poor Gracie is ignored. Without us she'd have no one.'

'Perhaps she just wants to see Italy,' said Madge with a shrug. 'After all, there's nothing wrong with wanting to go to Italy, is there?'

Once again Flappy put her head on one side and smiled patiently at Madge, whose bohemian clothes and unkempt grey hair more typically drew her sympathy. 'My dear, if it were anyone else we wouldn't be having this conversation, now would we? Of course, there's nothing wrong with wanting to go to Italy, or with simply *going* to Italy, I've been many times and it's a *paese incantevole*, but this is Gracie we're talking about. Gracie can't possibly go on her own. She can't possibly go. She's not up to it. It'll be a disaster. Gracie—' And at that point the doorbell went.

'Gracie!' Madge gasped, and as Flappy got up to open the front door four pairs of eyes followed her eagerly.